Wanderlust

"Fast-paced and thrilling, *Wanderlust* is pure adrenaline. Sirantha Jax is an unforgettable character, and I can't wait to find out what happens to her next. The world Ann Aguirre has created is a roller-coaster ride to remember."
—Christine Feehan, #1 *New York Times* bestselling author

"The details of communication, travel, politics, and power in a greedy, lively universe have been devised to the last degree but are presented effortlessly. Aguirre has the mastery and vision which come from critical expertise: She is unmistakably a true science fiction fan, writing in the genre she loves."
—*The Independent* (London)

"A thoroughly enjoyable blend of science fiction, romance, and action, with a little something for everyone, and a great deal of fun. It's down and dirty, unafraid to show some attitude."
—*SF Site*

Grimspace

"A terrific first novel full of page-turning action, delightful characters, and a wry twist of humor."
—Mike Shepherd, national bestselling author

"An irresistible blend of action and attitude. Sirantha Jax doesn't just leap off the page—she storms out, kicking, cursing, and mouthing off. No wonder her pilot falls in love with her; readers will, too."
—Sharon Shinn, national bestselling author

"A tightly written, edge-of-your-seat read."
—Linnea Sinclair, RITA Award–winning author

HAVOC

THE DRED CHRONICLES

ANN AGUIRRE

ACE BOOKS, NEW YORK

THE BERKLEY PUBLISHING GROUP
Published by the Penguin Group
Penguin Group (USA) LLC
375 Hudson Street, New York, New York 10014

USA • Canada • UK • Ireland • Australia • New Zealand • India • South Africa • China

penguin.com

A Penguin Random House Company

HAVOC

An Ace Book / published by arrangement with the author

Ace Books are published by The Berkley Publishing Group.
ACE and the "A" design are trademarks of Penguin Group (USA) LLC.

For information, address: The Berkley Publishing Group,
a division of Penguin Group (USA) LLC,
375 Hudson Street, New York, New York 10014.

ISBN: 978-0-425-25812-5

PUBLISHING HISTORY
Ace mass-market edition / September 2014

PRINTED IN THE UNITED STATES OF AMERICA

10 9 8 7 6 5 4 3 2 1

Cover art by Scott M. Fischer.
Cover design by Lesley Worrell.
Interior text design by Kelly Lipovich.

*For Courtney Milan, who makes me feel
smarter and more talented than I am,
just because she reads my books.*

Acknowledgments

As usual, I'm starting with Laura Bradford, my agent, partner, and friend.

Next I offer a hat tip to Anne Sowards for following me into dark places and never doubting that I'll write us out again. Thank you for making my books better. In addition, kudos to the team at Penguin for producing such beautiful books. Thanks also to my copy editors, Bob and Sara Schwager, who do such a fantastic job polishing my prose.

Over the years, I've been blessed with tremendous colleagues and amazing friendships. There's no space to articulate how much these individuals have contributed, so I'll name them in lieu of eloquence: Lauren Dane, Tessa Dare, Bree Bridges, Donna J. Herren, Vivian Arend, Megan Hart, Kate Elliott, Myke Cole, Leigh Bardugo, Courtney Milan, Robin LaFevers, Rae Carson, Lish McBride, and Yasmine Galenorn. You've all taught me something or led by example, possibly talked me down from a bad place or inspired me to keep going. So thank you all for being brilliant.

Thanks to my family for putting up with me. I'm trying to spend more time with you, and I hope that's a good thing. I appreciate how you listen to my ideas and give me new ones.

To my beta readers, Karen Alderman and Majda Čolak, there are no words to express my affection and gratitude. Through many projects, your excitement and enthusiasm fuel mine. I hope you know how much your support means to me, but the number of books I write—with you both cheering me on—should tell you everything.

Thanks also to my wondrous proofreader Fedora Chen. She always makes me look good, no matter how challenging the task.

Finally, all my love to you, readers, who make it possible for me to live my dream. Thank you so much for the letters and cards. I cherish them all.

◄ 1 ►

Party Crashers

Laser fire spattered the rusty floor like neon rain.

"What the hell—" Dred bit out, but there was no time for questions.

In ten seconds, she was fighting for her life. Along with Jael, Tameron, and Martine, she had come to wait for the supply ship. They'd been alerted as usual by the flicker of power just before lights out, so they'd hauled ass to the neutral zone in Shantytown to wait for provisions. Instead of bots unloading crates and barrels, a full squadron of armed men stormed out. She dove for cover, shouting at her people to stay low.

Why didn't I bring the Peacemaker? But she hadn't expected things to blow up like this. Some surprises couldn't be foreseen.

The smell of scorched metal filled the air as Shantytown prisoners ran amok amid the blasts. Most weren't sane to begin with, and it had been over two months since any provisions arrived. If the population hadn't been thinned so dramatically through the war with Priest and Grigor, Queensland would have already been on the verge of starvation, even with the hydroponics garden and the tetchy

Kitchen-mate. Dred could only imagine how bad things were here, with no rules or safety, just the law of tooth and claw.

Bodies dropped all around, and Dred crawled toward the corridor behind her. A few Shanty-men made it past the nose of the ship and attacked the helmeted squadron with ragged yellow nails and rusted bits of wall panel. Against full armor, they did no damage, and the soldiers picked them off with close-range shots. Their dying screams echoed in her head even as the assault gave her the necessary time to regroup.

"Fall back!" she shouted.

Martine snarled, but she could doubtless see how poor the odds were and how the Shanty-men were dying in droves. Along with Tam, she slid around the corner just behind Dred, while Jael covered their retreat. He swore as a shot sizzled against his back, but it didn't stop him. With a snap glance over one shoulder, she checked on him; anyone else would be on the ground in shock. His jaw clenched, but he ran through the pain, dodging lightning bolts bouncing off the walls behind them.

An inhuman-sounding voice crackled through the speakers on the helmet. "Let them go. We have plenty to clean up here first. We'll get them eventually."

That's what I'm worried about.

Dred sprinted until they reached Queensland; she didn't explain the rush to the sentries. Once she composed herself and discussed the situation with her advisors, she'd send Martine to update the rest of the men. Until then, they could wonder why there were no supplies. She beckoned Tam, Martine, and Jael to her quarters, where they were assured of privacy. She waited until the door closed behind them, then she secured the lock.

I learned something from the clusterfuck with Wills.

As the relatively new ruler of Queensland—it had been less than a turn since she killed Artan and took his turf—Dred had trusted Wills, a madman with a gift for prognostication, without realizing he owed his primary allegiance to

Silence. Their alliance was over now, and she knew she hadn't finished her business with Death's Handmaiden. For the time being, revenge had to wait. Once retribution had been her primary purpose, and it was the reason she'd ended up in Perdition. Time had taught Dred to be more judicious with her drive to violence.

"Report. Start with Tam." He was a slight man with brown skin and a cunning mind. From what little she knew of him, he had a knack for politics, skilled at seeing hidden snares and schemes, as well as planning his own. Since the disaster with Wills, she didn't trust him fully, but that applied to pretty much everyone in her inner circle. She didn't need to explain that she wanted to hear his observations.

The spymaster answered, "At least fifty got out of that transport. There was no room for anything else in the cargo area."

Martine added, "They all had multiple weapons, and their armor was top-notch. I doubt there's a weapon on board that could scratch it."

She was a small, dark-skinned woman with teeth filed to points to demonstrate how dangerous it was to mess with her. Though Dred hadn't always gotten along with her, in the past few months the other woman had proven her loyalty, at least as much as anyone did in a place like this. Martine was tough, smart, and honest. Like most, she'd hated Artan, and she took it personally when a raid took her men from her. At first she'd thought Dred was a coward for not pushing back immediately. Now she seemed to understand the need to evaluate resources and plan strikes accordingly.

I'm not claiming territory I can't defend.

"Apart from the turrets and the Peacemaker," Jael put in. "The uniforms had no logo, no emblems, no identifying details of any kind. That means this is black ops."

Jael was a former merc who was sent to Perdition because he was too dangerous to be allowed his freedom and too valuable to kill, mostly because he wasn't human. He was

Bred, the result of an off-the-books experiment. She didn't know how many tank-borns had survived, but Jael acted like he was alone in the universe. *Maybe he used to be. Not anymore.*

Possibly she didn't mind his difference because she had her own burden to carry. The first time she left the colony where she was born, her head nearly exploded with unwanted stimuli, a mad wash of deviant longings and murderous impulses she couldn't rightly call a gift. Things only got worse from there, and her story ended in blood, wound round with chains. *There's a reason he and I are here.* Dred controlled her empathy now, but the weight of it hadn't lessened over the turns.

Of all of her people, she relied on Jael most, probably because they felt the same, though she was far from comfortable with the development, and Dred was ready for him to turn on her, as people usually did, but it would hurt if she had to put him down; she didn't usually let people get that close.

Tam continued, "They also moved as a unit and were clearly taking orders from the one who called them back."

"Mercs," Martine guessed. "Highly paid if equipment is a gauge of earning power."

"Then what the frag are they doing here?" Dred demanded.

Jael wore a somber look. "Cleaning up."

Tam nodded. "That's my assessment as well. They've been sent to purge the facility."

She huffed out a breath, trying not to show how rocked she was by that conclusion. Things had been the same inside Perdition for turns now. Dred had no idea what political machinations had resulted in this new crisis, but they had to handle it. The worst part was, even if Queensland wiped out the first extermination crew, the Conglomerate had the budget to send more—more men with heavier weapons and deadlier tech. There was no telling what protocols were in place, however, or how long it would take before funds were skimmed and allotted to this kind of black op. It gave her limited ability to predict how much time they had between strike teams.

"The force fields never came up," Martine said, looking thoughtful. "It didn't register at the time, but usually when a supply ship docks, they lock the whole place down."

Tam paced a few steps—for him, quite a sign of agitation. "No need. They had the manpower to keep us from stealing the ship and taking off."

Jael wheeled and slammed a fist into the wall above Dred's bunk. The motion revealed the charred wreckage of his ruined shirt, nothing but smooth skin beneath. She understood how his lack of scars plagued him, a reminder that he wasn't human and never would be. In front of the others, she didn't move to his side. Didn't touch him. But her gaze lingered, silently asking, *What's wrong?*

"I've been sent on search-and-destroy missions. You go, burn everything down. Usually, it's because the territory's in dispute and someone else wants to take possession."

"They don't want to use this as a prison anymore?" Martine wondered aloud.

Dred shrugged. "It's probably getting expensive. They thought we'd kill each other off in a few turns, solve the problem without the Conglomerate's needing to dirty its hands by reinstating the death penalty."

Martine bared her sharp teeth. "But we beat the odds, huh? Carved out a little empire in here, so they're gonna take it back."

"Sod that," Jael snarled.

Dred shook her head. "We'll fight. I don't know how much good it'll do, but we know Perdition better than they do. Any schematics they brought are turns out of date."

"Equipment cannot compensate for cunning," Tam added.

She wanted to believe he was right, but based on the demolition squad wreaking havoc in Shantytown, his words might be bravado more than fact. "We won't go out easy. If they let down their guard, we might get a closer look at the ship, see if escape's an option."

Tam nodded. "We should keep our plans fluid, but there's no question we must defend. It's the only way to survive."

"Best defense is a strong offense," Jael said.

Dred raised a brow. "Did you see the heat they were packing?" She turned to Martine. "I need you to delegate five runners to carry word to all the sentries. Tam, circulate among the men and explain things. Ike can help, pull him from tinkering with the Peacemaker. This takes priority."

"What about me?" Jael asked.

"You're coming with me. I didn't see any of Katur's people in Shantytown, so he won't know what's happened. I'm hoping for some cooperation in exchange for the news."

"Good thinking. They might not be numerous in the Warren, but they're more trustworthy than Silence or Mungo's people."

She grimaced; that wasn't saying much. "Let's move."

The meeting broke up when she deactivated the electronic lock. Dred spied Calypso coming her way and dodged the questions by aiming Tam in the woman's direction; the spymaster could prevaricate with the best of them. With Jael at her heels, Dred raced back through the barricades toward the air ducts. It wouldn't take long before word spread among the Queenslanders, and she was relying on Tam and Ike to keep order.

Jael pressed ahead to scout. He gestured for her to move past him, and she went like a shadow, up the metal rungs and into the ducts. Jael pulled the panel shut after them, so nobody wandering close to their territory could easily see where they'd gone. From there it was a straight shot to the slope that led to the maintenance shafts. It was a long climb, and Katur's watchman met them at the bottom; he'd probably smelled them coming long ago.

"Why are you here?" The small humanoid had a deep voice with a hint of a growl, even when he spoke universal. Their native tongue had more guttural sounds, impossible for humans to reproduce.

"I request an audience with Katur," she said politely. "You can keep our weapons."

It was a small courtesy that cost them nothing. Jael was just as dangerous without a shiv, but Katur's people didn't know that. The sentry stripped them of their arms, then moved off, after admonishing them to wait. "If you stir, I'll know."

"So will everyone else," she murmured. A wrinkled muzzle and a flash of teeth met what she hadn't intended as a joke.

Then the guard continued until he disappeared from sight. Jael propped himself against the wall nearby, but she knew it was for a better vantage of the ladder they'd come down. He seldom relaxed all the way; the former merc slept less than anyone she'd ever known, and even when he did, he never seemed to be completely out. A whisper or a stray movement had him on his feet in a heartbeat, ready to fight. While she appreciated his wariness, he wasn't a restful bed partner.

"It doesn't make sense," she muttered, more to herself than him.

"What?"

"If they're tired of paying our upkeep, why not just blast the place?"

"They want to use the station for something else," he said. "There's no other reason to send in a cleaning crew."

"They want to retrofit again. Clear out the undesirables."

"And make the place turn a profit, if I had to guess. They might go back to refining minerals. Could also be an emergency station or a research facility for something too dangerous, unethical, or risky to be approved dirtside."

"The laws are smokier out here," she said slowly.

"Precisely, love. Whatever they want to use the place for, I guarantee it's not shiny or clean. Or the squad they sent would be sporting the Conglomerate logo."

"That doesn't make me feel any better."

"It wasn't supposed to." He offered a smile with razored edges and dark echoes. "They're in full assault gear. Nothing short of heavy weapons will penetrate. It's equivalent to durasteel but lighter and more flexible."

"Durasteel like the blast doors."

We have homemade blades and spears.

"Unfortunately, yes."

Before she could respond, Katur's guard returned. "He will see you. Briefly."

"Thank you for the courtesy." Tam had hammered it into her head that she had to treat each petty despot in here like a foreign dignitary even if she thought it was bullshit.

Dred had to admit, though, that Katur was the least insane of the lot, possibly including herself. But most of his people had been tossed in Perdition not for capital crimes, but for being nonhumans during a time unwelcoming to immigrants. So they had a better, saner group to build with, and their leader was the best of them.

Katur waited in a small room that still smelled faintly of machine oil. Once, this sublevel had been used for maintenance. These days, it was home to the aliens on board, but he kept strangers away from the rest of his people. Dred respected that caution. His mate, Keelah, was nowhere to be seen. The alien leader was short by human standards, with brindled brown fur and amber eyes, and he wore a shrewd expression as he studied them.

She recalled enough of Tam's lessons to say, "I greet you in peace."

"Likewise." Katur didn't ask about her errand.

"I'll make this quick since I need to get back to Queensland. The supply ship that just docked brought only soldiers. They're here to wipe us out."

Katur regarded her for two beats. "Why do you tell me this?"

"So you can make plans and aren't surprised by the heavily armed invaders above."

"Information is valuable. It seems unlikely that you've come out of kindness." His quiet tone said that humans rarely did anything from that motivation.

Sadly, Dred's experience dovetailed with Katur's. "I don't expect anything as formal as an alliance, but it might make things easier if we both rescinded our kill-on-sight policy—with regard to the other's personnel. It's about to get violent up in here."

"As opposed to the peace and prosperity we have enjoyed until now." The gentle irony in Katur's voice prodded a smile out of Dred.

"You make a good point."

Katur went on, "There's no question how you'll recognize my people, should they pass through your territory. But all humans look alike to us."

Jael smothered a chuckle, and she nudged him with an elbow. "You just enjoy saying that. Regardless of how we look, we don't smell like Silence's or Mungo's crew. We *bathe* occasionally in Queensland."

"Very well. The safety of your soldiers depends on their hygiene, then." That seemed to amuse Katur.

"I'll let them know," she said dryly.

"If you'll pardon me, I need to send scouts to verify what you've told me." The alien didn't reveal fear if he felt any. Maybe Perdition had burned it out of him.

"Thanks for your time."

"Thank you for the forewarning."

Dred dipped a shallow bow in response and followed the guard back to the ladder where they'd dropped down. As she climbed, she strained for the sound of laser fire but came up with only the normal groaning and banging of the ducts. Other machinery nearby made it tough to hear anything, so she wouldn't know if there was fighting on the deck above. Mentally, she mapped what she knew of the station.

They'll cross into Mungo's turf first. With any luck, his men will engage. She had no clear intel on what kind of offensive or defensive capabilities Munya could bring to bear, but they were numerous enough to slow the mercs down. She hoped. Silence's people worked best in the dark, but they would find it impossible to take out their targets through so much armor. Death's Handmaiden would have to find a workaround.

That will buy us some time.

In her mind's eye, she saw laser fire threshing the Shanty-men like wheat while the soldiers stood untouched in the armor. It reminded her of period vids she'd watched as a kid, about the dark time before humans were "civilized" and they stopped wiping out primitive people from Class P worlds with advanced weaponry. Even as a child, she'd known it was wrong, but she never considered how those people must've felt: how fear and futility came on, so powerful as to shatter the spirit. *At what point do you buckle and say, no more? This, I cannot fight.* In the vids, the doomed, noble tribe fought to the last man, then the wheels of progress rolled over him, and the credits began.

Dred didn't equate the plight of those inside Perdition with Class P sufferings, of course. Nobody here was innocent. But it was human nature to survive.

Once she swung out of the hole in the wall and down onto the ground, she glanced up at Jael. "What can we do to upgrade our defenses quickly?"

"You want my help, love?"

Though she might find it hard to speak the words with anyone else around, she said, "I need it. You're the only one with any tactical experience. The rest of us are just criminals."

His blue gaze locked with hers. "You're not *just* anything. But yeah, I've a few notions. I could use Ike's help and a crack at the parts we got as victory spoils."

"Whatever you need," she said grimly. "I have the feeling hell just got worse. And that shouldn't even be possible."

◄2►

Building the Walls

The supply closet was dark and jumbled with gears, wires, scrap metal, and lengths of pipe. Ike had some kind of organizational system with items sorted according to what could be built from each piece. Jael skimmed the make-shift shelves, narrowing his eyes to read the faded scraps of label at the bottom of each pile. Overhead, the single light flickered; when it gave up, there might not be another to replace it. He breathed in the scent of oil, dust, and the tang of hot metal, trying to focus on the blurry memory struggling to surface.

Ike interrupted his abstraction. "Something you need, son?"

"Are you busy?" Jael asked.

As usual, the old man was wrist deep in Peacemaker mechanical bits. He shook his head, wiping a hand across his brow, leaving a dark smear. "No more than usual."

"Have you heard?"

"That we have a new crop of killers among us? Yes indeed. I gather Dred wants us to tighten up security as much as possible?"

"That's the goal."

Ike nodded, wiped his palms on already stained trousers, and said, "Lead the way. I'm right behind you."

Out of necessity, Jael did the heavy lifting when they raided the parts store. Ike advised him on what would be most useful, and he loaded up. Then he headed for the first checkpoint. Jael dropped the parts and sorted through them with confident hands. Ike stood by with a weary expression. Lately, the old man had been moving with the stiffness of one who had aches and pains that defied classification. He hated the thought of seeing a man he respected just wither away, but there was no medical help available. Infuriating, when the outside world could fix Ike up right and proper.

His expression must've given him away because Ike said, "There's no cure for what ails me."

"Rejuvenex." That was an expensive antiaging treatment. Not everyone could afford it, but those who could often extended their life spans by close to a hundred turns.

Might be more, now. Jael wasn't exactly up to speed on the latest innovations.

"Not in here."

He was right, so no point in arguing. Jael put together the parts as fast as he could; there was a lot of ground to cover and no telling how much time. He'd built things like this before, when the outcome mattered less. But that was Perdition. Every day was life or death.

"Trip line, attached to a junk bomb?" Ike asked.

"Yep. Best I can do with what we've got."

"Some of that shrapnel might make it through the armor."

"I hope so. They've got the munitions to take out our Peacemaker."

"The turrets would probably cut through, too, if we could keep them pinned down long enough."

"Unlikely, unless we built blockades."

Ike looked thoughtful. "We could do it, but it would restrict our ability to leave Queensland."

"We might be trapped for the duration anyway."

The challenge came in the form of open corridors.

Eventually, he secured the trip line close to the ground and peeled back the wall panel to hide the makeshift mine. With luck, the enemy wouldn't expect convicts to be so prepared, but if their unit cohesion was anything to judge by, they wouldn't make the same mistake twice.

Still, if I can slow them down, that gives us more time to get ready.

"If you can spare me, I'll gather some of the big guys to haul junk."

Jael nodded. "We want them forced into proximity with the turrets as long as possible. We should build the barricades on this side. If they try to push past or climb them, the turrets will spin and catch them in the back."

"And pound them all the way down the corridor, until the first bend," Ike noted.

"That's the best we can do. Go. I can work and keep watch." He was fast enough to make it feasible.

When he wrapped up, Ike still wasn't back, so he moved on, installing the same security measures near each checkpoint. The sentries watched him, but they didn't try to interfere. His status as the Dread Queen's champion was secure, even more so with Einar gone. Crazy as it sounded, he missed the big man. Mercs in his unit had died before, but Jael had never minded. To him, people were a fungible resource, one easily interchanged for another. *Until Perdition.*

As he reached the third guard post, electronic feedback echoed from a sound system he hadn't even known was still functional. Doubtless it dated from back when Monsanto ran this place. The speakers popped as someone's helmet voice-software package synced with the ancient equipment.

"This is Commander Vost. I am now in charge of this facility. I've been granted authority to issue pardons to a select few, those who make themselves . . . useful. I've already seen that my schematics are outdated, based on certain renovations you've undertaken. If you want a Conglomerate pardon, the path is simple, and I have room on my ship. Help me clean this place up and be among the last five convicts standing."

"Mother Mary," he breathed.

It was an evil genius of a plan. Set the convicts to eliminate each other. When they whittled the number down to five, the mercs would mop them up. Jael wasn't gullible enough to fall for the promise of safe passage and a pardon, but he'd bet that a vast number of maniacs were. Hell, most of these guys liked killing. They were good at it. This was just an excuse to turn on each other.

Footsteps, along with the clink of Dred's chains, alerted him to her presence before she spoke. She wore metal links wrapped around her forearms, protection from enemy strikes and a potential weapon rolled into one. "It's going to be a bloodbath."

"Can you keep your people from turning on each other?"

"Don't know," she said tiredly. "The promise of freedom is . . . diabolical."

"I like my plan better. We kill the mercs and steal their ship."

"There's a lot of death between those points."

"Not ours."

She cautioned, "We don't know if it'll be possible with all of the mercs dead. We'll need launch codes most likely, and I doubt Vost will keep them on a handheld in his pocket for our convenience."

"Maybe Tam can hack the system."

"Maybe." But she didn't sound too hopeful.

"Hand me that line." No point in wasting time. The other zones might've already devolved into a frenzy of violence, but he didn't hear any chaos in Queensland.

Yet.

She did as he bade her, a good assistant. Dred folded down beside him, her knees jutting like the wings of a large and flightless bird. It was odd for him to think of her like that because she was so much predatory grace, wrapped in skin and bone, but she was also awkward angles and the tired slope of a spine that had no more steel in it. Briefly, he touched her shoulder because comfort was a foreign country to him. Then he got on with the business of mining their hallways.

"This next?" She proved she knew a little about bombs when she anticipated the part.

He nodded and installed it. With her help, the cache went together much faster than the others. Just before they left, Ike arrived with a team of muscle, all bearing junk that wouldn't be missed. It wasn't heavy enough to keep the mercs from shoving it down, but the onslaught from the turrets would soften them up before they did.

"Is the promise of pardons true?" a big Queenslander whispered to another.

The short one snorted. "You think that asshole'll stand by his word? When did anyone ever keep a promise to you?"

"You got a point."

Jael felt like a crisis had been averted. It was one thing to build barriers to keep the enemy out, another to find an adversary nearby, intending to cut his throat while he slept. A lifetime of expecting a dagger in the back had taught him to strike quick and hard, but Queensland would turn into a charnel house if that happened here. He'd be lucky to cut his way out and find a safe place to ride out the dying.

He set to work alongside the others, fitting debris in place like puzzle pieces. Too much heavy stuff on top, and the pile toppled. Soon, they blocked the passage, which made him feel trapped and claustrophobic, an uncomfortable flashback to his time in the Bug prison on Ithiss-Tor, when his whole world was bounded by an eight-by-eight hole in the wall. Perdition was big enough that he hadn't started to terror sweat yet, but now that they were closing Queensland off from the rest of the facility, the boundaries were shrinking. But he couldn't focus on weakness when there was more work to be done. Hours later, the territory was defended as well as he could manage, given limited supplies and time. The lights in this last corridor were malfunctioning, flickering, so that it gave the dirty hallway a derelict air. It was easy to imagine this place totally empty and himself as a ghost haunting it.

That'd be my luck, huh? I die, and I still can't get out of here.

Jael was careful not to reveal his uncertainty to Dred. She might have less use for him if she realized how much of a bubbling mess his brain was. Darkness and echoes and half-strangled memories from his time in the tank— and sometimes a voice in his head whispered that he *was*, in fact, a monster, so he might as well stop fighting it. Grim determination was sometimes all that kept him moving forward, along with the resolve to prove his creators wrong. *I won't come to nothing. I won't die in here.*

Dred came to check the fortifications as he turned back toward the common area. She paced around, inspecting the work, and he pulled her in for a kiss. To his surprise, she didn't stop him. He fell into her like a river of cool, clean water. Her mouth was soft and smooth, a panacea for the chains rattling in his head. Ironic, when she wore them around wrist and ankle. The metal felt cold and hard against his back when she put her arms around him.

"Don't do that in front of the men," she said quietly.

"You ashamed of me, love?"

"No. But it's not their business, and I don't want them wanking to it later."

"Hadn't thought of that. My prior incarceration didn't lend itself to such dilemmas." In the Bug prison, he had been the only humanoid, and while he ought to be used to being the only one of his kind, he never got used to the inhuman chatter echoing through the caves. "So what's the next phase of our strategy?"

He half expected her to pull away, but instead she put a hand over his heart. Nobody had ever done that before, as if she drew comfort from feeling the steady, reassuring beat. He almost made a joke about the thing being impossible to stop, but the sober look in her eyes kept him from it. Jael never imagined that he'd care whether somebody else felt like shit.

But he did.

She breathed out. "Not a fragging clue. Holing up feels like a delaying tactic at best, like we're just hiding and waiting to die. I'm not going out like that, so I need to work something out."

"Now you're talking." He barely managed to choke back some bullshit about the fight not being over until the last man's down. *What the hell's wrong with you?* If he didn't know better, he'd call it a brain infection.

"Supply run," she said, as if she'd been thinking while he studied her face. "We left things hidden in Grigor's and Priest's territories, thinking there was no rush on the hauling. But we might well need it now."

Jael nodded. "I'll assemble the others. Who do you want to take with us?"

She thought for a few seconds. "Tam and Martine."

"Not Ike?"

"He needs to stay and keep order. The men respect him."

That sounded like a good plan, so Jael let go of her and stepped back. "Then what're we waiting for, queenie? Rally the troops."

◀3▶

Blood for Blood

Once Dred gave all the orders, she went to find Ike to make a special request. "Is it all right if we borrow RC-17?" That was a boxy maintenance bot Ike had reprogrammed to do recon and help them bypass certain ship defenses. The droid's sensors might come in handy if the situation got dicey.

In answer, the old man turned the unit's remote over to Dred. "Be careful out there."

"Make sure this place is in one piece when I get back." She tapped the command button, and the unit circled her feet in response.

Ike rubbed his whiskered chin, wearing a wry expression. "Given what's going on, I make no promises."

She smiled as he intended and stripped off her chains. The skin of her forearms bore pebbled imprints from the metal; she shook her arms once, twice, getting used to the new lightness, then she bent to unwind them from her boots. It had been so long since she'd done so that she was surprised to see that the thin leather had faded in a pattern that matched the dents on her arms. Dred rubbed her fingers over her inner wrist, tracing the thorn-tree tattoo that wound up past her elbow. It was a delicate design, all black ink and pale skin—the only one she'd had done before she was sent to Perdition. The ancient symbolism had spoken to her, even then. According to the oldest tales, the thorn tree represented strife and challenges—with the promise of strength for those who overcame the odds.

"Thanks, Ike."

The old man stared at the circling bot for a few seconds, then glanced back up at her. "Two men were on the road together when they met a monster in the wilderness. One of them shoved the other down and scrambled up a tree. The second man lay there, terrified, and the beast came up to snuffle over him while the traveler held his breath and played dead. Surprisingly, that worked, and the monster went away, uninterested in carrion. When the other man dropped out of the tree, his former comrade killed him. Do you have any idea why?"

"Because he'd proven he'd turn at the first sign of trouble, and it was the wise man who knew to strike first." Dred couldn't remember where, but she'd heard some version of that parable before. "Is there some reason you're telling me this now?"

"Don't lean on anyone too hard," Ike said quietly.

"Is this about Tam again? Or Jael?"

"It's about no one in particular . . . and every man in the place."

"Not you," she said.

Tiredly, the old man shook his head. "Under the right weight, I'll buckle."

"Noted. Thank you for the story."

She signaled to Tam, Jael, and Martine, who were waiting near the center of the common room, and they joined her at a jog. The halls were eerily silent beyond the new barricades. Dred tilted her head, listening, and she didn't hear the usual scrabble of claws from the oversized rats that lived in the bowels of the station. She'd heard that the aliens hunted them for food, but they were tricky to catch and big enough to take on a normal-sized humanoid when they attacked as a pack.

More than anything else, their complete absence reinforced how serious the situation was. If the rodents had gone to ground, the mercs must be shooting up the place.

As if she shared Dred's concern, Martine muttered, "Wish we knew where those fucking mercs are."

"You're not alone." Tam slipped to the front of the group and headed off to scout.

"I'll go with you," Dred said.

Since she'd discarded her chains, she should be able to keep up, and Dred needed to keep her finger on the pulse of what went on in Perdition. While Jael shot her a look she found impossible to interpret, Tam only nodded. Soon they left the others behind, a deep sort of silence between them, born of shared trials and tragedies. Before Einar's death, she might've hesitated to call Tam a friend, but he was definitely more than an advisor.

The spymaster boosted into the ducts with her close behind and set a silent course to the nearest major intersection. Dred didn't hear the tromp of heavy boots that would indicate mercs but the *smell*—there was no nearby grille panel for visual confirmation, yet Dred was sure a large group of Mungo's men were moving nearby. Tam signaled a few things and she recalled enough from working with soldiers of fortune to understand he was indicating forty men, heading west. *Away* from Queensland.

Interesting.

She flashed her hands four times to confirm the number, and he nodded. *Not a threat we need to worry about today, at least.* Dred lifted her chin to indicate she got it, then Tam continued deeper into enemy territory. As they passed a duct panel, she glimpsed Silence's killers clad in black, moving like ghosts below. All of them had their garrotes out, which meant they planned to do some killing.

"They're headed for the Warren," Tam whispered.

Too bad for Katur and company, but Silence's choice of first strike gave Dred some room to maneuver. She experienced a pang of regret at reacting that way, but survival didn't offer the liberty of altruistic gestures. *In here, it's us or them.* Maybe, if she played her hand close to the vest, Queensland wouldn't be annihilated by the mercs. It was also possible that Katur would play a long game of cat and mouse, forcing Silence to a frustrated retreat. Nobody knew the bowels of the ship like the aliens.

"Nothing that will hinder us much," she said softly. "Let's go back to the others."

"Agreed." In private, he didn't use the faintly ironic "my queen" that he favored in front of other Queenslanders.

The return journey went much faster, now that they knew what to expect. Martine and Jael seemed edgy, though that might've been because their location had been more exposed. Jael paced forward three steps when he spotted Dred. She shook her head slightly; whatever he had to say could wait. Seeming oblivious to undertone, though doubtless that was only the impression he wished to give, Tam made a brief report of what they'd found.

Martine was frowning. "Can we circle around?"

Tam nodded. "It'll take longer, but yes. This way."

Farther on, Dred heard the distant echo of combat, but Tam veered away. Good call; she preferred not to waste time and resources on internal conflict when the mercs posed the greatest threat. If the other factions weren't completely psychotic, they'd see that themselves.

Both Jael and Martine were light on their feet. This time, if they were forced to fight, she'd opt for knives. Better if they weren't, however, at least until they had the cache.

The walls were gunmetal gray, etched with scars and encrusted with turns of grime. There hadn't been a sanitation staff since long before convicts took over the place. Ike had told her that drones like RC-17 were responsible for the cleaning, and some spots, the bots just couldn't reach. Turns of neglect had made it worse. Bulbs had burned out and not been replaced, so there were patches of shadow, loose wires dangling from broken ceiling hatches.

Tam's path took them through the neutral zone, down two levels, and out the other side. The smell alone told her they were getting close to what had been Grigor's territory. Farther on, blood smeared the walls, remnants of the battle where most of his brutes died. It had taken days to haul away the bodies.

"Left at the next turn," she said.

She sent RC-17 in to make sure no squatters had taken possession of the area, then she led her crew along to where the hallway widened into a great room. Through there and deeper in the zone, they'd hidden several crates. The stillness was making her nervous, so she quickened her step, not pausing until she opened the supply-room doors. Rubbish and empty containers were piled up in front, disguising the treasures hidden deeper within.

"Grab as much as you can carry," Dred said.

The hover dolly would've made this job easier, but it also would've been harder to maneuver, and it would've invited notice. Better to use manual labor and get it done the old-fashioned way. She and Tam scrutinized the supplies while Martine perched atop a box, reclining like a cat.

"Food first," Tam suggested.

"That's a genius idea." Martine was smirking. "Are you sure nuts and bolts aren't more important? If this death trap falls apart, we'll choke faster than we starve."

His dark eyes flashed at her. Dred left them bickering amicably as she prowled through the salvage. Once she designated the crates that needed to be moved right away, Jael piled four boxes in his arms, and she pretended she didn't realize he was showing off. She and Martine took two each, as did Tam.

"RC-17 can scout for us on the way back," Tam said.

"Agreed." She deployed the bot and let it scurry around corners.

It was programmed to beep in sequence, then speak an alert message if it encountered other life-forms. In here, it was best to assume they were hostile and respond accordingly. She moved cautiously behind the bot while they retraced their steps.

"Hard to believe this place was full of people, not that long ago," Martine said.

"Life is change." Jael wore his customary insouciant expression, the one that suggested he had no deeper feelings.

That look was a liar.

Dred drew him aside while Tam and Martine argued over the next supply priority. "What's on your mind?"

"Nothing, queenie. What makes you think otherwise?" The flat tone gave away more than he intended.

I know you better than that now.

"Don't lie to me," she said.

He pushed out a breath, his blue eyes unusually dark. "I'm thinking about Einar, all right? He was a bastard and a murderer or he wouldn't have been here, but I've not had so many friends in my life that I can just shrug him off."

"I know what you mean." She wanted to put a hand on his arm or run her fingers through his hair. That longing became a spike in her chest, but she didn't act on it. "I feel like I let him down."

"Me too," he whispered.

Before she could respond, Jael whirled in response to the RC-17 unit's beeping wildly. "Organics detected. Unauthorized personnel."

"Boxes down," Dred ordered. "Looks like we get to fight."

Martine dropped her burden and popped her neck on each side. "And to think I was afraid this would be boring."

"Since when?" Jael asked. "There's always the threat of imminent violence. That's why we vacation here."

Please don't let them be mercs. We're not ready to take on an armored unit.

Dred felt naked without her chains, but she swung around the corner with a blade in each hand. She was relieved to see four of Silence's killers, even odds. These men were dressed in black from head to toe, blood-whorl patterns on their forearms and their faces made up like skulls. Possibly they had broken off from the larger group and been sent on some dark errand.

A hunting party. Time to make them prey.

Like all of Silence's crew, this lot didn't speak. There were no growls of rage, no threats; the enemies just readied their weapons. Each one of them faced off against an opponent, though Dred knew from prior experience that Jael could've taken all four by himself. But she didn't like revealing his inhuman prowess, even to her inner circle. If anyone else figured out his healing trick, they'd cut him open just to watch him seal the wound. Queensland still had its share of sadistic bastards. In a place like Perdition, it couldn't be otherwise.

Dred's opponent was tall and gaunt with a spidery quality to his limbs. His long face, painted like a skull, along with yellowed eyes, gave him the look of a man who was already dead. As they circled, he flashed her a glimpse of his tongueless mouth, likely to intimidate her with his commitment to Silence's madness; his tongue had been severed at the base, so there was only a pink scar at the back. Revulsion did creep down her spine like scuttling, segmented legs, but she didn't let it affect her determination to kill the bastard.

When he lunged at her, she spun to the side, nearly slamming into Martine, who aimed a scowl at her. Dred was better with her chains than close-up with knives; she knew better than to let the man grapple. He had better reach, and Silence's crew was fast with their garrotes. He could slice clean through her throat if she gave him an opening.

She lashed out, first with her right hand, then her left, but he blocked both strikes. He nearly snagged her wrist, but she twisted out of the attempted hold and came out with her knife still in her hand. *You've gotten sloppy, relied on the chains too much.* Dred tried to remember old techniques and circled her knives so he'd be watching those instead of her feet. When she was sure he was waiting for a blade strike, she kicked him in the crotch. Silence's men still had testicles apparently; he flinched enough to give her an opening and she slashed a line across his throat. The skin peeled back in a wet red bubble, then he toppled.

Martine and Jael had already dropped theirs, but Tam was still working. He said without turning, "Feel free to wade in. We need to get those supplies back."

Jael ended the fight with a closed-fist blow to the man's temple. He didn't look strong enough for that to be a one-shot kill, but the enemy dropped like a stone. Martine regarded him with a speculative expression, gaze skimming down his lean frame, taking in the ropy musculature and the deceptive breadth of his biceps.

"Secret technique?" she asked with a raised brow.

Dred wasn't sure if the other woman could be trusted, but her options for lieutenants had shrunk with all the dying, plus Wills's betrayal after the massacre on Grigor's turf. The fact that they'd won in the end didn't change how many men she'd lost, and there would be no reinforcements. She was watching Martine, for sure, but she couldn't afford to cut her out of the loop. The woman was fierce and ruthless, and she wasn't psychotic, which was more than could be said for most of Perdition's inmates.

"I studied for decades with a bunch of monks," Jael said, straight-faced.

"I'm sure. Because our people are known for discipline."

"Our people?" Tam asked.

"Convicts. The lawfully challenged, if you prefer."

Jael laughed. "Lawfully challenged. I like that."

Dred interrupted, "The longer we stand here, the likelier it is we run into more trouble. Let's get these supplies back to Queensland before they decide we've abandoned the place, and Ike's facing a revolt."

"You think that could happen?" Martine wanted to know.

Dred shrugged. "In here? Probably. We need to be there, reminding the men that they can't believe that merc's promises. Otherwise . . ."

"It would be a massacre," Tam predicted.

She couldn't look directly at the threat of complete eradication without the shakes setting in. Though Tam had built the mythos of the Dread Queen, she wasn't a leader and never had been. Outside, she had been a solitary killer, a vigilante who hunted in the shadows. And she didn't know if she had the strength to hold Queensland together.

Not through this. But I don't know how to give up, either.

◁4▷

Echoes in Darkness

Queensland was in an uproar when they got back. Long before they reached the first checkpoint, Jael made out shouting voices, arguments raging in multiple corridors. *Too much to hope that they're all clever lads.* Though a few of the big brutes who had built the barricades might've seen through the empty promises, others weren't so savvy. *If this rot runs too deep, we'll have to cut our losses and run.* But Jael understood well enough that it would be the same as admitting defeat. While a smaller group might be able to hide longer, they'd have even less chance at taking out Vost's crew.

Dred wore a thunderous scowl as the sentry stopped them though they were obviously laden down with provisions. "Is what the merc said true? People have been saying it might not be a bad idea—"

"If you fight us," Dred cut in, "then you stop being a Queenslander. You can go join Mungo or Silence. They'd kill their own because an outsider said to. We don't."

"Artan did," the man muttered.

"And he's dead now. Maybe you want me to end you,

too." Dred took a step closer, and even without her chains, she was both terrifying and beautiful. She pulled a blade from her thigh sheath and set it gently to his throat. "Just say the word."

Dred flicked her wrist, and a pinprick of red appeared on the man's throat. Neither Jael nor Tam would dream of intervening. For her part, Martine looked downright eager.

The guard gulped and dropped his eyes. "No. Sorry. I'll man my post."

"See that you do," she said.

They pushed past with the supplies, then had to pass them across the barricades; the debris was piled nearly to the ceiling, with just a meter or so clearance, barely enough space for the crates. The last two containers, Jael shoved from the other side until the carton left scrapes on the ceiling.

"Put your back into it," Martine teased.

He leaned to the side to give her a look. "I shove any harder, and I'll pull off the ceiling panels."

She grinned back. "Men always overestimate their abilities."

Tam, Martine, and Dred wrenched hard from the inside, and centimeter by centimeter, the boxes shifted. At last they had the goods on the right side of the blockade, where their people could use them. A pang went through him. *What the hell. When did I start thinking of this flotsam as mine?* But he felt protective of this place even though it was a cesspool, maybe because of Dred. Her inner circle took their cues from her, treating him like a person, like he was worth something. This was the last place where he should trust anyone; intellectually he knew that. She'd probably kill him if it came down to his life or hers, but the hard facts no longer felt quite so incontrovertible.

"Where should we put this stuff?" Martine asked.

Good question, since with the bitching he heard in all corners, looting might be a problem. Dred looked thoughtful as Tam answered, "I know of a storeroom where the electronic lock still works."

"Nobody can hack it?" Jael asked.

"Unlikely," Martine said. "It would require high-tech equipment to bypass. It's not like an analog lock you can open with picks." At their collective stare, she added, "What? I had a life before I ended up in here."

Dred grinned. "Sounds like an interesting one."

"I did all right."

"Did the teeth come before or after?" Jael wondered aloud.

He expected the woman to threaten to bite him, but apparently she considered him enough of a friend to answer. "I filed them my first week in. Men were less interested in trying to rape me when word got around that I bite the penis off anybody who touches without permission."

"I take it you did that at least once, to prove a point?"

She smiled. It was impressive. And startling. "Doesn't taste like chicken."

Tam was regarding her with new interest. "We *must* get better acquainted."

"You serious?" Martine seemed surprised, but Jael heard the pleased skitter of her pulse. Tam had never shown interest in anyone that Jael had noticed—of any gender or species. *Until now.*

"Most definitely."

"What was it, the biting? Don't worry, I don't have to chew all the way through."

"I feel like we should leave these two alone," Dred said.

Jael nodded. "Likewise. You stay with the goods. Dred and I will make two trips, then you can lock up, Tam. Sound good?"

Ordinarily, the spymaster would help with the hauling, but he seemed quite distracted by Martine. *Right, then.* Since the other two didn't answer, Jael followed Dred down the hall to the storeroom. The low murmur of conversation started as soon as he stepped away; he could've eavesdropped, had he been so inclined, but there was no reason to spy on a personal exchange though he'd done it as part of a contract more than once.

"So *that* was interesting."

"I'd wondered what rang his bell," Dred said.

"Now we know. Do you think we should leave them alone for a while?" Jael spoke in a light tone, hoping the nascent spark between Tam and Martine would distract her, even for a little while.

Her smile was fleeting, and it revealed how troubled she was. "No time."

The door swooshed open at her approach. *Looks like the motion detectors are still working.* She slid into the room and carried her crates to the back wall before setting them down gently. Her careful restraint, so obviously a sign that she was holding on to her composure by her fingernails, made him feel . . . something, but damned if he knew what to call it. Tension rode low in his stomach, like he wanted to pull her close for a few seconds, but she wouldn't stand for it, even if he wouldn't feel like an arse doing it. They didn't have that sort of relationship, and he didn't even know if he wanted it. Each step closer to her made him feel like he was walking on razor blades with a pit of spikes below.

"Let's get the second load."

The next trip went quicker, as Dred seemed driven, like someone would steal the supplies if she didn't get them locked up fast enough. *Hell, maybe she's right.* Tam and Martine were talking earnestly, though the woman wore a pert smile. For his part, Tam showed more animation than Jael had witnessed from him previously, and his heartbeat was a little fast. Jael stopped himself from checking for other signs of interest.

Not my business.

Martine turned at their final approach. "You ready?"

Dred nodded. "Lock it down, Tam."

Jael expected that she'd leave them to it, but Dred supervised the securing of the storeroom. He tracked her eyes as she memorized the code. The door swished shut, and her shoulders relaxed. Tam stepped back, wearing a satisfied expression.

He turned to Dred. "If you'll excuse me, I have some matters to attend to."

"Mind if I tag along?" Martine wanted to know.

"Not at all."

With a tip of his chin in farewell, Tam led Martine away on some mysterious business. Jael didn't doubt it was important though, and beneficial to Queensland. He stretched, rolling his neck side to side. Then he flashed Dred a smile.

"Buy you dinner?"

Amusement flickered deep in her green eyes. "Why not? Let me get my chains first."

After she picked them up from Ike, they went to the common room, much emptier than it had been when he first arrived. As Jael headed for the meal station, he caught fragments of conversation.

"I'm telling you, it's a mistake not to jump on this—"

"You're a moron." The smaller man thumped a fist to emphasize his impatience.

The bigger one shoved to his feet, eyes veined in red. He had a fiery bulb of a nose that said he was a drunkard and on his way to liver failure. His knuckles were scarred from turns of issuing brutal beatings. "Let's settle this right now."

Jael saw the moment when the other man realized things were about to escalate. "That's exactly what that merc wants. You're playing into his hands."

Jael paused by their table, flattening a palm between them. At the interruption, they both turned with vicious looks that faded when they realized he was the Dread Queen's champion. That was a new experience for him; usually when he scared the shit out of other men, it was wholly due to his own nature.

"There's too much bullshit at this table and not enough eating," he snapped. "You want some help with that spoon?"

There was a long silence, then the little one answered. "No, we're good."

The rest of the room took a hint from the exchange, and the arguing died down. He leveled a long look across bearded faces, thin and sallow ones, bloodshot eyes, and sunken cheeks. Once he was sure they'd taken his message, he caught up with Dred, who was talking to Cook. Or rather, talking *at* him.

Cook was a big man, tall as Einar had been but without the bulky muscles; he was burly and broad-shouldered, with pale skin and a bald head that gleamed as if no hair had ever grown on it. His hands and arms were scarred from multiple knife wounds, and a red tattoo snaked out from his sleeveless shirt. Jael studied the characters but couldn't read the word. It wasn't in universal, and his formal education didn't offer a lot of variety.

"There are crates of organic in the storeroom," Dred was saying. "If you need to restock the Kitchen-mate, talk to Tam."

The chef's eyes flickered. Smart of her not to mention that he and Martine had the code, also. "So what's on the menu?" Jael asked.

The other raised both brows and gestured to the pot.

"I'll take a bowl." Because that was the only option.

Cook didn't do special orders or substitutes. And he wasn't fond of complaints either.

To nobody's surprise, the meal of the day was vegetable goulash with synth-protein stirred in. Cook slopped it into his bowl, but Jael had been eating scraps for so long in the Bug prison that the smell was faintly appetizing. Dred took her serving and stood, looking for a free seat. Really, she should commandeer one, but he sensed that she was feeling too tired to carry the Dread Queen crap at the moment.

Vix stood up near the back wall and beckoned. Zediah glanced up to see who she was signaling, and he offered a fleeting smile. Jael touched Dred's arm. "Over here."

"You know them?" she asked.

"Slightly."

"They're not much for fighting. No idea how the hell they ended up here."

That piqued his interest. "They came in together?"

"On the same transport."

"Wonder if they committed their crimes together out there," Jael whispered.

Dred frowned at him as they joined the other two. She set her bowl down and started eating at once. Jael winked at Vix as he took a seat.

Zediah said calmly, "Do that again, and I'll pop your eye out."

"He's protective. Don't mind him."

Jael knew a fleeting moment of curiosity as to how far back their connection went. Zediah hardly looked old enough to be incarcerated here, but it was possible he'd taken enough Rejuvenex to make him look eerily young. That would mean the man came from money, however, and had a fetish for "older women," but curious as he was, Jael respected the rules of Perdition, and he didn't ask personal questions while he spooned down the grub.

"Tell me the truth," Zediah said. "How long before the mercs kill us all? I'm not asking for false promises, mind you. Just an estimate of how long we've got."

Vix nudged him hard with her elbow. "Stuff the attitude."

Whatever Zediah might've said was forestalled by the alarm blaring throughout Queensland. "Incoming. Mungo's mongrels closing fast!"

◄5►

Enemies at the Gate

Dred raced for the nearest checkpoint. By the sound of it, they had incoming at three of the four checkpoints. She bit out a curse, and shouted, "Calypso, take some men to the east barricades but be careful of the turrets. They'll fire through the scrap."

"On it," the other woman called back.

She opened her mouth to give orders to Jael, but he was already rounding up some Queenslanders. "I've got the west. You're heading north?"

"That's the plan. All right, new fish, today you get to fight!" Though she'd told the men who used to belong to Grigor that they'd be on manual labor, no weapons, for a full turn, this was a special circumstance.

If they were smarter, they'd wonder why I'm letting them arm up.

Truth was, they needed the battle fodder. The dumb brutes roared with approval and jogged after her. Their path took them past the armory, and they chose some blades, then she sent them toward the checkpoint ahead. Tam didn't have to be right at her ear, whispering caution, for her to see

potential traps and snares; now it was second nature to consider all the ways people could betray her. Shit way to live,
but in some regards, each day was an unexpected bonus. If
nothing else, Perdition had taught her to exist in the moment
and make the most of each opportunity.

From all over the zone came the staccato fire of the turrets and shrieks of pain. She hoped the sentries had the
sense not to get shot. If they ran out of ammo before
Mungo ran out of bodies, however—eh, best not to predict
the future. When Dred reached the barricades, she saw
two guards standing well out of firing range and the towering wall of junk had holes blown through it, all the way to
the opposite wall. Dodging the sting of live rounds, she
sprinted up and snuck a peek through one of those rents to
scope out the situation. Eight big lunks stood behind
Mungo himself, eager to mix it up. He was a filthy, hirsute
brute with red hair growing wild all over his body, and he
bared his yellow, half-rotten teeth in challenge.

"Shut it down," she shouted to the guards.

We need to conserve ammo.

In reply, the guns fell quiet and junk tumbled from the
top of the blockade as Mungo and his crew shoved. Dred
shouted orders, and the new fish stared at her blankly.
Apparently, Grigor hadn't specialized in strategy, just
mayhem. *Never mind, then.* The wall came down with a
final massive push, and the first of Mungo's cannibals
breached the perimeter. On the other side, bloody corpses
assured Dred their measures had helped, but she couldn't
afford to waste bullets on Mungo. They would die easily
compared to Silence's killers or armed mercs.

As the cannibals charged, Dred slapped her chains into
the opposite palm and fell into a fighting stance. The first
three were injured so bad that they stumbled forward in a
slick of blood and dropped to their knees. Their comrades
paid them no heed, scrambling over their dying moans to
rush at Dred and her comrades. Drool trickled from their
mouths, as if they saw them not as an enemy to be con-
quered but a potential feast.

"Eat this," one of the new recruits snarled and slammed a blade through the mongrel's throat.

Up close, it had never been clearer to Dred how degraded Mungo's subjects had become. Their coordination was off as they swung in wild lurches, teeth snapping, and long strings of frothy spit surging each time they opened their mouths. *Are they . . . rabid?* Their eyes didn't seem to focus clearly, and their long, curled nails were encrusted with grime. The new Queenslanders pushed the defense, lashing out with the brutal strength that had been such a pain in the ass when they served Grigor. Since she hadn't let them drink, they were sober and angry, lots of pent-up aggression to work off. Mungo's men fell in droves, in no way equal to Queensland recruits. Dred held her own with a lash of chain and slice of her blade. Spilled Munyan blood reeked, as if the men were rotting from the inside.

She lurched backward, stumbling over a pile of entrails, and slammed into the wall. A begrimed fist smashed into the metal beside her head, hard enough to leave a dent. While they might be revolting, they were still killers. Dred swept with her chain, tripping her opponent, and as he struggled to keep his feet, she finished him with a swipe of her knife. The battle was madness all around, a cacophony of threats and screams, snarls and grunts from Grigor's former recruits that sounded almost like pleasure. A shiver went through her.

This truly is hell.

When his men were nearly gone, Mungo broke and ran. She considered giving chase and decided that was exactly what he wanted. It might even be an ambush, though that could be giving the monster too much credit. Possibly he was all hunger and instinct at this point. Once the dying stopped, she checked the turrets, careful to keep her reaction from the rest of the men. *Not much ammo left. I have to check on the other guns and see what we have in storage.* The drafted Queenslanders bumped chests hard and slugged each other with roars she recognized from Grigor's reign. *Damn. I wish I knew whether I should quell that. But it's not like it's a song glorifying his territory.*

In the end, she let them celebrate before saying, "There's something seriously wrong with Mungo's crew."

One of them turned with a look of thinly veiled contempt. "Yeah, they *eat* people."

"*Medically* wrong," she said icily.

"I read you can get diseases from eating your own kind," a guard put in.

She turned to him with increased interest. "Really?"

"Yeah, especially if there was something wrong with your dinner's brain."

That might explain a lot about Mungo's territory if they were all diseased and getting worse. It meant they weren't a threat long term, but in the short term, their actions would be impossible to predict. She made a mental note to ask Tam about it; the spymaster seemed to be fairly well informed about a wide variety of subjects.

Dred raised her voice. "Good work, all of you. Let's get this blood mopped up."

With luck, the rest of the checkpoints had held as well.

TAM was already some distance from Queensland when the sirens went off. He hesitated, and Martine said, "We can't turn back. They can drive off the attack without us, and if you're serious about scouting the other territories, this might well be the best time."

She had a point. With Mungo's forces committed to the run at Queensland, they'd be paying less attention to their own borders. "Then we'll continue on."

In the old days, prior to the conflict with Priest and Grigor, he would've needed to be far more cautious, as there would've been other scouting patrols coming this way to spy on Queensland as well. Before, there would've been traps and cloak-and-dagger games as he made his way toward his goal. But this time, the corridors were eerily deserted, just scarred metal and old stains marking days long past. Nonetheless, he couldn't stop checking behind them, as if the ghosts of enemies past might be stalking them.

"You've never taken anyone with you before, huh?"

That wasn't why Tam was edgy, but it seemed best to let her think she had him figured out. Being attracted to Martine didn't mean he wanted her to understand all his inner workings. "Is it so obvious?"

"You keep looking around as if you expect someone to stop us. But don't worry, I won't hold you back."

She was light on her feet, quick as a shadow as she boosted up ahead of him into the ducts. Tam listened, but he heard only the battle near Queensland before he vaulted up behind her. He used this entrance enough that he'd swept the dust away with his knees. Martine was waiting for him up ahead, where the passage widened.

"Which way, pet?"

Tam raised a brow. "Let's be clear, Martine. You don't hold my papers. Even should we come to an arrangement down the line, those private moments don't bleed over."

She stepped up to him, dark eyes fierce. Then she smiled and her filed teeth sent a frisson of anticipation through him. "If you're with me, they will because you'll never want anything else."

Damn. Maybe so.

With some effort, he forced a cool expression before deliberately dismissing her confidence with a tilt of his head. He slipped past her, moving toward Mungo's territory. Martine was quiet as they traveled. Tam didn't need to warn her that even a whisper could carry a surprising distance, and she was light enough not to make any noise as she followed. He hadn't gone this way in quite some time; for the last half turn, he had been watching Grigor and Priest.

Hard to believe they're no longer a threat.

The alliance with Silence had certainly been a devil's bargain. He'd calculated her treachery though he hadn't counted on Wills. *That mad bastard.* In the end, the strategy paid out as he'd expected, and they'd defeated Grigor and Priest with the Handmaiden's help. Now Queensland stood alone once more in midst of chaos and combat with a new threat burning like wildfire. *I'll reckon a way around it. I always do.*

But last time, it had cost Einar his life. Sheer inner steel made him square his shoulders and push forward, ignoring the pain and regret of that mistake. Tam slid down a level and paused. Though he hadn't heard any fighting for a while, the sounds of a fresh battle reached him. He glanced over his shoulder and gestured to Martine that they'd take a look before continuing on. It was tricky to find a vantage, but he managed and peered through the vent. Down below, mercs squared off against the mongrel horde. He might've guessed it was Mungo's men, as the whole area smelled disgusting: unwashed bodies, stale sweat, rancid meat grease, and scatological effluvia.

The close quarters slowed the mercs, but they fired point-blank, mowing down man after man. Bodies were thick on the ground already. Martine crept up beside him before he could warn her that was a bad idea, and the panel groaned beneath their combined weight. Her dark gaze met his, wide with alarm, then the grille gave way, dropping them into the middle of the battle. He landed on top of a dead body and immediately rolled to the side and drew it up as a shield. Two mercs shot the corpse, so the smell of burning meat filled his nostrils. Martine fared better as she immediately dove away and went scrambling around the corner, with laser blasts slamming into the floor behind her.

Clever girl. Save yourself.

Blade in hand, Tam slashed the hamstring of the nearest mongrel. The wound gushed blood as the leg gave way. Two mercs shot, and his victim jerked, dying. *Thanks for that.* But now the mercs were sizing him up, trying to decide if he posed a greater threat. In the end, they went for numbers, but Mungo's men had a description of the Dread Queen's spymaster, and they didn't care how many of them died as long as they took him with them. Laser fire painted his vision red, a strobe effect that reminded him of a bar he'd trolled, before everything changed. Before Tarnus.

Before I set things right.

He mistimed a movement in the wash of memory, and the bastard he was using as cover was too heavy for him to haul for long. A blade sliced into him from behind, a solid strike. *Another few centimeters, and I'm gone.* The pain crippled him. For a few seconds, he didn't see how he was getting out of this. And then Martine popped back around the corner, her blade sailing in a beautiful arc and slammed into a mongrel's forehead. The bastard toppled, giving Tam the opening to throw himself forward. A laser burst slammed into his calf as he scrambled toward Martine.

"You should've left me," he panted, as she hauled him forward.

The mercs took a few steps toward them, but the surviving mongrels seized that opportunity to renew their attack, so the mercs swung away and engaged. Two mongrels launched themselves at a single merc and dragged him to the ground, but his mates unloaded. The rifles went full auto behind them. Martine yanked him along despite his wounded leg and the blood gushing from his back.

"Not happening," she said cheerfully. "I owe you, was my fault we ended up like that. And if I get how these things work, we were on the verge of an understanding, yeah?"

He choked out a gasp of a laugh. "It would be my pleasure."

VOST strode through the command center, inspecting the facilities. The station was shot to shit, not worth the time it took to clean it out, but the payday had been too much for him to refuse. *Resistance has been heavier than we were led to expect, too.* But that was nearly always the case with bureaucratic assholes; they drew up mission parameters without regard for real-world conditions. They drew up charts, graphs, and budgets, then expected a miracle from their hired grunts.

He deployed the drone cams to keep track of the patrols. He watched a bizarre three-way battle, and he saw two of the combatants break free and bolt. The fact that they dropped from above told him that they weren't run-of-the-mill convicts; they had the brains to try and avoid his patrols, but something told him that wasn't their main motivation. Vost noted their faces as best he could and watched the fight for a few seconds before ascertaining that his men were wiping out the savages armed with blades and spears. A few of the prisoners seemed to be trying to attack with their damned teeth, useless against heavy armor.

Which means they're completely insane.

Shaking his head, he checked on the mainframe/handheld connection. This room had antiquated equipment, but he plugged in his own gear, interfacing where necessary to update the 'ware. Before he finished the job, his second-in-command, Casto, strode up. He was a tall man with mud brown hair and deep-set eyes. Not even his mother would call him attractive, but he was dogged and persistent, and he didn't break in battle, no matter how many assholes were coming at him. Vost admired those nerves of steel though he also wondered if the man was slightly brain-damaged. Fear was a normal response, one a soldier had to learn to overcome, hut Casto didn't seem to experience it. However, he also had a strong sense of self-preservation, and he didn't take stupid risks. That was part of why Vost had chosen him as his second. He wasn't likely to risk the men in some misguided desire to be a hero. No, Casto was too selfish for that. Given the option, the man would always choose to live and fight another day.

The lieutenant wore a frown and a thoughtful expression. While the former looked natural on him, the latter did not. "I'm not sure dividing the men so soon was the best idea. These assholes are more aggressive and more organized than they said."

Vost nodded. Well enough, he remembered the meeting with the Conglomerate drone in his expensive suit and his smooth Rejuvenex face. *"They've probably devolved into an animal state by now. It won't be a normal black op. It'll be easier, I imagine. Just like shooting a bunch of rabid dogs."* Then he'd made an offer so astronomical that Vost hadn't asked any more questions; he'd simply rallied his men the next day.

But he couldn't reveal misgivings this early in the engagement. "We'll clear this place. It'll just take a little longer than we thought."

Casto lifted one shoulder in a half shrug. "If you say so. Then, shall I take the rest and see how many I can kill?"

Inspiration struck. This initiative would counter the unwelcome surprise that the job might take weeks instead of days. "Sometimes I think you're smarter than you look, Casto. I've already got the morons mowing each other down. Now I need to motivate our guys."

"What?" Casto was young to be second-in-command of a highly paid merc outfit, and subtlety wasn't his forte.

But Vost wasn't talking to him anymore. He put on his helmet and activated the internal communication system. "Attention, all units. I hope you're keeping track of your kills. Use the helmet cam to document and the one with the highest body count will receive a 25 percent bonus on top of his usual cut."

An excited, collective "Yes, sir" came back to him, then he cut the comm connection, not wanting to distract the men hunting with wondering if he was listening in. Sometimes he did, of course, but they never knew about it. And he'd go on patrol next time personally, once all the equipment was set up. He couldn't lead these men if he wasn't as good at killing as they were. Better in some cases.

"You can go ahead and transfer that into my account," Casto said with a cocky grin. Then he whipped a quick salute and spun in tight posture to find his squad.

"And then there was one," Vost muttered.

He hated this part of an op, but since he was the best with the gear—and the mission would suffer from lack of reliable intel—he completed the installation and made sure all tech was shaking hands and playing nice. He whizzed through activating the drone cams and sent them out to map the facility. A few early missteps before they found the tech lab had shown him that the schematics he'd been given were hopelessly outdated. The cons had been inventive in making the station their own; there were traps and hidden defenses all over the place, and if it hadn't been for the damned expensive armor, he would've already been a man down just in setting up the command outpost.

One by one, his screens lit up with preliminary footage from his bots. They showed about what he expected, then he sent out a warning to Bravo team. "There's mooks on the move, twenty of them. No weapons that can penetrate your armor. Continue as you are, and you'll be on them in approximately 150 meters."

"Copy that," Bravo leader came back. "I can taste those extra credits already."

He watched as the unit engaged, and the battle was clean, surgical, even. Whoops rang over the comm as the last fell, then the men moved on. He watched as more images came in and wondered why he felt unsettled. *Probably because that Conglomerate asshole made this job sound too good to be true.*

Things that seemed that way usually were.

◀6▶

Best-Laid Plans

Mungo's crew wasn't quite to the west barricades yet. They came in, lurching drunkenly toward the wall, activating the turrets. From his vantage on the other side, Jael watched as the guns mowed them down, but there were enough bodies that they used the death of their mates to push forward. The wall of junk teetered as the brutes scrambled toward the other side, bullets drilling them from the back. Jael was taking a risk by defending close up; his men stood to the rear, waiting for him to kill the enemy or for the cannibals to leave the turret's range. One mongrel managed to ram his head through the gap, and Jael was waiting with a blade. He shanked the brute in the neck and left his corpse to block the way.

From behind, another of the brute's cohorts shoved until the body fell and he took his place. The screams of the dying men echoed until Jael's ears rang with them. The pressure eased as the rounds slammed into the enemy trying to breach their defenses. Jael killed a couple more who made it to the top and yanked them through so he could keep fighting, but the last one died on the floor in a spray of ammunition. The turrets fell silent.

He risked another look, and the hall was clear. *Must've been more of them on the other side*. In the corridor, there were fourteen bodies blown full of holes in various poses, starting from the beginning of the sensor activation all the way to the wall. Then they were piled high enough that he couldn't see for sure how many there were. Nothing for it but to climb over, haul the corpses, and start rebuilding the barricade.

"How many dead over there?" Dred asked, striding up.

Her checkpoint must've held. In here, good news was rare enough that he'd take this as a victory. But he was damned tired of the stench of blood and bodily functions, weary of the endless carnage. Before, it was only a job. Now he wanted out with a ferocity that made the recycled air taste coppery and thin, too tainted for breathing.

Jael lifted a shoulder. "We'll have to take inventory as we deal with the bodies."

"The barricades helped, at least." What she didn't say was how fast Mungo's men crawled over them . . . and how determined they were. Nothing deterred them. "I've got Grigor's louts tidying up on the north side. I'll send them over here when they finish."

"I'll get the work started," Jael said.

They had been hauling corpses for a while when Martine stumbled back toward the checkpoint. Jael saw her coming, dropped the dead mongrel he was carrying, and powered down the turrets. Tam was pale and sweaty, his jaw clenched with the effort of moving on an injured leg.

"A little help?" she shouted.

Jael ran toward them and lifted the other man without asking for permission. "I'll take you to Dred's quarters, and we'll see how bad it is."

Dred nodded. "Bunk there until you feel better, no arguments. It's the cleanest place in Queensland."

"Thanks," the man said hoarsely.

An hour later, it was clear Tam wouldn't be going on recon missions anytime soon. *We didn't count on this.* There was no telling how long the spymaster would be out of commission. He was resting at the moment, with Martine looking after him, but his injuries meant they couldn't include him in any plans for a while. Since his skill set was hard to replace, it put them in a hell of a bind.

Dred met him in the hallway. "We'll bed down in the barracks tonight."

"Understood."

He didn't sleep well, mostly because he wasn't used to being surrounded by other people. Though the room was sparsely populated, there were too many lungs pushing air in and out, too many hearts thumping away. He felt like shit when he rolled out of the bunk, and he definitely missed the private shower. The public facilities had a dank, yeasty smell.

"I think I've come up with a workable solution," Dred said after breakfast.

She filled him in. After he learned what she had in mind, Jael wondered if Vix and Zediah could really sub in for Tam and Martine. He'd never done field work with them, never seen them do anything at all outside the garden. Yet Queensland needed every advantage it could muster, and timing was critical.

"You sure about this?" he asked.

Dred nodded. "I asked a few key questions. They're both smart, the most technical-minded I could find on short notice."

"Then I can't wait to watch them work."

"Is everyone ready to go?" Dred asked.

"As we'll ever be," Vix murmured.

Despite her scars, she radiated a peculiarly peaceful air. She didn't seem like a woman who had done something so violent, so repugnant, that she ended up dumped in Perdition to keep her from repeating the offense. Zediah was harder for Jael to read; he maintained a perpetually opaque expression, and his vital signs seldom responded to normal stimuli. Either he was stoic beyond measure, or there was something . . . off about him.

No surprise in a place like this.

"Let's do it," Jael said.

This run was likely to be dangerous. While turrets might cut through the merc armor, the ones who scrambled over the wall like the mongrels had done wouldn't go down so easy, and they could probably take out the Peacemaker with collective effort. Then the personnel would be defenseless. *We need better odds.*

And there was only one way to make that happen.

"We set up in the main corridor leading to Queensland. There's no guarantee the mercs will make their approach this way, but the chances are good." She spoke as she ran, keeping the RC unit ahead of her.

Since it was quiet, that meant the bot didn't detect any life signs. Urgency pounded in his blood, an echo of his heartbeat. He'd already crushed a drone cam that the mercs had sent to spy on their territory. Dashing it against the wall had felt pretty fragging good, but it also meant he had to keep a sharp eye out for more. If Vost saw what they were planning, he'd warn his troops.

And then it's game over.

Jael was conscious that their time was limited, and he had no idea how well Vix and Zediah could perform under pressure. Each of them carried a bundle of parts necessary for the plan to succeed, and he was watching the whole time they moved—for mongrels, assassins, and mercs. At last, Dred stopped, surveyed the hallway, and nodded.

"Here. Zediah, hand me the cord."

With everyone working in concert, it became clear to him why Zediah and Vix had been included. They might not be on Ike's level of cleverness, but they both had some engineering aptitude. What had been a rough sketch on a dirty wall came to life with their efforts. Jael did the heavy lifting, hoisting the thing, then he helped Dred hide the tripwire. Triggering would bring the trap down from the ceiling; primitive, but it might disorient the mercs long enough for their primary aim to succeed.

"The ceiling won't hold indefinitely," Zediah said, replacing the last panel.

They'd chosen this stretch intentionally, as some parts

of the station had solid metal overhead instead of panels, but here, there was maintenance access, a space just wide enough for someone to crawl up to perform repairs. Which meant they'd wedged their trap above and run the line down the wall. If the mercs were paying attention, they'd spot it. Sweat beaded on his brow as he swung down, careful not to touch the wire.

Vix beckoned from the T intersection; they needed to hole up in the bot-charging alcove. If the plan failed, they only needed to retreat and haul ass for Queensland. It would sting to come back empty-handed but better that than injured—at least as far as the others were concerned. He'd noticed after the last battle, however, that his injuries weren't healing as fast as they used to. They still sealed, but it took twice as long, and the scar lingered before vanishing into seamless skin. He didn't care to ponder what it meant.

"Mary, I hope it's not Mungo's idiots who bring that down," Vix whispered.

Jael nodded, folding into a crouch. They wouldn't be able to see the enemy from here, but with his hearing, he'd be able to tell when they were approaching. It was likely smell would give them away, too. Mungo's mongrels reeked in a particular way, different from the necrotic rot that wafted from Silence's killers. She never seemed to require them to bathe, and since they lived with dead things, the decomp stench had sunk into their skin. So mercs should smell clean and sharp by contrast, all durasteel and oiled weapons.

In the end, the boots gave them away before he could smell them. The clomp was distinctive, unlike any footwear crafted inside. A guy in Queensland made boots out of rodent skin, but they were light and soft, no noise at all. Dred touched his arm, asking the question with her eyes. It was insanity how well she read him; he hadn't realized he had shown any sign, but she'd picked up . . . something. In answer, he nodded. The marching cadence came closer, until the others could hear it as well.

He leaned close to Dred, his voice little more than a breath in her ear. "Definitely them. Be ready to move."

"Quiet so far. No mooks sighted." As the merc made the report, he must've tripped the line. Cursing filled the air, and there was a huge clatter.

"Go, go, go!" Dred shouted.

They charged at top speed into a group of ten mercs entangled in the webbing and pinned down by the junk that had dropped on them. But they were slicing at the cords with utility knives. It wouldn't be long before they were on their feet. Jael snapped a kick at an armored hand; it was strong enough to bounce the rifle away. Vix grabbed it and sprinted back toward Queensland. Another merc brought up his weapon and opened fire. The rest followed suit, and Zediah ran.

Jael shoved Dred toward the others. "Get out of here."

Using his preternatural speed, he bounded between them, causing confusion. A couple of mercs actually shot each other while aiming at him, leaving scorch marks on their chest plates. He swiftly calculated the odds of stealing another weapon and decided he'd probably die instead. So he bounded after Dred. He took a hit in the back, and the merc who'd shot him exclaimed a startled curse.

"What the frag? Who runs away from a full shot?"

But he didn't wait around to hear what the rest of the unit would say. The others were well ahead of him, so he didn't see them, but halfway to Queensland, he spotted another drone cam. It tried to hover up out of his reach, doubtless in response to Vost's orders, but Jael used a wall to launch and snagged the thing in the air. He pushed his face up against it with an awful smile, and said, "I'm coming for you."

Then he dashed it against the wall until it was nothing but pieces on the ground. He pulled the screen and the processor out of the wreckage in case Ike could use them for something else. To his surprise, the burn on his back hurt like a bitch. Normally, it'd be gone by now, but he could feel the seared skin, throbbing with each thump of his heart. He rolled his shoulder blades, but that didn't help.

Get a move on. The mercs won't be far behind.

The turrets sat up at his approach, but since he was

wearing a magnetic bracelet, they lost interest immediately. It hurt scrambling over the wall, but Dred was waiting on the other side. Vix was parading around the common with the laser rifle. Since it was the first modern weapon they'd seen in turns, Queensland roared with triumph. The men threw Vix up on their shoulders, and she rode the crowd like a pro while Zediah gazed on with flat eyes.

Something about that kid gives me the creeps.

Dred vaulted onto the seat of the scrap-metal throne and signaled to Vix, who thumped on a man's shoulders until he delivered her—and the rifle—to the Dread Queen. The other woman slid down, evidently sensing that her moment had passed. Dred turned the gun over in her hands; Jael came up to stand at her shoulder with a military posture, inspecting it along with her. Automatic sighting, improved heat flow, larger battery pack to expand firing capacity. The rifle was a definite improvement from what had been on the market when he was a merc, forty turns or so ago now.

"We weren't sure how effective our weapons would be against their armor, but this is top-of-the-line," Dred called out. "And this is only the first of many victories. Now we just need to pick them off."

It would obviously be a lot tougher than that, but with those words, she put heart back into worried men. As she lifted the rifle, they raised their arms, and shouted, "Dread Queen, Dread Queen!"

That ought to hold them for a little while. But he knew better than anyone how fast human beings could turn.

◄7►

Adapt or Die

As the celebration continued, Dred dragged Jael to her quarters. He might think she didn't pay attention to the details, but it was obvious from the way he moved that he wasn't all right. Once inside, she was surprised to find that Tam and Martine had relocated. *Hopefully that means he's a little better.* But more likely, the spymaster had felt uncomfortable lounging in her private space. He had very regimented notions about what was proper, as if she really were royalty. That opened the door to all sorts of questions.

"Shirt off," she snapped.

"This is so sudden. I feel like we should cement our emotional bond first. Or perhaps you should offer a bride price for me?"

He was so ridiculous that she had to smile. Jael was the only one who could dig beneath the impenetrable mask she showed the rest of Queensland. She tapped her foot. "You were wounded back there. Let me see."

"Fine. But only because you said please so sweetly."

He pulled off the ragged shirt and showed her his back. She sucked in a sharp breath at the black, puckered skin in the center of his back. Mentally, she tabulated how long it had been since he had been shot. "Shouldn't it look . . . better than this by now?"

"I can't see, can I, love?" It was a blithe, slick reply.

As she inspected the wound, the mass of it shrunk infinitesimally. "It's healing, but . . . not like you normally do."

"I *had* noticed," he said dryly. "There's still plenty of pain."

That troubled her. He'd just about emptied his veins in saving her life; though normally a primitive transfusion wouldn't work, Jael had unusual healing abilities, acquired as part of his Bred heritage. Since then, neither of their bodies had been quite the same.

"This might seem like an odd question, but . . . what you did for me, have you ever done that for anyone else?"

He laughed. "I don't put out for just anyone, love."

"Don't flirt with me. This is serious."

"From my perspective, it just means I'm a few steps closer to normal."

"Normal people die in here," she said softly.

"Would that trouble you?"

A fist clamped around her heart. She didn't want to feel things, let alone admit them. So Dred squared her expression and offered him the same coin. "Obviously, it would. Where would I be without my secret weapon?"

To her relief, he didn't show disappointment in the pragmatic response. "Shoved down the chute, I reckon."

"You got that right. We're going to try an experiment."

"Does this mean you're taking your top off, too?"

"Not at the moment." Dred got out a slim blade that she kept in her boot and drew a line down her arm before he could stop her.

"What the hell is wrong with you?"

Blood welled up from the thin cut; it wasn't deep, so he was definitely overreacting. She said nothing. Instead, she counted in her head until the skin sealed, then she wiped away the red with her fingertips and offered him the blade. "Your turn."

"No offense, queenie, but this isn't my sort of thing. If this is what you want, you'd be better off with Tam."

"Did you want me to do it?" she asked softly.

His blue gaze burned into hers. "Be gentle with me."

"I'll do my best." She sliced with the same delicacy she'd employed before, then she counted off, watching his forearm the whole time. It was slow enough that she couldn't see the incremental improvements. When the wound closed, she shut her eyes.

"What's wrong?"

"Not sure what it means," she said, meeting his gaze, "but our healing rates are the same. I compared the seconds."

He actually took a step back. "I thought the side effects would fade."

"They don't seem to be," she said.

"You think by . . . saving you, I also gave away half of my ability?"

"Possibly. And I don't think I can give it back."

"I wouldn't let you bleed out for me anyway, love. You probably wouldn't fall into a coma. You'd just die."

"That's one exit strategy." Her voice was low.

"I didn't fight so hard for you to give up now. It's better there are two of us anyway. We can do impossible things together."

"Is that how you see this playing out?"

"I write my own ticket, always have. People don't tell me how things end. I prefer to determine it for myself." He shrugged back into his shirt. "And if it takes a day or two instead of hours to wipe this burn away, I can live with it."

"I wish you didn't have to." She wanted to wrap her arms around him and dig her hands into his pale hair.

But she squelched those instincts even as his emotions seeped into her consciousness. Before her arrest, she'd only picked up darker impulses, nothing clean or bright, but incarceration had given her time to perfect and expand on what genetics had bestowed. Dred wasn't trying to read him, but he was feeling something so strong, some memory, that it filled her head like a tsunami of blue. So much regret and sorrow, so much pain. It wasn't like guilt, but lonelier. If she let herself, she could drown in it. Jael was like the dark water at the bottom of the deepest cave, where light had never shone. The other prisoners didn't know she was Psi, and that was just as well. They'd riot in a heartbeat if they thought she was messing with their minds.

He said somberly, "Ah, but wishing's for innocents, love. People like us, we don't get the shiny."

A thump on the door interrupted whatever she might've said. "The Speaker is here. He's demanding an audience."

"What the hell does Silence want?" Dred snapped.

But she strode out the door and stormed to the common room, where the revels had fallen silent. Damned Death's Handmaiden, always thinking she could have whatever she demanded. After her failed power play, Dred hadn't expected to hear anything from her for a while, but the Speaker stood waiting for his meeting with perfect composure. She wanted to stab him, but their problems were already big enough without going to open war with Silence.

Now's not the time.

"What is it?" she demanded, omitting all courtesies.

"You've fortified Queensland. The Handmaiden will be reassured to hear that you fare well."

"I'm not in the mood for games. Say what you came to say or I kill you, shove your body down the chute, and tell the next messenger you must've died on the way back."

"She would never believe you."

Dred smiled and took a step forward. "But you'll still be dead. Talk."

"Very well, if you must be so brutish. You're turning into Artan."

That was the last insult that should've passed his lips. The former leader of this territory made Grigor look refined. He'd raped for pleasure and murdered for sport, taken prisoners as slaves and pets, and his idea of entertainment always ended in blood sport and torture. *I'm not like him. I protect my people as best I can.* Dred slammed a fist into the Speaker's stomach, then kicked his feet out from under him.

Once he was on the ground and understood just how precarious his existence was, she set her fingers gently on his throat. "You look better from this angle, Speaker."

"And your head will roll for this offense," he snarled. "To think I came to offer you the most sacred of honors."

"What's that?" She was smirking.

"The Handmaiden wishes to renew your alliance. In her infinite wisdom, she has foreseen that the only way we can withstand this invasion is to fight the interlopers together."

"Why does she want to survive it?" Jael asked lazily. "Isn't she all about death?"

The Speaker tried to roll out from beneath Dred, but she increased the pressure on his throat, digging in with her nails, sharp enough to bring up crimson crescents on his sour-smelling, pasty skin. "On her terms. In her time. She is Death's mistress, not a victim to be murdered by a mob of ignorant brutes."

Silence really is bugshit insane. After trying to kill me, after putting a mole in my inner circle, she thinks she can crook a finger, and I'll come running?

"It's a tempting offer," she said. "Let me think about it."

Jael made a noise, but she quieted him with a subtle gesture. She helped the Speaker to his feet, making sure her expression gave nothing away. Around her, other Queenslanders were watching, hardly seeming to breathe. Nobody shouted advice or warnings. She counted to ten, letting the tension build.

Eventually, Dred said, "I've come to a decision. Silence— and the rest of you—can fuck all the way off. I will not help you. In any fashion. If you show up near my territory again, I *will* kill you. Failing that, I hope the mercs burn everything down in that grisly slaughterhouse you call home."

Whoops rang out from the rest of the men, and she beckoned to Cook, who was the closest thing she had to visually intimidating muscle since Einar died. "If you don't mind, would you take out the trash?"

The chef grinned, threw his chopping knife at the opposite wall, and advanced on the Speaker, who backed up. He doubtless had a garrote on his person and maybe a poison knife, but Cook was too big to be taken like that, especially coming at a target head-on. The rest of Queensland stopped the Speaker's retreat and Cook yanked him up bodily and dragged him like a haunch of meat, so the emissary's head thumped against the floor. With a jerk of his head, the chef summoned more men, probably to help him toss the Speaker over the barricades. When he returned, someone scurried to retrieve his knife.

"That wasn't politic," Tam said from behind her. "But it *was* excellent theater."

She turned with a frown to confront his sallow, sweaty countenance. "You should be in bed, resting."

"He's bored," Martine said. Tam's arm was around her shoulder, more for support than in affection, Dred suspected. "He's not up to the sort of tricks he'd normally enjoy."

Tam wore an inscrutable expression, but Dred picked up a flare of strong emotion. Quickly, she shut her gift down, not wanting to spy on him. Whether it was anger or desire, she had no reason to delve further. More to the point, she was concerned about his recovery.

"Any sign of infection?" she asked Martine.

The spymaster scowled, as if he knew Dred suspected he'd prevaricate if questioned about his condition. But the shorter woman had no such compunction. "Not so far. He's going to have some impressive scars, provided he pulls through."

"It's not my time," Tam said.

His tone sounded as if he actually knew when he'd die, but Dred had met sociopaths who enjoyed screwing with other people's heads. Unsurprisingly, there were more than a few of that stripe in Perdition. Despite their relatively long acquaintance—in prison terms—she wasn't sure if Tam fit that profile. Martine was another enigma. Maybe that was why they gravitated toward one another. Interesting, because the partner the other woman chose before Tam had been his complete antithesis.

"Look after him," she told Martine.

"I plan to."

Tam raised a brow, but he didn't protest when the woman steered him toward the common room. There would still be goulash on the boil though it was probably down to mushy paste by now. It wasn't long until downtime, where most of Queensland retired, and only a skeleton crew remained on watch. Dred found it hard to relax during those hours because there was no way to be sure if the men on watch were truly loyal; it would be the perfect time for a traitor to let the enemy inside their borders.

Dred intercepted Jael on the way to the gardens. "Haven't you done enough today?"

He turned with the cocky grin that once drove her crazy. "Is that your way of telling me my services are required elsewhere?"

"If you wanted to discuss strategy, I wouldn't say no." She could use his perspective since he had some military background. Jael might have some insights about the best way to take the fight to the mercs before they dug in. Dred didn't have the personnel for a long siege. In a war of attrition, against superior firepower, in every scenario she ran in her head, Queensland lost.

Jael smirked. "Is that what they're calling it these days?"

◄ 8 ►

Willing Sacrifice

Dred was sound asleep, the rifle propped up against the opposite wall.

It was difficult for Jael to shut down under the best of circumstances, and tonight, he couldn't quiet his brain. They'd talked about tactics at length, considering and discarding numerous strategies, but he knew what he needed to do. Trouble was, he didn't want to. Once he'd been known for carrying out impossible ops, but he'd lost a few steps since then.

Gave them away, actually.

On the surface, there was no reason for him to stick his neck out for a bunch of lifers, and truth be told, he didn't care much whether they lived or died. But Dred . . . the idea that she could die here made him want to tear the ship apart with his bare hands, but that would kill her, too. He remembered the way she'd fought for his life like it was worth something, before she knew him at all, and how she treated him like a person, even after she learned the truth about his background. Women had been drawn to him before, but they saw only superficial features, the gleam of pale hair or the twinkle of blue eyes. All the while, he understood that they'd scream and try to destroy him if they learned the truth. Some of them had before he learned to strike first.

But not Dred.

She stirred, curling closer to him and pressing her cheek to his chest. He could hear her heart at rest, and he counted the beats as if the growing numbers could explain the mysteries of the universe. He lifted a hand, careful not to disturb her, and rested it against her hair. She wore the braids and trinkets on the sides, so the back was all messy curls. Jael looped his fingers in them as if they were ropes that could keep him from falling. But they might as well be gossamer. And he *had* to go.

One rifle wasn't enough to make a difference. He needed to snag more weapons and thin out the mercs. So he slipped from the bed with slow, careful movements. *It's you I'm fighting for, love. Not them.* Each time she stirred, he froze, until it felt like it took hours for him to slip out of bed. In her sleep, she moved into the space he'd vacated, possibly because it was warm. But it gave him an odd pang to watch it happen.

She'd miss me if something goes wrong out there.

With an odd ache in his chest, he crept out of her quarters. Queensland was quiet during downtime. He didn't see anyone until he reached the barricades; the watch posts had been moved to just inside the barriers. If the turrets went live, the man on duty would then alert the rest of the zone to the attack. His status as the queen's champion meant he could come and go as he pleased, so the sentry didn't seem surprised to see him.

"A little solo hunting?" the guard asked.

"You know it."

"That's a sweet rifle."

Jael nodded. "I'll let you know how it performs."

"Must be nice to rack up private time with the queen." It was the first time anyone had mentioned their sleeping arrangements, but people had probably noticed that since Einar's death, Tam no longer joined them at night.

"If I hear you talking about her again, duffer, to me or anyone else, I'll kill you." He was smiling when he made the promise, but the other man likely saw the truth in his eyes.

The guard dropped his gaze. "Sorry. No disrespect meant. Won't do it again."

"See that you don't."

Jael swung away without further conversation and hoisted over the barricade. The guard didn't say another word. He probably assumed Jael was going on some secret mission assigned by Dred, and remorse pricked at him for taking advantage of her trust. But he'd never told her to rely on him. In fact, if she'd asked, he'd have told her it was a bad idea.

I'm the villain. And you should've guessed that by the fact that I'm in here.

But even a villain was the main player in his own story, so if he could do some good before it all went to shit, he had to try. Hence the silent run during bunk time. He shouldered the rifle and jogged away from Queensland, determined to find a perch where he could use the rifle to its best advantage. Jael avoided the main passages, instead choosing to wend through secondary hallways designated for sanitation and maintenance. He went up a level and cut through the territory that used to belong to Grigor. Not long ago, this place teemed with bloodthirsty brutes, all ready to kill on a psychopath's command.

Now it was a warren of abandoned rooms. But it would take the mercs a while to search the whole station and figure out which areas were populated. If he had some drone cams, he could track their movements, but old-school recon would have to do. He found a roost on a beam above the cavernous space Grigor had used as a throne room. The climb pulled the sore spot on his back, but he was strong enough to scale straight up, then crab walk until he had a shadowed vantage of the whole room. The vertical joist provided cover, and if necessary, he could spin around it to avoid shots from the other side.

The worst part about an ambush was the "waiting" part of lying in wait. More than once, commanders of his merc unit had sent him to single-handedly secure a position while the rest of them hung back, allegedly guarding the rear. They'd learned quickly that he could deliver the impossible, and they didn't care how much he suffered in the process.

But they're dead now.

He settled against the beam at his back, stretching his legs out before him. Jael wished he could've packed some food, as there was no telling how long he'd be waiting before things got interesting. He listened carefully as he tilted his head back. Station noises came back to him: skitter of rodent feet, clang of pipes, whir of maintenance bots moving through vacant corridors. It was hours, and he was nearly dozing when he heard the boots.

Jael came awake in an instant and positioned himself with the rifle. The footsteps told him there were ten again, which meant that was a standard squad size. There had been fifty at the transport, so the commander had five patrols roving the station. If he were in charge of the unit, he would rotate them and have four out on duty and another resting. Even so, that was a lot of ground to cover for relatively few men.

I wouldn't want to be in their shoes.

He imagined creeping through Perdition, not knowing where the traps were and constantly finding deadly surprises. They had to know to stay sharp by now—that bad shit could come jumping out at any minute. Which meant his ambush had to be even tighter, timed down to the second. He had to drop one before the rest located him; and they were well trained, so it wouldn't be long.

When the heavy footsteps resonated throughout the room, he popped out of cover. A quick count confirmed what his hearing had predicted, and as they strode in, one of them gestured. The rest spread out to check different parts of the room. Jael did a quick sweep of all the men's locations and decided to take out the one standing guard by the door.

He's the farthest from the rest, so it'll take longer for them to notice when he drops. Then they still have to find *me.*

He crawled down the beam to get a better angle. After

getting into position and setting up his gun, he took aim in the middle of the merc's visor. Once he was sure, he confirmed through the autosight. The gun's computer chip confirmed the trajectory, so he took the shot, and a red burst snapped from his perch to the visor, shattering it on impact. Another snap shot exploded the glastique and fried the merc's face. His armor hit the floor with a noisy thunk when he dropped, alerting the rest of the men.

Two of them ran toward their fallen comrade while the rest spun, searching the ceiling for the shooter. Jael pushed to his feet and ran along the beam. The movement alerted them, but there was no other way to escape. Burning shots sizzled along the metal behind him, filling the air with the scent of melting steel. Part of him wished he could square off; he desperately wanted that fragging armor, but he had no chance of snagging it. Sparks sprang up behind him as he leapt from the ceiling to the wall. He hit hard enough to break some ribs; the snap sent pain down his spine like a lightning strike, but he ignored the gouge in his side and threw himself out the doors on the other side of the room. Merc shouts followed him, and the sound of pounding feet, but there was no way he was stopping. Nine men all with rifles identical to this one didn't add up to good odds, even for an inhuman bastard like him.

A drone cam zoomed past and this one, he couldn't catch but he eluded it by diving down a sanitation chute. Desperation drove him; if Vost was able to follow his movements, then the mercs would be on him in seconds. He fell with terrifying velocity, and he only caught himself a few meters before the recycling unit by jamming his feet as hard as he could against the opposite wall. His side gave, sending another wave of agony over him until his vision bled red. Jael hovered above the chopping blades, his entire body trembling.

Horror washed through him in a rushing wave. *Will I come back if this thing carves me into soup meat?* The worst part was, he could imagine it—being bound to the mutilated carcass with no way of dying. A deep breath, another, while his thigh muscles trembled and burned. Fear made him sweat, and his back slipped; he dropped a few centimeters, so the fans clanged against his boots.

No way out but up.

Winded, he shoved back up to where he had been and hung there, his body feeling like one huge bruise. The burn on his back must've split open like a smashed fruit, and hot blood slicked the metal behind him, making it damn near impossible to get any traction. With a stifled curse, he arched his back to use his shoulders instead and worked upward with his boots. He crooked his arms, shoved with his legs, and scrabbled with all his strength. Sweat broke out on his brow as he worked upward by the centimeter, conscious all the while of the disposal facilities beneath him. *If I slip, I go to pieces.* The joke didn't seem as funny when he couldn't get a deep breath, and the pain was constant, each time he shoved his body upward. *It was worth it. I dropped one. Forty-nine to go.* Red trickled down the wall, spattered by the whirring of the fan.

You can get out of this, mate. You've been in worse fixes. But for the life of him, he couldn't remember when.

◄9►

Tough Love

Dred wrestled with a colossal wash of rage as she stared at the sentry who had told her, unwittingly, about Jael's illicit departure. "What time was this?"

"Seven hours ago, give or take."

She couldn't let the guard know how far out of his jurisdiction Jael was operating, or it would look like she couldn't control her damned champion. *When I get my hands on him...* She nodded as if he'd had authorization to vanish with the best weapon Queensland had ever acquired. A small, bitter voice whispered, *You should never have trusted him. He's ripped you off and gone to join Silence or Katur.* She didn't think he'd be stupid enough to team up with Mungo. Silence, too, seemed unlikely, but maybe Jael thought he'd have a better chance of survival with Death's Handmaiden. Determinedly, she shook her head. *Bullshit, whatever he's doing, it's not that.*

The man went on, "But he should be back by now, right?"

"Probably," she said tightly.

"He's a tough bastard. I'm sure he's all right."

She offered an icy smile. "I'm more worried about the rifle. Inform me immediately if and when he returns."

Dred strode off to see if Tam or Martine knew anything, but they were both genuinely surprised to hear Jael had taken off. Their facial expressions were unstudied, and their emotions echoed what they said aloud. Sometimes her gift was useful though she never forgot it was also a bomb waiting for a chance to explode. Control was a tenuous, fragile thing, one reason she tried so hard to go numb and not feel anything at all.

Safer that way, for more than the usual reasons.

She was about to go searching when the sentry shouted, "The champion's returning."

With a soft curse, she jogged to the barricade, intending to verbally yank out his spine, but when he fell more than landed, she moved forward and pulled him to his feet. His face was pale and sticky with sweat, his eyes shining with incredible pain. He used the rifle as a crutch, something she'd deal with later. Frustrated, she dropped an arm around his shoulders. Queensland watched them go silently; it took all of her self-control not to tear into him in front of everyone. Rage throbbed in her head. Silently, she took the weapon from him and dragged him to her room.

"I should *kill* you."

His smile was shaky. "Just make it quick, love, I beg you."

"What the hell were you thinking?"

Jael's face tightened under what Dred took as a fresh onslaught of agony. "That something had to be done, and I'm the one to do it."

"Mission report." It gave her dreadful satisfaction to make him speak when she could tell he was having a hard time getting his breath.

"I hunted mercs. Took one out."

"One. And you look like this. That's disappointing. Did you retrieve any weapons?"

"It's lucky I didn't lose this one. Had to jump down a recycling chute to escape."

That gave her pause. "How are you still in one piece?"

"Strong thighs?" But he couldn't hold the light expression. When his breathing hitched, he went more green than pale.

"Let me guess, you're now even *more* injured. That's a brilliant move."

"Broken ribs. Not sure how many. And I think I might've punctured a lung crawling back out of the chute." He fell into a coughing fit that hunched him over, and as he straightened, she saw the blood spattering his lips.

Not for anything would she reveal how much concern was overtaking the anger. "You're an idiot. What if you can't heal this? Was killing one merc worth your life?"

"Depends on the merc," he managed.

But the blood on his lips had her shoving him down onto her bunk. He winced as he landed but seemed to relax when he realized she wasn't going to pummel him. Dred had no idea what to do for a punctured lung or broken ribs. Shit, they didn't even have pain meds, no medical treatment of any kind.

"If you weren't so hurt, I'd have you bound and be lashing you in public by now."

"What'd I say before, love? No time for sex-pain games."

"Is everything a joke to you? I won't have you undermining me like this. It's bad enough that we've got this shit to deal with. I can't have you—"

But he was already unconscious. It would serve him right if she left him to live or die on his regenerative ability, and she wrestled with the decision longer than she would've liked. In the end, she put Tam, Martine, and Ike in charge of Queensland and returned to her quarters with broth from the Kitchen-mate and a pot of sweetleaf tea. When she'd snuffed out so many lives, it was laughable that she was in charge of saving his, and it wasn't like when he was poisoned and she only had to breathe for him. But at base, she understood that she was the reason he was suffering at the moment—because he'd saved her.

Time to return the favor.

He was out for twelve hours, long enough for her to wonder if he'd wake up again. She remembered what he'd said about falling into a coma, though, so maybe his body was repairing the damage. Dred spooned broth and tea down his throat, knowing it was important to keep him hydrated. She was still angry with him, but it was hard to keep the rage at a fever pitch when you were responsible for someone else's welfare.

He's dulling my sharp edges.

It would be smarter to kill him in his sleep, before he breached her emotional perimeter completely. But even as it occurred to her, she knew she wouldn't do it. Prudence and caution had flown away when it came to Jael. He wasn't just the new fish she'd recruited because he fought like a demon. His speed and strength were beside the point. Exhaustion stole over her, and she lay down beside him, muted fury still simmering in her head.

It was the middle of the next downtime when he woke. Dred registered the change in his breathing even in her sleep and propped up on an elbow to peer at him. The lights were low, just lines along the base of the wall to keep her from stumbling fresh from sleep. In the pale glow, his color was a little better, and he was no longer soaked in pain sweat.

"It looks like I'll live," he said, sounding surprised.

"Possibly. You still have a lashing to get through."

"We both know that's not going to happen. If you punish me, everyone will discover that I acted without your authority. They'll think you can't keep your dog on a leash, love. And that'll wreck the image Tam's spent so much time crafting."

Dred rolled over him nimbly. "I didn't say it would be public."

His expression was . . . priceless. "You mean to do it in here?"

"You *will* learn to talk to me," she said quietly. "You will discover you can't make unilateral moves without consulting me."

"You think pain will teach me?" His mouth curved in a lopsided smile. "It's been my tutor every day of my life, and I never seem to learn. But if it'll make *you* feel better—"

Epiphany crashed over her. Normal discipline wouldn't

work on him. Tying him to a pole and going to work with a whip would only drive a wedge, make him more convinced he couldn't rely on anyone but himself. *Whatever he told himself, that's why he did this. To prove that I'll turn on him—that I can't be trusted. So what am I going to do with you?* It was obvious she couldn't punish him, and he was hurt already.

So she did the hardest thing imaginable. She told him the truth. "I'm angry because I was worried about you. I don't want to care, but I do. And it makes me sick to my stomach."

He lost the devil-may-care air immediately. In fact, he looked as if he'd taken a blow to the sternum. "Caring?"

"Especially about someone who has so little regard for himself, who seems to think he's disposable."

"Aren't I?"

"Not to me."

"Then you're too dependent on my freakish abilities for your own good, queenie." He made a valiant effort to rebuild his walls.

Not this time.

"Your physiology has nothing to do with why you're important to me. Let's have that shirt off."

Jael seemed stunned as she helped him out of the sweat-soaked clothing. Her gentleness had reached him. *He needs to feel like he matters, maybe more than anyone else in here.* Dred recognized the hunger; she'd known it a time or two when her parents were distracted with other problems. *He's never had anyone in his corner. There's always a price, always a point where betrayal becomes inevitable.* If discipline and punishment couldn't reach him, maybe kindness could. She'd had good parents. Dred remembered what it looked and sounded like. *Let this work. I don't know what else to do. I can't let him undermine me, and I can't defend Queensland alone.* In economical motions, she dipped a rag in cool water and perched on the bunk beside him. The covers revealed the deep bruising on his side, now faded as if it had been several days instead of hours.

"I've no idea what you're about," he said in a shattered tone.

"Just a quick bath. It should tide you over until you're strong enough to shower."

With careful motions, she washed every inch of him, and it was beyond intimate, done in silence. He watched her hands sweep over his body with a ravenous, bewildered expression, and that was exactly what she intended. By the time she finished, he was obviously stirred up. She sat back with a faint smile.

"I don't know if that was brilliant or diabolical," he murmured.

"Bit of both?"

"Definitely." He tried to pull her hands back to his chest, but she resisted. "Especially if you intend to leave me this way."

"That depends on you," she said softly. "I can make you very happy. Or I can leave you be. What happens next hinges on your answer."

"What's the question?"

She flattened her hands on either side of his head, leaning down so their faces were close. "Promise me you'll never do that again. Promise you'll talk to me first."

"If I do?" He raised a brow, trying to seem unconcerned, but she glimpsed his shaken aspect, echoed by the glimmering sparks of emotion streaming off him, too strong for her sixth sense to ignore.

"Then I'll forgive you, and we'll have make-up sex."

"And if I don't?"

"I leave you to recover and go about my business. But I'll never trust you again."

He seemed perplexed, slightly incredulous. "It's as simple as that. You'd believe me if I promised? How do you know I won't lie?"

"I can tell," she reminded him.

Jael drew in a deeper breath than he could when he first returned, another sign that his healing had kicked in, albeit slowly. "Then I promise. I won't go rogue again. And . . . I'm sorry." From the way he rushed the words, she suspected he'd never said them before.

"Forgiven. Scoot over." He did so, looking puzzled, but he was in no shape to orchestrate the sex she'd promised. "I'll be slow and careful with you."

"Then you *will* kill me."

Dred stroked her bare fingers everywhere she'd touched first with the damp cloth, and he shivered, lit up from the inside with longing. It was obvious he was ready to dispense with the preliminaries . . . but she wasn't. So she followed the path she'd blazed with fingertips with her lips, until he was trembling.

"Please," he whispered. "I've learned my lesson."

She smiled at that. "Have you?"

"I swear. I think I'd rather have the lash than another minute of this."

His hands came to her hips, hard and desperate, and she let him pull her up, but she was cautious, making sure she didn't put any weight on his chest. She sank down on him in an easy motion.

"I'll do all the work. I don't want you to hurt your ribs."

Frustration flashed bright as blue flame in his eyes, but he stayed still. Dred knew what she was asking of him—complete faith that she'd bring him to pleasure. That didn't come easy for a man like him. But she rode him and watched his face, and he let her see what he needed, shifts in pressure and pace, until they were gasping. She could've cheated and broadcast her desire so that he was swept into it. Instead, she took him there by centimeters, and when he arched, it was a tsunami of an orgasm. She fell just after, relaxing control only once she was sure of his. Then she rolled to the side, mindful of his ribs.

"Think you can leash me with sex, love?" His hand was gentle on her back.

"No," she said gently. "Because you don't need a leash. You need to *trust* me."

He drew her into his arms, whispering, "Mary help me, I'd walk into a fire for you."

◀ 10 ▶

The Sword They Die On

The sun beating down dried the mud on his skin into an itchy scale, but the boss man didn't slow the march. Ten men died in the last engagement, but leadership didn't care about things like loss of life. Every man who died in the killing fields increased the cut for survivors, so that meant nobody was too interested in guarding his brother's back. Jael hadn't known most of their names anyway, just taken the job to put paste in his gut and keep one step ahead of the Science Corp.

They passed from plain to forest, and the air thickened with the scent of damp, growing things. Thick canopy overhead, sharp needle green, interlaced with fronds, giving the others' skin a peculiar, sickly glow; glint of yellow in the foliage, slither-crawl of webbed feet slipping out of his line of sight. The marsh was alive with noises, most natural, chirps and croaks, crackles of snake grass and the sploosh of something sliding into the water outside his line of sight.

Told him this plan would never work. But I'm not known for brainpower.

"Jael, you've got the vanguard. Soften them up for us."

Since that was no different than most orders he'd received, he only nodded. He broke from the rest of the team, relieved to be away from their stink, now a permanent ache in the back of his throat. He could taste the tang of their sweat, the mildew growing in their boots. Most of them hadn't bathed in weeks, unless you counted sluicing down with standing water, after first scooping away the algae on top. It made it harder for native wildlife to track them, but Jael never adjusted to the smell. Fragging enhanced senses.

He ran silently through the tangle of jungle vine, ducking where necessary, leaping the pools of stagnant water that rippled lazily with things hidden beneath the brown surface. A scanning gaze showed him minutiae that other people wouldn't notice: a cocoon on the underside of a leaf, the bulge of eggs laid in the dense clay at water's edge, and the twinkle of a silver charm. Cold washed over him, and he didn't want to kneel to pick it up. But he didn't control his muscles anymore and he stooped to retrieve the small jewel, a sparkling blue stone banded in silver and dangling from a broken chain.

He spun, pulled by the echo of laughter. It rang on and on like a bell even as his heart raced. Jael sped up and broke from the undergrowth into the burning heat of the noonday sun. This was supposed to be a stealth mission—what the hell's a kid doing out here? *A cluster of houses had sprung up, nearly in the battle zone, prefab units that said they belonged to hopeful settlers who didn't think the reported conflict was serious.* Or maybe they didn't have the money to go farther. *Then he saw her, a little girl with brown curls. She had on a yellow dress, and the sky was blue and cloudless overhead, just the burning orange sun blazing down.*

"You found it!" She sounded so happy.

"Get out," he called.

But she didn't seem to hear him, and he glimpsed the shine of light off the barrels of enemy guns. Jael sprinted toward her, knowing he would be too slow—

He came awake with a smothered cry. Dred stirred behind him and roused with a sleepy frown. "Problem?"

Jael metered his breathing, eyes shut against the memory. "An old one. Don't know why it's bobbing to the surface now."

"You want to tell me about it?"

His voice came out in a rasp. "The last job I did before retiring as a merc, there was this little girl in middle of the hot zone. I was supposed to clear a path for my unit, and there she was. Both sides unleashed on us, and I ran. Landed on her. I took the hit, hurt like hell."

"Did you save her?" Dred asked softly.

"That's the shit of it, love. I didn't. When I rolled over, I had a big-ass hole in my back and blood all over her. The blast went all the way through. She died anyway. I got into salvage work after that."

She didn't say anything. Maybe she could tell he felt like a big exposed nerve, and no words would do. *She has that bloody Psi whatever-it-is. First time I've ever been glad somebody could rummage in my feelings.* Instead, she lay beside him in silence until he felt like he could stand being touched, then he wrapped his arms around her and didn't let go.

FIVE days after the failed recon mission, Tam could limp about with relative facility. Things had been fairly quiet since Mungo's mongrels died outside their border, and the mercs hadn't made any moves on Queensland. Frankly, the silence worried him. He was the one who gathered intel, so at the moment, they were operating blind. Tam tried to tell himself that Vost's men were engaged elsewhere, and they'd turn their attentions on Queensland soon enough.

To distract himself from futile foreboding, he circulated, listening to the populace. He overhead scraps of conversation: gossip, bets regarding which zone went out first and how long it would take for the mercs to wipe out Mungo's mutts, idle chatter and the usual shit talk among men with too much time on their hands. But there was little aggression, much less than when Artan ran the territory. Most convicts had settled down and were no longer whispering about the benefits of Vost's offer. It seemed as if the majority of Queenslanders knew a baited trap when they saw one, and they were capable of convincing their comrades, with a clenched first if necessary.

He was less sanguine about the recruits they'd acquired from Grigor. While they had desperately needed the numbers—and that was the only reason he hadn't protested Dred's clemency with them—he suspected they wouldn't quietly yield the unchecked violence they'd enjoyed under Grigor's rule. *They didn't in Queensland, either.* So far, the fresh meat had offered complete obedience, and he hadn't caught any of them with contraband weapons, but he didn't have the time to police them exhaustively. Sooner or later, that situation would explode, but the mercs made it impossible to turn his gaze inward; instead, all of his skill had to go toward ensuring their survival.

Or all of your plans will go to shit.

They might anyway, of course. For the moment, they were on hiatus, as the balance of power had shifted, not just with Jael's arrival. The decimation of two territories and the advent of the mercs made prior plots no longer viable. Frustrating, maddening, even, but in a place like this, it was impossible to calculate the odds with complete precision, as things had a way of shifting by the day. As his mother had been fond of telling him, *That which cannot be changed must be borne.*

His sullied schemes certainly fell into that category, so he went to assess the new training program; this was Jael's innovation, initiated after a planning session with Dred. *"If you want them to fight as a unit, you need to teach them how. You can't expect a bunch of convicts used to fighting for their own lives suddenly to care about the assholes next to them."*

Though Martine had come in a few minutes before, he wasn't actively spying on her. Since he couldn't collect information on the other zones, he could analyze the internal dynamics, so as to offer Dred the best advice when it came time to plot their next move. Tam stood by the door, watching the men spar. Training occurred without weapons, and Calypso, Mistress of the Ring, was in charge. There hadn't been any death matches lately—too much real fighting for the men to build up rancor over grievances real or imagined—and she had been chafing over her lapse in personal prestige. So it made sense to give her this responsibility. She officiated the games because she was fierce enough to defeat any man in single combat, so if the fighters cheated or objected to her authority, she ended them. Before the coup, Calypso had served Artan, one of the few women who never shared the man's bed. Tam recalled her efficient brutality when she performed an execution.

Martine stood near the other woman, talking quietly. She was the last person he could've imagined being attracted to. Other men fantasized about the Dread Queen, but he'd never shared Einar's infatuation, possibly because he'd played such a large role in her creation; it would be too much like onanism, fine as an outlet, but it seemed like a waste of time with a partner. Those factors aside, Dred didn't share Tam's interests, rendering her useless as a potential bed partner. Mary, it was difficult enough getting her to play the part in public; she was unlikely to take up the whip for fun.

Before Perdition, he'd preferred a sort of icy elegance that masked a predilection for dominance, and gender was less important than other aspects of sexual compatibility. Martine was bold and brassy, not in the least elegant, but she had . . . something, a puzzle he lacked the time and opportunity to explore. As a man whose inner life was primarily intellectual, he could go turns without being drawn to a potential partner, and he didn't mind the long gaps. In short, his libido had picked an odd time to come to life.

Using the perimeter, he moved closer, hoping to overhear what had Calypso looking so pensive. Martine was still speaking earnestly, her hands moving with a fluid grace. You could tell a lot by a person's hands, whether they had passion or restraint, what sort of work they'd done or crimes committed. The lack of scars on Martine's told an interesting tale.

". . . don't think that's a good idea," the smaller woman was saying.

"Of course you don't," Calypso answered. "You've thrown in with the little man and the would-be queen."

Tam froze, wondering if he was about to hear the mistress of the ring propose what amounted to sedition. The tall woman called out a few suggestions regarding the form of the men sparring nearby. The pairs she singled out redoubled their efforts, likely hoping to impress her. Then Calypso glanced at Martine. Her face in profile was lovely and stern, like a woman laser-etched from dark marble.

"That's not why," Martine argued.

"Yeah, you *say* so. But *I* say it's time to break away from big groups. We could wait out the fighting, just the two of us."

"That's not a permanent solution. The mercs need to die, end of story."

"I can tell you never lived through a war, my sweet. The first thing you learn is to get out of populated areas. They take the most damage in a firefight."

From what Tam could extrapolate, Calypso wanted to leave, not stir up a rebellion, and Martine didn't think that was a smart plan. Hiding wasn't a bad strategy in the short term, but it didn't resolve the core problem. With any luck, Martine could convince the mistress of the ring to stay, as the training program would suffer without her.

The tall woman turned, pinning Tam with a mordant stare. "Did you overhear anything good, little man?"

"Not for us," he said honestly. "You'll be missed if you go."

"But you won't beg me to stay or try to convince me I'm wrong?" Calypso raised a brow, her dark eyes glittering with suppressed emotion.

"That sounds unproductive. While I'll be sorry to lose your expertise, I would never force a person to act against his or her conscience."

"Does he ever take that stick out of his ass?" Calypso asked Martine.

"Oh, lamb, you know I never kiss and tell." She snapped her teeth playfully at the other woman, and the heated expression on Calypso's face made Tam relatively sure they had been lovers at some point.

"You trust them to get us through this?" Calypso asked quietly.

Martine nodded. "I'm not the gullible sort. The outlook's bleak, but with this lot, I reckon we'll take out a fair number of those sodding mercs before they get us."

Calypso straightened as if she'd come to a decision. "Then I'll fight with you until the end." Then she moved to instruct the men training nearby.

Tam had the awful feeling that he was holding the sword these women would die on.

"EVERYTHING all right, boss?" Redmond was a grizzled veteran with a lazy eye and a lazier nature, but he had impressive patience and a good sense of humor. Both skills often proved invaluable on extended ops.

"The guys are ready to blow this place to particle dust over Gerardo."

The other man nodded. "I've heard the chatter. He was Casto's pal."

"Is he heading up the complaints?" Vost asked, low.

"Are you asking me to inform on my mates?" Redmond was grinning.

"Asshole." He waited two beats before tapping his foot.

"Yeah, Casto's talking the most shit. He says it's your fault the scumbags got the drop on the patrol, therefore Gerardo's death is on you." Redmond shook his head with a scornful twist of his mouth. "If they're too dumb to search for snipers without being expressly ordered to do so, well . . ."

Vost tended to agree, but he couldn't side with one grunt over another. "That was a solid tactical strike. I'm guessing the shooter set up hours before our men arrived. That takes patience, plus he had to be able to predict that we'd eventually pass through. And he had some skill to make the shot at that distance."

Redmond inclined his head. "Two hits, both in the same place. Sounds like an opponent we need to worry about."

Vost nodded and stepped out of the command post, where his men were waiting. "Stay with me, double time," he called.

He was glad to be out and seeing some action; monitoring the fights wouldn't get the job done. The Conglomerate wanted the place purged with facilities and equipment intact. Mr. Suit and Tie hadn't told him what the place would be used for going forward, but they needed the criminals out yesterday. *I'll do my best, you colossal twat.*

This time, the op would go smooth as s-silk. Vost sent out a drone cam to locate the closest enemies, soft targets that would let the men burn off some of the need for revenge currently clouding their heads. If they didn't chalk up a win, it would lower performance and morale, so he watched the crackling image on the screen until he spied a likely group of drooling, pockmarked cretins from the lower levels, at least forty of the ugliest creatures Vost had ever beheld. The beasts were united in their aim, however. For some reason, they were moving, not to attack his unit, but another territory. That decision didn't make sense unless they took his bounty seriously, and they thought they'd wipe out the other cons before doing away with each other. If that was the case, it made him want to laugh.

"Silent run, gentlemen."

His men nodded. They'd learned that their boots gave them away in this echoing cavern of a station, so they wrapped them swiftly to muffle the sound. Vost never led from the rear, so he took point, rifle in hand, laser pistol on his hip, and a couple of knives in sheaths on his thighs. The armor felt heavier than it used to, dragging on joints that had been injured more times than he cared to count. It was hot inside his helmet, too, and his breath smelled like the paste he'd swallowed for breakfast. He skimmed the update in green just inside his visor. EIGHTEEN DEGREES CELSIUS. NO ORGANIC LIFE WITHIN FORTY METERS. SCANNING PERIMETER.

Then the feed scrolled with new information. THIRTY-
FIVE METERS, FORTY-TWO HUMAN LIFE SIGNS. WEAPONS:
PRIMITIVE. THREAT: NEGLIGIBLE.

Vost didn't need the armor to tell him that. The sound
of turrets banging away told him the filthy bastards had
engaged. Until now, he hadn't realized that the cons
had repurposed certain station defenses. Good to know, as
that misstep would've cost them.

"Hit them. Stay in cover, don't draw the automated
emplacements."

"Yes, sir."

The team arrayed itself on either side of the corridor.
When Vost peered out, he saw the animals clawing at each
other, using bodies as a shield, in the attempt to breach the
makeshift barricade the denizens had built. The turrets
spun inward, firing toward the territory, and the ballistics
tore through the scraps, sparking cries from those on the
other side. *You'll have to rethink your strategy or rebuild
the barrier every time from new materials.* And in here,
there was a definitely a dearth of resources.

On his signal, the men opened fire. It was precise and
economical—ten shots, ten kills. Now there were only fifteen left, given the ones the turrets had mowed down. The
installation was top-notch; someone had the capacity to
retrofit tech with the same efficiency as the initial installation, an uncommon skill and one that made him wary.

I need eyes on the other side of those barricades. This
was the one zone he hadn't scouted; some athletic bastard
kept breaking his tech. *And when I get my hands on him,
I'll pull his head off.*

"One more time." Another burst of red, and ten more
brutes dropped dead. The turrets took out the other five,
and he signaled for his squad to fall back. "That's it for
now. We don't go in there until I have more intel."

"Makes sense, Commander."

After what happened to Gerardo, the guys were hungry
for payback, but they weren't stupid. It might take a little
longer, but the time he spent gathering information would

be worth it when the last murderer died at their feet. Fifty million credits went a long way toward excusing the fact that the job hadn't been as easy as described. At that price, he ought to have known it wouldn't be a quick in and out. These men were the worst of the worst, and they'd had the run of the place for a long time. *They won't surprise me again,* he vowed, as he led his men away. The turrets spat a few rounds, activated by the retreat, but his unit wasn't in range. On the way back, they shouted out a marching song, buoyed by victory.

Vost smiled. *I'm coming for you, assholes. And then I can go home.*

◄ 11 ►

Havoc Unleashed

It was two days after Mungo's last attack, thwarted unexpectedly by the mercenaries.

The mass of attackers had been thinner than the first strike, so they took some casualties due to rounds blowing through the barricades and into defenders trying to hold it in place. That was collateral damage she hadn't predicted, and she was hearing complaints from the injured. A few of them probably wouldn't make it, especially the man with a massive hole in his gut, currently moaning in the makeshift infirmary. There were no nurses; nobody was looking after them unless they had friends or lovers willing to take on the burden.

"This wasn't your fault," Tam said.

He met her as she came out of the secondary barracks, now purposed for the wounded. The reek of septic wounds and unclean bodies nearly choked her, even out in the hall. *I don't want to know that the last man on the left's just pissed himself.* She strangled the dying scraps of human decency that made her want to go back in and take care of people; that wouldn't serve Queensland, and it sure as hell didn't fit the Dread Queen.

Sometimes I hate that bitch.

"Doesn't matter," she answered. "Everything comes to rest at my door, whether I could've prevented it or not."

"Price of power." Seeming to realize she was in no mood for a prolonged conversation, Tam limped away, likely to pursue his private intrigues.

Dred went looking for Jael. He wouldn't see the wisdom of her next move, but she had to use every tool in the armory, even one that horrified her personally. But since she'd coaxed a promise out of him, she couldn't take off without informing him. Trust had to go both ways. So while she wasn't asking for his blessing or permission, she did intend to offer full disclosure. For obvious reasons, she chose mealtime because he couldn't react too strongly while they were surrounded by Queenslanders.

Jaw clenched, Jael listened with palpable, growing incredulity, then he shook his head. "If you do this, I'm coming with you."

"You can't. Not because I don't trust you, but I *can't* risk that you'll be affected. If you go nuts and attack me, that won't help."

"Do a test run, see if I'm susceptible."

"The whole zone will run amok, pretty lad. I don't think you understand the scope of what I'm capable of."

His blue gaze skimmed the room. "There has to be somewhere we can be alone."

"Jael . . . I appreciate your loyalty, but it'll be faster if I just *do* this."

"On your own. After your blistering lecture, too." He wore a thunderous scowl, lips clamping to a thin white line.

"The difference is, I'm not crawling out of bed and sneaking away. You don't have to understand, just keep things together until I get back."

There was a long silence. The susurration of other voices rose and fell around them. Utensils clinked against tin plates; laughter rang out, along with the occasional curse. She leveled a frank gaze on Jael, waiting for his response.

"You really think this is necessary?" he asked at last.

"We have no armor. One rifle. And the turrets out front are running low on ammo. There's enough in the storeroom to reload once. After that . . ."

"I take your point," he said.

"Yes, I think it'll bolster our position."

"Then go. Do it fast before I realize how stupid I'm being . . . and how much you're putting on the line for a bunch of gits who don't know or appreciate you."

Dred pushed to her feet, dinner untouched. There was no way she could eat anyway; the prospect of what happened next churned in her stomach like dread. Jael caught her wrist, circling it with his fingers. His thumb and forefinger traced lightly over her pulse, then he kissed the heel of her hand.

"Come back, right, love? I'm just getting used to your face."

"Will do my best," she said.

He didn't let go immediately; he held on just long enough to make her wonder, then he opened his fingers in a deliberate gesture. *I'm trusting you. I'm letting go.* She smiled and walked out of the common room, careful to look as if she had no pressing business. The last thing she wanted was a shadow. If the men knew her secret, they'd probably burn her as a witch. Convicts were generally a superstitious lot. It was one thing for her to be ruthless and hard to kill; any whisper of Psi, and she'd be done as the Dread Queen.

The sentry saluted as she went over. Blood smeared the flooring outside; chunks of Mungo's mongrels were slowly decaying. The men had hauled the corpses off earlier, so at least the station had plenty of organic to recycle. *At this rate, there will be nobody left, but the Kitchen-mates will be full.* The stink from battle lingered with every breath she took.

Dred wished she had Tam with her to scout, but he was still injured, and she couldn't risk him any more than she'd risk Jael. So she took the RC unit to alert her to nearby battles without drawing undue attention. There were other maintenance bots still roving the station, repairing what they could reach. Using the remote, she programmed the bot on a long maintenance cycle, added a beep sequence that wouldn't give the plan away to the combatants, then she followed it silently. Once more, her chains remained in Queensland since brute force was inadvisable on this mission.

Corridors closest to Queensland were clear, and the going was slow because RC-17 kept stopping to scrub at bits of grime it encountered along the way. In stop-and-go fashion, they moved in a pattern created by some long-ago tech. It seemed to take forever—and she was cognizant of how impatient Jael must be—but halfway to Silence's territory, RC-17 beeped in sequence, then it went on cleaning. She was far enough behind that she heard only muffled signs of battle, but that was her to cue to make her approach. It didn't matter if they saw her because seconds after she deployed, they wouldn't be thinking rationally.

Dred took a deep breath and strode toward the shots fired. Rounding the corner, she interrupted a firefight between ten mercs and twenty mongrels. They all turned toward her, but seeing a lone woman, they didn't disengage. Nobody fired on her. The mercs went back to decimating Mungo's guys while she unleashed the rage she kept coiled in a diamond-hard ball. It crackled outward, tingeing the whole world; the power felt like the detonation of a bomb she'd swallowed long ago. Though she couldn't see it, the effects were visible at once.

One of Mungo's mongrels let out a demented roar and turned on the man next to him. He went for his eyes with hands curved into claws. The mercs took longer to sink into the bloodlust, but when they started tossing down their weapons and pulling off their helmets, she knew it was working. Men in the throes of her dark empathy wanted the hot rush of blood on their skin. If it went on long enough, they'd feast on the dead. The power blazed out of her until her eyes burned, and her hands curled into tight fights. If she stopped projecting, they'd recover their senses and come for her, so she'd hold until the fight ended.

Doing this repeatedly had gotten her kicked out of the ultramax prison on New Terra. Oh, the authorities hadn't known for sure what she was doing or how, but they *had* connected her to the riots. Back then, she hadn't cared if she lived or died; it was enough that she could take some murderous bastards with her. But mad as it was, she had a place here and people to protect. *I've got Jael, pacing the floor, waiting for me to come back.*

A few of the mercs fought the madness, gouging at their own heads instead of attacking, but that only meant their comrades killed them faster. They used hands and teeth, ripping at each other with brutal glee. As she held the onslaught, emotion slamming from her head in waves, the mercs tore off their armor.

Just a little longer.

Once the last died, she'd loot the bodies and haul as much as she could carry back to Queensland. But as the final two squared off, RC-17 beeped. *No, not now.* The unit had moved on, cleaning past the mob brawl, and it was unmistakably telling her she had more bodies incoming. From the other side of the intersection, the merc commander shouted, "What the *hell* is going on?"

His timing was uncanny. She bolted as another unit crashed onto the scene. Vost fired on her, shots pinging off the walls and singeing the tips of her hair. Dred sprinted around the corner, listening for the sound of pursuit. It came at once, several pairs of boots thumping in cadence. Shouts rang out behind her as she came into the straightaway.

"Take her alive," Vost ordered in ringing tones. "I want to know how one woman reduced my men to that."

Since she wasn't broadcasting anymore, they'd regain their senses soon. *Didn't get any gear, but I killed eight mercs. That's almost a whole unit, added to the one merc Jael took out.* She mapped the corridors ahead, trying to figure out how she could get back to Queensland without being captured or shot. The answer came when she glimpsed one of the missing ceiling panels; as the mercs closed the gap behind her, she took a running start and grabbed onto the bare metal, slicing open both palms. The blood made it slick and tricky, but she swung upward and landed above the ceiling. It wasn't the ducts, and this extra space might end sooner rather than later, but she could run for a while up here, and she didn't think their rifles would shoot through metal with one blast.

"She went up," Vost said.

Damn him.

"Listen, she's on the move, sir."

"Do you want us to go after her?" another of his men asked.

"No telling what's up there. We'll track her from the ground and take her when she emerges."

In answer, Dred let out a mocking laugh, which echoed a lot more than she realized it would. She could tell they were keeping pace. Maybe it hadn't been smart to come up here because she couldn't run as fast, but there had been no cover at all down below. She would've ended up shot in the back and chained up in their command post while they opened up her brain to see if they could figure out how she made their men go nuts.

Dred rounded a corner, hunched low, and came up against a solid wall. No way to continue up here, so she went for it and dove with all of her strength, hit the ground in a tuck and roll amid a flurry of laser fire. She took a shot in the shoulder, and she was thankful for it because even though her arm was on fire, she was able to scramble to her feet and keep running. It felt like they were almost close enough to grab her.

"She's tough as hell," one of the soldiers said.

"They have to be in here." That was Vost.

She was close now, but they just kept coming. Dred had almost made peace with the idea that this mission was a failure when she skidded into the home stretch. As she popped into the mined and turreted hallway, she dodged their defenses, then dove on her belly, sliding all the way to the barricade. Vost's mercs gave chase even as he was shouting at them to fall back.

As she scrambled over the blockade, a shrapnel mine exploded, and the turrets came to life.

◀ 12 ▶

The Wounded Queen

Jael had been pacing for hours.

You matter, he said in his head. But it would sound like bullshit if he ever said it out loud, especially when they were at war. They had to live in the moment, even if each one thrummed with the bittersweet resonance of mourning drums. He drew in a breath, as if he could hold her in his lungs, as if he could keep her with him always. But she always felt like starlight in his palms, dazzling but ephemeral. Anxiety welled up, haloed in fear. He understood now what she'd meant when she said, *I care, and I don't want to. It makes me sick to my stomach.* Just then he felt like puking. *Imagine how bad this would be if she hadn't talked it over with me first.*

So when Dred came tumbling over the barrier and violence exploded on the other side, he was torn in his impulses. He wanted to kill the bastards chasing her, but he also wanted to squeeze her until she couldn't breathe. One was more urgent than the other, so he bounded to the top of the scrap wall, found a place to brace his rifle, and opened fire. The merc commander shouted furiously at his men to disengage, but one of them had been badly wounded by the junk bomb. His helmet was scattered around in him several pieces, his scalp gushing blood. His comrades made several runs to try to save him—brave, loyal bastards—but the turrets pushed them back. While they hovered just outside the kill zone, Jael took aim and finished what Dred had started. The downed soldier's face sizzled and burned while his mates looked on, roaring with murderous rage.

Jael called, "Come on in! Don't let the turrets stop you."

He peered down at the body. *Damn.* The armor was too damaged from the explosion to be used though Ike might be able to jury-rig something from it. He couldn't see the man in charge until one merc edged forward as if trying to retrieve the body. Jael took aim, and the soldier dove for cover, swearing so he could hear it even over the firing turrets. *I know that voice. That's Vost. Kudos for trying not to leave a man behind.*

"Time to cut our losses and regroup." The merc commander seemed to be making sure Jael could hear him, too.

He respected the man for keeping his temper in the face of provocation. It was easy to blow off steam and rant threats you had no means of carrying out. The fact that Vost hadn't done that, had instead calculated the odds and chosen to fall back, didn't bode well for Queensland long term. It meant he was a smart leader, one who plotted his battles and achieved success through patience and planning.

"Help me," he said to the sentry, once he was sure the mercs were gone.

The man went over the barricades with him, no questions, and together, they hauled the fallen merc and his gear over to the Queensland side. Close up, the armor was beaten to shit, helmet worthless, but his squad hadn't been able to retrieve his rifle. Jael turned to Dred and lifted the second rifle in a triumphant gesture. She leaned against the wall, one arm crooked as if it pained her, but he knew better than to draw attention to the injury.

"How'd you do?" he asked, loud enough for others to hear.

"Took out eight mercs and around twenty of Mungo's men."

"No fragging way." The sentry actually took a step back.

Martine shoved the guard from behind. "Why do you think they were *chasing* her, genius? To chat?"

"Backup squad?" Jael guessed.

Dred nodded. "They showed just as the fight was ending, tried to run me down. Too bad. Five minutes more, and I'd have come back loaded down with presents."

Instead of shot up and pale with pain.

But it was more than that, actually. Her eyes had dark circles beneath them, and her lips were dry and cracked. She *looked* as if she'd been in the wilderness for a week with little food and water. *Is that what your power does, love? Burns you out like a branch alight at both ends?* Small tremors shook her from head to toe; at this point, she seemed to be standing more through will than strength.

"Why didn't you just kill them, too?" the guard asked.

It was a good question. If the sentry believed she'd taken out eight mercs, plus twenty brutes, and had barely a scratch on her, what was ten more mercs in heavy armor? They need to scotch those inquiries, or the men would argue that Dred should go out alone and kill the enemies herself. Sometimes a legend swelled so big, it became unwieldy.

"She's not a machine," Ike said testily, bending to examine the armor. "Just look at her, she's exhausted. You would be too if you'd fought that hard."

The guard seemed to come to the same conclusion after a quick inspection. "No, I'd be dead," he said with what Jael judged to be impressive self-awareness.

"Exactly, so stop bitching that she didn't kill *all* the mercs in one go, you moron." Any other Queenslander, himself included, would be guaranteed a fight with those words, but Ike had apparently earned some respect due to his longevity.

"Sorry," the sentry said.

But Ike wasn't paying attention; he was already stripping the armor off the body, probably to see what he could do with it. Nothing went to waste in here. With everyone else occupied watching the old man, Jael turned to Dred and wrapped an arm around her shoulder, making sure it was a casual gesture. He also took care to stay on her uninjured side.

"Let's get these rifles to the armory," he said.

As soon as they left the common room, he cupped her face in his hands and kissed the hell out of her. Her lashes fluttered shut, and he listened to the thrum of her galloping heart. For the first time, it moved him knowing he could make somebody else feel that way. Before, he'd always used it as a tool for gauging potential success or failure of emotional manipulation. Then she shoved him away, and he saw stark terror in her green eyes.

"It's a good thing the mercs don't know how little ammo we have left for the turrets. Or they'd have stayed and baited them until we ran out. Then they storm the place."

His satisfaction in her success died a lonely death. If she'd taken out eight, and he'd dropped two, that only equaled one squad. There were still forty mercs on station, and they wouldn't go out easy. Vost would make sure of it. He'd learn from his mistakes and fight smarter, going forward. Jael also suspected he'd be able to predict their strikes better. An experienced commander was gifted at assessing his enemy's tactics and extrapolating.

It only gets harder from here.

"How bad are you hurt?" he asked quietly.

"Just a laser bolt. I'll live."

He'd never heard anyone shrug off injuries like he did, and in a strange way, it made him feel less alone. No longer was he the solitary monster. Maybe he should feel bad about doing that to her, but instead he wanted to swing her around until they were both dizzy. But there was no time be playful, hardly even a moment to breathe. Life was a constant state of crisis—without any of the small pleasures that Perdition had previously allowed—like downing a drink with some mates over a bowl of Cook's goulash.

"Can you move your arm?"

She showed him. "Hurts, but I can."

"It'll burn like a bitch for about two days if my back is anything to judge by. Then you should be all right."

Dred gave him a fleeting smile. "Let's hope for a couple of quiet days then. It would be nice if Mungo and Silence kept the mercs away for a while."

"They won't do it on purpose, that's for sure."

"No, I've been failing at diplomacy lately. Not that Mungo ever *sent* envoys."

"And from what I hear, he'd eat any that you dispatched."

"I saw him a while back, before he turned into such a beast."

"Yeah?" Jael invited her to elaborate with the question in his tone.

Her tone was cool and remote, as if she were relaying events she'd heard about long ago. "Artan had taken me to the neutral zone to recruit . . . always attracted more men by putting me on display. Back then, he kept me shackled to him by a five-meter chain, and he held the end of my leash."

"Ownership," he said, hoping his voice didn't give away his utter rage.

"Precisely. That day, Mungo came to recruit in person though that's probably the wrong word. He had half a dozen bruisers with him and they carried off ten men. Didn't talk to them, just claimed them like slabs of meat." She paused, gazing inward at that memory. "I remember thinking he had dead eyes, even more than Artan. It was the first and only time I was ever glad I let him take me."

"You can choose not to answer, but . . . why do you wear the chains? If Artan—"

She took a step forward, reaching for weights that weren't there. The gesture told Jael more than she likely realized. "After he died, I made them mine, so they're not a mark of how he owned me anymore. They're the way I kill anyone who tries."

"I understand." He did, probably better than she realized.

"These rifles won't store themselves." She moved around him and headed for the room now serving as the armory.

Though he wanted to, he didn't offer to help her. She

maneuvered the weapon with one arm and keyed in the code to unlock the door, then stowed the gear with stilted movements that told him more clearly than any complaint how much pain she was in. Times past, he could've offered her a wide variety of chem to dull it, but those days were long gone.

"Why is there a still, but nobody's taken to manufacturing pharmaceuticals in here?"

"Short version? No skilled chemists have washed up in Queensland. Silence might have product, but she's not one for free trade."

"Probably just as well. Chem brings its own share of problems," Jael said. "Wonder what Ike's decided about the armor."

Dred brightened. "I'd love if he could patch it together somehow."

"I wouldn't rule it out. He's a clever devil."

"If I know him, he'll say, 'Quit bothering me, you're in my light, I'll tell you when I know something and not a minute before.'" Dred deepened her voice, adopting a gruff tone that actually resulted in a fair imitation of the old man. "Still, I have to make the effort. I need to have an accurate picture of our resources."

"You *are* the Dread Queen after all." But the words didn't come out teasing, as he intended. To his chagrin, Jael heard a sort of reverence instead.

Fortunately, Dred was too preoccupied to notice. It was better if she never realized how close she was to holding his heart in her hands. They went to the supply closet where Ike did his best work and found him already tinkering. The old man was on his knees beside the armor, cursing it roundly as he failed to mend it with a scrap of metal.

"Need a damned soldering kit. Might find one down in the repair bay . . ." Ike glanced up from beneath bushy white brows. "What do you want?"

"To know whether we'll be using that gear in any capacity."

"How am I supposed to know? I just got started on it." He made a shooing motion. "It's too small for all three of us in here. If one of you wants to stay to lend me a hand, have at it. Otherwise, scuttle."

"I might prove useful," Jael said.

By Dred's expression, she knew he'd offered so she had an excuse to rest. "Thanks. Keep me posted."

"Always do, your highness." Ike was already back to work, barking orders.

It took all of Jael's self-control not to watch her go.

◄ 13 ►

Immigration

The next morning, the burn on Dred's arm was red instead of black. It still hurt, but she could manage it. *No weakness allowed. You're damn near invincible. So go prove yourself.* It had been late when Jael slipped into the bunk, after long hours he'd spent working with Ike, and they didn't talk. He was gone when she woke up.

She was about to go spar with the men when a commotion at the eastern barricade demanded her intervention. The sentry was shouting his head off, so she went at a run, expecting to find an invasion force at the very least. But to her astonishment, she found the guard spinning wildly, trying to defend against the bulk of Katur's aliens.

She had *no* idea how they'd gotten past the barricades, but they must know of secret secondary passages from time spent exploring the station. Dred spotted Katur and Keelah standing toward the back, guarded by a couple of Rodeisians. There were only three or four of the oversized species left alive; there had been more before Grigor went hunting. Counting quickly, she tallied twenty-two bodies. Some were small and furry; others were slim and scaled, and there was an alien with tentacles on its head, each one moving with the hypnotic grace she associated with sea creatures. There was even an Ithtorian among them. In vids, they had been popular even on the backwater colony where she'd grown up, something to do with a famous Ithtorian bounty hunter turned war hero. Her grasp of history, particularly as related to the Morgut War, wasn't all that it should be.

"Stand down," she told the agitated guard. "I've got this."

"I greet you in peace," Keelah said courteously.

Dred returned the words, studying Katur. His whiskers twitched in what she took for alarm. On second glance, she noted that some of the aliens were wounded, leaning on one another for support. *Whatever's going on, this definitely isn't an attack.* When she met its bulging eyes, the tentacled alien bowed low, an unquestionable sign of respect in any culture.

"When I suggested we rescind our KOS policy, I didn't know you'd bring the village for a visit," Dred said to Katur.

He inclined his head. "I have a story to tell, Dread Queen, and a request to make."

She didn't want the guard eavesdropping, and it seemed like a bad idea to march so many aliens into the common room. There was a space behind the hydroponics garden, once dedicated to R&D but now mostly full of cobwebs and dust. It wasn't the most impressive place to host a summit, but it offered privacy, at least.

So she beckoned the group and led them to where she could entertain Katur's petition.

"I'm listening."

"After the mercenary leader left Queensland, I suspect he needed blood to reassure his soldiers of their superiority and put the heart back into them. Since there aren't many of us, the mercenaries marched on the Warren."

"Shit." Dred thought she knew where this was headed.

Katur went on, "Since you'd warned us, we had an escape plan, but we didn't have the numbers or munitions to fight the mercenaries."

"How many did you lose?" she asked.

"Twenty-six." Keelah gave the number with a hitch in her breath. Her furred hands twisted together in a small pantomime of grief. "We're all that's left."

Regret went through her like a blade. "I'm sorry. What's your request?"

Keelah and Katur exchanged a look, and then the female spoke. "Sanctuary. In return, we will teach you what we've learned of the station's hidden places. Some of us are crafters. Others are technicians. We can help. We won't be deadweight."

They didn't accuse her, but Dred bore a portion of responsibility for what had happened in the Warren. She'd enraged Commander Vost, and he'd gone on a killing spree, seeking the softest targets to restore his unit's nerve. The aliens had been caught in the cross fire, and she couldn't let them be wiped out. With the losses she'd taken in the conflict with Grigor and Priest, she had room for twenty more.

And then some.

Dred didn't need to consult with anyone else to know the right answer. "You can stay. Welcome to Queensland. There are a few rules. No fighting, unless it's a sanctioned grudge match . . . I'll tell you more about the games later. They've been suspended indefinitely for the moment. No stealing. Sleep with whomever you please as long as he or she is willing. Follow the work roster, complete tasks as assigned, and practice decent hygiene."

"That's all?" the Ithtorian asked.

Since she'd heard their native tongue in vids, he must have a vocalizer implanted. "Yeah, why?"

Katur explained, "There were a lot more rules in the Warren, mostly to do with respecting each other's culture."

Briefly, Dred wished she'd thrown in with the aliens rather than taking Artan's bait. It sounded like life had been much better down there. *But if I had, they would've had no place to go, as Artan's realm wouldn't have lasted long against the mercs.* So she hoped that maybe things happened for a reason even though she suspected that belief in a benevolent power was the last refuge of a lazy mind.

She answered apologetically, "You won't find that here. Many of these convicts are left from Artan's days, and they're brutes."

"So they're likely to pummel us for praying?" Katur asked.

"If they catch you? Count on it."

She wasn't sure how anyone could hold on to faith in a place like this, but maybe this was where a man needed it most. A long-forgotten memory bubbled up—usually she tried not to remember her parents, to wonder if they were alive or dead, or how ashamed they must be—but she remembered her mother's murmuring over the evening meal a litany of thanks to Mary and pleas for the health and comfort of her loved ones. *Hail Mary, full of grace. Thy spirit is with me. Blessed are we among all people, and blessed is the fruit of thy womb, this world. Holy Mary, Mother Goddess, pray for us sinners, now and at the hour of our death. Amen.* It seemed she could recall the words in their entirety; but then, her mother had spoken them each night before bed, murmuring beside Dred's bunk.

They must be old now. If the Science Corp hasn't tracked my dad down. If they're still alive out there. But framing the mental question hurt so much, she had to stop. Most days, it was best to consider Perdition the beginning and the end of the universe, as reminders that it used to be so much bigger and more beautiful could kill her with the longing.

With effort, Dred put aside the unusual introspection and beckoned to the newcomers. "It'll be best if I introduce you right away."

"Thank you," Katur said.

She didn't kid herself that this would be a smooth and seamless integration. Nonetheless, she strode into the common room with the aliens in her wake. Men froze, then scrambled to their feet; most had weapons in their hands before she could speak. So she vaulted onto the nearest table and let out a bloodcurdling war cry. The shock stilled the Queenslanders for a few moments, then she unwound the chains from her arms and slammed them three times against the tabletop, chipping off bits of resin.

"Are you listening, men? I'm in no mood to repeat myself."

"Yes, my queen!" The reply didn't come as neat in unison as it ordinarily did, but since no combat had broken out, she'd call it adequate.

"Today, you join me in welcoming new warriors to Queensland. You will *not* judge them by their skins. You will treat them as any other comrade. Is that clear?"

"Filthy alien-loving bitch!" From her vantage, she couldn't identify the malcontent, but Tam and Martine tag-teamed him, dragging him out of the crowd.

Jael followed them, but he didn't intervene. *Just as well.* The rest of the men needed to see she had support from people she wasn't sleeping with.

With a sharp smile, Martine kicked him in the gut, and the scrubby man bent double. He was almost as old as Ike but less prepossessing, with greasy iron gray hair and a matted beard. From the way his mouth had sunken in, Dred didn't imagine he had many teeth, and his cheeks were veined from years of hard drinking. His small eyes shone with hatred over being asked to cooperate and cohabitate with nonhumans.

So many years after the Morgut War, after aliens saved us, and we still hate like this.

Though she could scarcely afford to lose a single man, Dred had to make an example of him. "You're saying you'd rather die than follow my edict?"

She scanned the crowd to see how they were taking this, and they seemed more interested in the prospect of a sudden execution than the arrival of a few aliens. That was good. The spectacle would probably grind the edge off their xenophobia. She wouldn't goad someone to this point, but this Queenslander seemed to have a death wish.

"Damn straight." He screwed his mouth up as if to spit on her, and Tam backhanded him so hard, the old man hit the ground with a spatter of blood.

When he climbed to his knees, practically snarling, his lips were split and stained against his gums. Dred didn't let pity move her. Yes, he was decrepit, but he could also sow hatred and rebellion among her people. *It can't stand.*

So she merely nodded, and said to Tam and Martine, "Hold him."

They complied, one on each arm, and she could tell that Martine in particular enjoyed keeping the captive on his knees. She kicked him as he fought to rise. The severity of his situation didn't seem to have sunk in yet. While she ran a less bloody regime than Artan, it didn't mean she was the forgiving sort.

She turned to Cook, who was standing nearby with his chopping knife. "Get Einar's axe, please."

They kept it hanging in a place of honor on the wall, so the chef jogged across the room. The axe was a huge weapon, crafted especially for the big man who had fallen just before the battle with Grigor, out of scrap metal and honed to razor sharpness. The steel haft had leather wrapped around it to make it easier to hold, and it was stained dark from so much blood. She suspected the cost of rebellion must be sinking in when the old man pissed his pants.

Cook made a production of the retrieval, pulling it off the wall with great ceremony, then he lofted it a few times, just so the spectators had a sense of how bloody huge the thing was. Dred took it without revealing how much the weight pulled at her injured arm. *Hope I've got enough range of motion to see this through.* She'd lose credibility if she had to summon someone to perform executions, now that Einar was gone.

Miss the big guy.

"Hold him for me," she instructed Cook.

In reply, Cook forced the old man down and shoved a chair under his cheek to serve as the chopping block. Dred took a couple of practice swings and then cut clean through the old devil's neck in one slam. The head bounced away in a red streak while his neck jetted blood all over the floor. She kicked the body down, then raised the weapon.

"Anyone else want to debate immigration policy with me?"

◄ 14 ►

Burying the Dead

After leaving Ike and Cook in charge, Dred convened a meeting. Jael, Martine, and Tam followed her to the training room, currently unoccupied. That was likely a good call, as four aliens came with them. Her quarters weren't big enough to comfortably accommodate everyone, and circumstances had changed. The room smelled like sweat, but it was reasonably clean; Calypso insisted.

Jael closed the door after them. There was no lock, but he doubted anyone would be crazy enough to snoop so soon after the execution. In fact, that was all anyone could talk about as they left the common room. They'd set a few of Cook's assistants to cleaning up the blood and disposing of the body. With luck, it would be done before the late meal.

"Let me introduce my lieutenants," Katur said. "You can trust them." He gestured to the tall Ithtorian with a speckled mud carapace and triangular head with a notched mandible. Jael noted the particular scarring on the thorax, as if it had survived a bombardment, or fought in numerous battles at bleak odds. "This is Brahmel Il-Charis, my first."

For the first time, Jael stared directly at the Ithtorian,

nearly drowning in a wash of revulsion. For so many turns, he'd heard nothing but the chitter and hiss of their native tongue, known nothing but the company of Bugs, if it could even be called that, given they were all confined to separate caves. He fought off the tide of memory, rooting himself in the present instead. Intellectually, he knew it wasn't fair to dislike Brahmel Il-Charis strictly on the basis of his species, but Jael did *not* have fond memories of Ithiss-Tor.

"Just Brahm," the Ithtorian corrected. "I'm not permitted to use my father's name."

Jael frowned, wondering where he'd heard the name "Charis" before, but he dismissed the curiosity as Katur went on, indicating the Rodeisian female on his other side. "This is Alaireli. She's our best warrior and my second."

"You can call me Ali," the female said in a deep rumble of a voice.

"I wish I could say it's a pleasure," Dred said, "but under the circumstances . . ."

Keelah inclined her head. "We feel the same. This isn't how we'd have chosen to deepen our acquaintance."

"How long ago did you leave the Warren?" Jael cut in.

There was a reason for his question. If it hadn't been too long, the merc unit might still be exploring down there, checking for hidden resources or survivors in hiding. With a quick enough reaction, it was possible they could retaliate before Vost saw it coming.

Katur answered, "A few hours, give or take. We fled when it became clear we couldn't win, but they couldn't tell how to follow us."

"Who wants to see if we can do some damage?" Dred asked.

"Me," Ali said at once.

Brahm inclined his head. Both Katur and Keelah took a step back, so Jael guessed it was too soon for them to return to the Warren—too many dead bodies, too many memories. Tam and Martine both nodded, and the spymaster was healed up enough that he shouldn't slow them

down. Dred's burned arm would have been an issue for anyone else, but by today, she should be sound enough to fight.

"Let's stop by the armory and move," she said.

"I'll show you how we got from the Warren inside your
territory without passing your borders," Brahm said.

Tam frowned. "I've done a complete survey, and I was
sure there was no shaft access inside our perimeter."

"You were wrong," Ali told him.

Martine chuckled. "I think I'm going to like her."

At the armory, Dred passed out weapons, though both
Brahm and Ali opted to use their natural defenses. Then
Tam locked up, and they rolled out. The Ithtorian led
them toward the eastern barricade, but then he turned off,
moving down a corridor that Jael was pretty sure ended in
a blind. He had surveyed the zone fully when he first
arrived, looking for weaknesses, and he hadn't seen an exit
this way.

"There's no—" Tam started.

Ali held up a hand to shush him. Then she said, "None
of you sees it?"

Jael skimmed the walls, ceiling, and floors. "It's dented
right there."

"So it is." The Rodeisian female reached up, flattened
her hands on the wall panel, then pulled with pure brute
force. The metal folded inward, revealing a hollow behind
the wall where pipes and wires had been ripped out.

Jael was stunned into silence. Leaning forward, he
peered into the tunnel that had been excavated and shook
his head. "That's not on the original plans."

"I get bored," Ali said.

Tam slipped inside and followed it back a few meters. "It
continues on, joining the natural gap between the walls."

Brahm stepped in and signaled with four long talons for
everyone else to do the same. "Ali will come last to close it up.
She's quite remarkable. Once she's done, a cursory inspection
won't reveal the passage."

Dred frowned. "I need to know if there are more
passages like this. If the mercs stumble on them from the

Warren . . ." She trailed off, but Jael knew what she was thinking.

He wouldn't sleep well until he was sure Vost couldn't lead a raid straight into their territory, bypassing the turrets. With that troublesome thought in mind, he watched Ali close up the wall. *Her hands are strong enough to crush a man's skull. She might even be able to do it through one of those helmets.* Unfortunately, the merc armor wouldn't fit her, or she could be an unstoppable killing machine.

It was dark inside the wall, redolent with musty smells. More disturbing was the crunch underfoot as he moved. His vision adapted fast enough for him to identify the crackling whiteness underfoot as small skeletons, and by the shape of the skulls, this was where tons of rodent-creatures had crawled to die. *Or maybe the Warren-dwellers thought it was hilarious to dump their trash right outside our doorstep, so to speak.* But that was probably an unworthy thought about their new allies.

"How many turns did it take you to achieve this?" Tam asked as they moved.

Ali replied, "I couldn't even tell you. But I had help."

Jael registered the smaller man's curiosity as they moved. Tam was counting, trying to determine when they left Queensland, but despite twists and turns, he wasn't sure. The tight space confused Jael's senses, too, and left him feeling as if they'd been in here for hours, and the number of bodies shifting in the dark exacerbated that impression.

"This is the border," Ali whispered eventually.

Ali opened the wall, this time near shaft access, but it was a different set of maintenance ladders than the ones they used. In fact, Jael had never *been* in this part of the station; permanent force fields, a Peacemaker, and active turrets blocked it off. But the aliens had found a way in. Jael went third, climbing down the rungs toward the Warren. It was a tight fit for Ali, but it made sense to let her take point. By this point, even their breathing seemed loud. He winced at each footfall as they stepped off the ladder.

From floor to ceiling, this part of the station bore signs

of the people who had inhabited it. The walls were etched in symbols and patterns meaningless to Jael, but they doubtless held great significance for those who had painted them. Ali caught his gaze skimming over the art on the walls.

"This was the closest thing we had to a temple. We gathered for regular services."

"You have a spiritual leader?"

"We did." Her tone became melancholy.

Jael suspected the priest or shaman, whatever they called him, had died in the attack. "What does this symbol mean?"

"Place of prayer."

"And this one?"

"Reverence for the dead." Ali roused from reverie long enough to explain, "Some of the people in the Warren believe in ancestor worship."

"This may seem like an ignorant question, but the alien with tentacles—"

"You're not familiar with his species?"

"No. I've traveled a fair bit, but not recently."

She managed a rough chuckle. "That applies to all of us. And he's Kelazoi, from a planet in the Outskirts. They don't travel much, tend to be treated poorly when they do."

"His incarceration supports that allegation."

"He was with us on New Terra, my mate and I, when we were rounded up and sent to internment camps. We were there for half a turn before they responded to the outcry." Her breath hitched, and Jael was surprised that he wanted to comfort her. Instead, he just listened. "They promised the media that they'd release us, but instead they sent us to Perdition."

"That's enough chatter," the Ithtorian cut in.

Brahm took the lead from there, signaling with a clawed hand for the others to fall in behind him. It took a while, but they searched the Warren completely. Though the place had obviously been ransacked, and there were dead bodies scattered from the failed defense, they were too late. No mercs. Ali slammed a massive fist into the wall and hung her head.

"I'm sorry. It seems we were too slow."

"Perhaps not," Tam said. "We'll help you deal with your dead, then I'll tell you what I have in mind."

"That would be greatly appreciated," Brahm answered.

Dred nodded. "You can't just leave them. I know you'd probably prefer to have a service, but—"

"No, it's enough not to leave them where they fell," Ali said softly.

It was backbreaking because the corpses had to be hauled up two levels to the nearest recycler, and a few of them were too big for anyone but Ali to manage. From her body language, Jael guessed she had been close to one of the fallen Rodeisians, but she didn't say a word from the moment she slung his body over her shoulder until Jael helped her push him down the chute. To make matters worse, it was a tight fit, and they had to shove, breaking bones in the process.

She pressed both palms against the chute door after it closed, then she whispered, "Good-bye, my love." Her grief and sorrow were palpable.

Jael had no idea what to say to her, and it was bewildering even to contemplate what words might be right for the occasion. In the end, he simply followed her down to get the rest of the bodies. Afterward, Tam laid out his plan, using dust from a little-used passage to sketch in the particulars. Brahm and Ali agreed at once while Dred looked thoughtful.

"What's the goal here, Tam? Revenge, carnage, or equipment?"

Jael nodded at Dred, indicating he wondered the same thing.

"Why does it have to be mutually exclusive?" Brahm asked.

"If we're fighting to kill, we'll go into the battle differently than if we're planning a snatch and grab," Jael answered.

And the Ithtorian acknowledged the truth of that with an inclination of his head.

"I want them all dead," Tam said quietly. "It's the only

solution that will serve. But we don't have the firepower to kill ten armored mercs with two rifles between the six of us."

"So this is a robbery," Ali said.

Jael had once known a Rodeisian female fairly well; she had been mated to a merc he called a friend. Despite their size, Rodeisians were typically calm and gentle unless you hurt their loved ones. And then there was no shelter from their wrath. So he was surprised to read bitterness and not rage in the twist of her generous mouth.

"Is that a problem?" Martine asked.

Ali shook her head, sorrow in her glittering eyes. "I was just thinking that it's ironic. It took sending me to prison and murdering my mate to turn me into a criminal."

◄ 15 ►

Baiting the Trap

"This thing is sodding huge," Martine bitched.

It had taken them hours to haul the gear up from the sublevel. Dred expected one of the men to respond with the obvious joke, but they were all focused on heaving the girder into place. The lattice of tension wires didn't look strong enough hold the contraption, but Brahm was monitoring the process, and he seemed to have an engineering background. Ali heaved, shouldering the front of the metal beam as Jael shoved.

"Can't do it with two of us," he grunted.

Dred stepped underneath; Tam, Martine, and Brahm followed, but she didn't feel much of a difference. *If we had couple more like Jael and Ali, this should work.*

With a moan that sounded as if she'd ruptured something, the Rodeisian lowered her end of the metal beam. "Need a break. I think we have to try this another way."

"I can build a harness," Brahm said. "It'll take longer. Tam, can you scout and give me an idea how much time we have until they get here?"

"Certainly. I can extrapolate based on the numerical

mean of their patrol times." The spymaster took off, running lightly along the footbridge.

This cavernous space gave Dred the creeps. The common room was the largest place she was used to, and she could do without the long drop, too. She spun in a slow circle as Brahm muttered over the supplies. Then he tapped Ali's arm with his talons, and she went to work with him, weaving scraps together, presumably to construct the harness he'd mentioned. As they worked, Dred developed an idea how the thing would work once it was finished.

"What can I do?" she asked the Ithtorian.

"See if you can find some rope."

That might be easier said than done, but she moved toward the other side of the footbridge. Jael strolled after her, and she turned with a quirk of one brow. "You don't think I can find salvage on my own?"

"It's better with company, love. Plus, I'm a professional, you know."

"You mean because you gave up being a merc to work salvage?"

"Who says you don't listen?"

"Not you." She flashed him half a smile as she strode into the offices. Hairline cracks threaded the glastique that had once shielded the managerial portion of the station from the industrial part. The lights were almost entirely broken, shards of glass crunching underfoot like the discarded husks of long-dead insects. A foul smell permeated the room—blood, sweat, urine, and dust. She climbed across an overturned desk and reached a hand back to help Jael. He took it with a bemused expression.

It's like he doesn't believe in . . . this, whatever it is. But it's not going away.

"You think we'll find anything in here?"

She was dubious. Rope was something they'd most likely find in the repair bays, but that was too long a trek. There was no way she and Jael would be back before the patrol arrived. "Maybe not rope, but something similar. Cables or cords we can loop together?"

"Sounds like a plan."

Dred rummaged while Jael did the same across the way. She tried to be quiet, but the broken furniture made it tough. Occasionally, Jael swore softly as he ran into obstacles; she gave him a hand in pulling the junk out of the doorway. After scrutinizing each piece, she sorted them into piles: broken and worthless versus Ike might be able to do something with this gizmo.

Jael tilted his head. "Always thinking ahead, hey?"

"Can't do otherwise, can I, pretty lad?" But her tone was soft, making an endearment of what had first been mockery.

"Hurry up!" Brahm shouted. "Tam says we've got ten minutes to put this together."

THE trap was finished.

Based on what Brahm had told him about patrol routes, Tam had picked the perfect place to set it up. The station was divided, and the industrial side was separated from cleaner, corporate offices by a footbridge that connected the two hemispheres, and it was a long drop to the repair bays below. Mungo had laid claim to the offices, but once he trashed them, he evidently decided they were too small to be worthy of his empire, so he'd moved on, leaving the rooms reeking of blood, feces, and urine. That miasma didn't improve after festering, either. So now nobody came through there.

But the mercs don't know that. Now Tam just needed to bait them. Everyone else knew to stay out of sight until the squad committed.

The armor felt heavy; he wasn't used to it. Hopefully, if the mercs noticed any damage from a distance, they'd assume it came from the firefight that killed their mate. Up close, it wouldn't pass inspection, but Ike had patched it together enough that when the merc unit spotted a fallen comrade on the walkway, they'd investigate. Since this trap relied on muscle and not hidden wires, the mercs could inspect the area before approaching; it didn't matter if they came in slow and cautious, only that they made the approach. Tam glanced up at the other five perched on the level above. Without Ali's strength, this wouldn't work, though Jael seemed to be holding up his end.

Timing is everything.

Without further delay, he dropped facedown on the walkway, facing the direction Brahm said the patrols walked. He didn't need to *do* anything; the others would handle it, but nerves pulled him tight. If their timing was off, if the mercs rolled him over before his team struck, then he'd take a laser blast to the face, and it was lights out. But the mercs would all recognize Dred, and Martine was too small to be credible as a merc—Tam himself was borderline—while Brahm and Ali were out for obvious reasons. Jael had the misfortune to be on Vost's radar due to multiple encounters with his drone cams, so he was likely on the Most Wanted list alongside Dred.

Since it had taken quite a while to get the apparatus in place, he didn't lie there long. Some distance off, he picked up the muffled clomp of enemy boots. It wasn't loud compared to other machine noises echoing on station, and he actually felt their steps more than heard them. Beneath his cheek, the metal vibrated as the mercs stepped out onto the walkway, but he was careful not to move. They halted; Tam wasn't sure how close they were.

He tried to regulate his breathing; holding it would only result in a perceptible swelling of his chest when he lost the battle with his reflexes. His skin twitched, a psychological reaction to being studied. Tam suddenly had an awful itch in the center of his back, but he resisted the impulse.

At any moment, they could see through the ruse and shoot me.

"Who is that?" a merc asked.

"Not sure. But Vost's gonna be *pissed*. If a squad lost a man and didn't report it, didn't take the body with them—"

"The team leader will end up spaced."

"That could be fun," another merc said. "I hope it was Alvarez. I hate that asshole."

"I warned you when you first signed on, man. He cheats when he's playing Charm."

The first merc laughed. "So do I."

"Apparently, he's better at it."

This didn't sound like a top-notch squad to Tam, but evidently their boss agreed. A thump sounded, as if he'd hit someone to shut the man up. "Stow it, both of you. We have to call this in."

"I'm glad that's your job." That was the merc who cheated at cards.

A new voice spoke. "Wait, do you see anything? Vost will want to know which way the mooks went. Scan the area for life signs."

Tam tensed. He hadn't counted on the mercs being this smart or cautious. The machine beeped.

"Shit, he's still *alive*. Let's get him back to the medibot."

The others must be out of range.

Relief left him limp as care for their wounded mate drove the mercs forward, forgetting their initial caution. They were close enough that he could smell them—hints of sweat and gun oil—when a loud clang resonated as his team dropped the boom. The massive girder swung from the level above, suspended on tension wires, and it swept through the mercs like they were made of marzipan. Tam held still, feeling the breeze of the thing as it flew over him.

One merc sailed over the side and screamed all the way down. The others were luckier; they fell backward, but a couple of rifles went bouncing down. *Dammit. The armor might be all right, but those weapons might be broken. But maybe Ike can fix them.* Tam bounded to his feet and raced for the other side of the bridge. The mercs were already recovering, firing wildly, but before they refined their aim, Jael and Dred unloaded. They laid down cover fire, so he made it to where Ali and Brahm were waiting in case this turned into a hand-to-hand fight.

"You make good bait," Ali said.

Tam shook his head. "I was hoping we'd kill more of them outright."

Brahm spread his clawed hands in an open gesture. "I'm happy with one. And the others are hurting. The beam cracked their crunchy coating."

"That *is* good news," Tam said as they moved to meet up with the others. "Maybe we can take some more of them, now that we've softened them up."

He crouched, taking cover from the barrage of laser fire coming in hard on his six.

"They're not following," Ali reported.

"Vost's reaming their ass," Jael said, coming around the corner. Nobody asked how he could hear the conversation; they just listened as he repeated what was being said on the other side of the bridge.

"It's not over yet," Dred muttered. "We still have to beat them to the bottom and retrieve the gear."

VOST was nearly dozing from staring so long at the drone cams when his comm crackled. "Commander, it's a soup sandwich out here. I'm a man down."

He froze, then counted to ten, but it didn't staunch the rage throbbing in his head. Anytime a unit encountered the convicts—and he wasn't personally in charge—it immediately went to shit. This was the most chaotic op he'd ever run. Too much space, too few grunts, and the inmates they had locked up in here were *not* just murderers and madmen. *They're fragging smart, smarter than* these *idiots.*

"What happened?"

Delta leader went over the scenario concisely, but it didn't do anything for Vost's blood pressure. "You actually fell for the injured-ally trick?"

"We scanned to see if it was an ambush," the other man protested. "There were no life signs apart from the man on the bridge. In *our* armor."

"They stole some of our gear, genius. And the scanner has a range of forty-five meters. It's a tool, not meant to replace independent thought."

"Orders, sir? They killed Higgins. Or least, he fell and is presumed dead."

"Get your ass to the bottom and get his body. Before those scavengers strip him of armor and weapons. I guess it hadn't occurred to you that's the plan?"

"We're pretty beat-up, sir. Trevino's armor has a fracture across the chest, and a bunch of us have broken ribs. That thing hit us fragging hard."

He swallowed a curse. It wasn't his imagination. The men were losing their will to run around this massive station, chasing rats into holes where they disappeared, only to be blown up the next time they turned around. *This is the kind of mission that could cost you everything,* he thought. But for reasons deeper and greater than pride, he couldn't withdraw.

"My unit's en route. Get back to base camp and put the medibot on those injuries. I need you up to speed as soon as possible. And stop losing your equipment, assholes. There's a limit to what we have for replacements."

"Copy that, sir."

They shouldn't be able to kill us. We're better prepared and battle-tested.

In a normal engagement, his men destroyed the enemy, but Vost knew a pang of unease. Most of their jobs were easy, unexpected strikes on the unsuspecting. Maybe he didn't have an accurate picture of the unit's capabilities. They'd never been tested in a situation like this one. The enemy kept surprising him, time and again, and not in good ways. Problem was, they fought like clever animals, not trained soldiers. Now he thought he had their measure. *My mistake; I judged them by what Mr. Suit and Tie said. Won't happen again.*

He stomped into the server room, where his men were bunked down with thermal blankets and polymer bedding. Vost slammed a palm against the wall, and shouted, "Wakey, wakey, it's time to do some business."

They were dumb enough to protest, and he *wished* he had time to work on company discipline, but he had a mess to clean up first. Plus, he reminded himself it was impossible to expect military-grade performance from a bunch of self-taught fighters who had never served. They were mercs, not soldiers. The difference might cost him this station.

Not happening. He shoved the thought down with ferocious determination. The men sobered up fast when he said, "Higgins is DOA. We're on a body-retrieving run."

"We can't let those animals eat him," a merc named Frankel said.

That was actually the least of Vost's worries. The cannibals died without much trouble. It was that other nest, the one he couldn't scout with drone cams, spearheading the attacks that cost him men and equipment. But if it made the rest feel more willing to work, he could pretend this was a mercy mission and not damage control.

So he ran with that assumption, painting a gruesome picture. "We're racing these convicts to the repair bay. If they get there first, they take Higgins, use him as a trophy, cook him, and put his head on a spike. Are we gonna let that happen?"

"No, sir!" his men shouted.

It would be better if all his squad leaders had the ability to keep their men on task or the judgment to be wary. While he wouldn't have shot the man on the bridge on sight, he would've called for a medibot and sent it in to wake the soldier up, then he'd have demanded name and call number before letting him off the ground. Any deviation would've resulted in a laser blast. Still, it was too late to change the outcome. Now he had to make sure those Mary-forsaken mooks didn't benefit from this.

"What's our strategy?" Frankel asked.

"That's need to know, but if things work the way I've planned, we'll beat them there by a wide margin, giving us time to lay a trap of our own. How do you feel about payback?"

"That's my second favorite kind of pay, sir!" That came from Kinsey, a bit of a smart-ass, but he kept the men laughing during the rough patches, so Vost didn't curb him.

"Moving out, double time!" He set a grueling pace toward the cargo lifts.

Vost had been tinkering with them for a while, but parts had been stolen, and it took time to locate replacements on this wreck of a station. Plus, there were security protocols to override. If he could use station defenses, things would be a lot easier, but something had gone wrong with the subroutines, and the codes his employers had given him no longer worked. The inmates had stripped so many parts from the mainframe that the defenses that were still functional were running off pocket nodes, each with random overrides, changing every sixty seconds. While he worked on the control panel, his men paced and talked shit behind him. They didn't need to remind him that every moment's delay could cost them a critical victory, but luckily, he didn't choke under pressure. Twenty minutes later, the doors slid open, and cheers rang out.

He fixed a hard look on his men. "Let's do this. We retrieve Higgins's body, protect his gear at all costs. And we get the bastards who ended him. Are you with me?"

The answering outcry nearly deafened him.

◄ 16 ►

Fish in a Barrel

The mood was grim and quiet.

Brahm didn't insist on silence because the mercs knew where they were headed, but nobody had the breath to speak. They had been running steadily downward for the better part of an hour; even maintenance drones didn't make it to this part of the ship. Another of Ali's shortcuts had taken them past some defenses that would've netted them some impressive resources, but Jael understood why the aliens had kept these caches to themselves. Other territories had reckoned them confined to the Warren when the truth was, they'd had supplies stashed all over the station.

Jael leapt the last few rungs and scrambled out of the way so the others could follow. He peered down with incredulity. "We're only halfway?"

"Do I need to remind you of the station's size?" Tam asked.

"That'd be great," he answered with a sharp grin. "Do you think you could sketch me the schematics while you're at it?"

"Internal conflict won't solve anything," Ali cut in.

Dred nodded. "We'll take a short break, catch our breaths, and rest up. That should put us in prime condition to finish the run."

The Rodeisian female didn't look winded to Jael, but she propped herself against the wall near Brahm, her eyes dropping half-shut. Her ears swiveled independently, doubtless listening for pursuit. While the mercs were the primary threat, that didn't mean Mungo or Silence's people couldn't crash the party.

"I'm sorry for your loss," Brahm said softly to Ali.

Jael didn't mean to eavesdrop. The aliens were speaking softly enough that he gathered their words weren't meant for him. He exchanged a look with Dred that told him she shared his discomfort. *Sorry, love. There's no way to shut it off that I've found.*

"You fought bravely," she said. "I know you tried your best to save him. You've been a good friend to us."

"No more than you both were to me on New Terra."

Ali choked out a laugh. "You see how well that ended. Instead of smuggling you to safety, we all got caught."

"It's a cesspool, no mistake," the Ithtorian said. "But you make it bearable."

Jael had never heard friendship proclaimed like that. In his experience, such words were kept under lock and key. You didn't tell people they were important because they might see it as a weakness to exploit. Better still, you didn't let people get close.

Ali's chin drooped. "I don't expect to get out of this alive, but I hope you make it, Brahm. You deserve better from life than you've gotten."

It was tough as hell to work with a Bug. After turns imprisoned on Ithiss-Tor, he hated them and himself, too. Once, he might've only loathed that he'd failed to kill Charis Il-Wan, as Ramona Jax had paid him to do, but now regret burned inside him like the sun. *What would my life be like if I'd turned her down? I probably wouldn't be in Perdition. I might still be traveling with—*

No point in such thoughts. He distantly recalled vowing

vengeance on those who had seen through his bullshit and left him to rot in prison. Now, if he managed to escape, he wouldn't waste his time or energy hunting them to settle old scores. *I blamed them, but truth is, I turned first. I played my cards, and I lost.* The admission didn't come easy to him, but a certain comfort came with it. *It's over, then. There's only Perdition now. And Dred.*

The Ithtorian made a chittering sound deep in his throat, a noise Jael associated with profound disagreement, the kind that defied words. "A deviant like me? This is precisely the end my father predicted."

At that, her head swung up, and she touched the Ithtorian's claw. "That's not true, my friend. Love is love."

"Everyone ready to move?" Dred asked.

"Shit," Martine said, skipping past the lot of them to peer over the railing. "Is the lift . . . moving?"

"That's the cargo elevator," Ali said. "We tried to get it working. And failed."

Dred swore in low and virulent tones. But before Jael could decide how dire their predicament was, the mechanism holding the box shuddered and gave in a cascade of orange sparks. Brahm let out a trill that Jael recognized as laughter from his time incarcerated on the Ithtorian homeworld.

"That's a break for us," Dred said.

The lift swayed as a cable snapped, and the winch holding it in place groaned. Given the state of repair on the rest of the station, it didn't take a genius to guess that the mechanism must be rusty. There was no way to check from the inside of the compartment though Jael could see the discoloration on the metal when he narrowed his eyes.

"If we're lucky," Ali growled, "they fall to their deaths."

Martine shook her head. "None of us can count on luck, lamb. But while they get out of that mess, it gives us time to maneuver."

Brahm set a rapid pace down the skeletal stairs that led to the next level. The sound of laser fire exploded across the way, the lift rocking even more, then a merc crawled out the top. *They're not waiting for the cradle to fall.* Jael ran faster and he almost slammed into the Ithtorian, who had stopped for obvious reasons: An amber force field blocked the way. He turned, expecting to see Ali pulling at the wall, but she was still, hands balled into fists. The expression on her face was familiar to Jael, despite their differing physiology. *Impotence. Regret. She's thinking if we stall here, there will be no more forward momentum, no justice for what happened to her mate.* And there might never be, but that was a fearful thing to confront in the company of strangers.

"What's the plan?" Martine asked.

Tam rapped his fist on the metal plating to the left. "This is solid."

"Can we kick a hole on the other side?" Jael demanded.

Ali shrugged. "Probably. But I don't know what's over there or if there's a way back to this corridor. The repair bay is directly below us, toward the external wall."

"On the left," Dred said.

"There has to be a way to turn this thing off," Martine said, pacing.

Jael retraced his steps far enough to see the mercs scaling down. It looked precarious as hell, but they were free-climbing. *Crazy bastards. I wouldn't want risk that with no rope, wearing full armor.* On the plus side, a man with good balance and strong shoulders had a good shot of making it without being pulled down by a less coordinated comrade.

"Sorry to rush you, but they're making tracks on the other side. Whatever we're doing, we need to get a move on, or this becomes pointless."

"We have more time than you think," Brahm said unexpectedly. "They're on the other side, and there are active ship defenses, turrets and force fields, to keep them from crossing over. Ali has created alternate pathways over here. The mercs have to find their own way to the repair bays."

Dred grinned. "Stalemate; best news I've heard all day."

"That's assuming all of them survive the climb," Tam pointed out.

Jael watched the mercs inch downward. "I don't know

what call I'd make. Vost can't let us have the weapons and armor, but there comes a point when an op offers diminishing value and you're better off conserving strength and resources."

"I don't care," Martine said, baring her teeth.

"Fair enough. You talk it over." He moved over to Dred and hefted a rifle. "Want to shoot some fish in a barrel?"

She beamed, as if he'd bought her a necklace shining with precious gems. "Love to."

"This way, love." The endearment slipped out, and he waited for her to bitch at him, but the complaint didn't come. Actually, the others were too deep in discussion about how to circumvent the force field to pay attention when Dred and Jael moved to the balcony and knelt, rifles braced on the railings.

"Mooks at nine," Vost shouted.

The merc commander swung over the railing on the other side and landed, yelling at his squad to do the same. That probably wasn't where they meant to get off, but if they didn't get to cover, Jael would melt the armor off their backs. Most of them made it. Two fell.

"That was fun," Dred said, grinning.

To his ears, Vost's cursing was audible across the gap. Jael had the pleasure of knowing the mercs were rattled because he and Dred both fired two bursts each before the soldiers returned fire. Laser blasts singed the metal he was hiding behind, so it burned his skin when he brushed against it. The red glow came again and again, filling him with delighted euphoria.

"You know how long it's been since I was in a proper firefight?"

"No clue," Dred said, popping up to return fire.

She nailed a merc who had the bad timing to risk a shot at the same time, but his chest plate caught it. Jael yanked her down with enhanced reflexes before the answering blast could end her. Maybe she had enough of his healing to survive more than a glancing shot, but he didn't want her suffering through days of agony while the burn healed.

"I can't even remember, but it's pretty glorious."

"You're a madman," she said, as a shot slammed close to his head.

Dred huddled beside him, smiling. God, he loved this. He stole a kiss as he settled the rifle into a steadier position on the rail, sighted manually, and fired. Jael didn't trust the autosight. Maybe it helped those with lesser hand-eye coordination, but he had an excellent internal trajectory-calculating system already on board. He missed only because Vost saved his man, just as he'd done with Dred.

He stood up and etched a mocking salute, then dropped a microsecond before the barrage. *Just what I intended. Focus on me, assholes, not her.* The laser fire came in waves. *I'd love to unleash the Peacemaker on these guys. Just imagine the look on their faces.* But he understood why they couldn't take the mech on the offensive; it was the last defense for Queensland, and the mercs couldn't know it was there.

Jael and Dred settled into a firing pattern, gauging the openings with ultimate precision. There was something almost sexual to it, the perfect synchronicity of their bob and weave . . . in and out of cover in absolute harmony. His shots followed hers like day after night. Then Dred unleashed on an electrical box nearby, and the explosions sent shrapnel flying everywhere. She laughed softly and kept firing. Her pleasure in the fight rivaled his own.

Once the smoke cleared, he counted and was disappointed to see there were still eight mercs across the way. But as long as they were pinned down, they weren't getting any closer to their fallen men at the bottom. Hopefully, their crew was making some headway on the force-field problem, as his ammo meter read halfway, and Dred couldn't have much more.

She timed her next shot, after the merc's clip gave out, while he was scrambling for the next one. Jael admired the neat way she threaded the needle through the gaps in the railing, hitting the soft spot she'd created before. The second hit was fatal; the soldier slid sideways and dropped his rifle.

"Nice shooting," he said, as she ducked down next to him. "You got one."

Three. Vost must be livid.

A cry of rage came from the surviving soldiers, and they renewed the onslaught so hard that the railings glowed. Dred dove for the hallway and Jael crab walked after her. They burst into sight, startling the others. Martine threw Jael a roguish smile.

"Did you have fun?"

"More than," Jael answered. "Any luck?"

Tam replied, "We'll have to work around the outside of the wall and short out the electrical system powering the field."

"The mercs might have something to say about that." Dred frowned, pacing toward the railing, so she could see the conduit that controlled the force field some distance up the wall. A flurry of shots slammed the ground near her feet, and she danced back. "Maybe we shouldn't have taunted them so much."

"I regret nothing," Jael said.

"Stay out of sight," Brahm snapped.

Ali nodded. "They'll surmise that we've moved on and remember their mission."

"Vost won't let them linger long. Five minutes at most." Jael pulled Dred away, so even her shadow wouldn't be visible from the outside.

Martine prowled among the group, examining each in turn. "Now we just need to decide who's doing the climbing. Who's a nimble monkey?"

"It's not my strength," Ali admitted.

They talked it over for a few moments, but then Dred held up a hand, ending the debate. "It should be me." Jael opened up his mouth to protest, but she leveled a hard look at him.

Right, she's the Dread Queen. Doesn't matter if she has a burned arm.

"Are you sure you can handle it?" Martine asked.

Dred lifted a shoulder in an eloquent shrug. "Near enough. When the coast's clear, I'll get out there and do my part."

◄ 17 ►

Falling Hard

Ironic. If we had been shooting from a level up, I could've gotten the mercs to destroy the conduits for me.

Dred made sure not to look down as she climbed. Part of her wished she could find a good vantage and explode the thing with a rifle, but she couldn't take the chance that the shot would echo, drawing the mercs back. It was unlikely she'd get to cover before seven angry soldiers unloaded on her, and she didn't intend for this to be a suicide mission.

So she inched up the wall, digging into rusty notches and hauling herself up by cables that might not be strong enough to bear her weight. Just as she thought that, the cord snapped and she plummeted a few meters, then caught herself on a jutting rivet. The metal bit into her palm and cut into it, so blood slicked her fingers. Dred curled one hand around the bolt, her heart thumping in her chest. *Hope Jael's not watching this.* Deliberately, she wiped the blood on her palms, ignored the burning pain in her shoulder, and reached up with her other hand.

It took all her strength to scramble back up to where she'd

been when she fell, then she pressed on. Her eyes were fixed on the conduits above. Her heartbeat slowed as she neared the goal. *Ten meters to go. Five. Don't think about falling.* When she got her feet on the railing, her palms on the conduit, she took a few deep breaths. Then she carefully drew her knife and went to work. It took long moments to short out the circuits, and the resultant shock rocked her so hard, she almost dropped off the wall.

Her head spun, and she leaned her cheek against the metal while waiting for the numbness and tingles to subside. She was sure the conduit wasn't firing anymore, but she reached in and pulled out the wires just in case. Then she clambered down the wall. Her injured palm throbbed, and so did her burned arm. She had been a little surprised when Jael didn't pull her aside to argue that she wasn't strong enough to get the job done.

When she finally fell onto solid ground—what seemed like hours later—Jael was there to pull her in. His arms went around her, and he put his cheek to her hair. Her hands settled at his waist; it was like the world went away. She didn't hear the station noises or the others milling around in the hallway past his shoulder. There was only his heartbeat thudding beneath her ear.

He stroked her back, and whispered, "You just sliced a few turns off my life, love."

"Did it work?"

"Like a charm." He kept his arm around her and moved into the next hallway, where no amber force field hummed. "See?"

Dred nodded, patted him once on the hip, and strode onward. The others followed as she ran toward the internal stairs. From there it was a clear shot to the bottom. The repair bay where the merc had fallen wasn't too far off. *Hopefully, the rifles the mercs dropped aren't completely beyond repair.* She could taste those weapons when she rounded a corner and skidded to a stop. *There will be armor, too. If it's damaged, Ike may be able to salvage it.* Even then it was a close call, as the turrets came to life, pelting the corridor with rounds. She dropped instantly, and the shots flew over her head, slamming into the back wall.

"Don't come any closer," she shouted.

"We noticed the welcoming committee." That was Jael's voice.

She lay still, scanning the door behind the turret. It looked solid as hell, but there was a keypad beside it. They might be able to hack their way through the lock, but first they had to deal with the turrets. *But I don't want to damage them. We could use them in Queensland. Unfortunately, these aren't coded to recognize our mag bracelets.* Ike had worked on the other salvaged turrets, so they recognized VIPs. There weren't many, but it helped when she, Tam, or Jael were coming in hot after a mission.

The others stood out of range of the motion sensors, debating her predicament. She scooted backward in infinitesimal movements, relying on Jael not to panic. She'd been in worse situations *today*. Getting away from the automated defenses just required patience.

"Scatter," Jael said to the rest of the group.

Then hands yanked her back faster than she could blink, and the turrets came to life, sweeping the hallway again. The high-velocity rounds slammed into the wall behind them. Jael rolled with her, and the ceiling spun over walls, floor, and back again, until they were safely beyond the range of the turrets. Her head spun a little as she stared at the dents in the metal where all the rounds hit.

"Those will definitely chew through merc armor," Martine said.

"Ruin it, too," Ali muttered.

"That's assuming they don't have some way to shut off the turrets," Tam pointed out. "They may have been given overrides."

Jael sighed. "That's all we need."

Dred pushed to her feet. "We can't worry about the mercs right now. So, new problems. Active turrets, not tuned to our magnetic bracelets, plus a sturdy door."

Jael paced away from the turrets and back to the limit of

their range. "Bloody station seems almost sentient. It wouldn't surprise me if it throws up new obstacles the moment our backs are turned."

Martine shivered. "Don't even joke."

"As long as the mercs aren't faring any better on the other side, we have time to deal with this." Brahm was studying the turrets.

"I can blow them up," Jael said, "but I know how Dred feels about wasted resources."

She shot him a dark look without disagreeing. "If it comes down to it, we'll have to decide if the weapons and armor on the other side of the door are worth destroying these. But let's put our collective minds on a bypass."

The Ithtorian squatted, his segmented limbs popping in a sound that sent a slight shiver through Jael. Though nobody else noticed, Dred took a step closer and set a hand on his arm. His palm skimmed down her arm, and he laced his fingers through hers. The touch of skin on skin was unexpected, a shocking warmth. Surreptitiously, she explored the texture of his hand thoroughly, running her fingertip along the curve between his thumb and forefinger. He made a noise, a soft rumble in his throat, and she slid him a sly smile.

"I have an idea," Brahm said, pushing to his feet. "Someone needs to donate a shirt to the cause."

"I'll do it," Jael said. "Mine's already shot up."

Dred stepped back, hoping nobody noticed that she had to let go of him. He pulled the shirt over his head and offered it to Brahm. The Ihtorian opened up a nearby wall panel and jerked out the wires, then he stuffed the fabric into the sparking recess. When the cloth was smoldering, he plucked it out and chucked it down the hall toward the turrets. The movement made them perk up, but evidently the shirt didn't register as a person, and the smoldering intensified into an actual fire. Since the shirt was synth, it smoked up the hall.

"Was your plan to choke us out?" Martine asked.

"Watch," Brahm said.

As the haze filled the air, Dred made out tiny slivers of light that gave away where the sensors were placed.

The Ithtorian nodded with satisfaction. "It will be tight, but if someone can negotiate the sensors before the smoke clears, we can deactivate the turrets."

"I can do it," Martine said easily. Dred regarded the other woman in surprise, but she only shrugged. "Hey, I told you I had a life before."

From what she'd said, Dred suspected Martine had been a gifted burglar, and she wondered how a thief ended up in Perdition. *Doesn't matter, I suppose.* As if on cue, everyone stepped back, likely not wanting to get caught in the blast radius if Martine missed a step. After making an obscene gesture, Martine closed her eyes, rolled her neck to each side, then ran for the turrets, but just before she would've activated them, she leapt forward in a roll, came up tight, and did a little hop into the next blind spot. Her subsequent performance was . . . awe-inspiring. Dred hadn't known she possessed such skill and coordination. Martine teetered a little at the last flip, then she was behind the turrets, both arms in the air.

"Let's hear it, bitches."

Tam was the first to applaud; everyone else followed suit as she turned off the defenses. Dred turned to Ali. "Can you and Brahm work on getting those out of the floor? I'd like to take them with us now."

"Before someone else finds them," the Ithtorian guessed.

"That's the idea."

Tam slid past as Jael was stomping on his shirt. "You think I can still wear this?"

"I'd say no. But there are perks to being the Dread Queen. I'll hook you up when we get back."

"You'll spoil me," Jael said with a wry smile.

Yeah, yeah.

Deliberately, she brushed by him and joined Tam, who was bent over the keypad. She couldn't hear anything from the other side of the door, but that didn't mean the mercs hadn't already gotten there. Dred couldn't guess if Vost would stay to fight or if he'd grab the gear and fall back. He knew they were a small group, and his surviving seven men had better weapons and armor. Still, he might not want to risk losing more men since preventing them from getting their hands on the supplies was his goal.

After a few minutes of tinkering, Tam shorted out the lock, and the doors popped open with a clang. The repair bay had the musty smell of a room long closed, and in the middle of the floor lay three dead mercs, along with a scattering of their equipment. Dred led the way at a dead run, knowing they were lucky as hell the mercs hadn't gotten here first.

But just as she was thinking that, the bay doors on the other side popped open, and Vost opened fire.

◄ 18 ►

Desperate Measures

The group scattered.

"How the hell did he get ahead of us?" Martine demanded.

"No idea," Dred answered. "Maybe he disarmed some of the defenses?"

Jael figured that was as good a guess as any. *The bastard hacked the cargo lifts when none of us could, not even Tam.*

He hit the deck and whipped out his rifle. "How doesn't matter. Get to cover!"

A bolt came in close enough to singe the hair atop his head, keeping him pinned down. He crawled forward on elbows and belly until he reached a better position to return fire. There was no time to see how Dred was faring, but it bothered him a bit that he wanted to. The mercs used the corner by the bay doors as cover, and they were doing a stellar job of keeping Jael's crew away from the salvage.

"You can't win this fight," Vost shouted. "You're outgunned."

Jael laughed. "Don't ever tell a desperate man that he's got no hope!"

Trusting the others to cover him, he pushed up on hands

and knees and sprinted for the rifles and dead mercs in armor, the center of the room. The mercs popped out to unload on him, but Martine and Dred drove them back with a tight barrage of shots. Laser fire burst all around him, bolts narrowly missing as he sped along a random path, swooping low, grabbing some gear, then whirling for the retreat. The asshole in the body armor was heavier than he expected, so his escape took longer than he'd calculated.

A merc nailed him in the back, full on, and the pain sent him tumbling forward. The equipment—and the body—bounced toward the Queenslanders, at least. Hands reached for him and hauled him back behind a broken-down lifter. He was grateful that they didn't roll him over. His back blazed as the nerves died, then there was just this sweet numbness. When Dred touched his head, he recognized the feel of her fingers stealing through his hair.

"He's dying," Ali said softly.

"Give him a minute. He'll shake it off."

"That's impossible," said the Ithtorian.

Death was getting a bit closer, a little less impossible, all the time. One of these days, he'd push it too far, miscalculate how much he could heal. *I'm still taking risks according to how I used to be. Before Dred.* With a groan, he rolled over on his own, but he couldn't feel either of his arms well enough to shoot.

"Someone else have a go." He nudged his rifle and the one he'd grabbed toward the others.

There were still two bodies in armor, and a couple of rifles, but Vost's men had their helmets down and rushed, just as Jael had done. One man grabbed his fallen comrade; another followed suit. Dred and Martine opened fire while Brahm and Ali snatched up the extra weapons. Dred hit one of the mercs, but it wasn't a kill shot, not through the plating. It singed the back, but one of his mates shoved him forward and took the next shot. The polymer smoked, but they didn't go down. As a unit, they moved their comrades out of the line of sight.

"They probably didn't even feel that," Martine bitched.

"We need to fall back," Dred answered.

Jael tended to agree. Now that the mercs had secured the rest of the gear, they'd push to finish the fight. He yanked the helmet off the dead man, seeing the bruises on his pale face. His eyes were open and staring; the aliens took a step back, but Tam and Martine set to work, helping him. He thought they probably knew what he had in mind. As they removed each segment, Dred scrambled into it.

Not squeamish, love? That's my girl.

Quickly, Dred snapped on each piece as Jael heard Vost calling orders regarding the gear they'd kept from enemy hands. Jael was waiting for the order to charge, and the rest of his team must have been, too. They had more rifles now, but without more sets of armor, they would be at a disadvantage. *It's not time to make this a stand-up fight.*

Once she was geared up, she motioned for the others to move. "Get behind the blast doors. I'll cover you."

"You can't—" Martine started to say, but Dred sliced the air with an armored hand.

The other woman seemed to grasp that she wouldn't change Dred's mind, so she turned to Jael instead. "Can you walk?"

"I can run, bright eyes." That might have been overstating the case, actually, but with Tam and Martine each under an arm, he managed a speedy stumble.

The mercs responded at once, but Dred stood between them and the rest. Her bottom half was hidden by the lifter and the rifle spat red light at their enemies. Jael watched until Tam jerked him forward, out of sight around the corner. He heard the heavy tread of Ali following and the chitinous click of Brahm's retreat.

"We're clear," Jael called.

That was apparently what she had been waiting for. Dred backed up, firing the whole time. She took a solid shot to the chest, but her armor caught it. She ducked and spun low, narrowly avoiding a shot to the faceplate. Jael knew from experience how quick those cracked. Tam went to work on the lock, hacking to seal it so the mercs had no choice but to circle the long way. With luck, that would be long enough to get back to Queensland.

"It wasn't a complete success, but I'll take it." Dred's voice sounded strange, coming from the merc helmet, touched with tinny reverb.

"Nobody died," Martine put in. "That's more than I expected."

Ali was staring at Jael. "Why *didn't* you? What you did should've been suicide."

"I'm tougher than I look," he said lightly.

Dred moved toward the stairs. "We don't have time to chat. Each second we stand here, the more time we give Vost to catch up."

"She's right," Tam said.

Martine pushed past everyone else to take point. She handled the rifle with near-military precision. Jael was curious about her background; she'd said a few things that made him think she had been a thief, but she also fought like a former soldier, a unique combination to say the least. He leashed his curiosity with the understanding that she wouldn't question him about why he could take a laser in the back and stagger away.

The climb was exhausting, but at least this time it wasn't a race. Now that they had the rifles, and Dred had the armor, it didn't matter how long it took them to get back. With some quiet, remote part of his mind, he wondered if the repeated injuries to his back would be enough to create a scar. *At what point does the damage grow so great that I can't heal it?* It was the mark of a disturbed mind, he supposed, that he wanted to find the line.

He heard something, a ping, a whir. Jael threw up a hand, listening. Everyone stilled. Though he spun in a slow circle, he couldn't find whatever it was. Now there was nothing but the station noises and the sound of other people's breathing.

Inside the Warren passages, Ali took the lead, and the return went smoothly enough. Nobody spoke, remembering Brahm's caution from before. But when they stepped out of the wall to make the last jog, where they would emerge safe behind Queensland lines, Vost was waiting. Beside him, a drone cam hovered, and Jael bit out a curse. *That's what I heard. He was spying on us, tracking our movements.*

The merc commander opened with grenades this time; and then he pulled out the heavy weapons. When the gun emitted a low hum and started to vibrate, Jael ran. Energy exploded outward, scoring the floor in a smoking circle. The metal softened and exploded, shards of synth shrapnel raining down.

"What I wouldn't give for a rocket launcher," Brahm muttered.

Again, Jael and Tam deployed laser shots, then ran like hell before the weapon could vaporize them. It slanted over Jael's head, so he felt the buzz of the energy on his skull. *Close call. Too close. Never seen anything like this.* It was small enough to be used by one man with two hands, but it was powerful enough to qualify as antipersonnel. If Vost wasn't careful, he'd blow a hole clean through the station.

Vost's men went with grenades, too. Three exploded in quick succession. Then Dred shouted, "Dammit, my clip's running low on juice. Push past them."

"How the hell are we supposed to do that?" Ali demanded.

"Watch me!" Dred took off, charging the mercs.

"Are you out of your mind?" Jael yelled.

But she didn't listen. She ran for it, leaping, ducking and sliding, until his throat closed with fear. This woman had no caution, no sense of self-preservation, maybe because she was stuck here, and she felt like she had nothing left to lose.

You have me, he thought.

But perhaps he didn't weigh heavy enough against the mission. Fear threatened to paralyze him, but he fought it back. He opened fire, trying to draw their attention away, but she was right there, and the armor wouldn't save her forever. Even the healing ability she'd acquired from him didn't make her immortal.

Mary curse it.

"We don't have armor," Martine called. "We can't follow."

There was no question about that. While Dred had managed to blow past the merc blockade, the rest of them would die trying. Jael hoped she knew the way into Queensland, the back way as excavated by the Warren. No telling what dangers lay between here and the border; could be Mungo's mongrels or Silence's assassins creeping around.

"Then fall back. Find a place to bunker down. I'll bring help, I promise."

Jael pushed out a breath. "You heard the woman. Let's get to defensible ground."

One Good Man

Dred felt like shit abandoning the rest of the group like that, but if she hadn't done something, between the grenades and that sonic whatever the hell it was, Vost would've killed them all. Pain blazed in her sternum with each ringing stride, each step carrying her farther from Jael. And the others, of course.

I'm not far from Queensland. They can hang on. They have to hang on.

Her breath sounded extra loud inside the helmet, and she was rushing toward the barricades when she realized she must look like a lone suicidal merc. Though she couldn't see the sentries on the other side, she called, "It's me. Stand down. Get Ike immediately and tell him to bring the Peacemaker."

Though it wasn't ideal, it was the only solution she could think of. Nothing else provided sufficient firepower to defeat Vost now that he'd dug in and brought out the heavy artillery. She didn't like revealing the territory's secret weapon, but maybe it would make him wary of a full-scale invasion. *He might imagine we have more of them.*

If only we did.

"We'll have to dismantle the blockade for the mech to get past," the sentry said.

"It's fine. Just make it fast."

Next, she gave directions to where she'd last seen the merc unit, then she ran back the way she'd come. *Ike will find us. If I can hit Vost from behind, I might distract him from the others.* Scraps of strategy whirled in her head, but she didn't settle on any one solution. In this armor, it was impossible to be quiet, and the rags the soldier had wrapped around the boots reduced traction. Dred felt clumsy and frantic as she ran.

Battle sounds echoed from some distance away, the boom of grenades and the unearthly hum of the weapon that had melted a hole in the floor. It wasn't a laser, but Dred had no idea what it could be. Disruptors were smaller, so far as she knew, but maybe they had upgraded them during her turns inside. *Just what the universe needs.* She was afraid that they'd all be dead when she got back—that Ike and the Peacemaker would arrive too late, but the cadence of shots fired and rounds returned steadied her shaky nerves somewhat.

When Dred ran the fight down, she saw that the mercs had shifted, splitting their forces to cover the passage and keep her stranded people from getting past. The corridor was a T, with the mercs on the right and the rest of her people around the corner to the left. At the base of the straightway lay the entrance to Queensland, complete with turrets and barricades. It wasn't the checkpoint she had approached before, however. *This is east. Hope Ike gets here fast. We don't have much time.*

The merc laid down a line of intermittent red light, pinning her in the hallway on the wrong side. She returned fire, but her single rifle wasn't enough to penetrate good cover, especially not against armored targets. Someone—Tam or maybe Jael—added to the onslaught, but the mercs had a good position.

Maybe they can circle—but if I call it out, the mercs

will hear. Wish we had some way to communicate over distance. Given time, Ike might jury-rig something from the merc helmets, but he would need to use a different frequency. Otherwise, the enemy could listen to all updates. *That won't help.* Ike might also be able to assemble a device that would knock out the mercs' frequency. That would cripple their ability to scramble teams across the station, a definite boon for Queensland, but there was no way to know until she talked to the old man about it.

She situated herself close to the turrets and took aim each time an enemy popped into sight. But they were skilled with the bob and weave, and she did nothing but drain her ammo charge. An eerie hum vibrated the flooring, and Dred tensed. *He's using the big gun again.* If fate was kind, the thing would explode in Vost's hands, solving the problem. But no such luck. She heard a whine, then there was screaming. Her stomach swam with sickness and fear. The Dread Queen would never feel this way, but Dred was panicked. *He's going to kill them all if Ike doesn't get here soon.* Then the reassuring clomp of mechanized footsteps echoed throughout the hall. *Thank Mary, he's coming from behind. He must've circled around from the south, where I was before.*

"What's that?" she heard a merc say.

Don't waste time with the usual warnings, she willed Ike. *Put the thing on manual.*

The mech could be programmed with facial recognition, but urgency didn't allow for such finesse. Better for Ike to just operate the bot. To her vast relief, the Peacemaker unit stomped into view and immediately went to work with the Shredder. The rounds tore through the walls as if they were made of butter, slamming into mercs and armor with equal facility. Shouts of pain rang out.

"Pause," she told Ike, low. "Let's bring our people home." If he didn't stop the Peacemaker, the rounds would annihilate the Queenslanders, too. Then she yelled, "Jael, push, push now! But stay low."

In the confusion, the rest of her team slammed past the

mercs. They brought weapons to bear and before she could tell Ike that their people were clear—to get the guns going again—the first soldier shot him full in the chest. The remote bounced out of his hand and she dove for it in reflex, even as horror and disbelief overwhelmed her. *He's the only one who didn't belong here. The only one who should've made it.* Rage filled her in a towering wave. If her own people hadn't been so close, she would've opened her brain and let a tsunami of bloodlust drown them.

You're lucky, assholes. Today you don't pull each other apart with your bare hands.

With shaking hands, she took up the remote and activated the Peacemaker. Its broad back provided cover fire in retreat, even as Jael knelt to lift Ike's body. Everyone was stunned, silent, as they moved away from the mercs. Vost was yelling something at his men, but they didn't want to fight a Peacemaker. Dred didn't blame them even as she hoped to see their bodies fall, just as Ike had.

He came out to save us. And he died.

It was just so impossible, so awful, that she couldn't look directly at Jael. The old man's silver head lolled against his shoulder. Her ears rang from the roar of the Shredder, and as she turned, a grenade landed at her feet. Jael was fast enough to boot it back and the explosion rocked the corridor behind them. Smoke and cursing filled the air, so she keyed the follow command for the Peacemaker and let its huge back cover their escape.

"That shouldn't have happened," Tam said quietly.

"No talking until we cross the border." Her voice was stern because it had to be.

If she spoke of Ike right now, she'd crumble, and the others would see that the Dread Queen was a myth of other people's making. They would glimpse her feet of clay, and maybe they'd stop following her orders. With the mercs coming in hard, Mungo on the warpath, and Silence wanting to cut her throat and drink her blood, she couldn't afford to show weakness even if each step hurt as if she had spikes embedded in her heels. With each breath, she inhaled a dead man's fear, a dead man's sweat, until she wanted to tear off the helmet and cast it aside and just scream until her throat bled.

She kept it locked down.

The sentries stood, looking worried, as the Peacemaker knocked down the east barricade. Wordlessly, she escorted her crew past, stepping over the wreckage as if the mission had been a success. Jael came last, with Ike cradled against his chest. The old man's chest was a black hole, the shirt fused to his skin in a charred pucker.

"I can rebuild the junk wall," Ali said.

The Rodeisian female seemed to carry the weight of the sacrifice on her broad, furred shoulders, and she must be of the opinion that she needed to give something back. But nothing could ever be enough. Dred just nodded as the Ithtorian set to work beside Ali. She trusted them enough to see the job done properly and continued on to the common room, with Tam and Martine flanking her.

The Queenslanders cheered when they noticed her decked out in full merc armor, even more when Martine and Tam lofted the rifles they had recovered. But the crowd fell silent when Jael stepped forward and laid Ike on a table. He leaned down and touched his brow to the old man's, a quiet moment that probably meant things she didn't understand. Then Jael straightened and closed Ike's eyes for good.

With the last of her self-control, Dred pulled off her helmet. She hoped she was wearing her Dread Queen face, not revealing all the pain and sorrow she felt at the loss of the only good man inside Perdition. There were so many things she wanted to say—and so few would fit the image she wore like a crown of thorns.

"How many among you did Ike help?" She paced among the men.

A rumble of affirmative answers swept the room. Their faces were shocked. Ike wasn't one you imagined would die in battle, defending the territory. And in truth, it had been more of an execution.

Congratulations, Vost. You gunned down an old man.

She went on, "The question is, what're we going to do about this?"

"Take the fight to them!" all of Queensland shouted.

Easier said than done.

But she gave away none of her fear, none of her reservations. She didn't mention the grenades or the big guns. The Dread Queen took over, preaching blood and retribution. She spoke in ringing tones until the men were calling her name over and over. It didn't bring Ike back, but it drove the shock and horror out of their faces, replacing it with righteous anger. Perdition might be a hellhole, but she'd carved out a place, and she would defend it with her last breath.

There is nothing more ferocious than men defending their homes, Commander. I hope you're ready. As Martine would say, it's about to get bloody up in here.

◄ 20 ►

Death and Remembrance

"That . . ." Jael squinted at the man who was struggling for words. He couldn't recall the lunk's name, but he suspected he was one of Grigor's leftovers. They tended to be hulking, though nothing to compare with Einar or Cook. Still, he had hefty arms and hairy shoulders, a fact he seemed proud of.

"What?" he finally prompted.

"You'd never have seen something like that where I came from. Grigor used to have us fight each other for a place at his table, a chance to eat decent food."

"To the death?"

The other man nodded. All around them, men were singing rowdy drinking songs in honor of Ike, though truthfully, his demise was just an excuse to bust out the still, and that roused a bleak, deep rage in Jael that he couldn't explain. *So bloody unlikely that I'd meet a decent man in here, but there you are. And he died for us.*

"Never anything but." The other man had a deep voice, gravelly, and beetling black brows that met over a hooked nose.

Ugly sod.

"Sounds pretty hellish."

"You get used to anything." The man wore a thoughtful expression. "Under the Great Bear, you'd never witness anything like what that geezer did for you lot, either."

"Let me guess—he thought it was weakness to stick your neck out."

"More or less."

"It's not like that here," Jael said, trying to ignore the three men at the table who were slamming their fists on the table to punctuate the raucous noise they called music.

A vein in Jael's temple throbbed.

"So I see. I need to talk to the boys." But he didn't tell Jael what he was thinking because he was turning to pound somebody when Calypso vaulted up onto a table.

"While I love a party, we need to honor a brave man, Queensland-style."

"What've you got in mind?" someone shouted, while another asshole hooted at her, too far into his bottle to realize what a bad idea that was.

She leapt lightly down and stalked toward the poor idiot; Jael almost felt sorry for him. But at least the noise died down in her wake. The shit-faced dimwit had the temerity to grin up at her, like catcalling at the mistress of the circle was a good idea. Her smile was feral as she swung back an arm and backhanded him out of his chair. His booze spilled as he hit the floor; nobody said a word as he scrambled backward.

"Yeah, proper respect, that's what I'm talking about." Calypso swept the room with her dark gaze, then added, "For Ike, of course."

"Of course," Jael murmured.

The woman hopped onto the nearest table, ignoring the men who had been drinking there, then she raised her voice in a rich and lovely alto. "His day is past and gone / The evening shade appears / Oh, may we all remember well / A night of tears draws near."

Almost timidly, a few voices chimed in. Apparently,

this was a well-known song though Jael hadn't heard it before. The slow, mournful memory opened up a hole in his chest as Calypso nodded, encouraging the others to join the chorus. *She's right. Ike would like this better than the wake we gave Einar.*

She sang on, "We'll lay his garments by / Finally, he is at rest / Death will soon disrobe us all / Of the little we possess."

Depressing as hell, that. Having caught the tune, Jael hummed since he didn't know the words.

"Mary, keep us safe this night / Secure from all our fears / Her spirit guard us while we sleep / 'Til morning light appears."

The mistress of the ring bowed her head, and the rest of Queensland did likewise. For the full space of a minute, Jael heard nothing but convicts breathing, quite a rarity with his senses. Nobody whispered or coughed; a few men even had their eyes closed, as if they might be praying. *Closest this lot has come to a church in turns, no doubt.* The thought held a certain dark charm.

Then she flashed the others a big grin. "Back to drinking, you sots. That's enough reverence."

TAM could hardly bear to stay at Ike's service.

When Einar died, it was bad, but he'd known Ike even longer and had come to realize that he didn't belong in Perdition. Yet like all the rest, he had no hope of escape aside from death. After Calypso's serenade, Dred spoke all the right words, honoring his memory, and they carried him to the chute. For a man like him, there should be something more, something better, but Ike went like the rest, down, down, down, meat to feed the beast that was Perdition.

Tonight, the still was unlocked, and most of the men were drinking themselves stupid—with Dred's blessing— leaving a light crew on watch. He didn't agree with the decision, but he knew better than to question the Dread Queen. *Perhaps she's right. The mercs probably won't move on us again for a while. They'll be wondering how many Peace-makers we have, how well fortified Queensland is. They also need time to rest and regroup.*

So do we.

He was in no mood to watch criminals get soused, how-ever, and partner up in an orgy supposedly in honor of Ike. So Tam went to Dred's quarters to bathe. She wouldn't mind—or she never had in the past—as long as he tidied up after himself. In some corner of his brain, he hoped the san-shower would wash away the profound feeling of fail-ure. If he'd planned better or noticed the drone cam track-ing them, Vost wouldn't have gotten the drop on them.

Ike wouldn't be dead.

Martine surprised him when he stepped out of Dred's quarters. He'd expected she would be drinking with the others. But instead, she was propped on the opposite wall, arms folded over her chest. He tilted his head.

"Can I help you?"

"I'm thinking it's more the opposite."

"In what regard?"

"You don't think I can tell you got a knife buried in you blade deep? Figuratively speaking."

Tam was speechless for a few seconds. "I don't see why you'd notice. Or care."

"Funny thing about arrangements. We've nearly come to one, don't you think?"

He nodded. In here, sex was entirely separate from emotional entanglements, however. It was better and safer that way. Since he wasn't in the mood for games, he didn't see why she was waiting for him.

"That means *you're* my business, and I look after what's mine."

Her tone sent a frisson down his spine. There was no beginning or end point; he couldn't remember a time when that hadn't been the case for him. In some way, he'd always known he was meant to serve, and it gave him pleasure. It didn't even have to be sexual in nature though that was best.

"What do you mean?" he asked though he knew.

"I can't have you whipping yourself over Ike. That's my job."

"Not today," he said politely.

"I wouldn't have thought you'd be so literal. Come on."

"Where are we going?"

"You think you're the only one with secrets? Trust me."

That was an impossible request, but when she put out her hand, he took it. Then she pulled him along, past the hall to the common room, past the hydroponics garden and the armory, past the dorms. The only thing back this way was the ladder to the next level. They had so much space to protect now that it almost wasn't even worth it; numbers in Queensland had diminished to the point that they no longer needed to expand.

It might be dangerous to break away from the pack like this, but the promise of silence lured him on, almost as much as the neat sway of Martine's hips. She cast a look back every now and then, making sure he was still with her. He appreciated her silence, too. They emerged in a narrow hallway he'd never seen before, almost as if this were between levels on the station.

She read the question in his eyes, and answered, "I think this is where the maintenance crew hid from their supervisors."

"Back when it was a mineral refinery?" It amused but didn't surprise him. Tam could well imagine men holing up here to take a nap.

The ceiling was low enough that he and Martine had to hunch over. She continued down to the end, then darted into a small room that was more of an alcove, with odds and ends in it, things she'd scavenged and hidden away for her personal enjoyment. He examined the items, including the cushions and the electronics affixed to the wall.

"Portable entertainment unit, broken when I found it. Ike got it running for me."

Now Tam understood. This was a quieter homage than was going on currently in Queensland. "That's Ike for you. He could fix anything."

She nodded. "It has sixteen old vids on it, and I've watched them so many times that I can quote all of the lines. Some of them are truly terrible, but I thought you might like to watch them with me."

Tam considered refusing. This was a sort of closeness he'd eschewed for turns. Instead, he let her draw him into the nest she'd made, then Martine flicked on the screen. For the first time in longer than he could recall, he didn't feel alone.

"**THEY** have a fragging Peacemaker." Casto slammed a fist into the wall, rattling the sensitive equipment stacked on the shelves above. "Any other surprises, Commander?"

"I'm sure there will be many before we're through here." Vost kept his tone mild.

"This is bullshit. I say we cut line and bug out. Who's with me?" The flash of teeth presented the words as a joke, but those eyes were dead serious.

Mary curse it. Casto was skating pretty close to mutiny, and Vost was hanging on to his men by the scruff of their necks. This wasn't the in-and-out, easy money they had been promised. But since when did anything ever pan out that way?

"We won't be dividing up into patrols anymore." He spoke over the rumble of discontent, hoping to reassure the mercs. "Given what we know of our enemy, we can't assume that a small squad will be sufficient to take them out."

"Wish you'd made that call before so many of us died," Casto muttered.

Too far.

Vost knew exactly what he could tolerate—what could be written off and what had to be dealt with. Casto was now an obstacle to overcome. He whirled and slammed his lieutenant to the ground in a move that he'd learned on Nicu Tertius. The other merc didn't look so cocky staring up from his back with a man's boot on his chest.

"You think I'm looking for a performance review from you, soldier?"

Casto looked like he wanted to shoot Vost in the face, but he got the respectful words out. "No, sir."

"Then you shut the fuck up and listen." Vost glanced around the room, seeing the right mixture of awe and respect back in his men's faces. "Any of the rest of you have something to say?"

They shook their heads.

Pointedly, he didn't let Casto up. *This is what you get when you cross me.* "I don't like dissent among the ranks. I know this op has gone to shit. Trust me, I'm very aware. That just means we have to adapt. Or do you agree with Casto that scumbags armed with forks and spears are too much for us?"

"Like hell," Duran said.

"Exactly my point. We patrol together from here on out. And fuck the Conglomerate's ban on weapons that'll fuck up the facility."

"Does this mean I get to use the grenade launcher?" Redmond asked.

"Why not? I don't give two shits how much it costs the suits to patch this place up once we're done with it. They try to dock our pay for damages and we'll . . . discuss that difference of opinion."

"Just like you did with Casto?" Duran grinned.

From the twist of Casto's mouth, he was plenty pissed. *Good. Remember how it feels when you cross me.* Vost leaned down. "Next time I hear anything like that from you, I don't knock you down. I take you out and promote from within. Understood?"

"Yes, sir. Sorry, sir."

Vost then showed he could be a good sport by towing his lieutenant to his feet. "Redmond, you lead the watch. The rest of us will catch forty winks."

"You got it, sir."

Wearily, Vost moved down the hall to the room he'd apportioned for the barracks. The men who weren't standing guard followed suit. Nobody said much as they stripped out of their armor, but they were all professional enough to secure it before crashing out. Like everyone else, he had a thermal blanket to roll up into. It seemed like forever since he'd had a hot meal or a proper wash. He was wary of using too much water as he didn't control the facility resources.

Yet.

Nearby, his squad dropped off quicker than he did, turns of soldiering combined with the fact that their decisions didn't mean life or death for men depending on them. Vost tried to turn his brain off, and he succeeded in dropping into a light sleep. That readiness saved his life. When the blade shinged down toward him, he rolled before his eyes were open.

That fast, he was fighting for his life. His rifle would do more harm than good in close quarters, so he drew his knife as men shouted in the dark. Someone hit the lights to reveal sixteen silent killers, all with war paint on, eyes dark as bottomless pits. Their blades flashed in an elegant whirlwind of death. Blood spurted from the merc next to Vost—up-close carnage—and he was already screaming in his head at the watchmen who'd let this happen.

Unless they're all dead.

Grimly, he squared off against three assassins. There was no time to gear up, no time for tactics. *Right, then. Bring it.*

Soon the command post rang with the screams of dying men, but it was more horrifying to watch the ones who died without so much as a whisper.

◀ 21 ▶

Sex-Pain Pleasure Games

Dred left the wake early.

It didn't surprise her when Jael broke away from the group he was drinking with and went with her as she left the common room. Her stomach roiled with grief and cheap liquor; the stuff they produced in the still barely qualified as a nontoxic substance. But it would've been out of place if she'd refused to drink in Ike's honor. The Queenslanders would continue all night, getting drunk and telling stories.

"I'm not in the mood to talk," she said, without turning around.

"Neither am I."

"Yet here we are. Talking."

When his hand came down on her shoulder, she reacted. She spun and slammed him against the wall. Pain and regret lashed her like gale-force winds, and she was barely holding together. She had no patience for his bullshit at the moment. Whatever he had in mind, she just wanted to be left alone. The scene kept playing through her head while she tried to figure out if there was a way she could've saved everyone.

"Tell me to leave you be." His blue gaze was steady.

I never looked for this. I don't want it.

But she couldn't speak the words, so he slid his hand down her arm and laced their fingers together. She didn't ask as he pulled her toward what had become *their* quarters. Once inside, he secured the door and stepped back. Dred stripped off her armor, each movement emphasizing her mood. She wanted to chuck the pieces against the wall, but since Ike had died as part of their retrieval, she set them down carefully. Each time she clicked the segments into place, she'd feel the weight of Ike's death.

"Scream if you need to. Hit me. You can't cut loose out there, where everyone can see. You're the Dread Queen, immovable and infallible."

That was the crux of the problem because she so obviously wasn't. With better planning, Ike would be alive and installing the turrets they'd brought back. That was a problem she'd deal with later; she had no idea if anyone else could make the tech work. Vix and Zediah were probably the next best with such things.

"You think I can cry on command?" Quite the contrary— her eyes burned bone-dry even as loss and regret rose and fell within her like the sea.

"Hey, I'm trying. This isn't my forte."

"Then get out. Go drink some more."

"Now that's just cruel, love. You'd send me to my doom because I don't know the right words for the occasion?" He paused, apparently watching her face, and added, "That shit causes liver failure, and I don't heal like I used to."

A reluctant smile escaped her. "You're not going anywhere, are you?"

"You're a clever thing." His tone was soft.

"And you're wrecking me." She spun away, feeling as if she had glass bones. Dred sucked in several sharp breaths before she felt able to face him again.

When she turned, he was too close. "Excuse me?"

"I stand alone. That's the way it works."

"Then maybe it's time to change the system. Before it

breaks you." He took a step toward her, and she shoved him in reflex.

He caught her wrists in his hands and pulled her toward him. She fought without even considering why she couldn't stand his warmth. When it became clear he wasn't letting go, she went limp in his hold, startling him into loosening his hands. She folded into a ball, arms wrapped tight around her knees. The urge to scream as he'd invited rose, an endless clamor in her head. She couldn't count all the times she had brought a problem to Ike, who'd always listened with infinite patience and kindness.

To her chagrin, Jael knelt and wrapped his arms around her taut back. She clenched her teeth until her jaw hurt, then she slammed her head back against his shoulder. He grunted, but he didn't let go. Dred hovered mere millimeters away from losing all control. She strangled the urge to pummel Jael and rake his face with her nails, not because she truly wanted to hurt him but because he was *here*, and he wouldn't leave her the frag alone.

"You don't know how to take a hint," she growled.

"It's never come up. I have encounters, not relationships. So nobody's ever asked me to go, mostly because I was already gone."

"Then why are you still here?"

"Hell if I know." His hands were gentle, at odds with his offhand tone.

She sucked in a shuddering breath and realized there was one thing he could give her that would shut off her brain for a while. "Would you mind if I objectify you a little?"

"Just a little?" His mouth quirked in a half smile.

"Until we're exhausted and can't think anymore." She followed the words by going in for a kiss, and he met her halfway.

His lips were a blaze of pure fire, kindling all of her cold and desolate spaces. She wrapped her arms around his neck and bit down in surprise when he rose with her in his arms. *I always forget that he's stronger than he looks.* Jael carried her to the bunk, and she pulled off her clothes in reckless urgency. *Better to be stupid like this.* Once they were both naked, she pushed him back and came down on top of him.

"One of these days—" But she didn't let him finish.

A hungry kiss. Another. Until his hands dug into her hips, and he moved beneath her with ever-increasing need. Dred poured everything into him, making his body a canvas upon which she painted all the fear and grief, all the loss, and it transformed into the pulse of desire. She ran her lips down his neck, then bit. He twisted under her, hips bucking.

Dred took him then, but the moment she did, he rolled, so they were facing one another. It wasn't enough like Artan's preferred posture of ownership to mess with her head, but it was strange and intimate. She made a sound of protest, then he stole her breath with a long, determined stroke. Their legs were tangled; this position was a little awkward, but it took away the pretense that she was in charge. This way, he wasn't either.

Jael drew her closer still in a haze of soft, drugging kisses. His hands played down her back in teasing patterns, so she pricked his shoulders with her nails, a demand or a reminder, she wasn't sure which. It was hard to think with the pleasure drumming in her ears. He pressed deep and held; she cracked open like a ripe fruit, spilling cries and tears. Dred didn't realize she was crying until he pulled back, leaving only his arms to hold her. She wept into his bare shoulders, smearing him with salt and sorrow. He was still hard, pressed against her belly, but he seemed more focused on comforting her than searching for satisfaction.

"There's something wrong with you," she whispered.

"I know, love. People have been telling me that for ages." His voice sounded deep and low through the tangle of her hair.

"That's not what I'm talking about."

"Enlighten me."

"You let me use you. But you didn't—"

"That's not the beginning and end of everything. It's a

flicker, really. As it turns out, I appreciate other pleasures more."

"Such as?"

"Feeling you come apart in my arms, knowing you trust me with your fear."

Oh, Mary. The truth of it hit her like a metal ballast. But even as she choked on the realization, he was kissing her face gently. Each brush of his lips felt like it might pull her apart, snapping bones and sinew until she was a series of disconnected components. Desperate to reassert control, she shoved him away. He moved as if to leave the bed, but she put a hand on his chest.

"I believe in fair play. It's your turn."

If he had protested, she would've stopped. But she glimpsed cognition of her motives in his blue eyes, which made it simultaneously better and worse. Jael settled against the pillows as she went to work with her mouth. He twisted and writhed, just as he was supposed to, but even when he lost control, arched in a perfect bow, hands tangled in her hair, she never lost the sense that he had won this battle—that something had permanently shifted between them.

Afterward, he drew her up into his arms. Shaken, she rested her head on his chest and listened to his heart. Nothing unusual about the sound, no sign he was anything but human.

"Do you think you can sleep?" he asked.

"Probably. The better question is if I *should* be able to."

"If I thought it would help, I'd tell you it wasn't your fault. It was bad timing or luck or some combination of the two. Ike wouldn't blame you."

"If I could, I'd ask him," she said softly.

"I know."

She sighed, rolling onto her side to face him. "This is so backward."

"What is?"

"*This.*" Dred gestured at their proximity. "Everything about us. I need to stay away from you, but I never follow through."

He flinched, such a fleeting expression that if she hadn't been so close, she would have missed it. And the words sounded as if they were being dragged out of him with hooks and wires. "If you really think this is a mistake—"

She put two fingers to his mouth. "Against my better judgment, yes, but . . . I'd be lost without you, Jael."

He kissed her hand, then pulled it away from his mouth, so he could tuck his face against her neck. "I should've realized I needed to go all the way to hell to find my soul."

The Past Is Another Country

A day later, they were still mopping vomit off the floor and blood from the walls. *Hell of a send-off. Ike might even approve.* After Jael left the common room with Dred, the populace apparently ran amok, with the usual results and casualties. People were still sullen, nursing grievances that sprang out of nowhere. Or at least, it seemed that way to Jael.

Maybe it was more accurate to say that liquor gave men the courage to say shit they'd never otherwise admit. As a result, tensions were high today. A number of Queenslanders had only pretended to accept the admission of the aliens, intimidated by the example Dred made of the man who disagreed with her decision. Since nobody wanted to end up like that, their complaints had gone quiet, confined to whispers that stilled as soon as Jael approached.

Good thing they don't know I can hear them from here.

"I can't believe we have to share bunk space with those freaks," a Queenslander was saying.

"They're eating up our food," someone else complained.

"If I'd known the Dread Queen was such a sympathizer, I'd have—"

"What?" Brahm stood behind the group, talons splayed.

At his back, there were a number of aliens from the Warren, some of whom Jael knew by name, like Ali. The rest he had no experience with, so he couldn't be sure how quickly this situation would escalate. And he wasn't sure of his role anyway. Maybe Dred would be pissed if he stepped in, like he held actual power.

But Cook solved the problem by hurling his knife. It thunked into the table where the xenophobes were sitting. The handle quivered as the man stalked over to retrieve the weapon. He paused for a few seconds in silence before picking it up. Not surprisingly, the malcontents found other places they needed to be. Satisfied, Cook went back to his pot.

"Sorry about that," Jael said to Brahm.

The Ithtorian still gave him the creeps, but he knew better than to blame Brahm for the shit he'd gone through on Ithiss-Tor. It was a personal bias, one he was struggling with, and he didn't intend to make a public issue of it. But the alien regarded him for a few seconds out of side-set eyes without speaking.

"You have a problem with me," he said.

"Not like *they* do," he answered, defensive.

The Ithtorian clicked out a laugh. "No, your issue is specific to my kind. I don't notice it around the rest." He turned to his companions and waved them away. Ali seemed most reluctant, but she eventually moved off, presumably so Brahm could speak to Jael in private.

Once they were alone, relatively speaking, Jael said, "It doesn't matter. I won't move on you if that's what you're worried about."

Brahm tilted his head, mandible moving in a way that Jael recognized as being a thoughtful gesture. He'd learned a lot about Bug body language during his long incarceration. He wished the cues didn't make him want to pull Brahm's head off.

"I'm not. You seem to have more honor than that."

"*Seem* being the operative word."

"The Dread Queen relies on you. And we've noticed that her advisors are a cut above the rest of the population."

Jael wasn't sure where this conversation was going. "Thanks. I think."

"But you're naïve if you think our assimilation will pass without bloodshed."

"That's not something I've been accused of before." The Ithtorian wasn't wrong, though. He saw the tension growing as the days rolled on. Sooner or later, it would explode.

"I imagine not. The interesting thing about you, downright intriguing, in fact . . . is that I've been speaking Ithtorian for the last few minutes."

Now that Brahm had pointed it out, Jael registered the clicks and chitters that comprised the Ithtorian native tongue. The alien stood there, silently awaiting an explanation, and Jael gave it reluctantly. "I spent some time in the Ithtorian penal system. They chipped me, so I could understand orders the guards gave me."

Mostly it had consisted of *turn around, present your limbs to be shackled*, and *step out of the cave so we can hose it down*. Not exactly scintillating conversation. But limited interaction was better than nothing, better than silence. Yet Brahm went still, his mandible locked in a position Jael identified as tension.

"You're the one."

Before he spoke, he suspected. "Pardon me?"

"You're the man who tried to murder my father."

Shit. Brahmel Il-Charis. Charis Il-Wan. There *had* been a reason the name sounded familiar, but it'd been so long. Jael didn't take a step back even as the Ithtorian moved forward. He blocked when the Ithtorian reached out slowly with razor-sharp talons.

"If I was a better scion, I'd cut your throat," Brahm said in universal.

The men nearby froze at that, and Jael knew they'd back him if it came to a fight. *Can't let this escalate.* Ali stood with the rest of the aliens, but she was clearly paying attention to

Brahm. At a gesture from him, they would wade in. He didn't see Katur or Keelah anywhere, so that was a blessing. Their presence might put the stamp of approval on a bloodbath, so far as the rest of the aliens were concerned. While they were loyal, they lacked the ferocity necessary to kill everyone in the room.

That's because they're not killers by nature.

"I could make excuses," he answered. "Say it was just a job, nothing personal. But it *is* personal for you. So that wouldn't help."

"You took the coward's path, poisoned him."

Jael wanted to ask if there was a *good* way to murder someone, but levity would only worsen the situation. A couple of Queenslanders pushed to their feet and came to stand at his shoulder. By the smell, it was the ones who had been complaining about the aliens. *Yeah, they'll love it if this explodes.*

"This is between him and me," Jael said over one shoulder.

Then he faced Brahm again. "What will square this? A grudge match?"

The Ithtorian spread his claws. "I bear you no malice. My only regret is that you didn't succeed."

"What the hell—"

"I did say *if* I were better. I loathe Charis Il-Wan, and I wish *I'd* poisoned him." So saying, Brahm shocked the shit out of Jael by offering his claw, human-style, for a clasp.

Recovering, Jael shook his hand, wondering exactly what the Bug politician had done to his offspring to make Brahm wish he'd killed his old man. The tension seeped from the room like air slowly escaping a balloon. Little by little, the Queenslanders went about their business, and the aliens left the hall entirely.

"I can safely say I didn't see that coming. How did you end up here anyway?" Maybe Brahm was the exception, an alien who had been locked up for capital crimes.

"I was banished from Ithiss-Tor. It was bad luck that

landed me here, got caught up in immigration sweeps on New Terra, like everyone else."

"I don't understand that," Jael said. "Why not just deport the lot of you?"

"Most of us know something about the current administration. It would be . . . inconvenient to have us revealing that information."

Given what he knew about the government, he wasn't surprised. "Pardon me. I shouldn't have pried. That goes against the code."

"You'll note I didn't volunteer anything about my exile."

"Noted."

With a parting nod, Jael excused himself and went to join a card game. He played for several hours, while the men around him gradually relaxed. There was nothing for winding convicts up like the promise of violence. But the common room was much emptier than it had been when he first arrived. Full tables sat vacant, chairs never to be filled. When you looked at the conflict as a war of attrition, it was hard to imagine anything but inevitable loss.

The crowd thinned even further as the hour got later. He wasn't paying full attention to his hand, so he lost more than he won. No, it was the activity among the alien-haters that troubled him. They slipped in and out, never more than one or two at a time, and they had the shifty look of assholes up to no good. One man stole up to another, whispered in his ear, then left. The other one waited for a couple of minutes before taking off after him. *Yeah, that's a sure sign they're rallying.* Cook turned off his equipment and headed for the dorm, so there would be no backup from that quarter.

Quietly, he threw down his cards. "I fold."

The rest of the gamblers hardly glanced up when he slid out of the hall. The conspirator glanced both left and right before bearing left. The training room was this way; so was the armory. Jael half expected the man to stop and fiddle with the lock, but instead he kept moving, quickening to nearly a run, as if the anticipation had grown too much to bear.

He grabbed a man who was on his way to his bunk, and ordered, "Go find the Dread Queen. Send her to me immediately. If you fail, you'll wish you were dead."

Gulping, the drafted messenger took off at a run.

Jael didn't know what he expected to find, but the reality was worse. The men had captured an assortment of aliens, Keelah among them, and they were bound to support beams in the training room. The bastards had grabbed the weakest among them, too, so Ali and Brahm were both conspicuously absent. Some of them were bleeding while others trembled in anticipation of pain to come. Now he understood why they had been traveling in pairs, better to pounce on a single target and drag him off.

He slammed a palm against the door as he strode through. "I'm damn sure the Dread Queen didn't approve this. Which means it amounts to treason."

◄ 23 ►

Let the Games Begin

"So it does," Dred said.

When the runner Jael had sent showed up, panting and out of breath, she'd known something must be wrong. She stalked toward Keelah, blade in hand, and cut her loose. Then she offered the knife. "Free your people."

It was better to show complete support for the newcomers. Though it was technically the middle of downtime, she couldn't let this ride; there would be no delays to justice or waiting for the rest of the territory to wake up on its own. Some offenses had to be tried immediately in the court of blood and bone. Once the aliens were released, she turned to the treacherous Queenslanders, all of whom looked half a second from pissing their pants.

"Perhaps I didn't make the rules clear," she snarled, pointing at the tallest of the lot. "What are they?"

There were eight of them, yet they didn't try to fight. She had the Dread Queen's reputation to thank for that. Instead, they stood frozen beneath the weight of her wrath, and one of them even moved closer to Jael, as if he thought he might find mercy there.

You don't know him very well.

Jael shoved the man who was supposed to be answering her question toward the rest and added a kick for good measure. The impact sent him reeling to the floor. Nobody moved to help him up. He shoved to his feet with a defiant air, but he couldn't hold her gaze long. He pushed out a wavering breath.

The man thought hard, brow furrowed as sweat dripped down one cheek. "No stealing, no unauthorized fighting. Bathing. Do your work—"

"Then you have *no excuse* for this offense, cretin. Not even ignorance. You tortured your fellow citizens. Did you think I'd let that go?" Long strides carried her over to where alien blood smeared the ground, not always red, but unmistakable. Kneeling, she swiped her fingers through the sticky droplets, then she returned to the criminals and painted the backs of their hands one by one. "Now their blood truly is on your hands. Remember this feeling. Remember this mistake. It will be your last."

"They're not really Queenslanders," another spat. "Just look at them."

That moment of bravery didn't last long when she turned her gaze on him. He stumbled back a step, cowering with the rest. Ignoring them for a few seconds, she turned to Keelah, who had blood smeared on her muzzle. *Katur will want their heads, and I don't blame him.* She could ill afford the loss of grunts for the front line, but better to keep the aliens, who weren't utterly awash in prejudice.

"As the offended party, I'll give you the option on what I do with these wretches. I can cast them out—to be killed by Silence or eaten by Mungo's lot. You can execute them yourselves if you prefer. Or we can enjoy their misery in a series of death matches."

The alien female didn't ponder long. "The latter sounds fascinating."

"We're not fighting!" one of the traitors shouted.

Dred turned with a wicked smile. "You know the rules. The winner gets to live."

It was a measure of her depravity that she enjoyed how fast the bigots turned on one another. Jael had to pull them apart, or they would've started the killing before she roused Calypso and summoned an audience.

She nodded at Keelah. "Can your people restrain them?"

"Gladly."

Leaving Jael to manage the situation, she ran off to wake Calypso. The mistress of the ring wasn't amused at being disturbed until she found out it was in her official capacity. Then her white teeth flashed in a delighted smile. "It's been too long." She yawned and stretched, then nudged her bedmate out of the bunk. "Go fetch the others. Tell them it's time for the blood sport."

A slim, brown-skinned male who bore a passing resemblance to Tam darted out of the room, his eyes lowered submissively. She noticed the fresh marks on his back, but as long as bed play was consensual, this didn't fall under the heading of harm. *Best to check.*

"He's a willing participant, yeah?"

"I don't make them cuddle with me afterward, dear heart," Calypso said, smirking. "That's *his* choice. So that should tell you plenty about how he feels."

"Point taken. I can't believe we have to do this. I wish we weren't sheltering such animals, but—"

"What more can you expect from Artan's loyalists?" Calypso rolled out of bed, unconscious of her nudity, and dressed quickly. Her entire outfit had been crafted from cured skins, harvested from the rodents infesting the ship. It gave her an earthy, musky smell, unique among the rest of Queensland.

"What do you mean?"

"You didn't think they all threw in with Lecass? There are those who miss Artan's cruelty and chaos. They just weren't brave enough to try to depose you."

"Comforting," Dred muttered.

"If you're looking for solace, my queen, well, you won't find it here."

Except that I did. From Jael.

"Don't call me that. I can't tell you how much I hate this *Dread Queen* crap."

"The men need something to believe in. If they thought you were an ordinary woman, they'd put a blade through your heart."

"None of us are normal, or we wouldn't be in Perdition," she pointed out.

But there *were* more men than women incarcerated here. Dred wasn't sure if men were naturally more prone to criminal behavior or if they just got caught more. Ego made her want to believe the latter. But since *she'd* slipped up, it was slim consolation.

Calypso took up her staff, an impressive feat of scrap engineering; the thing didn't look like it had any smooth edges, so it must cut into the other woman's palm, but she showed no visible signs of distress. The mistress of the circle didn't check her reflection, merely strode out of the room ahead of Dred.

"You'll get the hall set up?" she asked.

"Of course. Bring the prisoners in a quarter hour or so."

Nodding, Dred jogged back to the training room, where the traitors had been forced to their knees. They wore the same bloody cords they'd used on their victims, and the refugees seemed pleased with the resolution so far. Katur had joined his mate, but Dred couldn't read anything from his demeanor. His coppery fur was flat, his eyes dark in the low, downtime light, as Dred ran the zone on half power while most of the populace was sleeping.

She made eye contact with Jael, silently asking how much of a bomb they were sitting on. He shook his head, and she took that to mean the newcomers were satisfied with the swift and merciless judgment. But this wasn't wholly about protecting the refugees; it was also about reminding the men that she held the power, and while she might be less of a lunatic than Artan, it still didn't pay to cross her.

Dred presented herself before the alien leader and tilted her head down, not quite a bow, but he should recognize it as a gesture of humility. "I apologize for the harm to your people. I said you're Queenslanders now, and I meant it. The guilty will be punished."

"I look forward to the show," Katur said. "We have never permitted such barbarity in the Warren."

That's definitely a reminder of who the civilized people are in this room.

She only nodded. "This way. I'll explain the rules."

By the time they reached the common room, Calypso had the makeshift arena set up and her bed partner had rousted most of the Queenslanders to serve as the audience. Though some looked sleepy and surly, the bulk reacted to the prospect of bloodshed as Calypso had, as if it were the delivery of a much-anticipated treat. *I can only do so much with what Artan left me.* But she was aware of the silent aliens standing at her shoulder, likely thinking she was no better than Mungo or Silence. For obvious reasons, that turned her stomach.

She said, "Pardon me," to Katur, then sent a number of men, led by Cook, to assist Jael in escorting the combatants. The chef chucked two men bodily over the scrap framework that made up the ring. They hit the floor with a metallic clang, and one skidded into the barricade, prompting raucous jeers from the spectators.

This is how I hold them. No matter what I tell myself about rules or order, it's the promise of violence that keeps the rest in check.

As if he suspected her thoughts, Jael put a hand on her arm, and she covered it with her own, a quiet moment of secret solidarity. Or maybe he was exerting ownership. She preferred to imagine otherwise.

Once everyone took their places outside the circle, Calypso thumped her staff against the floor three times. That was the cue for the games to begin.

"These men are charged with bringing harm to other Queenslanders!" Calypso shouted. "And so it is we who have a grudge to settle with them. Do you trust them to watch your backs or fight alongside you?"

A resounding *no* rang out.

I could take lessons from her on working the crowd.

"In her infinite wisdom, the Dread Queen has decided it is fitting for these traitors to fight among themselves. For your entertainment!" A prisoner groaned, receiving a clout from Calypso as a reward. Then she went on, "Eight men enter the circle. Only one will emerge victorious. Do you understand these rules, gladiators?"

They each nodded, reflecting different degrees of agitation and fury. Using her staff, Calypso vaulted out of the ring, leaving the two men to eye one another warily. They wouldn't fight until the mistress started the match officially. Dred took their measure and decided neither would last long. They were both thin with the sallow complexions of men who drank too much. Loose skin at their throats said they had been hardier once, but Perdition had carved them down to skin and bones.

And vile instincts.

In the crowd, she caught sight of Vix and Zediah, standing together. The look on their faces struck her as odd, avid even, but they weren't watching the ring. Dred followed their gazes and saw that they were staring at Jael. He seemed oblivious though their interest was odd. She put it from her mind as the mistress of the circle raised her staff.

"Then let the games begin!" Calypso shouted.

◀ 24 ▶

Something from Before

The first match kicked off with an attempted knife-palm to the throat. Jael watched as the second man dodged and came in low. Their technique was sloppy, more suited to a bar brawl than life-and-death combat, but regardless of how badly they fought, one of these men was leaving the arena feet first. Around him, Queenslanders were betting, offering goods and favors, and Calypso seemed to be making book.

"No wonder she likes this job," he muttered.

The mistress of the circle wrote furiously in a sheaf of bound pages, nodding as she set up the terms. Her action on the side was more interesting than the fight. The smaller man rushed the other and took him to the ground, then they rolled, scratching and gouging. Other Queenslanders probably couldn't hear the growls and groans of pain with the roar of the spectators, but Jael registered each gasping breath and how one man lost traction, revealed in the stink of terror in his sweat. The fighter on the bottom took an elbow to the face, and his nose crunched, spurting blood. There was hesitation from the second man as he smeared it into his opponent's eyes, and that gave him the advantage he needed to finish the fight by digging his bare fingers into the blinded target's eyes. Jael didn't flinch from the wet pop, and the victor drove deep, until the other stopped twitching. Amid a flurry of shouts and cheers, he stumbled to his feet and raised bloody arms high in the air.

"Winner, first match!" Calypso called out. Then she moved the metal aside to let him pass out of the circle. "Wait here. You'll fight the next soon enough."

At her orders, the cleaners removed the body and mopped the floor while Queenslanders paid off their wagers. More than a few looked pissed off at their luck, and some of them spat on the dead man as the sanitation crew carried him out to the chute. They stomped their feet, eager for more blood sport. A shiver of revulsion went through Jael.

Zediah caught his eye, a long look broken only by Vix, who put her hand on the other man's arm, then smiled. She nodded once. Jael had no idea what that was about, but it prickled his skin every bit as much as the bloodlust emanating from the crowd.

Men like this made *me. Told me I'm a monster until I acted the part.*

He gazed out over the avid, bloodthirsty faces and shook his head. Dred touched his arm. "What's that about?" she asked in a low voice.

Always surprises me, the way she pays attention. Hell if he knew why.

"I used to wish to be human," he murmured. "I hated that I wasn't. But . . . now? I'm rather glad I'm not."

"Since this is all we see, it's easy to forget there's another sort of people."

"Kind, gentle, and selfless?" he mocked.

Dred shook her head. "Normal folk. They live their lives, and they don't harm anyone. This isn't the usual, Jael. You *must* know that."

"I haven't had much contact with them. But I'll take your word that they exist."

"Isn't that your dream? To break out of here and hide among them."

In all honesty, he hadn't planned that far. His current goal was to survive killing the mercenaries. Then he had a half-baked notion of escaping this place. To do the impossible—break out of Perdition—*that* was the goal. His vision cut off after that.

"Nobody's ever asked me what I *want* from life."

"Do you know?"

He watched as Calypso signaled for the next match to begin. "Not this."

In the end, the eye-gouger emerged victorious, despite vicious injuries. Still, the man raised his arms as if he expected people to cheer. As for Jael, he was waiting for Dred to reveal the crook in her plan. He didn't credit for a second that she intended to release this bastard after what he'd done.

Calypso kicked the ring down and stepped closer to the winner. "Behold today's champion of the games."

"Shit. I thought Arndt had a shot of going all the way." A Queenslander spat and paid his lost bet with a set of hand-carved blades. "I never would've bet on Errol."

"He's a sneaky bastard," the winner said smugly.

"I won! Someone bring me a drink." Errol was grinning.

"Not yet," Dred said.

"We're done," the man bit out. "I passed your test."

The rest of the Queenslanders fell silent, waiting to hear the verdict. Dred joined Calypso, and the two women towered over him. "I said I'd let you live if you won. Not that I'd permit you to stay. From this moment forward, Errol the Skinner is an enemy to Queensland, and we kill him on sight."

"Understood!" the rest of the men called.

The victor only had time for a choked gasp before Jael cut off his air. He lifted the rat by his throat and dragged him to the barricades. The sentries made no attempt to stop him. Errol landed with a painful-sounding thud, and Jael detected a snap. *Broke some bones, on top of the injuries he had already. Won't last long out there.*

That was the point.

When he returned to the common room, the cleaners

had already removed all traces of the arena and were carrying the last corpse to the chute to be recycled. Sometimes Jael had the feeling that the station was alive and eating them one by one. He silenced such mad-tinged thoughts and crossed to where Dred stood, making further apologies to the refugees.

"I hope this redresses the offense sufficiently," she concluded, as Jael stepped up.

"How can we be sure there are no more enemies hiding among us?" Keelah asked.

Jael respected Dred's honesty when she said, "You can't. So exercise caution. I'll punish additional offenders, but some damage can't be undone."

"This is true," Katur replied. "And you've dealt more fairly with us than anyone since before our imprisonment. We will be watchful."

"I should've acted sooner," Jael murmured.

Keelah inclined her head, leaning on her mate for support. "We all have regrets."

The Ithtorian nodded at that. "I wish I hadn't lingered on New Terra. But I didn't think the sweeps were anything to worry about."

Jael understood how the Bug felt though it was a reluctant empathy. He knew all too well what it was like to be hunted due to circumstances beyond your control. For the aliens, it was how they looked that made them targets. For him, it was his bioengineering. Sometimes he wondered if there were any survivors from his pod; they would be the closest thing he had to family, but he'd never gone looking for them. The truth might do his head in; it was one thing to suspect you were alone in the universe, another to have it confirmed.

"You have our sincere gratitude for the swift justice you delivered." Katur put his hands together, then signaled for his people to withdraw.

That was probably a smart tactical move, before the rest of Queensland remembered that the death matches took places because some of their number hated aliens. The atmosphere in the common room was rowdy. Death matches were apparently excellent for morale, not something Jael would've anticipated, but that was why he wasn't in charge.

"It used to be like this all the time," Dred said quietly.

"Artan held matches more often?"

"I only do it to settle grievances or in lieu of a trial. He did it for fun. There was a daily lottery, and unless you were one of his favorites, anyone could be chosen."

"Sounds like a barrel of laughs. I wish I could stab him between the eyes."

At that, she slid him a sideways glance and a half smile, then she stepped closer slightly, enough so that her arm was brushing his. "It's enough that you want to."

"Tell me something else about you. Something from before."

"Before I wreaked havoc on so many psycho killers and turned into one myself, before I was sent to Perdition for my crimes?"

"Yeah. I want to know something about who you were."

She tipped her head forward. "I barely remember." This was why he didn't get close to people. Jael turned, ready to head for the hydroponics garden, when she spoke again. "I always wanted to travel. I hated the Outskirts and the small colony where I grew up. Since my dad was hiding from the Science Corp, my parents were always lecturing me on being careful, not taking risks."

"So you grew up wanting adventure."

"That's why I took the job on the freighter. I . . . always wanted my own ship. I can remember sitting with my dad on the roof of our housing unit. I wasn't supposed to crawl up there, but I was never big on rules, even as a kid. Go figure, huh?"

Jael smiled, hoping she'd never stop talking. The background noise receded; he filtered until there was only her voice. "Somehow, I'm not surprised."

"And as an . . . apology, I guess, for being the reason that we were trapped on Tehrann, he spent hours teaching me astronomy. I can see the night sky in my head, even now, picture all the constellations. I can hear my father's voice, repeating the names." She paused, gaze locked on Jael's. "To this day, that's the way I fall asleep."

"By holding the stars in your head?" he asked softly.

"Yeah. Stupid, I suppose. I haven't seen them in turns."

"You will again." It felt like she'd given him a part of her to keep with him always. Nobody else knew that the Dread Queen named faraway stars when rest eluded her, a wisp of a secret binding them together, but he held to it as if it were more than gossamer.

"I'll ask you for a truth one day soon," she said then. "Quid pro quo."

"And I'll answer." There was no mockery in his tone, only another promise.

◀ 25 ▶

Truth or Dare

"You seem really sure Tam will succeed," Jael said to Dred, as they carted a table from the common room one level up.

Getting the thing up the shaft was a bitch, but for the work that would go on up here, they needed privacy. The men shouldn't know all of their secrets and plans. On that aspect of strategy, Dred stood with the spymaster. *Sucks to be the grunt in that scenario, but I don't give a shit about their feelings.* It was hard not to, sometimes. Caring about Jael had opened a floodgate, reminding her of the person she used to be, before she left home.

I can't let Dresdemona come back. Not yet. We need the Dread Queen.

"He's not known for failure," Dred answered.

"Haven't you noticed that he seems different lately?"

Come to think of it, she had. With a grunt and a final shove, she nudged the table onto the floor, letting Jael haul it up. *He has the strength for it.* She arched her aching back, wishing she could afford to trust someone else with the heavy lifting, but her inner circle had already expanded enough.

Before she replied, she let Jael pull her up, then she took up her end of the burden again.

"Yeah, it started when Einar died . . . and it's just gotten worse with Ike."

"He seems more . . . human now," Jael said.

Yeah, less of the cool, calculating tactician, more fallible man.

"Let's hope it doesn't fuck with his ability to scheme like a cold-blooded bastard and get the job done when our lives are on the line."

"He's also got Martine now. Maybe she's warming him up."

"I hope so . . . if that's a good thing. But there might come a time where we need him to be icy and devious."

He didn't speak as he moved backward. Dred jerked her head, signaling that they'd reached the door that led into the vacant space that would become the lab. "Here we are."

Inside, there was already a bunch of stuff she'd raided from Ike's storeroom. Doing that hurt so bad. Dred dropped to her knees and touched a knot of copper wires, petting them for a few, ridiculous seconds. There was no point to it; it wasn't like these bits and bobs contained any of Ike's spirit, but Mary, she missed him.

I didn't realize how much I listened to him, relied on him, until he was gone. Even more than Einar because I always knew the big man wanted in my bed.

Aloud, she said, "Ike . . . he didn't want anything, except to feel useful."

"He'd want us to kick their asses," Jael said.

"Definitely." She forced a toothy grin and pushed to her feet.

"Don't do that. Don't lie with your eyes. I'm usually bollocks at knowing when people mean what they say, but your face is plain to me."

"Is it? What's it saying then?"

"That you're bleeding like hell over that old man."

Dred swallowed hard and nodded. "It's worse because—"

She couldn't say it, couldn't get the words past the knives in her throat.

"I know, love." His arms were around her without her ever seeing him move. That fast, a blink, and he was there, only his racing heartbeat giving a hint that he might be suffering, too.

"I shouldn't care. The Dread Queen wouldn't."

"She's a straw man, an effigy made for burning. Tam knows that even if you don't, and he'd be the first to tell you not to let the role swallow you."

"Would he? I wonder."

The old Tameron probably wouldn't have, actually. He'd have used Dred until she broke, then found another piece to move about the board. The new Tam? Dred had no idea what he was capable of—but she hoped for a great many things.

"I can see why you came to me," Martine said. "Sounds dangerous."

Tam nodded. "We need an advantage now that we've lost the element of surprise with the Peacemaker. The mercs now know the full extent of our capabilities, and Dred has her hands full keeping order in Queensland."

In the days since the death matches, there had been a few abortive runs by Mungo's monsters, and Silence had tested the turrets as well. With Ike gone—the thought sent a fierce pang through him—it had been a struggle to get the new turrets installed. Even now, they didn't work correctly and didn't recognize the mag bracelets half the time. One of these days, a native would end up mowed down by their own defensive measures.

Calypso tilted her head. "You're sure we don't have what we need here, little man?"

She called him that because it was supposed to bother him. He was supposed to get angry and defensive, but the truth never troubled him. Lies were another matter though they were sometimes politic and necessary. So he merely offered her a level look.

"I've checked all of our storerooms. For my plan to succeed, we must retrieve chemicals currently in storage elsewhere."

"How far are we going?"

"Priest's domain. We prioritized on our last trip and took what we needed most. But circumstances have changed."

"There are three separate factions that want to kill us wandering the station. Or had you forgotten that?" Calypso didn't look eager to venture out.

And honestly, Tam didn't blame her. But he needed people who could fight and haul a significant amount of weight. He and Martine could manage the former, but their upper-body strength wasn't up to dragging multiple bottles of chem across the station. So he couldn't complete this mission solo, and his usual crew was busy. Which was why he'd asked Ali if she minded helping as well. The Rodeisian female was fair in a fight, and she'd be able to bring back plenty of components.

Ali joined them a few minutes later, just as he convinced Calypso that the benefits outweighed the risks, and she had Brahm with her. "Are we going?"

Tam swept a hand toward the barricades. "Stay close."

The downside of this group was that they couldn't travel through the ducts as he normally did. Ali couldn't fit comfortably, and even if she squeezed through, the noise of her passage would alert anyone to their presence. Best to stay on the ground and fight through if necessary. They each took rifles, but because there wasn't enough armor for everyone, and Ali couldn't wear it in any case, they went without. Dred and Jael saw them off, but Tam could tell by their expressions that they were worried about something and trying to hide it. He didn't derail the mission by inquiring. Timing was everything in such matters, and he was skilled at choosing both his moments and his battles.

Since he didn't want Calypso to know about the secret way in and out of the territory that the aliens had devised, he led the group out the east barricades. Sentries helped pull down some of the junk so Ali and Brahm could pass, and as soon as Tam's people climbed over, they immediately started rebuilding. *It appears that the death matches had a meritorious effect on the work ethic.* Some of them doubtless recalled how different it was under Artan's regime.

On the other side of the barrier, Tam powered down the turrets and signaled for the women to move out of range. There weren't enough magnetic bracelets to go around; since he had one, this was the only way.

"Someday you'll have to tell me what a proper little man did to end up here," Calypso said, as Tam moved toward the intersection.

"That's unlikely," he said politely.

Newly broken pipes and wires torn from the walls showed that someone had been here recently, some forty meters from the end of the turret range. The destruction suggested to Tam that it had been Mungo's lot. Silence's assassins tended not to yield to rage if they were frustrated in an objective; they were colder and more disciplined. The sentries couldn't see what happened past the barricades, but they should've reported hearing the damage.

"I don't like this," Martine said.

Calypso nudged the other woman forward. "We're exposed. We need to move. If the brutes are still around, we'll spot them soon enough."

"Rather fight them than the mercs," Ali put in.

"Agreed," Brahm said.

Tam concurred. Even if there were a lot of cannibals between here and Priest's abandoned territory, his crew had laser rifles, so they should be able to take out a fair number before the monsters closed to hand-to-hand. He moved past the wreckage and set out, aware that Queensland's survival depended on the success of this mission.

THINGS had gone better since Vost stopped dividing his forces.

They fought and won four consecutive battles, a boost to morale, and subsequently decimated the fetid-smelling humanoids. The men were much bolstered by uncomplicated killing. Vost knew better than to trust a sudden change of fortune, however; luck could be a fickle bitch, loving one day and kicking you in the junk the next. So he was wary as he led the men on patrol. He didn't like leaving the command post unattended, but he couldn't assign a man to keep an eye on the gear, either. After a successful enemy incursion, it was critical to prevent additional loss of life. If he lost too many men, the mission objective would become impossible.

As it was, he'd caught Casto shooting him furtive looks as he went around talking to the men, just out of Vost's earshot. They always shut up the minute he approached and insisted they were talking about *nothing*, which always added up to trouble. There was precious little Vost could do about it, however. The terms came down from the high-ups in the Conglomerate—that they go in and clean house without alerting any outsiders as to what was going on in Perdition. The tragedy would be "uncovered" later, and the story would be disseminated that the inmates had fought each other to the death, freeing the facility to be repurposed after it underwent a thorough sanitizing.

If we take off before the job's done, we don't get paid.

He couldn't permit that failure.

Vost fought down the memories, knowing they weakened him and lessened his concentration. In here, he needed to be on point all the time. He stopped at the fourway and held up a hand. His helmet had sense-boosting capabilities, and he heard something at fifty meters out, a good number of targets, moving fast. Casto shoved forward, likely to say something, and Vost slammed a palm up, demanding silence. Then he signaled for the men to move in quietly—or as near as they could manage. The heavy suits weren't designed for stealth. There was gear that helped with it, but it didn't offer as much protection, and they'd gone in with the intent of resisting primitive blunt and bladed weapons.

"Looks like we caught a battle under way," he said, low. "Let's get in and mop up."

Casto hefted his rifle. "Fragging brilliant. It's about time we got to shoot some fish in a barrel."

Redmond said, "Have you *seen* these scumsuckers? That's being unfair to fish."

"Enough chatter. Get ready." Vost led the charge down the hall, which bore sharp right and opened into a wider room.

The scene puzzled the shit out of him. A group of the filthy humans was fighting a better-equipped team; the latter was badly outnumbered, but they were carrying Vost's own damn rifles. That burned him even as he stared at all the barrels of chem stashed around. *That's why they're not shooting.* He couldn't be sure what was in them, but a stray shot might light up the world, depending on what they contained.

"Melee only," he ordered.

"You heard the man," Casto shouted.

A frisson of unease skated down his back. *Since when do I need backup from him to get the guys to follow my lead?* But he couldn't pause to ponder the implications. That would come later in the postbattle analysis. His men rushed in, laying about with knives and clubs they'd fashioned from station salvage.

A small, dark-skinned man glared at him from across the room. "Mary curse you for being everywhere I don't want you."

That sounded oddly personal to Vost, as if he'd thwarted some critical scheme. *Best news I've had all day.* He sank a blade into a filthy belly, yanked it back out with a burble of blood. Some of the targets attacked with teeth or bare hands; that was how far they'd fallen. For all their savagery, however, it was easy to take out men who lacked the sense to swing a length of pipe at your head.

There's a reason we started using tools, assholes. We lack the natural weaponry of, say, that Ithtorian.

Bugs were nicely evolved with talons and chitin to protect their squishy bits. He kept a watchful eye on the small squad with the rifles, making sure they weren't about to open fire, and as he fought the bestial prisoners, he watched the Ithtorian drop four in quick succession. *That's a worthy opponent. It'll be an honor to put him down.*

It was almost like a wary truce, as they fought the primitive convicts together while he kept an eye on the smaller force. It wouldn't take long to mow them down once the rest were dealt with. But as if the small man anticipated his plan, he turned his rifle on the barrel nearest to him, as Vost's men killed the last cannibal.

"You withdraw, or I blow us all to bits." The man had an educated voice, with a hint of accent that Vost couldn't immediately place, but he knew he'd been there.

"You're bluffing."

The other man smiled. "You can't afford to take that chance. *We* have nothing to lose. We expect to die here, and I'd enjoy taking you with me. Your mercs, on the other hand, are already looking squirrelly. They think they're going home. Who's right, Commander?"

Before he could reply, Casto said, "Let's go."

And the rest of the soldiers followed him. Redmond and Duran took a long look at him first, but they went, too, and it was a blow since they'd served with him the longest. Vost was left scrambling to follow, as if it were *his* decision, but deep in his gut, a kernel of emotion popped to life.

Dread.

Something Deep and Strange

In the twenty-four hours since Tam had returned with the chemicals, with Dred's help, Jael had finished the upstairs laboratory. Once apportioned for dorm use, so many Queenslanders had died—and no more coming in—that they didn't need the space anymore. The aliens had their own quarters now, better for keeping the peace. A lot of the men were stupid brutes, and out of sight, out of mind worked on them. It was shitty for the refugees in the sense of fair and equitable treatment, but it was better for them to be safe.

"How much experience do you have with explosives?" Tam asked as he stepped into the new lab.

"I've used plenty."

"But no background in building them?"

"Bombs more than grenades," Jael admitted. "But I've steady hands."

"That should do. First we have to make the shells." Tam sighed. "This would be a lot easier if Ike were still around."

"So many things would be."

"Truer words. But we'll make do. I've jury-rigged a

smelter . . . since I've done this before, it's best if I handle melting down the scrap and pouring in the molds."

"You've been planning this for a while."

Tam nodded. "It was impossible when everything was scattered and too well protected for me to acquire what I needed, but I've long known that what I needed to upgrade our armaments was theoretically available, just not easily acquired."

"Now we're set?"

"Yes, the last run took care of the missing components."

"Then just tell me what to do."

Tam handed him a list. Jael skimmed it; his reading was sufficient for this though he found it tedious to digest longer documents. That weakness had plagued him through a career as a merc, as he occasionally signed things he didn't understand, which screwed him later. Word got around that he wasn't the brightest bulb—that he was easily tricked—and it made life tough as a soldier of fortune. Just as well he'd gotten out of the private-army business and gone to work on salvage instead.

But that didn't end well, either.

"Make sure to follow the directions precisely. Mixing the chemicals out of order could result in unpleasant results for us. And put on this helmet."

Though the other man must've noticed that Jael didn't stay injured as long as other people, he decided it was better not to admit that poisonous fumes might burn his lungs but wouldn't kill him. So he snapped the headgear in place and got used to the filtering system. The enhanced sight and hearing array took him a little longer since it was working on preternaturally acute senses.

For a while they worked in silence, with Tam preparing the grenade casings and Jael measuring and mixing the chemicals. Jael finished his part much sooner, however, because the scrap had to be melted down before Tam could pour it into the molds, then there was cooling time.

"Come back in four hours," Tam said. "We'll finish up then."

At that point, they took a break, and Jael went to the hydroponics garden. He'd noticed that his name no longer appeared on patrol rosters or work lists, but he had to pull his weight, or the men would notice. Sleeping with the Dread Queen wouldn't keep six pissed off felons from jumping him, and he'd hate to kill even more of their men. They might be needed as battle fodder later.

Vix and Zediah were hard at work when he arrived. Neither one was much for chatting. Wearing an odd, excited expression, she pointed at some plants that needed tending, and he got to work. As he did, he considered Dred's question from a few days back—about what he saw himself doing once they left Perdition. He'd never been a dreamer, let alone a planner. *Maybe that's part of the problem.* But forming ideas about the future seemed oddly treacherous, like a mist-wreathed mountain path where he couldn't see what lay ahead.

"So how did the two of you end up on permanent plant duty?"

"It was the best solution," Vix answered. "Zed kept killing men for looking at me wrong. Artan was going to execute him when I convinced him we'd be more useful in here and that he'd eat better, too."

That's surprising. He would've guessed that Vix was the more dangerous of the two, but more than once, he'd gotten an odd vibe from Zediah. Possibly his intuition was dead-on, reassuring since he wasn't always the best at reading people. Idly he wondered what kind of body count Zed had racked up—and why these two were here, together.

Jael moved a plant, as all of these had to be relocated in order to flush and clean the pipes. "So the garden wasn't producing before you took over?"

"Not efficiently," Zediah answered.

"I can see you want to ask," Vix said unexpectedly.

He glanced up in surprise, his hands still dripping from extracting the next herb. "Is that an invitation?"

The two exchanged a look, then she nodded. "I don't mind telling you. We've been working together for a while."

From what he understood of Perdition customs, this was tantamount to declaring formal friendship. If a convict was willing to discuss his past, he meant he trusted you enough to want you to know more about him. Jael felt strangely honored.

"Right then. What happened?"

"He was my student," she said quietly. "I taught advanced sciences. We met when he was fifteen turns . . . and I was twenty-eight."

"I loved her instantly," Zed added with creepy intensity.

Though Jael had met some strange blokes in his time, he could tell by the gleam in Zediah's eyes that he was more than in love with Vix; he was utterly obsessed. The scar on her face hinted that the story had some twists and turns, especially considering it had started in a school.

"Never went. Go on then." He continued working, as if he weren't intrigued.

That seemed to settle Vix down; she got back to business, too. "I was married, and I knew it was wrong when Zed paid attention to me. But . . . he made me feel special, and my husband was often . . . unkind."

"Did he do your face?" Jael asked.

She touched her cheek, her eyes shadowed with remembered pain, then offered a single nod.

Zed put in, "We were lovers by then, and I knew he'd kill her if he found out. So I did him first." His tone was cool.

While that was fragged up, it wasn't the kind of thing that landed people in Perdition, especially not Vix. "There has to be more to it."

"Much more," she said softly. "There was a scandal . . . and a long trial. I lost my job. And people persecuted me until I went a little mad."

Zediah paused in his work, his eyes flat and dark. "I can't stand when people hurt her. They have to pay."

I see where this is going.

Vix was smiling a little dreamily. "So . . . we hunted them down, one by one. Everyone who said I was a whore

for falling in love with Zed, who said I deserved everything my husband did to me. *Bitches like that have it coming*," she repeated, deepening her voice so Jael figured she
was quoting a man they'd killed. "How long did it take him
to die?"

"Thirty-six hours. That was fun." Zed was officially the
most terrifying person in the place. "There were 112 in all.
There would've been more because the bastards just never
got tired of talking shit about Vix."

"But the law eventually caught up with us." She lifted a
shoulder, as if that were an inconvenience, not the end of
life as they knew it.

"I'm surprised they sentenced you together," he said.
Given how obsessed Zed was with her, it seemed like the
judge might've punished him by separating them.

"Our attorney made sure the court officials were aware
that if they sent us anywhere but here, anywhere apart, that
I'd find a way to kill them."

Damn.

That fast, it wasn't as restful to tend the plants with
these two. Before, he'd thought their devotion was sweet, if
slightly strange, but now there was no doubt in his mind
that both of them were unhinged. It just wasn't obvious,
like with some Queenslanders. He supposed the benefit
was that Zed's mania was really specific, so to avoid prod-
ding him into a killing spree, you just had to be distant and
courteous to Vix.

"I should go see if Tam's ready to finish the grenades,"
Jael said.

"You'll share your story next time," Vix said. "I really,
truly like you, Jael."

Somehow it sounded like a threat, and he didn't enjoy
being the object of her interest when Zed was watching
with those dead, cold eyes, like he had no emotional
responses to anything or anyone who wasn't Vix. *Disturbing. How does that happen? And I thought I was fragged
up.* Still, he murmured something noncommittal before
heading back up to the lab.

"Damn," he muttered.

"Problem?" Tam asked.

"Vix and Zed are cracked, aren't they?"

"It's not immediately obvious, but yes. I'd stay away from her. I've heard she makes a sex game of it, trying to make Zediah jealous. If she succeeds, the man dies."

"And that would be why I'm the only one who volunteers to help in the garden."

"Somebody should've warned you."

Jael sighed. "Dred probably thought it was funny. *Let's see if the new fish is clever enough to survive the land mines.*"

"I'm sure she had other things on her mind, and she knew you could handle yourself."

Better to give her the benefit of the doubt, I suppose. "That's the best possible interpretation. Let's finish these grenades."

"After this, I need help with another special project if you're interested."

Jael grinned. "I *could* use the work since I won't be gardening."

◄ 27 ►

No Greater Love

"I hope this works," Dred said.

Recent intel indicated that the mercs traveled as a single unit, so there could be no more hit-and-run strikes. With Tam's new weapons, this was the first time they would engage them en masse, and she was nervous. *Not that I don't trust Tam, but . . .* It was a big risk to take while using untested weapons. She would've preferred to engage with Mungo's men first to make sure the grenades would work as intended, but since they only had so many of them, after some discussion, they'd decided to do a field test.

With luck and timing, we take out a good number and get away clean.

She might not be able to do anything about the former, but she could work on the latter. Dred strode among her forces, giving last-minute orders. For this to work, it had to be an ambush, and they needed the high ground with some cover. A straight-up fight would end badly for her side, so Tam had watched Vost's movements for a full day, timing his routes, and they were now set up just outside the command post.

She had twelve people with her, a mix of aliens and humans. Some were armed with laser rifles, others had the poison grenades, and the last four were using the crazy-looking carbines Tam had jury-rigged out of scrap and chem. There was no way to be sure if the plan would go as intended, but she hoped so. Though they'd managed a few successes, the way the mercs were mowing through Mungo's horde, it wouldn't be long before they finished wiping that part of the station and moved on to Queensland.

"We should be set," Tam reported.

Dred turned to her people. "Everyone clear on their orders?"

A series of quiet nods came in response to the question as they were already set and focused at the railing. The odds were three to one against them if the mercs found a place to hunker down, and even worse if they closed since most of her people didn't have armor. *But we do have vicious cunning and desperation, the stuff dreams are made of.*

She took a deep breath, listening for RC-17. They'd placed the bot for surveillance, and it would signal when the mercs were near. It didn't take long before the whistles and beeps rang out, and she knelt alongside the rifle division. *Grandiose word for five of us.* Dred fought the urge to utter more cautions and explanations. *They know the drill. We can do this.*

As soon as the mercs stepped onto the platform below, she opened fire, aiming for the faceplates. She let Jael take Vost since he was a better shot, and it took her three tries to crack the glastique on one. The mercs returned fire, forcing her down. Around her, others fared better, taking out targets, while the carbine users unloaded with the acid pellets Tam and Jael had fabricated. They exploded with a hiss as they hit armor and immediately went to work on the structural integrity. If the stuff wasn't washed off, it would eat through the skin.

Once a good portion of the mercs were wearing helmets with compromised filtration systems, her people lobbed the gas grenades. On impact, they shot off clouds of green gas, and she waved the retrieval crew in. Jael led the run, along with those in all the helmets they could spare. The gas reduced visibility, leaving the mercs who could still breathe firing blind and worried about hitting their comrades while their cohorts staggered and wheezed and yet others were scrambling desperately out of armor that was dissolving on their skin.

"Grab as much as you can carry," she shouted. "No more. We need to fall back."

The point of this strike wasn't to kill all the mercs in one go. She lacked both the firepower and manpower for a full-out assault. No, this was another guerilla strike, aimed at surprising and demoralizing them. *If we whittle away at them when they've started to feel safe, it'll erode their confidence.* It wasn't just a ground war she was fighting; she was also trying to break their spirits. *Artan taught me something about that at least.*

"Don't let them take your weapons," Vost choked out, but since Jael had smashed the faceplate on his helmet, he was also inhaling the gas, so his words were strangled by the wheeze and whine of his labored breathing.

"Move, move, move!" Dred called.

Her people were hauling multiple bodies, clad in armor, and others had weapons. A barrage of laser fire came in hard and Ali threw herself in front of Brahm, who was running with his head down, rifles in both hands. The smell of burning hair filled the air as the Rodeisian female went down. Even from this vantage, Dred could tell it was serious. The concentrated laser fire burned a hole clean through the fur and into Ali's spine. Her hands and feet spasmed, and her breath went fast and shallow. She tried to turn over and failed, a small whimper escaping her.

"Brahm?"

"I'm here." He dropped to his knees beside her and took a shot in the back. It cracked the chitin, and Dred yanked him into cover with a muttered curse.

"I'm sorry," Ali whispered.

Another minute of this, and they'll rush us. Then we die.

She positioned her rifle on the metal lip and fired back, but the citrine cloud hindered her as well as the mercs. Her shots went in wild, slamming the floor in a laser light show that probably did little more than make them dance. She glanced at Jael, who came in at her side to focus fire. He aimed at the stairs, trying to keep the area too hot for the enemy to push.

"She's gone," Tam said.

There was no way they could transport Ali's body, as well as haul all the armor and weapons. Martine and Calypso stripped the undamaged pieces as fast as they could, while Dred and Jael fired at the mercs down below. A few made it past, staggering toward the stairs, and she shook her head, laying down a tight line of red. She hit their leg armor so they had to fall back or lose the segment with another shot, but they were hungry for payback. One death on her side wasn't nearly enough to satisfy angry soldiers.

"We can't stay here. Are we ready to roll out?"

"Nearly. Give me a minute," Calypso answered.

Brahm was still and quiet on his knees. Dred knew nothing about Ithtorian expressions, but he didn't look all right. "She knew I can take a hit. Why didn't she let me?"

"Reflex," Calypso said. "Caring makes you weak. On your feet, bug man. I'm not dying today." With that, the mistress of the circle hauled him up, and he didn't resist, or she probably couldn't have budged him, despite what Dred knew to be exceptional strength.

Jael hurled another grenade at the stairs, so the men with damaged faceplates couldn't follow. That left the mercs the unenviable decision of whether to split their forces, which had proven to be a bad strategy, or to let their attackers go. The argument sounded behind her, but she didn't glance back to see which side was winning. *If we get back to Queensland with this haul, we're home free.*

Ahead of her, she saw ichor trickling down Brahm's back. *Does cracked chitin heal?* She figured it might seal over time because it probably renewed itself somehow, but she had no scientific information to back up the theory. No medicine to help him, either. If the wound got infected, she might have to put him down. Triage was her least favorite part of leading Queensland, worse even than living up to the impossible standards Tam had set for the Dread Queen. It was hard as hell to look into a man's eyes, then end his life and call it kindness.

They didn't stop running until they hit the barricades. A few times, she felt like she was being watched, but nobody attacked. That made Dred think it was Silence's people like rats in the walls, spying and spinning schemes. But she didn't have time to worry about that when the mercs would be out for blood, and Mungo's men were still trying to breach the perimeter in the hope of winning the promised pardons.

They're so stupid it hurts.

Dred blew toward the turrets at a run, and her mag bracelet kept her safe. She turned off the defenses long enough for everyone to pass, then she powered them back up. It was sobering—and awful—that they didn't have to deconstruct the junk pile for Ali. That would never happen again. *This is what it's like to be hunted.* Back on Tehrann, she'd known men who liked to go out and shoot things for sport. While she'd disapproved in principle, she'd never considered how the animals must feel—one minute living their lives and the next interrupted by a danger they had no hope of surviving.

But I can't give up.

To make matters worse, Keelah and Katur were waiting when they came out in the common room. Queenslanders roared in approval of the new gear, but the alien leaders searched the group, then Katur stepped forward. "What went wrong?"

"She saved me," Brahm said, lowering his head.

"Ah." Keelah raised him with a hand on his mandible. "Then she died as well as anyone can in this place. I'll inform the others and arrange for her service."

◀ 28 ▶

Dark and Darker

When Jael awoke, he was strapped to a chair.

The last thing he remembered was drinking with the aliens in their private dorm, a quiet farewell to Ali, whose body had been gone when they backtracked to retrieve it. He didn't want to say so, but the chances were good that she had been taken—as food. The mercs would have no use for a Rodeisian corpse, and Silence's killers only revered the death they caused personally. Which left Mungo's roving monstrosities.

He couldn't see anything because there was a cloth wrapped around his eyes, thick enough that he glimpsed nothing but darkness. Listening provided slightly more information; the noises were familiar enough that he must still be somewhere in Queensland. The pain at the back of his head told him he must've been jumped; they must've cracked his skull to knock him out. He'd been taken prisoner before, tortured extensively. On a few occasions, he'd been so close to death that it probably counted.

It just never sticks.

His heart raced as he tried to figure out who would've

done this. And why. It could be someone with a grudge against Dred or some asshole who didn't like Jael. Mary knew, he didn't have the knack of winning people over with his endearing personality, and he'd played enforcer in the common room more than once. Soft footsteps approached, too light for it to be a big person. Inhaling, Jael drew in a familiar smell; he just had to place it.

Then he knew. And he wasn't reassured at all.

"He's waking up. I think he recognizes your scent." That came from Zediah.

"I thought you were wrong," she said softly. "I thought he just liked the garden."

"I know when a man wants you."

No, you really don't. Psycho. Jael reckoned Zed had killed a lot of fellows who were completely indifferent to Vix, but Zediah's reality didn't allow for that being possible. In his eyes, somehow, she was an irresistible temptress. At that point, he would've spoken up in his own defense, except for the strips of leather wound around his head. Jael bit down, working on chewing through them. In time he'd manage it, but there was no telling what they'd do in the meantime. Trying to be surreptitious, he struggled against his bonds, but they were good and tight, more leather reinforced with durasteel.

"I don't want you to hurt him." Vix sounded unsure, however.

"Why not?" Jael heard a world of warning in that tone. *Don't say you like me again. Don't.*

But since Tam had given him an inkling of how this game played out, Jael had a feeling about what came next.

"He's always been so kind to me. I'm fond of him."

We've hardly spoken.

"How fond?" Zed's voice grew husky. "I could let you have him. Once. Then—"

"I know. He has to die, or he might come between us."

Yeah. This is why people give them such a wide berth. How long have they been quietly continuing their murder spree inside? Vix had said that Zed used to kill the men who paid her too much attention openly; did this mean they'd simply continued in secret? He was surprised at the cunning and intricacy of this game. It was also galling to be captured by this pair. Since they didn't *seem* as dangerous as the others, he'd judged them superficially.

A costly mistake.

"Let's ask him what he prefers," Zed murmured. "A quick death after one night with you, or a slow one as punishment for refusing you."

Shit choice. I'll take option C.

The blindfold came off, then the gag. Jael spat to clear the sticky, dry feel of leather cleaving to his tongue. Vix regarded him with what looked like genuine concern, and he wondered why he hadn't noticed how absolutely mad she was before. He *had* picked up the complete lack of . . . anything in Zediah, but Jael wasn't used to considering himself vulnerable since he could shake off injuries, plus he was strong and fast. Since halving his abilities with Dred, he was constantly overestimating his own strength.

That has to stop.

"You may have played this game before," he said, "but Dred will ask questions."

Zed seemed unmoved by the potential risks. "She'll receive no answers. This is a dark hole, and people disappear all the time."

"Don't you think I'm pretty?" Vix asked.

"Zed will pull my tongue out, no matter what I say."

The younger man smiled. "You're smarter than the ones we usually play with. So which is it to be?"

"Neither. You unfasten me, and I'll let this go as a misunderstanding."

"But it isn't one. You came to us in the garden. There's no other reason you'd have done that if you didn't want to play. Everyone else steers clear . . . and I saw the way your eyes followed her."

Jael was fragging hamstrung because any repudiation of Vix controverted Zed's reality, where she was the sun, the center of everything, and the most desirable woman in the world. But he had to try since straining against the bonds wasn't working. *It'd be nice if Dred was looking for me about now.* He had no idea where they were in the cycle, if this was during downtime, or how long he'd been missing.

"You know how you feel about Vix?" he said, instead of a straight answer.

Zed nodded.

"That's how I feel about the Dread Queen. I realize you think I was panting after Vix. And I would be, if I wasn't already on someone else's hook."

Let that be just crazy enough to make sense.

The two exchanged a look, but Jael couldn't interpret it. Then Vix said, "There's only one way to test it."

She straddled his lap and he pulled his head back, but her face came closer and closer until she was kissing him. The woman tasted of fresh herbs, and her lips were soft, but he wanted nothing more than to shove her off him and beat the shit out of her insane lover. He also sort of felt sorry for her because she was so obviously broken. They were like a pair of antique windup dolls locked in a permanent dance, where they circled and circled and could never leave the track. It was all he could do not to chew her lips off.

Jael had *never* felt quite like this. He didn't want her on top of him, didn't want this kiss. Mad as it sounded, he wanted to scrub every inch of himself. And it would be worse if it went further. With enough handling, she could probably make him respond, and then—his heart leapt at the horror of that thought. There were *so many* ways this could go wrong. Fear and revulsion warred in him, and Jael prayed for his body not to react. This was mad because desire wasn't dictated by physiological response. Other things could trigger it; or if a person had strong self-control, they could smother what was there.

Eventually, Vix sat back, looking surprised. Maybe the other men had been so desperate for a woman's touch that they all showed her what she wanted to see and gave her the excuse to use them, then turn them over to her lover to be murdered.

Beyond crazy.

"He's telling the truth."

"You're the first," Zed said.

Then the man actually unstrapped him, like he'd passed a bizarre initiation ritual, where the stakes were life and death. "I'm sorry we misjudged you."

Jael could've killed them so easily, snapped their necks as soon as he was free. He rubbed the circulation back into his wrists as he stood up. A long moment passed while he gazed at them, mentally wrestling. In the long run, it might be better if he did. But without them to tend the hydroponics garden, food supply would diminish. *So I let them go on killing their fellow Queenslanders when the mood strikes?* That didn't seem right either. In fact, the scenario appeared to have no correct solution, and he wasn't good with philosophical matters.

"Your head wound has already healed," Zed said.

The other man's eyes were dark and calculating, as if he realized that they shared a secret, what used to be called mutually assured destruction. If Jael revealed what had happened, then Zed and Vix would be punished, but likely not before he revealed Jael's fast healing. There would be problems from the others, who hated aliens and would hate a Bred thing just as much. With a half smile, he touched the spot that had hurt when he woke up but wasn't bothering him anymore. His hair was sticky with blood.

He pushed out a breath, troubled by the impasse but unable to resolve it. "I see no reason why we can't part as friends."

Big fragging lie. But what else can I say? Now I get to go find Dred and pretend nothing's wrong. If she finds out, they'll die. That was the brightest spot of this mess; he had no doubt she'd execute these two for this. And then Queensland would suffer.

But maybe I can find a way to tell her about their . . . hobby.

"No permanent harm done," Vix agreed. "I hope the Dread Queen appreciates your loyalty. You seem like a good man."

"We hope to see you soon." Zed smiled as he stepped back, waving farewell.

Jael strode past them and out the door, waiting for the surprise attack that never came. *But why would it? Zed thinks he has a hold on me. And the worst part?*

He does.

◀ 29 ▶

Whispers in the Dark

"So where's the old man?" Martine asked.

Dred lifted a shoulder. "No idea. I left him drinking with Katur and crew."

"Then you probably won't see him again tonight."

Calypso refilled their glasses and dropped down at the table with a weary sigh. "I don't understand why you two limit yourself to a single man. We're like goddesses here, and I can pick and choose, a different slave in my bed every night."

"If they hadn't sterilized us before we came in, I'd worry about you," Martine said.

"Why d'ya think the strapping one threw herself in front of the Bug?" Calypso asked.

Dred had been wondering that. "They were close friends, I suppose. Is there anyone you'd die for in here?" she asked Martine.

The smaller woman laughed. "Not hardly."

Dred had been monitoring the situation in the common room, but with the aliens in seclusion, things seemed to be relatively calm. The watchmen on patrol weren't idiots, either, at least by Queensland standards. So she pushed to her feet.

"I've had enough of the public eye. Come on."

Calypso raised a brow. "Party at your place?"

"Depends on how much we drink." Martine grabbed Calypso's hand and dragged her toward Dred's quarters.

She realized then how long it had been since she'd spent any time in the company of women. Back on Tehrann, there hadn't been many girls her own age, and her dreams had been too big for a small colony, where most wanted to grow up, go to work, and help populate the company town. Dred had dreamed of nothing but getting away. And after that, the freighter crews were comprised mostly of scruffy men. Beyond that point, she hunted alone, where everything boiled down to stalking and slaughter. There were no friends or even allies, only people she used to make the kill.

They left the common room and went to Dred's quarters. It would be interesting to see how long the party lasted before Jael interrupted and what he said when he found three women waiting for him. You could tell a lot about a man by how he reacted to such surprises.

She ushered Martine and Calypso in. "Make yourselves at home."

"It's smaller than I expected," Calypso said.

"The lock works on the door, at least."

Martine flung herself on the bed without waiting for an invitation. Dred let it go because if she wanted actual friends—and she wasn't positive she did—she couldn't be all Dread Queen in private moments, too. So she crawled past Martine and sprawled against the wall, leaning her head back with a weary sigh. Calypso settled on a chair nearby, stretching out her long legs.

"I feel like we should be playing a game," Martine said, grinning.

Dred raised up enough to ask, "A drinking game?"

"Might not be wise, but it could be fun," Calypso said.

Martine raised her glass. "I'm down."

"I'm too tired for anything complex. Keep the rules simple."

"We used to play this game when I was a little girl," Calypso said, sounding thoughtful. "You tell two lies and a truth about yourself. If we guess the truth, you take a drink. If we don't, then the others do a shot."

On the surface, it was a silly childhood game, ridiculous among hardened criminals, but on another level, it was also a gateway to things that normally stayed hidden. It wasn't like any of them could acknowledge being lonely or being sick of having so many assholes around them night and day. That was the same as admitting weakness, something that would get a woman killed if word got around, and neither Calypso nor Martine were soft.

"Why the hell not?" Dred said.

"I'll start." Martine crossed her legs as Dred focused on her face. "I was born to wealth. My favorite color is pink. And I killed my first man when I was fourteen."

She's a good liar.

"I say the third thing is true," Calypso said.

"Is that your official guess?"

Dred just nodded, figuring the other woman knew Martine better.

Martine laughed. "Wrong! There's nothing wrong with pink. It makes me feel pretty." Her tone rang with a self-deprecating note. "Not that I've seen the shade for a while. You lose, bitches. Bottoms up."

"My turn." Calypso frowned, seeming thoughtful. "I've loved only one person in my life. I killed her. And I've never spent a day in school."

Dred considered for a few moments. "The last thing."

Calypso raised her glass and tipped back a mouthful. "Good guess. I wonder, do I not *look* educated, oh Dread Queen? Beware of judging by appearances."

"Not going to school doesn't mean uneducated. You might've grown up on a remote colony and did coursework via VI."

The mistress of the circle quirked her mouth in an

expression of approval. "Got it in one. I see why your coup succeeded when so many others failed."

There wasn't one. But she wasn't about to ruin Tam's hard work by admitting she'd murdered Artan and the spymaster had turned it into a change in regime after the fact. So she forced herself to smile through the dismay. "Before, there were too many conspirators. The fewer people who know a secret, the less risk of betrayal."

"I'll drink to that," Martine said. "Your turn, I think, queenie."

She didn't bitch at the other woman for borrowing Jael's irreverent nickname, not that he used it much anymore. These days he was more likely to softly whisper *love*. She told herself it was just a word and that she couldn't let him worm too deep into her head. *He's a bed partner. That's all.* And she was matching his loyalty by paying him in the same coin.

After thinking about what the other women had revealed, she offered, "I killed 224 men before they caught me. I'm an only child. I miss choclaste more than anything else about the outside world."

"The last thing can't be true," Calypso said with a shiver.

"Agreed. No sane person would miss it when there are so many better things."

Dred shrugged. "I'm not telling you. Make your official guess already."

"You don't relate well to people. You're not a charmer." Martine's expression was unexpectedly shrewd. "That tells me you grew up lonely, not much company. So I say the second fact is true. Calypso?"

"No rebuttal."

In answer, Dred downed her shot. "You two are good at this."

"When you grow up on the streets, you learn pretty fast to read people. Who'll feed you, who'll report you as a vagrant, who'll try to take you home and chain you up." Martine rubbed a hand across her face. "Man, this shit is strong."

The game went on for a while. Eventually Dred and Calypso fetched more booze. It was the middle of downtime, so only the sentries moved in the hallways. Dred was feeling the effects slightly by then, though not as much as the other two. *That's probably because of Jael. And where the hell is he anyway?* After the fourth bottle, Martine was bleary-eyed and Calypso was singing. Dred enjoyed the warm buzz as she settled in her quarters again.

"You're terrible guessers," Martine mumbled.

"Maybe you're just an excellent liar," Calypso said.

"That I am. Always have been."

"I like that you're proud of it. A woman should celebrate her strengths." Dred closed her eyes.

Calypso let out a snore. It was the first time anyone had passed out on the floor since before Einar died. Casting back through muzzy memories, she realized Tam had been avoiding her quarters for quite a while, and that it had become a haven for her and Jael. She weighed her reaction to that, as the closeness had crept up on her. Between the rotgut and the surprise, a queasy feeling roiled in her belly. Attachments were the surest way to get hurt in here. They offered leverage to her enemies.

And there's a fragging lot of them at the moment.

"I was a free bird during your trial," Martine said unexpectedly.

"So you know more about me than I do you." Her trial had been a circus, with coverage all over the bounce.

"I know what the talking heads reported. But that's probably not true."

"Are you asking to hear my side?"

"Your call."

Dred wasn't drunk enough to tell the whole truth. So she said, "I was hunting killers. The authorities take it badly if you do it without proof."

"But you got caught up in it. You fancied the rush, or you wouldn't have done your last victim in front of his little girls."

"I just didn't want him to get away." But their faces haunted her, even now. To them, *she* was the monster, and it was in that moment that she realized she hovered on the knife-edge of turning into exactly what she hated most.

That was when she knew she had to stop and take whatever punishment they doled out.

"Lie to yourself if you want, queenie. Don't bother with me." Martine rolled onto her side and lifted her feet until they touched the ceiling above the bunk. She swiped her feet back and forth, as if she were running. The motions were rhythmic, almost hypnotic. "We're all some shade of devil up in here."

"You, too?" Dred closed her eyes and collapsed more than lay down beside Martine. If either woman wanted to take Queensland, now was the time. She was too tired to fight. In fact, in this moment, she'd happily step aside so the mistress of the circle could take over.

But Calypso seemed to be out cold. If anyone had asked, she'd have guessed that the tall woman had a better head for liquor than Martine. *And I'd have been wrong.* The little sharp-tooth was full of surprises. *Jael calls her "bright eyes."*

"Me especially. Oh, am I supposed to whisper what I did now?"

"Do you want to?" Dred murmured.

"Evidently so. Pour me another drink, and I'll tell you a story."

In reply, Dred emptied out the jar into the other woman's mug. Martine knocked it back and closed her eyes, as if that would make it easier to speak. "It starts with a man."

"Usually does," Dred said.

Martine smiled wryly. "Unless it's a woman. And in my case, it was that, too."

"Sounds fascinating. And complicated."

"The best things are. I mentioned I grew up rough, yeah?"

"You said something about learning quick on the street." It was a prompting line, providing a place for Martine to start.

"I was thief early in life. Had to be. If I failed, I didn't eat. My skills called me to the attention of a powerful underlord, the man who ran Novus." Martine paused, then added, "That's a neighborhood in Ankaraj on New Terra."

"Thanks. I'm not from there."

Martine aimed a pat at her arm. "I can tell by the accent. Anyway, Darak's goons dragged me into his office. I expected to be executed."

"Obviously, that didn't happen."

"Instead, he offered me a job. Those were good turns actually. I stole what he told me to, received a fair cut, and had protection."

"So what happened?"

"I fell in love with an honest man, a lieutenant in the New Terra militia, and I was young enough, *crazy* enough, to enlist, so I could stay close to him. But I wasn't cut out for that life. Darak offered me a certain amount of freedom as long as I got the job done. He cared about results more than procedure, so I wasn't good at following orders, especially when they were stupid."

"Doesn't seem like you," she said, curious how Martine had gone from thief to rebellious soldier to Perdition.

"Things didn't last between us. He was too gung ho on protecting and serving. I was too ho hum on the propaganda. But I tried to stick out my term because by then, I was head over heels . . . for my commanding officer's wife."

"Are you making this up as you go along?"

The other woman grinned. "Sounds that way, huh? But no. Truth is stranger than fiction, or some shit."

"Was it mutual?" she asked.

"Unfortunately, yes. It didn't start out personal, though. She came to me because I'd been vocal, complaining about her fascist husband's policies."

"Came to you with what?"

Martine's dark eyes were grave. "Proof of Conglomerate atrocities, incursion on civilian civil liberties, and evidence that they were ignoring due process."

"Shit. War crimes?" This wasn't what she'd expected at all.

"Exactly. Against Nika's wishes, I went public with the information, and they labeled me a traitor. She was taken into state custody, detained indefinitely." The other woman took a deep breath, as if the memories hurt even now.

"So you cut a deal to save her."

"Yep. I go quietly to Perdition, and she goes free. Traitors are the worst of the worst, you know. It doesn't matter what the government does to its citizens, apparently. They're above the laws they write to govern us."

"So you'd never killed anyone before you went inside?"

"In combat, sure. I saw some action in a few skirmishes, doing colony work for the Conglomerate. But that's . . . different."

She wanted to reach out, but she didn't know how to connect with anyone besides Jael. It was kind of a huge deal that she wanted to. Besides, the other woman might not welcome a hug or a pat or whatever the hell women did to comfort each other. This would have to do, just listening in the half-light.

"I hope Nika's safe," Dred said finally. "And that your sacrifice wasn't for nothing."

Martine's voice was so quiet she could barely hear it. "Me too."

◄ 30 ►

Hide and Seek

Jael stopped outside the quarters he shared with Dred, listening to the rise and fall of female voices. *Seems like she has company.* He continued to the common room, where a handful of men were snoring. A few were propped up on the tables; others had passed out underneath them. Between Ike's wake and the celebratory revels, Queensland had been liquored up a lot lately.

Cook was the only man who looked remotely sober, so Jael headed for the herbal teapot. He wasn't ready to face Dred in any case; he still had to figure out what he was going to do about what had happened with Vix and Zediah. The taller man greeted him with a jerk of his chin. It seemed to Jael as if he was always around. *Does he ever sleep?*

Silently, the chef poured him a cup and raised his brows. "You're playing bartender?"

The other man shrugged.

He considered unloading his troubles but he didn't know him well enough to be sure he could be trusted, and the sort of vague advice he could receive without telling Cook everything made it seem like a waste of time. Moments like this, he missed Einar most, as he might've turned to the big man. But he could already imagine what Einar would say: *Tell Dred. Someone else will figure out the hydroponics garden.*

But with Ike gone, there was no guarantee anyone was smart enough to keep food production up. So he'd sit on this problem and hope it didn't get worse while they dealt with Vost and his wrecking crew. He had been sitting alone long enough to see the bottom of the tin cup through the yellow liquid they dubbed tea when the beetle-browed recruit ambled into the common room. Jael glimpsed an interesting exchange between him and Cook, just a quick gaze, a nod, nothing more, but it made him wonder. There were always silent intrigues going on, and Tam used to be top-notch at keeping track of them.

To his surprise, the lout came over and sat with Jael. "Not drinking tonight?"

"Somebody has to keep a clear head."

"Did the Dread Queen kick you out of bed?" The other man smirked.

Jael barked out a laugh. "If she had, you're the last one I'd tell, mate."

"It's an interesting setup you've got here. Name's Pietro by the way." He didn't seem to take offense to the rebuff.

Something about this conversation struck Jael wrong, but he couldn't put a finger on why. "How come *you* aren't drinking?"

And why are you roaming around during downtime?

"I was playing cards with some of the boys earlier. Won a bunch of chits from the ones who *were*." A glib answer, convincing even. "I won't be on watch for a ten-day stretch now. That's what I call being a gentleman of leisure."

He couldn't find anything to object to in that statement other than the obvious smugness, but hell, he'd enjoyed hustling a mark in his time. There was a certain satisfaction in proving that you were smarter than other people thought, and if you could get people to underestimate your abilities, all the better. This was certainly no worse than anything else he'd heard in here and better than a lot of it.

So why's my skin crawling?

Past experience had taught him to pay attention to these moments, so he half closed his eyes, paying attention to the unsteady skitter of Pietro's pulse and the sour tang of nerves percolating beneath his skin. Once Jael zeroed in, he took in the nervous tic in the other man's jaw, along with the faint sheen of sweat on his brow. Pietro drummed his fingers on the table, but before Jael could call him on it, the convict pushed to his feet.

"Nice chatting with you, but I'm late for an appointment with my bunk." Pietro hurried out of the common room, as if he'd successfully stalled him.

That was enough to send Jael back to Dred's quarters at a run, but to his relief, he still heard the rise and fall of her voice, along with Martine's. He closed his eyes on a sigh of relief and turned away.

Lucky bastard. You get to live another day. But I'll be watching you.

"CAN you find out for me how much the mercs have hurt Mungo and Silence?" Dred kept a hand on her head, making Tam think that, like Martine, she had a raging headache.

"How much did you drink last night?" he asked.

"Unimportant. Can you do it?"

"Absolutely. I won't engage . . . I'll just go on a fact-finding mission to discover how many men they have left."

"That would be useful information."

"As you like. Feel better, my queen." The gentle irony in his tone prompted a scowl from the woman, then Tam headed toward the barricades. Ordinarily, he would take Martine out with him, but she couldn't move without moaning, not an asset on a silent run.

Halfway across the common room, Katur stopped him. "I overheard your assignment, and I wish to accompany you."

"Why?" It was best to understand a prospective ally's motives.

"Though my people have been assimilated into Queensland, I'm still in charge of their safety. If I lack knowledge regarding our enemies, it compromises the effectiveness of my leadership and my decision-making abilities."

He didn't ask if Katur could move quietly; the alien had been slipping around, probably inside Queensland itself, without Tam's knowledge for turns. So he nodded. "Will you show me the best route to Munya?"

"Of course."

"Then welcome aboard."

"One moment, please." Katur signaled to his mate, who nodded. "I'm ready."

"It's impressive that you two maintain a close relationship, in spite of all of the challenges," Tam said, heading for the barricades.

"Our love would be a pale, weak thing if it couldn't survive privation as well as plenty."

While that might be true, Tam had often seen couples devolve into spitting accusations over lesser trials. Katur took the lead, showing him an alternate route three levels up. Though this was part of Queensland, they no longer had the men necessary to protect it, so the corridors had an abandoned air. Dred had made the right decision when she tightened up their boundaries, but she'd also yielded a fair amount of territory to protect her citizens.

Katur tilted his head, presumably listening for movement. "There's a patrol one level down, directly below us."

He raised a brow, impressed. "Hold or move?"

"We don't want to be out in the open if they climb to this deck, so get to cover as quickly and quietly as you can."

Tam followed the other male, boosting silently into the ducts, then he pulled the grille back in place. The repair work made a metal ping, and, beside him, Katur froze. That might be enough to alert the aliens, but—then he heard voices.

"My audio picked it up, too. This way, I think." Tam recognized Vost's voice, and soon the full group of mercs appeared.

He took a head count and was dismayed to see how many were left, despite all of their small victories. Beside him, Katur was so still as to seem catatonic, hardly even breathing. *If they find us, we're dead meat up here.* Since rifles added weight and weight added to the sound of passage, both he and Katur were armed only with small knives in case fighting became unavoidable. Long moments passed while the mercs tromped beneath them.

"There's a trail in the dust leading off this way," a merc said.

"Looks like one of the maintenance units."

Vost sighed. "Then maybe that's what we heard just now."

"Probably. We're not gonna find a hidden way into this zone, so let's go kill some more of those smelly mooks. Their turf isn't nearly as well defended."

Dred will be glad to hear that. Tam counted it as a blessing that the mercs couldn't find the paths the aliens had carved because if they woke up some morning to find this many armored soldiers wreaking havoc inside their borders—with only a single Peacemaker for counterattack—then the game would be done, and he hadn't yet put all his pieces in play.

Katur waited a full five minutes after the mercs departed before moving or speaking. "It bodes ill for us that they've decided we're too strong for a frontal assault. Sooner or later, they will find a vulnerable gap, some weakness no one has foreseen."

"Unless we kill them first," Tam said grimly.

The alien's eyes gleamed in the dark, hinting at better-than-human night vision. "How do you propose we do that? It has taken some of our finest people and all of the resources we can scrounge to kill a few."

"I'm not sure yet," he admitted. "But it's been proven time and again that if one is cautious and watchful, the opponent will make a mistake that proves to be his downfall."

"The same could be said of us," Katur murmured.

Interesting. He's a pessimist.

Tam didn't address those words. If you focused too hard

on the dire nature of reality, it could paralyze you. "Let's get the intel for Dred and warn her that we spotted mercs pretty close to our perimeter. I have some plans to make."

VOST led his men away from well-defended territory. So far, he'd found only abandoned rooms and corridors though some of them showed signs they had seen recent use. *Guess we've forced them to tighten the border.* It was small comfort when his men had expected the facility to be clean by now; none of them had predicted losing a full squad to the scum incarcerated within, convicts with primitive weapons, no less. Vost led the column through the corridors, checking each turn while he mentally mapped the facility. He was down to his last few drone cams, and he still didn't have an accurate picture of the layout given the way the cons had barricaded some shafts and hallways and cut holes where there had been no passages before.

"You all right, boss?" Redmond fell into step with Vost. Since the unit moved two by two, nobody seemed to think anything of the maneuver.

If he wasn't the unit commander, he'd admit to being worried. But even though Redmond had been with him for a lot of turns, he couldn't say so out loud. An odd sensation skittered down his spine. "Fine."

"I feel like someone's watching us."

"Me too." That much he could acknowledge. "Probably some enemy scouts have eyes on us."

"I don't like it. I don't like any of this. You think maybe we should pull out? There will be other jobs."

None that pay like this one.

"We've taken some losses, but we're not out of the game. Once we wipe out the other two pockets of resistance, we can fix full attention and resources to burning down the bastards who hit us with the poison grenades and acid pellets."

"If they've got the know-how to build shit like that, I wonder what else they can come up with," Redmond said.

It was a prudent concern, one Vost shared. "They also have that Peacemaker. The suit never said anything about their having heavy droid defenses."

"They must've hacked it," the other man guessed.

"There are others on station. If they can, *I* can."

"Is that your plan to minimize losing more men?" Redmond asked.

Vost nodded. "We'll go kill some mooks because they die fast and easy. Too bad there are so fragging many of them. After that, I'll program my last drone cam to look for a Peacemaker. Even a broken one would serve. I'm sure I can get it running again."

"Then we'll send it in to soften up the smart ones?"

"That's the plan. While it draws their fire, we can roll in behind and wipe them out."

Redmond smacked his armored fist against his palm. "It'll be fun to see their faces when we surprise them for a change."

"Agreed. I've had enough of their ambushes. This may be their home ground, but I've won harder battles against cleverer men."

Redmond seemed to take heart from his tone, and when he punched the air in anticipation of triumph, the rest of the men followed suit. The mood was much improved as they moved toward the stinking compound full of carrion eaters. Vost had encountered cannibals before, and now he wondered if eating human flesh made you stupid, because these men had no grasp of strategy or tactical advantage whatsoever.

Then a stink hit him, so foul it almost made him puke inside his helmet. He choked down the bile while quickly adjusting the filters on his sense array. *No, definitely don't want to smell this.* The stench made him think there must be a group nearby, but instead his unit stumbled into a huge room full of grisly artifacts. There was human skin stretched across a tanning rack and a pile of polished bones on a crafting table. Through his faceplate, it looked as if someone once used this place to create armor and weapons out of the dead.

"This . . . this is seriously fragged up," Casto said. "No wonder the Conglomerate wants these monsters dead."

"They should've just been executed in the first place," someone else muttered.

"If we execute people who kill, we become murderers, too." Casto seemed to be imitating the political commentary of some talking head. By the tone, Vost guessed Casto thought they should bring back the death penalty.

"We must've taken a wrong turn," he said. "This doesn't look like the way."

"I think we're close to the silent watchers," Redmond put in.

Duran muttered, "Those bastards are creepy. They cut out their tongues."

This place sent a chill down his spine. In his time as a merc, he'd seen some awful shit, but superstitious as it sounded, this place felt *saturated* in evil. He gestured for the men to move out by whirling his finger in the air.

"There's no battle here. They're watching, but they won't engage in a stand-up fight."

Casto shook his head. "Man, I hate this place. We can't leave soon enough."

"I understand. But we finish the job done first."

I hope.

◀ 31 ▶

The Storydance

"Between 100 and 120 of Mungo's left. You can't be sure on Silence?" Dred paced, rubbing her temples. The headache had receded, but she didn't like hearing that Silence had gone to ground.

Tam shook his head. "Her entire zone was deserted. I've spied on them before, but they're definitely in hiding now."

"Probably to stay away from the mercs," Jael guessed.

Dred nodded at him. "But it's bad for us not to know how many of them have survived the chaos."

Jael said, "If I know anything about Silence, I'd say most of them. Her people are like cockroaches. They scuttle into the walls and skitter out when it's dark and you least want to see them."

"Good analogy." She turned to Tam. "Did you stay for the fight between the mongrels and the mercs?"

He shook his head. "The mercs were still a ways out after we completed our survey of Munya. I thought you needed the intel as soon as possible."

"I hate the fact that they were right upstairs, and we didn't know it." Dred balled her hand into a fist, but there was no outlet for the frustration. "They have drone cams, armor, rifles, kinetic grenades—"

"I could liberate some of their equipment while I know they're busy in Munya."

Dred stopped pacing. "If you can do it without being caught, then move. Take as much as you can carry."

"I'll see if Calypso and Martine feel up to some light burglary."

"Thanks, Tam."

The spymaster paused. "You might wish to consider letting the men cut loose as you did last night. Open up the still and let them celebrate."

"Is that a good idea?" Jael asked.

"We have a little breathing room. Mungo should keep Vost busy for a bit."

Tam's opinion was enough for Dred. With a nod in parting, she beelined for Cook, who had taken over from Ike in terms of provisions. "Do you feel like throwing a party?"

The chef cocked his head in silent inquiry.

"The mercs have turned their attention to Munya, so we're safe for now."

Cook nodded at that. Some Queenslanders lived for moments of drunken forgetfulness, and as long as Dred doled them out regularly, she could keep them in check. If the liquor dried up permanently, however, she might have a riot on her hands.

At Dred's signal, Jael vaulted up onto a table as Cook sent his assistant to retrieve bottles of rotgut. "Thank the Dread Queen, gentlemen, for tonight she's hosting a party."

"What's the occasion?" someone shouted.

"In honor of dangerous bloody bastards who have the interlopers running scared."

Not surprisingly, a cheer rang out as Jael jumped down, both at his words and the booze being wheeled into the common room. Queenslanders grabbed bottle after bottle. Dred hoped that the sentries realized they weren't allowed to get shit-faced and that patrols needed to continue as usual, but what the hell, she'd deal with the fallout later.

Since she disciplined offenders consistently, chances were good that Queensland could survive one more revel.

Personally, she'd love to withdraw, but part of the job required being a badass alongside the men, so she joined a table and knocked back several glasses. *My liver may never forgive me for doing this two nights in a row.* Then Dred remembered that she had Jael's enhanced healing ability. *Does that go for self-inflicted damage to organs, too?*

For his part, Jael was quiet though he put away his share of alcohol. She noticed that he shook off the effects much faster than other men. That might be why her hangover had dissipated in a few hours instead of leaving her with a full day of misery. There were so many unanswered questions regarding his nature, but he was touchy on the subject. *With anyone else, you wouldn't care. You'd demand answers.* The softness that existed in relation to him felt like a wound, one she had no hope of healing.

"I'd give a lot to know what put that expression on your face," Jael said softly.

She slid him a layered glance. "Make me an offer."

"But you already have everything."

The words hit her like an armored fist in the sternum. Dred was actually grateful when the men started chanting, "Dread Queen, Dread Queen!" and made it impossible for her to reply.

With a smothered sigh, she pushed to her feet and strode to the center of the hall. "Music!" she demanded.

The Queenslanders responded with makeshift instruments: pipes of synth tubing, drums from cloth stretched over a metal frame, and their stomping boots made up the rest of the rhythm. This had been Tam's idea, a ritual that belonged only to the Queenslanders, unique to her territory. *Give a stupid man the pretext of power,* Tam had said, *and he will never question whether it's the real thing.* So in such moments of revelry, the citizens had the right to demand a storydance, which might be a real thing somewhere but sounded like bullshit to Dred. Jael was watching, brow furrowed in puzzlement, when she began to move.

She kept time to the pace the men set, twirling in a pantomime of the night she killed Artan. The storydance unfolded in silent verses with each lash of her chains, each stomp of her feet, each clockwise turn. Though it was simple choreography, it was important to keep an eye on how the ritual impacted her audience. A few looked bored, as they'd seen it before, but others seemed enthralled with the sway of her hips. Most knew they'd never make it past the door of her quarters without dying, so this was the piece of the Dread Queen they claimed.

Einar used to roar out a song as I danced. Not a very good one, but meant to evoke the glorious nature of the deed; the big man had written it himself. In comparison, the storydance seemed oddly somber, performed without his accompaniment. As if the men sensed that same lack, someone in the back started singing:

The queen in waiting, she bided her time,
Watching, plotting, and waiting to strike.
While the brute, he ranted and roared,
Never seeing the danger in her.

There were several verses, though nobody but Einar had memorized them. So the men got lost around the third stanza and started making up their own. She didn't let the terrible poetry distract her from finishing the performance, so she spun into the last moments of the dance with increased intensity, stomping and whirling, chains flying over her head until she thought she might strangle herself. By the time she finished, her arms and shoulders were aching, and the common room rang with the chants of "Dread Queen."

"Explain to me what that was about," Jael said, as she sat down. Quietly, she filled in him in, and when she finished, he was frowning. "You're not a performing pet, Dred."

She shrugged. "Take it up with Tam. They don't ask often enough for me to care, usually just at celebrations like this."

"If you don't mind, it's not my business."

As time wore on, the men got drunker, but the patrolmen

abstained. The louder it got in the hall, however, the more she wanted to escape. Jael laced his fingers with hers and pulled her away from the table, where two men were arm wrestling. She let him because she'd given the public enough for one night. *Time for peace and quiet.*

"Do you mind if we check on the sentries?"

"That's probably a good idea. Tam said this is safe enough, but if I was Vost, I'd think this was the perfect time to attack."

"Presuming he knows."

Jael nodded. "I've been busting his drone cams as fast as I spot them, and he can't have an unlimited supply."

As they headed for the north border, Dred spotted Tam, along with Martine and Calypso. They each carried an armload of miscellaneous articles, and Calypso had a crate. "Mission accomplished."

"What did you get?" she asked.

"Ammo and replacement parts mostly. They didn't leave much for us in the command post." Tam didn't seem surprised. "I wouldn't either."

"He probably moved their more valuable gear," Jael said.

Dred offered a half smile at that. "If he's started hiding his goods, creating caches, then he's going native."

"We barely made it out," Calypso put in. "The assholes came back singing. Seems like it went well in Munya."

"Is there a party on?" Martine cocked her head, listening to the racket coming from the common room.

Dred stepped aside and made a sweeping gesture. "Have at it. They're gambling, too, so you should be able to hustle a bunch of suckers."

"Come with me. You're a genius at spotting tells."

Jael didn't move, but Dred knew he was expecting her to accept the invitation. She found that she wanted to surprise him—in a good way. It had been so long since she gave a damn about anyone else's feelings. This was both liberating . . . and terrifying.

"I've got other plans," she said quietly.

"Oh?" Martine grinned. "Don't do anything I wouldn't do."

"Fortunately, that gives me a lot of leeway."

Martine grinned. "Seems like we've bonded, queenie. I approve."

Dred put a hand on Jael's arm. "Let's finish our rounds, then retire."

"Sounds good, love." He wore a light expression, but she saw that he expected her to bitch about the endearment, used in front of people.

Instead, she waved at the others and went to make sure the sentries were sober.

◄ 32 ►

Coming in Hot

At the east checkpoint, the sentries reeked of rotgut and could barely stand upright. Jael bit out a curse. "I doubt there's a sober man left in the place to relieve them."

"Not who isn't already assigned elsewhere." Dred scraped an angry hand through her tangled hair. The trinkets clacked with the movement.

"Then we'll have to finish their watch."

She sighed. "It's not how I wanted to spend our night, but it's necessary."

"I don't mind." He could've said that was because he had her with him, but it seemed like too close to a confession. Though he'd promised to help her escape, they'd never talked about a future. In here, such a thing didn't exist.

"I appreciate it." She turned to the drunken guards. "Get to bed. Now. If I find out you went to the common room to keep drinking, you'll get worse than a flogging tomorrow."

Jael could see that the men believed her, and they stumbled off, leaving their post. Dred took up the weapons they'd left behind and handed one to Jael. He'd never stood watch like this, and he guessed it had been a long time for her, too.

"Did Artan ever station you here?" he asked.

She shook her head. "He preferred to keep me close."

So do I.

It was a long night, listening to distant shouts from sotted Queenslanders. And when relief turned up, they were visibly worse for the wear and stunk of liquor.

"Are you two sober enough to stand watch?" Dred demanded. She put them through a series of a tests and eventually gave grudging permission for them to take over. "If there's an incursion on your watch because one of you passed out, you better hope the enemy kills you before I do. I guarantee it'll be faster."

"We'll keep each other awake," the soldier promised.

"You almost made him piss himself," Jael said, once they moved off.

"That's my job."

Together, they walked in silence to her quarters. Things had died down at last in the common room, the din replaced by periodic snoring. "I can only imagine how long it'll take to set the place to rights."

"Cook will see to it. He'll kick the ones awake who passed out in the hall and make them clean."

"That'll teach them not to drink themselves stupid."

"It hasn't so far."

After Jael stepped inside her quarters, she sealed the door behind them. "Not in the mood for company?"

"Just yours. Let me shower; and then . . ."

"And then?"

"We get some shut-eye."

"Really?" He tried a mocking smile. "Don't I deserve a reward for keeping you company tonight?"

"Maybe you just needed to ask."

She slipped into the bath, then he heard the water running. If there was more space, he'd join her, but the sanshower was designed so tight that one person of average size could barely fit. It wouldn't be seductive to get wedged in there. So he waited for her, sprawled on a chair while his eyes burned with weariness. He didn't sleep much at the best of times and he was still mulling what had happened with Vix and Zediah. Keeping such a huge issue from Dred didn't feel right, but he couldn't let Zed spill his secret, either.

When she stepped out a few minutes later, she was clad only in a threadbare towel. Jael didn't stir, letting her come to him. And once she dried off, she did.

"Did you want a turn?"

"I probably should."

But Jael made his ablutions quick, an effort of necessity rather than luxury. She was already in bed waiting for him when he stepped out, and the lights were down, wreathing the room in darkness. External noises made him think downtime was almost over, but Queensland could get by for a few hours without them.

"I'm tired," she said softly.

"Then we can sleep." He'd be lying if he said he wasn't disappointed, though.

"I find that a workout before bed helps me to relax."

Jael grinned. "Don't invent reasons for sex, love. Just tell me that you want it."

She propped up on an elbow and reached for him. "Not it. *You.*"

It took him two seconds to reach the bed, but she flipped him as soon as he touched her. "You smell good. Clean."

"I do what I can."

Heat simmered in Jael's head, making it difficult to lie still. Dred was all shadow and hollows, but the play of muscle beneath her skin hinted at strength—and that he liked, very much. She was fire and vengeance. Blood. Sex. The two swelled around her until the two urges melded; she was carnal death, kneeling over him. He ached. She smelled luscious as she leaned down. Her mouth brushed the side of his throat.

He turned his head with a little growl, allowing her better access. Then she gripped with her teeth. The mock-threat should've been laughable; there was no way she could hurt him. But pleasure rolled through him regardless, particularly when her tongue traced where she'd bitten. More softness and heat. Desire careened in his veins, spiraling along nerve endings that could scarce contain its breadth.

He shifted, already wishing he could push her down and seize control. Never had he permitted a female to take charge of him like this. Yet there was a delicious, addictive quality to her softness—the way her hair fell across his throat as she ran her lips around to the other side. He breathed her in, delighting in her closeness. Dred bit her lip with her curious, blunt teeth, and phantom pleasure stole through him; he registered the bite as if to his own body.

"Ahh." He arched. It was all he could do not to overpower her right then. Yet this was not a game of dominance, but something else, frightening and new. Jael trembled with the need to reach for her; closing his eyes helped a little.

"So you like that. Good to know."

"Please tell me you're not stopping."

"I'm not." She lowered her head.

Hell. If another woman in here got near him down there with her teeth, he'd scramble away, especially after Martine's story. Her silken hair brushed him, and his whole body jerked. A snarl escaped him. Pleasure approached pain—and not because it actually hurt, but it was too much, too good, and he didn't understand what he'd done to earn this extra gratification. Before, his encounters always ran on expected lines.

Not with her, never with her.

The first brush of her lips made him roar and draw his knees up. It was . . . indescribable. Her tongue followed. She teased up and down, using both in a sweet, maddening pattern. He pushed up, twisting and growling. This teasing would kill him.

She lifted her head, and he saw her lips were swollen, so red and shiny that he wanted to bite them. Jael pushed up to meet her, nipping with feral need. She welcomed it, opening her mouth to let him use his teeth on her tender flesh. *Oh. Ohhh.* She had her hand on him again, squeezing, stroking.

"I yield." Maybe it was the wrong thing to say, but in his head, he was babbling other words, promises, offers of devotion.

Somehow, he strangled them.

In answer, she swung a smooth leg across his body and came up on her knees. Her muscles flexed, tightening her stomach as she curled her hand around him again. Even that proved almost more than he could take.

"Hold my hips," she whispered.

Jael did, his hands digging in, and she dropped, letting her weight do the rest. His breath went in a strangled gasp.

Her body clung—all heat and demand. He pushed up to meet her on each downward stroke. The sensation maddened him, but the position let him watch her build.

Her groans grew guttural. Dred breathed faster, exhaling in lovely gulps through her open mouth. And then she drew his fingers down. Despite his own madness and need, he took careful note as her whole body tensed; she sobbed out his name, her skin shiny with sweat. In response, he pulled her down hard.

"Is it too much?" Jael didn't know whether he could stop, even if it was.

As he gazed up at her, the awareness exploded through him, wonder and amazement mingling with the furious delight. *This is Dred, the woman who saved me.* He was shaking when she lay down on him, tucking her face into the crook between his neck and shoulder.

"Can you sleep now?"

"Mmm," she murmured.

When her breathing evened out, he had his answer. The specter of Vix and Zediah surged to the forefront of his brain. *I don't need this shit.* Between Silence's disappearing act and the mercs who would invade as soon as they put down Mungo's cannibal dogs, he shouldn't have to worry about internal threats, too. But in a place like Perdition, it came with the territory. While Queensland was better than the alternatives, it still wasn't populated with honorable, trustworthy men.

Much like you.

Despite the worry, he slept for a few hours. Jael never rested for more than four. Dred was still passed out when he rolled out of bed and got dressed. He was silent as he went, but before he got out the door, the alarm sounded. Klaxons had Dred out of the bunk and on her feet, scrambling for her clothes before he unlocked the door.

"What the hell's going on?" she demanded.

"No idea. I'll go find out. Catch up when you can."

Jael went at a run, blowing past other men scrambling toward the north barricade. Tam and Martine met him, sprinting hard, but he shot by to where the sentries lay in a bloody heap. From the look of the hallway, it had been ravaged with heavy rounds, not laser fire, and the junk that formed the barricade was practically shredded. He moved closer to the rubble to see what the hell was lurking outside.

A weapon unloaded just beyond his line of sight, and he grabbed hold of the sentries, towing them back toward cover. They might be dead, but he couldn't be sure. A ballistic round slammed through a metal plate and nailed him in the leg. Pain rocketed outward, followed by a trickle of hot blood. Gritting his teeth, Jael pulled harder.

His iron grip prompted a groan from one of the guards, and he opened his eyes. "Get back. Mercs, *all* the mercs. And they brought a Peacemaker."

◀ 33 ▶

Red as Blood

When Dred hit the scene, she registered infinite carnage.

A score of Queenslanders were already dead or dying. Since Ike's passing, she had charge of the Peacemaker unit, and she deployed it, but there was no safe haven for this battle, no place to shelter. The mercs came in hot behind their mech, mopping up with laser fire the men trying to crawl away in trails of their own blood.

It might be too late to defend her territory, but she could use one bot to take out the other. She keyed the commands on the remote and listened to the heavy tromp of her unit responding. Between the cries of pain and the rapid exchange of weapons fire, she had no idea where any of her closest comrades might be. Jael had dashed out of her quarters to investigate the alarm, and she hadn't seen him since.

"Scatter!" she shouted. "Find a place to hide. It's a big station. If they can't find you, they can't kill you. I'll announce on the comm when it's safe to return."

If it ever is.

A chorus of assent came from those not too wounded to evacuate. Hiding might not be daring or glorious, but her people knew Perdition better than the mercs. It would take forever to search them all out, and maybe in the meantime, she could come up with a plan. From the moment the mercs jumped out of the transport, she'd known this day was coming—that there would be a time when they invaded.

They picked the perfect time to strike. Everyone's got a hangover.

"They're running like rats," one of the mercs said.

"Don't let them get away." She didn't recognize the voice. *But it's definitely not Vost.*

The merc Peacemaker was older than the one Ike had restored, banged up around the edges and with weapons that whirred and whined when they fired. *Still enough to do us in.* Across the way, she spotted Tam and Martine with rifles. They'd flipped a couple of tables in the common room and were creating a cross fire, permitting other people to escape. There were more weapons locked up in the armory, but only she and Tam had the code to retrieve them. There were also more acid carbines and the remainder of the poison grenades.

Have to get to them.

Leaving the Peacemaker to hold the room, she sprinted across and slid beneath a barrage of laser fire into the hall beyond. She skidded several meters on her knees and bounded to her feet, pushing to full speed. Calypso was outside the armory, kicking with all of her might. She had ten or twelve men with her. When she glimpsed Dred, she stood back with a huff of relief.

"Thank, Mary. I've rallied a few of the boys, but they need guns and whatever else you have stockpiled. This is not the time to hold back."

"I know." Quickly, she keyed in the code and darted into the storage room and tossed weapons out for Calypso to distribute.

The booms and rat-a-tat-tat from the common room told her that the Peacemaker was still intact, still firing. If they were lucky, the two mechs would take each other out, leaving the mercs in a position of vulnerability. *They still have weapons and armor.* Dred would feel better if they weren't scrambling to regroup, but maybe all hope wasn't lost just yet. *We can play cat and mouse all through the territory. I just hope the men armed only with shivs have the sense to stay hidden.* If there was no chance of winning a fight, there was no shame in avoiding it.

After she emptied the armory, she led the run back to the common room and returned just in time to see her Peacemaker fly back. One of its arms was missing, the one with the Shredder on it, and a big hole gaped in the center of its chest. Still, the mech fired a powerful laser burst; the heat made the other droid's chest plating burn red-hot.

"Get to cover," she called out. "Then let's disable the Peacemaker. If they take ours out first, we're done."

Dred moved first, drawing the attention of the mercs who were bunkered down behind their mech. She took a couple of glancing shots, and the resultant burn lanced straight through her nerves to numbness. But the diversion allowed her people to charge in behind her and flip more tables. Calypso popped up and nailed the merc Peacemaker with the carbine. The acid pellets were strong enough to eat through metal, softening the droid for their Peacemaker's next shot.

"I need some of you to focus on the mercs. Try to keep them pinned down."

"Happy to help, love." Jael appeared on the other side of the common room, and she had never been more relieved. He had Tam and Martine with him, so she signaled for them to fan out and create a cone of fire to pin the mercs down.

"I wondered when you'd visit," she shouted to Vost. "How's your armor by the way? It was looking ragged the last time I saw you."

The only answer to her words came in the form of a volley of laser fire. It scorched the table she was hiding behind until the metal glowed red, and the hole appeared in the center. Dred slid along to the other side. *Maybe trash talk is a bad idea.* Two more acid pellets hit the enemy Peacemaker, then her unit followed with a barrage. With Jael and company keeping the mercs contained, she dove for the Shredder and rolled to the next overturned table. She banged hard on some fallen chairs, and the clatter drew the other droid's attention.

This is gonna hurt.

As the Peacemaker targeted her and cycled to weapons hot, she raised up on her knees and opened fire with the Shredder. It was awkward, and it cut her fingers since it wasn't a weapon meant to be operated by hand, but the heavy ballistic rounds tore through the other Peacemaker's softened armor plating. Calypso and the others added laser fire as blood dripped from Dred's sliced fingers, and she didn't let up until all her ammo was gone. The bot staggered back, then went boom in a shrapnel explosion of armor plating and cascading orange sparks. Their own mech was in a hell of a mess, barely able to trudge forward, but it still had one functional weapon.

"Broke your toy," she called to the mercs. "Come on in, and we'll talk about it."

Most likely, she wasn't supposed to be able to overhear their conversation, but thanks to Jael, her hearing had improved. Her gaze met his across the common room and his slight inclination of the head told her he was eavesdropping, too. She ducked down and cocked her head, wryly amused.

"We don't know what kind of defenses they have inside the barricades." That was the voice she hadn't recognized before, the one who said, *Don't let them get away.*

"Or how many."

"We should push," Vost said. "They're disorganized and at a tactical disadvantage. We *heard* her call a retreat."

"That doesn't mean anything. She might've moved the support staff out of the line of fire. For all we know, she's got military training."

"Someone does," Vost admitted. "Her traps and ambushes have been top-notch."

Dred stifled a smirk. If she kept quiet long enough, the mercs would talk themselves out of the attack. *Seems like I've made them wary of me.* That felt like an accomplishment.

The other man went on, "*And* they took out our Peace-maker. That was supposed to be our free pass to burn this place down. Unless you want all of us to die, maybe we should scour the facility for more of them."

"They'll burn the armor off us again," someone else said. "And there are no more replacements on the transport. I'm *not* fighting these savages in my shirtsleeves."

"I still can't breathe right from whatever they put in those grenades." To Dred's ears, the soldier sounded worried. "The medical droid can't fix it, either."

There was a silence, as if Vost was weighing the best course of action. To goad him, Dred called, "I'm getting bored in here. Are you coming to play with me or not?"

Vost shouted back, "Another time. This was just a trial run. The next time, I'll bring special gifts to remember me by."

Shit. If he finds and recovers more Peacemaker units, we're done. Ours is just about busted, and I don't know if anyone can fix it with Ike gone.

For the sake of those who had her back, Dred infused her tone with more confidence than she felt. "Things haven't turned out like you expected, have they, Vost? I guarantee that will continue. In fact, it'll only get worse. See, you're fighting people with nothing to lose and a lifetime of experience at surviving despite all odds. Your men *already* want to go home. As more of them die, it'll only get worse."

Vost didn't reply to her, but his voice buzzed with tension. "Move out."

Dred lowered her head, resting her brow against the cool underside of the table. Footsteps sounded behind her, and she recognized Jael's tread before his warm hand dropped to her shoulder. *Can't believe I held them off Dread Queen–style.* She was too drained to feel like celebrating, however, because if the mercs had pushed, they would've found fifteen poorly equipped men and women, easily killed, easily overcome.

What the hell's going to happen next time?

◄ 34 ►

A Shadow Falls

"That was some of the most bullshit cowardice I've ever seen," Martine snarled.

Jael agreed with her. Considering their advantages, if he had been leading that group, he'd have rolled in and finished the job. "No doubt, bright eyes. They used the Peacemaker to soften us up, then bailed without losing a single man."

The common room was an abattoir. So many Queenslanders had been mowed down, aliens and humans alike. A number of them were moaning and weeping, lying in puddles of blood. Dred gazed about at the wreckage with an expression so open and broken that he wanted to caution her against showing that much vulnerability. While she trusted Tam and Martine, hopefully him and Calypso, he didn't know the other men that well.

"We have to rebuild as fast as we can," she said tiredly. "Mop this place up and deal with the wounded."

"The mercs have a medical droid," Jael murmured.

Tam shot him a curious look, as if wondering how he knew. No point in explaining, no benefit, either. Dred shook her head.

"It wouldn't be able to help them."

"Then I'll take care of triage if you get started on cleanup." Jael produced a knife and knelt beside a man whose guts were spilling out of his body.

"I'm sorry."

But the Queenslander just closed his eyes, turning his face to the side. Jael had done this before, on other battlefields, usually at his commander's behest, like he was a monster, not a person, and it didn't trouble him to cut human losses. *I don't know your name or your story.* The knife went in clean, and the man gasped out a last breath. Raising his head, Jael signaled to Calypso and her men to haul away the body.

But he wasn't prepared to find Brahm among the mortally wounded. The Ithtorian wheezed for breath, his chitin cracked in half a dozen places. Added to the injury he'd already sustained, he had no chance of recovery. His talons flexed, stirring the ichor spilled from his sides. The smell carried Jael straight back to Ithiss-Tor, until his gut churned with revulsion. *It shouldn't be me. Someone else should—*

"Jael?" Brahm rasped out.

"I'm here."

"Death . . . is a funny thing. Sometimes . . . people die bravely. Honorably. Other times . . . they just die."

He had no idea what to say. "That's true."

"I'm so . . . sorry Ali died . . . for nothing."

"I doubt she would agree."

"I'm ready. Do it. Up through my neck, beneath the mandible."

Jael readied his knife, but it was harder than he'd expected. *I tried to murder the father, and now I* am *killing his son.* He opened and closed his fingers on the haft several times—and only the pained noise the Ithtorian made drove him forward in the end. As instructed, he sank the blade deep, lodging it in Brahm's brain. The alien shuddered and fell still beneath Jael's hands. Ithtorians enjoyed natural longevity, so this felt like a crime rather than a mercy killing. Guilt swept over him as he recalled his initial response to Brahm, the instinctive prejudice he couldn't control.

It shouldn't have been me to send you to your rest.

But he couldn't stay there forever. There were too many other men who needed the kindness of a quick death. So Jael carried on with a blade until all the dying were dead. Then he joined the others in removing corpses to the chute.

Seems as if that's all we've done lately.

Cook came into the common room at some point thereafter and he stood, staring at the sea of red spilled on the battered floor. He spun in a slow circle, gauging the damage to tables and chairs, then he strode toward Dred, who was standing next to Jael. It took all he had not to reach for her, not to wrap an arm around her shoulder and stroke his hands down her back, when he could see she was on her last legs.

When he spoke, because he did so rarely, the chef's voice sounded rusty. "We cannot continue this way. How do you intend to fix this?"

Dred pushed out a sigh. "I don't know."

A flicker in the other man's eyes made Jael uneasy. Maybe she shouldn't have been so honest, but she couldn't be the Dread Queen every minute of every day. These men needed to stop being such lazy bastards. *If more of them fought, we wouldn't have lost so many today.* But given the lack of weapons that could hurt an armored merc—or a Peacemaker—they couldn't have done more than die, like the ones caught in the initial onslaught.

Cook just nodded and signaled for the sanitation crew to bring out the mops. Little by little, Queenslanders came out of hiding. Jael set a number of them on rebuilding the broken barricade, though everyone knew at this point how little protection it offered against a mech. The mercs would be slowed by it, however, maybe long enough for Queensland to prepare.

Her eyes shadowed, Dred sent runners to search for those who had fled when she called the retreat. With the mercs still a threat, despite what she'd said before, she couldn't risk an announcement on station comms, where the enemy could overhear. It might spur another attack.

Soon after the scouts left, the aliens came out of hiding to help with the damage control. Katur and Keelah oversaw repairs to furniture, patching things as well as could be expected, given limited supplies and resources. By the time the common room was set to rights, it was obvious there had been a hard-fought battle. Even the flooring was permanently dented and scarred, marred with bloodstains that no amount of scrubbing could wash away.

As Jael stretched, the Dread Queen beckoned. "We need an emergency council meeting. This way."

She led them all to the training room. A quick glance identified Keelah, Katur, Calypso, Martine, and Tam as the ones invited to this planning session, whatever it might entail. The resistance had managed to kill a few mercs, damage some armor, liberate a few supplies, and steal some guns. Compared to what the mercs had done in one strike? Laughable. Jael didn't see how this could end well.

"How many did we lose?" Dred asked Tam quietly.

"I'm still counting, and I think some of the men might be in hiding on the upper levels. But . . . it looks like we're down by half."

Dred sucked in a sharp breath, and that time, Jael couldn't prevent himself from stepping up behind her. He was beyond gratified when she leaned, not so anyone else would notice, but it felt like a silent message. *Yes, I do need you at my back. Don't let go.* Maybe that was wishful thinking, and he should be beaten for such notions in the middle of a crisis. But it was a rare, incredible feeling.

Nobody's ever needed me before.

"What's your plan?" Katur asked.

"I wish I had one. The mercs are planning to look for more Peacemakers before they come back. Ours won't last through another firefight."

Jael wished he could offer to tear them apart with his bare hands, but Einar was gone, and he didn't have the same strength, speed, or healing as before. He didn't regret saving Dred's life, but he didn't much like the limits on his capacity. Caution had never been part of his battle strategy, and it was strange, suddenly having to think about risking injuries too severe to heal.

"There are five on station," Katur said.

"You took an inventory?" Calypso asked.

Keelah nodded. "It's wise to know what dangers exist, even if you can avoid them."

"I don't suppose you marked the locations?" Tam wanted to know.

"In fact, I did."

"That's the best news I've had all week," Dred said. "Tell me."

Katur elaborated and drew a map, but he cautioned, "Three of these units, I don't think the mercs can reach. They're behind turrets and force fields, and I haven't been able to bypass them."

"He's a good hacker," Keelah said uneasily.

"If he can get them, we're done," Martine muttered.

"That might be good for us," Jael put in. "If they *can't* reach them, they can't send them against us."

Calypso frowned. "Unless Vost figures out a way around the station defenses. I wouldn't have suspected he could acquire his own Peacemaker so fast."

"We can't underestimate him," Dred agreed.

Keelah rubbed her chin. "Ali tried to hack a few of the stations, but the algorithms were too complex to manage it without specialized tech."

Tam paced, five steps away, five steps back. Since the spymaster didn't usually give away such insights regarding his mood, Jael reckoned he must be pretty agitated. "I've calculated the odds. Queensland can't survive another attack like that. If we don't resolve this, we'll end up hiding in isolated pockets, easily wiped out. I can steal parts from two of the Peacemakers, provided I can get to them before Vost, but—"

"We no longer have the numbers to defeat the mercs," Dred said.

"Not without better armor and weapons." Jael didn't like being the bearer of bad news, but there was no point in ignoring reality.

"Tam, can you hack the Peacemakers instead of disabling them?" Keelah asked.

The spymaster shook his head. "Would that I could, but my expertise lies elsewhere."

Ike probably could have. But that thought didn't help.

"How is it that Vost can do it but not you? I thought you were a genius." Martine seemed disappointed.

"I suspect he has special equipment to aid him. I have . . . very little." The admission appeared to hurt Tam, as if he loathed confessing to being ill prepared.

Apparently not enough to crack station defenses, thank Mary. But the Peacemaker operating systems would be considerably less complex. *Bad news for us since he can manage with the gear he brought with him.*

"Well, we can't just sit here, licking our wounds and waiting for them to slaughter us." Jael restrained the urge to punch something. "What now?"

Tam stopped and faced the group, his expression somber. "This idea might not *save* us . . . but it offers vengeance. It's not easy to acknowledge the potential for failure or that death may be inevitable. I think we've reached that point. Yet there's a certain satisfaction in knowing that even if we lose, so do they."

Dred smiled. "You have my complete attention."

◀ 35 ▶

Karma Is a Stroppy Bitch

Katur made it clear that there were minute design flaws in Perdition, conduits that could be targeted to make a force field fail before the system backup kicked in. And in some cases, the backup had been stripped for parts, like the force field down below. There was no way to be sure, however, unless you shorted things out. Tam was ready to move.

After considering for a few seconds, Dred nodded. "Do it."

The others scattered shortly thereafter, each with business regarding the protection of Queensland, but she couldn't bring herself to get moving just yet. Calypso stuck around, too, her strong features set in a pensive expression.

"Tough call," the other woman said.

Dred nodded. While she saw the benefits, it didn't mean she liked acknowledging that the retributive strike would only happen after the mercs wiped them all out. "I haven't ceded the battle yet. It's a fail-safe, that's all."

"That's the spirit. We're doing better than I expected. To be honest, I tried to get Martine to run for it a while back."

Dred hadn't known that, but she wasn't surprised. "I'm glad you stuck around."

"I'm a sucker for lost causes. That's half of why I ended up in here."

Though she'd learned Martine's story, Calypso had dozed off before they started talking seriously about LBP—Life Before Perdition. "Oh?"

Calypso propped herself against the far wall. "Do you know anything about the Human Initiative?"

After a moment of poking around the cobwebby corners of her brain, Dred came up with, "Some kind of propaganda campaign? I don't remember much about it."

"Conglomerate brainwashing manifesto—about how we needed to complete our diaspora and get out there, populate the universe with lots and lots of humans. So they started a drive toward colonization. There were incentives and—"

"I'm with you," she said. Whatever the hell this was about, it was a welcome distraction from the seemingly hopeless odds in Queensland.

Calypso went on, "When corporations saw there was money to be made, they got involved, offered complete settlement packages based on income. I'm from a desert colony myself. Shit place to develop, but we couldn't afford a more hospitable climate."

Dred knew shit about the Human Initiative, but she did understand profit and loss, supply and demand. It didn't take a genius to work out that the private sector wanted to compete with the Conglomerate. History didn't support the idea that it was possible to have one governing body in charge that didn't eventually succumb to internal turmoil, nepotism, and general corruption.

"I'm from a pretty small outpost, too." That seemed like a safe, neutral reply.

"Things were hardscrabble, but it was a decent life. Until we discovered uranium on our claim."

"Let me guess, things went to shit after that." Dred could envision any number of ways that could go wrong.

"Suddenly, the company we bought the property from found errors in our documentation and the deed, along with mineral rights, reverted to them."

"I'll just bet," Dred snorted.

"We didn't yield," Calypso said quietly. "That land was ours, and we fought to the last. I killed so many men over that rocky patch of ground. The struggle honed me and made me strong, and when we lost, when I was the only one left hiding in the hills, half-starved and wild with grief? They sent me here."

"Damn." Inadequate response, but she had nothing else.

"I told myself then, I'd never sign on for another lost cause. I'd never fight to the last. From that point forward, I'd only look out for myself."

Ah. She got it then. "You think that's what we're doing here?"

"I hope not. I wouldn't have your job on a bet, but the others see something in you. So don't make me sorry I stuck around."

"I'll try not to," she said softly.

But Calypso was already gone.

TAM tapped his foot at the delay; he had a job to do. He frowned at Martine, but she wore a stubborn-as-hell expression that said she wouldn't budge until he heard her out.

"I can help," she said.

"There's more likelihood we'll be caught. I can do this on my own."

"You can. But I won't let you." She caught Tam's shoulder and dragged him close for a kiss that stole his breath.

He didn't like being pushed outside the bedroom, but by the time she let him go, he was ready to make an exception. "You're a distraction."

"I'm your backup. And I know a thing or two about security systems and engines."

"Of course you do. Hurry up then."

Only the fact that she didn't gloat let him accept the situation with equanimity. Instead of making for the Peacemaker units as previously discussed, he cut a path directly for the transport bay. A few times, Tam heard the sound of combat, but he circled it, heart pounding in his ears. There would never be a more critical mission.

"Sounds like Silence is killing some of Mungo's rotters."

"Good," he muttered.

"This should be fun."

She's got an odd sense of what's entertaining.

For him, it was pure adrenaline, mingled with visceral terror. He'd undertaken missions like this one before, where he never relaxed until the job was done. They had no rifles, no armor. This was a quick in and out. If they were discovered, they died, so he led Martine at a dead run. She was fit, so she didn't flag or fall behind, and she was lighter on her feet than she had been in the beginning. *Not that she was ever loud or clumsy.*

"You didn't have to come with me," he said quietly.

"Of course I did. You're my man, yeah?"

"Am I?" A few bed games didn't constitute a commitment.

"I'm not having this conversation with you now, Tameron. Watch ahead."

"Yes, ma'am."

Despite the tension locking his spine, he stifled a smile. With caution and stealth, he skirted the danger zones and guided them to the power conduit that kept the force field up. While the mercs had the code to shut this down when it came time to leave, they probably hadn't considered that somebody could circumvent the security and go after their ship.

"Is there any way we can just steal this and take off?" Martine asked.

"It's late to be asking, isn't it? I thought you had background in this sort of thing."

"Not ships." She seemed to read a question in his eyes though he hadn't been aware of one. "Jewels, paintings, sculpture. On New Terra, I pilfered pretty, expensive things. That's probably why I'm drawn to you."

He raised a brow. "You think I'm pretty and expensive?"

"Aren't you? That accent doesn't come from the streets."

She's too clever by half.

Tam turned to study the ship through the force field. He

couldn't start the transport without the piloting codes, and the system would be too sophisticated for anyone to hack without special gear. Plus, there was the additional problem of needing override codes to open the bay doors. Otherwise, he'd have led the others here, and they could've hopped aboard, leaving the mercs stranded. Tam regretted the impossibility of that scenario because it would be such poetic justice. *Hoist with their own petard, as they say.*

"If Katur was right, I should be able to interrupt the field protecting the transport bay by shorting this out."

As the alien had said, this was definitely a design flaw, as some of the fields could be powered down by localized power outages. It was a temporary solution, obviously, as he had to be fast, darting in before the backup engaged. But a few seconds should be all they needed.

"Wait here," he said to Martine. "And be ready to move when the force field flickers."

Bracing himself, he opened the box and yanked out a handful of wires. No finesse, and the resultant shock blew him backward. He slammed into the wall and shook his head to clear it, seeing only blurry movement. He had no sense of whether Martine was safe, but his heart pounded in his ears. Tam stumbled toward the force field. *If she was too slow, it could've hurt her.* But Martine danced in triumph on the other side of the amber light, arms in the air. Then she curtailed her celebration to power the field down for him to pass through.

"I took a quick look at the ship . . . and I can't even get inside."

Tam smiled. "I don't need to."

He scrambled underneath the transport and went to work on the wiring. It didn't take long to frag up certain functions, so that when the mercs started the vessel, all power would be immediately routed to the engines, causing an instant and critical overload. Tam wished he could be here to see the results of his handiwork. Between the grimspace drive and fuel in the tanks, the explosion should take out the whole bay.

"That's impressive," Martine said, as he crawled from beneath the ship.

"Thanks. Now let's find the force-field codes, so we can activate it from the outside."

She stretched out a hand and pulled him to his feet. "Agreed. If we cover our tracks well enough, they'll never see this coming."

"THIS is bullshit, Vost."

Casto was asking for a beatdown. He had been insufferable since the attack on what some monster had told him was called Queensland, and he hadn't gotten better after they failed to acquire more Peacemakers. When the Conglomerate sealed this place up, they did so fairly tightly, and the prisoners had already stolen everything that was readily available. He'd spent hours trying to work around the corrupted overrides, but they kept changing before his limited equipment could solve the problem. Other assets offered potential acquisitions, but it would take time, and Casto had the patience of a brain-damaged kid.

"We're getting nothing accomplished here," his lieutenant said. "We could spend half a turn crawling over this place and not stamp out all the maggots."

While he was an asshole, he wasn't wrong. There were too many decks and levels, too many bolt-holes. When they'd hit Queensland, half the populace disappeared. Oh, they'd gotten a good number of them. The stink of blood and shit from dying men was ingrained on his brain, so he knew when he'd led a successful strike.

You didn't lead it. You butchered them with a Peacemaker.

He'd been a merc long enough to recognize that there was no such thing as honor in combat. You iced your targets, and you went home. End of story. But that fight had been one-sided enough to send a pang of regret through him. Their leadership had shown enough craft and cunning to make him feel like they were worthy opponents, regardless of crimes committed. It was an odd fragging situation, to be sure.

"Here's what I propose," Casto went on. "You stay here

with Duran and Redmond. I'll take the rest of the men to mop up those skin-eaters. I don't think there are more than fifty of them left. We can handle it."

Vost shook his head. "We're not splitting our forces. I'll go with you."

"With all due respect, Commander, the last time we all went out, the scum crawled up our asses and stole our shit. We need you here to guard what's left . . . or we'll come back to an empty command post."

Starvation was a real danger. They'd packed enough paste for a three-month campaign, but prisoners had stolen it in the robbery, along with other critical equipment. Vost tapped a hand angrily against his thigh. Sometimes it felt like no decision was the right one.

"I don't like it, but you have a point."

Casto saluted. "I'll be back as soon as I've wiped out the mooks."

Once the men rolled out, Redmond strolled up. "You sure about this, boss? I wouldn't trust him to wipe his own ass."

"Then you should've taken the promotion when I offered it to you." Vost would've preferred Redmond because the man was solid, but he was also lazy as shit.

The other man snorted. "Like that'll ever happen."

Duran glanced up from taking inventory of what was left. "By my count, we've got two weeks at most. We need an alternate food source."

"There's a Kitchen-mate in one of the abandoned zones," Vost said. "It might still be functioning. I'll take a run to see once the others get back."

"Do we even want to think about what organic might be powering it?" Duran asked.

Redmond made a gagging sound. "Probably not. This is a crap gig. I don't think I've been so skeeved since we did that village on Tarnus."

That wasn't one of his brighter memories, but being a soldier of fortune didn't come with a guarantee that all the jobs would be good for the soul, and he had bills to pay. The thought sent a pang of worry through him so hard that his hands actually curled into fists in reaction. *Can't think about him. Eyes on the prize. It's not going as fast as expected, granted, but we're making headway.*

With a sigh, he sent his last drone cam on patrol with orders to track Casto. It was just good strategy to make sure the patrol didn't encounter more resistance than it could handle. Worst-case scenario, Vost might not be able to do much about it, but a commander should have complete situational awareness. As the cam skimmed through the halls, he saw about what he expected, pockets of prisoners skulking about, occasional combat between warring factions. *Shit, if we wait a week, they'll whittle each other down even more for those "pardons."* He stifled a laugh.

Then he froze in his chair. "Redmond, come look at this and tell me what you see."

The soldier ambled over to his shoulder. "Looks like Casto's heading for the transport bay, not the mooks."

He shot to his feet, pure rage swamping. "That bastard's leaving us behind."

They had too much of a head start for Vost to catch up, so he could only watch, jaw tight, as his lieutenant powered down the force field. The mutinous fuck actually waved at the drone cam, likely knowing his commander could do fuck-all to stop this. He'd set his plans too well. Vost wheeled and slammed his armored fist through a broken vid screen.

The rest of the men boarded the ship like hell was at their heels.

Ten seconds later, the drone cam went off-line in a fizz of static as an explosion rocked the whole station. Sirens blared like it was Armageddon, a constant shriek of alarm.

"What just happened?" Duran asked. "What the *fuck* just happened?"

"Payback." Shaken, Vost scrubbed a hand over his face; and then, despite himself, he began to laugh.

Rats in the Walls

"Alert, the facility may be under attack. All executive personnel please proceed to shuttle pods on alpha deck. There is a hull breach in the transport area. All support systems are compromised. Main power is off-line, backup engaged. Bulkheads are now sealing decks eight through ten. Emergency repairs are required." The station VI voice sounded eerily calm. "Maintenance supervisor, please dispatch immediate assistance."

Jael had always found virtual intelligences creepy, which was probably an unfair bias, given his own origins. But with biological life-forms, there was always a common imperative and some kind of emotional response. The Perdition VI didn't care if the whole station imploded, taking her and everyone else with it.

"Holy shit." Martine paused with her spoon in midair, aiming a shocked look at Tam.

"Why would the mercs try to leave?" Dred asked.

Jael shrugged. "You got me. Maybe the transport overloaded on its own?"

"Not unless someone powered it up."

Calypso was grinning. "Wonder how many of the ass-holes we took out."

Tam pushed to his feet. "Impossible to say, but I can check the command outpost, see how many men are in there."

Dred seemed to consider. "Might not provide a definitive answer—there could be some on patrol—but find out what you can. Carefully."

The alarm went on for hours before the VI must've figured out that nobody from maintenance was coming. Then she made a new announcement. "Decks eight through ten permanently compromised. Access revoked to all personnel. Have a nice day."

"That happened sooner than I expected," Jael said.

He was alone with Dred, relatively speaking. They were sitting in the common room, keeping an eye on the men, who were agitated by the station damage. According to Tam, the average Queenslander wouldn't understand the reason they'd blown the transport; most of them would see it as a wasted opportunity, like it really *was* that easy to steal a ship and take off. Then again, most of them were dumb as broken data readers. Jael agreed with the necessity of keeping the explanation for the explosion under wraps. The last thing they needed was a rebellion from men who believed their leaders had trapped them on station out of a misguided thirst for vengeance.

Dred nodded. "I thought we'd all be dead when they left."

A Queenslander whose name Jael couldn't recall approached the table. "My queen, do you know what the mercs are doing? Why they blew up part of the station?"

Jael admired her poker face as she replied, "Maybe they were trying to get into a restricted area and set off the top-tier defenses."

That was bullshit, but the convict didn't know that. "Then we need to be careful on salvage ops, huh?"

"I'd say so," Jael put in.

The man bobbed his head in a sort of bow, then hurried back to his table, likely to spread the news. Jael watched as he whispered, and other men glanced their way, looking simultaneously relieved and worried. Within a few minutes, the same prisoner was moving among other groups, warning them about the fact that Perdition could blow up if you tinkered with the wrong wire.

Dred sighed. "They'll be scared to leave Queensland at this rate."

"Better than the alternative." Which was rioting and death. "And at this point, we've lifted just about everything we can use."

"That's true." Her tone was bleak.

"We're in a better position than we have been for a while. So what's put that look on your face?" Jael couldn't believe he was *asking* that, inviting confidences.

Sucker.

"I don't want to think about the future." By her tone, she didn't think they had one.

And Jael had to admit, sometimes it was tough to imagine a way out of here. At the moment, his nebulous escape plan hadn't coalesced; more immediate problems kept cropping up, but hope flickered inside him, a tiny flame that couldn't be extinguished. Jael knew what true darkness of the soul felt like. He'd fallen into that abyss in a small cave on Ithiss-Tor, deep within the ground.

When they pulled me out of that hole to extradite me, I barely remembered my name.

"What then?"

"I'm calling in the mark I mentioned before. Quid pro quo, Jael. Tell me something . . . not awful."

Horror stories he had aplenty, tales of vice, betrayal, and bodily harm. Jael racked his brain for a thing of beauty, but most of what he had, that he cherished, had come from her. *That's probably not what she's looking for, though.* He imagined that she'd punch him the head if he said it out loud. *And I'd have it coming.*

"When I first broke out of the lab," he said slowly, "I had never seen direct sunlight before. My education wasn't all that impressive, either."

"So you thought it was a fire god?" She was smiling, teasing him.

Who the frag ever teased me? He wanted to hug her for it. The feeling that rose up in him when he looked at her face made him feel like he was choking. Only not in a bad way. *I've finally lost what little mind I have left.*

"No, queenie, I knew about the sun. In theory. But I'd never seen it. I should've been running, getting as far away from the facility as possible, but instead I climbed to the highest hill I could find to get a better look at it. And as I reached the summit, I saw my first sunset."

Jael still remembered that moment of breathless surprise when the sky melted into a sea of colors: pink, orange, yellow, and clouds streaked through with light. Dred seemed to be riveted by his expression, and he tipped his head back, fighting the urge to run. There was physical nakedness, but this was . . . something else entirely.

"And it was beautiful?"

"Spectacular. But that's not the point. In that moment, I realized I was free—that nobody could do anything to me without my permission. No more drugs, no more needles, no more tests. After that, sunsets represented freedom to me, and I hate being indoors. It's part of why I became a merc though it wasn't like I had many other options."

"So it's worse for you, being here."

"I haven't seen the sun in almost fifty turns. I don't know if it was calculated or coincidence, but even when they moved me, they kept me in containment units."

"Come on." She pushed to her feet and held out her hand.

For maybe the first time in his life, he hoped she wasn't leading him away for sex. It would feel like a pity move, and he didn't want it on those terms. But he took it anyway and let her pull him up. Instead of heading for her quarters, she led him on a meandering path through Queensland. They ended in what looked like a storage closet, but inside, it had been appointed like somebody's personal retreat.

"That's an old vid console," he said.

"Yeah. This is Martine's hangout, but she showed it to

me the night we got really drunk together. I *think* that means I have permission to be here."

"You sure? I realize you're the Dread Queen and all, but I'm not sure you want to piss off bright eyes."

"Why do you call her that anyway?"

"Because this place hasn't ground the life out of her yet." Some convicts, you could tell with one look that they'd given up, yielded to despair and acceptance. Not Martine.

"She's been here almost as long as I have." With a gesture, Dred seemed to dismiss the subject of Martine though Jael hoped the sharp-toothed woman wouldn't appear in a rage when she discovered them trespassing. "Sit down, I want to show you something."

With a growing sense of curiosity, Jael folded into the cushions next to her. She wore a concentrated look as she fiddled with the remote. Eventually, she got the menu up, though the quality was terrible. Lines ran through the picture, making the vid look like a canvas of geometric art. He was patience itself, though, waiting for the reveal. Dred skimmed a number of titles, then she picked one and keyed through it. All at once, he understood. On the screen was a brilliant sunrise, the colors shimmering and lovely despite the screen defects.

"This is what I've got," she said softly. "It's not freedom, but—"

"It's more than anyone else ever gave me."

That wasn't true in the strictest sense. There *had* been women—often wealthy—but their gifts didn't compare. He'd sold the timepieces and jewelry almost as soon as he left them. But this wasn't the kind of present that could be pawned or taken away. Warm with gratitude, he leaned over to kiss her, and she met him halfway. Her mouth was a galaxy to explore, sweet beyond the telling, and it almost hurt when he tasted him in turn, her breath mingling with his until he wanted to breathe only her. *This can't happen. Not like this.* He pulled away, shaken, because it was so much more than sex. When Martine pulled Tam into the room, then stopped short, Jael was grateful.

"What the hell?" Martine demanded, her expression pure outrage.

"It's my fault," Jael said. "She just wanted to show me a sunset. We're leaving now."

Martine scowled at Dred while Tam eyed the ceiling. Jael stepped out into the hall, measurably cooler than the smaller space had been. Ten minutes later, he knew something was truly wrong when his breath showed in a puff of smoke.

"That . . . is a problem," he murmured.

Dred swore. "Someone's gotten to Queensland's climate controls."

While nobody could shut off life support, enemy territory could be made profoundly uncomfortable, dangerous even. *Like when we poisoned Grigor's water supply.*

"Come." Jael beckoned with a smile that he hoped looked confident. "Let's deal with the rats in the walls."

⊲ 37 ⊳

A Cold and Creeping Doom

"This is Silence's work," Dred snapped.

Jael offered no argument. "Most likely. Even I'm aware that Mungo isn't known for his planning capacity. So where's climate control from here?"

"Four decks down."

"In the unused part of the station. Should we assemble a team?"

Dred shook her head. "It's too cold now. The others need to huddle and wrap up."

"Ah, so my monstrous DNA comes in handy once more. You must think you got a bargain in me, queenie."

"I don't think, I know." But she didn't have the time to devote to more reassurances. "Hurry. If the ambient temp drops any more, hypothermia could set in."

"I've heard it's a pleasant way to die."

"Not in the mood, Jael."

"I don't think we've been together long enough for you to say that, love."

"It's not dictated by length of relationship, just by how much of a pain in the ass the man is being."

"That explains a lot."

She knew he was trying to lighten the mood, but this was a serious problem. Even battles at impossible odds could be won, but if the environment itself turned against them—well, she wouldn't entertain thoughts of failure. Dred quickened her pace, running past the sluggish sentries. And from what she'd seen running past, the same could be said of the rest of her people. *They won't be any good if we're attacked.* That was her worst fear—that this might be an unholy alliance between Mungo and Silence.

Her joints ached, as if every injury she'd ever taken had rebounded with a vengeance. She remembered how slowly her father had moved on chilly mornings, and the realization that the cold was slowing her reactions made Dred step it up even more. She threw caution aside as she raced to the shaft that led down to the control room. In days past, there would've been guards here, but all of the recent losses made it impossible to guard anything but the heart of Queensland itself.

Another instance of losing by attrition.

"Don't get yourself killed," Jael called.

"Like I can die," she shot back. "You saw to that."

"Are you *blaming* me? And trust me, you're not invincible."

"Shut up and follow me." She put two hands on the sides of the ladder, braced her feet and the bottom, then just let herself slide.

The rough metal scraped the skin off her palms, but the descent was lightning fast. Blood slicked the path even more, so she was dripping red when she hit the designated deck. Jael was yelling something, but she ignored his words of caution. Her skin itched while it healed over, slow enough not to be visible to the naked eye, but five minutes later, as she closed on the control room, her skin was fresh and new. She swiped the sticky blood residue on her pants.

"You're insane," he snarled, catching up to spin her around with a hand on her shoulder. "If you think I'm going to watch you get hurt—"

"Feel free to watch," the Speaker said.

He emerged from the shadows with ten of Silence's trained, tongueless killers. Dred jerked away from Jael, incensed that she hadn't heard or smelled them. The usual reek of death was missing, which made her think they'd started bathing as camouflage. All eleven of them wore the white face paint that marked a hunting party, and the Speaker was smiling.

"I've been looking forward to reclaiming the honor you spat upon when you treated me like one of Mungo's mongrel dogs."

"How do you plan on doing that, you ghost-face asshole?" Jael stepped up beside her.

"By holding the two of you here long enough to make sure that the rest of Queensland freezes to death, then delivering you to the Handmaiden for a slow, satisfying death."

Dred laughed. "I don't like your chances."

"We shall see." As they charged, the Speaker blew two darts in quick succession.

"What the frag . . ." Her tongue felt stiff and numb, her limbs paralyzed.

"Happy news. We learned recently that rodents that infest the station have a gland that can be crushed to create a paralytic poison. Don't worry, I didn't use enough to kill you, though it *is* possible, per our early experiments."

Dred toppled forward, her chains clanking on the floor. Jael hit behind her, though she heard him trying to curse through a choked throat. *If he hadn't healed me, he'd be able to shake this off in seconds. Let's hope we both recover fast enough to keep the rest of Queensland from dying of frostbite.*

"The ambient temperature is not safe for human personnel. Decks twelve to twenty-four are now limited to automated workers."

Thanks for the tip, VI.

"Ten minutes should do it, I think. Don't blink. Or you might miss the end of everything you've built." The Speaker leaned down, his fetid breath wafting across Dred's cheek.

"But the Handmaiden tried to show you the true path. There is no end but death."

It was hell not being able to respond to his bullshit. If rage could help her burn the poison out of her system faster, then Dred should be set. Behind her, Jael made incomprehensible sounds of fury, almost like he was strangling on it. *Shit, is he all right?* But she couldn't turn to check, couldn't see anything but the yellow sclera belonging to the Speaker. When he shifted, she got to study the smeared white paint, his pores, and the prickles of whisker on his sharp chin.

A few seconds later, he straightened, leaving her to gaze at the scuffs at the base of the wall. Her chains were tantalizingly close, but she couldn't move. *You'll pay.* Yet there was only the sickening impotence of dead limbs, nothing she could use to enforce her will. The Speaker leaned over her, and for a few seconds, she thought he meant to assert dominance in a particular way. But instead he only trailed grimy fingers down her cheek. *It's a mercy I can't feel this.* Jael managed to make an animal noise in his throat, and she wanted to warn him not to reveal his weak spot.

Me.

"Lucky for you that the Handmaiden gelds her favorites. It was a hellish ordeal, but in the end, I'm grateful for the blessing. It frees my mind for higher pursuits."

Death instead of sex.

She'd never known revulsion could crawl inside a person, but it slithered through her innards like a nest of snakes, tangling in her lower stomach, until she was afraid she'd be sick. When the Speaker turned toward Jael, she understood the sound he'd made earlier. Whatever the Speaker chose to do, it would be worse if she had to witness it. *Better to take the wounds and suffer the pain.* It was a surprising realization but one she couldn't deny.

"I think I'll start the pain for my mistress, bring you to her with the sweet scent of blood on your skin." The skull-faced devil produced a blade.

The feeling came back to her fingers first, but she didn't

give any sign. The Speaker drew a line across Jael's palm, and red sprang up, trickling between his fingers. *He can't feel it right now, and it'll heal.* But the time was ticking away for the rest of her people. Worry chewed its way through her stomach and started on her spine.

*It must be freezing in Queensland. There must be some-*thing *I can do.*

In fact, there was.

But I can't take the chance. If she unleashed her murderous broadcast, the enemy would tear each other limb from limb, but the effect might not wear off Jael before the poison did. *If he goes after me—no, I can't. I can't risk it. So come on, body, shake it off. Can't move too soon. Have to be sure I can fight.*

Mustering all patience, she waited. Her heart ticked away the seconds, and gradually, the feeling started to come back, much sooner than the jackass could've expected. With a grunt, Dred struck, yanking the Speaker's ankle, and he fell backward. The rest of the killers were on her, so she rolled, snagging her chains. *If they all have poison, I'm fragged.* But the low-ranking ones only had shivs, better for her to keep them away as she scrambled back on the floor. She staggered to her feet, whirling her chains in a clumsy circle. Jael was there, teetering but up. He slammed a kick into the Speaker's stomach to keep the asshole from sticking them with another dart.

"Impossible," the Speaker wheezed.

"I'll fight," she said to Jael. "You get to the control room and fix the temperature."

To her relief, he didn't argue. Jael took a few steps back, and, with a running start, launched into an awkward flip over the rest of Silence's assassins. A few turned as if they'd follow him, but Dred got their attention with a slash of her chains. Two went down beneath the force of the blow, and she kicked out twice, snapping bones with each strike. *Eight left.*

Movement seemed to help loosen up her seized muscles and joints, so she jogged in place, twirling her chains before.

The silent killers encircled her. Rage blinded her, so she lost track of what she was doing to whom, and when her head cleared, the Speaker was gone, and his ten men were dead at her feet. She bore multiple cuts and bruises, all over her body, but she had no memory of receiving them. Dred took a step and was surprised to discover her hamstring had been cut. *Mother Mary, what's wrong with me?* Jael rushed out of the control room, and he was fast enough to catch her before she hit the ground.

"What happened?" he asked.

"I won? I think."

"The bodies on the ground point to yes. But . . . you don't remember the fight?"

Reluctantly, she shook her head.

Jael wore a troubled look. "Has that ever happened before?"

"Not even remotely. Does it happen to you?"

"No. But I wonder if your Psi ability is reacting somehow with my gift."

"Turning me into a berserker from the old vids?" Dred pushed out a sigh. "Why not? I could use another idiosyncrasy."

"Did you get the Speaker?" Jael seemed to understand that she didn't want to discuss her . . . episode, and she could've kissed him.

"He took off."

"Cowardly sack of shit. I regulated the climate control, and I'm going to lock the door. Can you hang there for a minute?"

Blood trickled down the back of her calf, so Dred leaned against the wall. "I'll be fine. Just need a minute."

"Now you sound like me." Jael went to work on the keypad beside the door to the control room. "The security's shit, but I can rewire it so the hacking solution is counterintuitive, and if they try to get in again, they'll set off station alarms."

"That would give us a heads-up, at least. Thanks."

Once he finished, Jael wrapped an arm around Dred's shoulders. She leaned on him until the blood dried on her leg, and she stopped feeling the injury. Curious, she bent to examine it. "Already sealed."

There was still a deep red scab where the knife had sliced through, but the tissue beneath had already knitted together. Her limp disappeared as they approached Queensland. The air was already a bit warmer though she could still see her breath when she exhaled. The rungs of the ladder were cold as she climbed back to the heart of the zone.

As she reached the right deck, she cocked her head. "Do you hear . . . combat?"

Jael nodded. "Fucking Silence—"

"And her two-pronged attacks. It's not as much fun when we're the target. Judging by the smell, we've got Mungo's monsters all over the place, too."

◄ 38 ►

Chaotic Crush

Queensland was in chaos.

Fifteen meters from the checkpoint, Jael spotted the first of Mungo's cretins, only five of them, hardly any opposition. They didn't turn as he and Dred approached. He was good and pissed at the incursion, but when he came up to the group, he saw what occupied their attention. They'd killed one of the sentries and were busy sawing him into shareable pieces. One cannibal had an arm; another was working on separating thigh from hip. Jael had seen some horrific shit in his time, but this—

"No fragging way," he bit out.

He launched at them and opened two throats in a rapid sweep of his blade. Those two dropped, leaving the other three to charge him with deep-throated growls. Like Silence's crew, this lot didn't talk much either, at least not that he'd heard, but these things were more like animals than humans. It was like they'd forgotten their words along with all sense of moral compass. *Not that I'm a saint, but shit, I never* ate *anyone.*

Dred laid one open with a slice of her chains. The links

whipped past Jael and glanced off his arm, but the pain didn't stop him from breaking another's neck. Blood spattered from the last one's mouth; he and Dred took the brute together, leaving only the chunky meat and bone remnants of their victim.

No time to deal with the dead. Have to save Queensland first.

"I'm afraid we're the only ones left," she whispered. "You, me, and the monsters."

The promise burst out of him like a river too long dammed. "Doesn't matter, love. I'll keep them from you, even if it *is* just you and me rattling around this place. The only way they touch you is if my head's on a pike, and somebody's eaten my heart."

"Smooth talker. But . . . you're not as tough as you used to be."

"Better men than Mungo have tried."

She smiled. "Thanks for the pep talk. Let's go kick some ass."

It was a cesspool of a station; Perdition always hovered on the brink of disaster, with shit being stolen, people shanking each other in the dark, transports exploding, and mercs arriving to execute all the meat bags incarcerated within. Jael wouldn't change a minute of it, so long as he got to fight at her side.

They hit hostiles almost as soon as they rounded the corner, a barrage of shots coming in hard and hot. Jael dove for cover. Through his enhanced senses, he identified merc armor, but these guys didn't seem to be shooting to kill. *More like they're just adding to the confusion.* He could respect Vost for capitalizing on Silence and Mungo's joint assault, if it wasn't so damned inconvenient. The VI was crackling with some old propaganda announcement, the first time he'd heard that, some shit about the Monsanto Corporation.

"Is this new?" he asked Dred.

She nodded. "Someone's been in the mainframe."

"How do you know?" Jael asked, ducking low to move along the wall toward the common room. He thought the shots were coming from around the corner, but he couldn't be sure. His hearing was scrambled with all the competing noises.

Battles all over the fragging place. I don't like it.

"Stands to reason. And I'd bet money that it was Vost."

Jael sniffed. He smelled a number of things, including Mungo's mongrels, along with burning wires, hot metal, carbon and cordite, sweaty prisoners, and melting durasteel. The air was a melting pot of interesting stink, most of which meant they had a long fight on their hands. It wouldn't be an easy run to save Queensland, but he hadn't expected it to be, either.

"Huh." Dred vaulted over a pile of junk. Head down, she went in a graceful run and slid under a slash of laser fire.

Dammit. He hated when she did that; only skin and bone stood between her and a splatter fest. But she was fearless. If they needed to push, she ran for it, and it was up to him to keep up. Jael sprang after her and pressed on.

"They got past us," he heard a merc say. "Orders, boss?"

Vost answered, "Let them go. We'll get to a safe distance and watch the festivities."

"Asshole," he and Dred said at the same time.

Despite himself, Jael grinned. "I could get used to sharing certain things with you."

"Just some, not all?"

He didn't answer; it wasn't the time. But on the whole, as long as she let him watch her six, he had no complaints. They fought through a host of cannibals before coming up on Cook decimating the enemy. He didn't turn when they reached the battle. He just kept fighting, his chopping knife a blinding silver arc. By the look of him, he had hard-core battle experience, though he seldom showed it. None of his assistants seemed to have made it; Cook alone was holding this part of the zone.

"You all right?" Dred asked him.

The chef nodded. "It's worse farther in."

Taking that as an indication of numbers, Jael glanced at her. She beckoned with a jerk of her chin, and he readied his weapons. Past the tumbled barricades, the common room was a wreck of a place, with broken chairs and tables, and it was full of crazy, man-eating loons.

Whatever Mungo was trying to accomplish, he couldn't be permitted to succeed. Jael didn't think the nutter had a master plan, actually. He operated on the *kill, kill, kill* managerial style, just as Silence brainwashed her people and cut out their tongues.

No wonder Dred didn't try to talk me into joining up.

"Mother Mary," Dred breathed.

"Where are the others?"

"No fragging clue."

Jael hoped they were holed up somewhere, waiting for the right time to strike. The cannibals didn't give him a chance to say as much, however. They rushed in a mob, no finesse or battle tactics whatsoever. There had to be twenty of them in here, and they all looked hungry. A few gnashed their red teeth as if at the promise of the grisly feast to come.

"I don't think so," Dred said.

She slammed her chain away from her body, nailing the closest monster in the face. The blow broke his nose and knocked out some teeth. Since he needed those for chewing human flesh, the enemy let out a scream of pained rage. Around him, the others responded, pressing closer until Jael had them all snapping and grabbing at him. It was hard to fight in close quarters, so he opened things up by wrenching free and flipping backward. Dred covered his movement with another lash of her chains, and two of the prisoners went down. She stomped on their faces even as another one sank its teeth into her arm.

Funny, "it," not him or her. They don't even look human anymore.

Some of them had film across their eyes, open sores oozing pus, and others were losing their hair, like their grotesque habits had imprinted on their flesh. He shuddered and rushed back into the fight, before they surrounded Dred. Their grasping nails dug into her arms, gouges that healed before his eyes.

She's stronger, I think. Good. She needs to be.

Jael dropped another one as Tam and Martine burst into the room. Calypso was close behind, along with some of Katur's aliens. Relief surged through him; he was happier than he expected to see the others. *What the hell's wrong with you? Do you* like *these misfits?* But the cannibals didn't turn. Like animals, once they focused on their prey, they didn't think about the odds of winning. These things were wholly driven by hunger and impulse.

"How does it look elsewhere?"

"There's fighting everywhere," Tam answered.

"Help us with these, and we'll get to work clearing the place." Dred sounded confident, exactly what her people needed to hear.

"My pleasure," Calypso said.

The mistress of the circle was a dervish of death, bare-handed, and she snapped two necks by the time Jael took down his next one. *It's because of the poison,* he told himself. In truth, it was a pleasure to watch the woman fight. He doubted there was anyone who could counter her rapid-fire strikes and sweeps. For her height, she was incredibly agile, one moment before, the next behind, and she ended her next brief fight by strangling one of the brutes with her bare hands.

Strong, too. Good to know.

Martine and Tam fought as a unit. Since they were both small, they assisted each other and took out targets with brutal efficiency. Reassured, Jael went back to killing, and soon Mungo's mongrels lay dead on the floor, along with the rest of the rubbish. Dred held out her hand briefly; nobody else would've noticed that it was shaking. To cover, she curled her fingers into a fist and propped it on her hip.

"We saw Mungo's men coming in. Is Silence here, too?"

Martine nodded. "They're ambushing us left and right. Strangled two men right in front of Tam and me and took off."

Dred muttered a curse. "You won't get them to face you straight up, so make sure you have someone to watch your back. They'll probably strike in dark hallways while we're fighting Mungo's people." She sighed. "It'll be tough as hell to clear them all out."

If it's possible at all. Everyone wore an expression that suggested they shared his skepticism regarding the impossibility of this task.

But nobody spoke his or her doubts aloud. Like Jael, they'd follow Dred until the end.

◀ 39 ▶

Honor Among Thieves

Dred split off with Tam and Katur. Jael didn't like it, but he seemed to understand her reasoning. They needed to spread their strength around and clear as much ground as fast as possible. Otherwise, Queensland might never recover. The fighting went fairly well for a while. Despite her weariness, it was no trouble to kill cannibals or Silence's killers when they stumbled on them. The room they stepped into next, however, held three mercs, all fully armored, geared up with heavy weapons.

She froze.

The distance between her and the merc group was such that she could get away, but she was less sure about her companions. Tam and Katur stood at her back and neither of them wore armor. If the mercs opened fire, she'd survive, most likely. The other two would not. Slowly, she lowered her weapon.

"Why don't we settle our grievance, Perdition-style?"

"What did you have in mind?" Vost asked, flipping up his visor so she could see his face . . . and he could read hers, human instincts replacing technical assessments. She'd heard

Vost's voice crackling through the old emergency announcement system now and then, but in all of their encounters, she'd never seen his face. He was older than she'd expected, square iron jaw and lines about his eyes, black-and-silver hair shorn down close to his skull. Old bruises dotted his face in various hues from blue to green; cuts had scabbed over on his left cheekbone. He had hazel eyes with crow's-feet radiating outward; they spoke of long turns squinting into the sun, not smiles or laughter.

She didn't like realizing that she was looking into the eyes of a decent man. "Grudge match. Usually, it's to the death."

"It's smarter for me to kill you all." His men raised their weapons.

"You could try. The rest of my people will likely be here at any moment, and there's so few of you, unless you're hiding the rest. Wonder how many mercs went boom . . . I suspect it was all of them but you three."

A flicker in his eyes told her she was right. Dred repressed a smirk. This wasn't the time to muck up the negotiations by being an asshole. The fact that he was talking instead of shooting told her he might be amenable to an alliance if she gave him the right opening and an opportunity to save face.

He wore a hard look. "The fact is, those men made their choices."

Her eyes widened as she realized what happened. "They betrayed you. They were stealing the ship, stranding you here. That must really piss you off."

"Nothing I can do about it now."

"It's smarter to face me than deal with everyone in Queensland. You can trust me to keep our agreement. The rest? Not so much."

He hesitated, glancing at his surviving men as if trying to take a quick census. "If I accept, I set the terms."

"I'm listening."

"If I win, you grant us clemency for past offenses."

That sounded dangerously reasonable. "And if *I* do?"

"You can kill me, if you promise not to harm my men."

"Boss, no."

But Vost held up a hand, eyes steady on hers.

Dammit. His actions sprang from a desire to protect the soldiers loyal to him. Vost had to know he was in a tenuous, disastrous position, stuck on a station where the natives hated and wanted him dead. Yet he was trying to buy his men a better position with the currency of his own life.

"As long as they're willing to take orders from me, they can fight for Queensland. But the penalty for disloyalty is high here. Infractions start with flogging, continue to castration, and end in death."

"Iron fist," one of the mercs muttered.

She ignored him. "Well, Vost? It's a limited-time offer. I hear others approaching."

"Yes. Bring it, Dresdemona."

It had been a long time since anyone called her by her full name. Probably the last time she'd heard it, her mother had been aggravated with her about something. Likely, his knowledge was meant to rattle her and put her off her game. But she had been looking forward to this moment since he arrived on station, talking about how he controlled the facility. *Wrong, you bastard. This is* my *house.*

"Armor off."

His men started to protest, but he waved them away, and there was an oddly ritual air as they stripped the plated segments and piled them nearby. He was strong and fit, better built and nourished than most of the men in Perdition.

This won't be easy.

Ordinarily, there would be a bigger audience, Calypso holding court in the circle, but this would have to do. She felt a twinge of guilt over the fact that he was offering his life as a bargaining chip, but it wasn't enough to stop her from raising her chains in challenge. One end wrapped around her wrist with a length hanging loose between her hands, and the other tail sat in her palm, waiting for her to flick it outward. The comforting weight of the blade in her boot reminded her that she could repeat the tactic that took down Grigor, if necessary.

Vost pulled two knives with long, wickedly serrated blades, superior to any shiv crafted in here. By the gleam of the metal, they looked like durasteel. *I'll have to be fast.* She wasn't afraid of pain, and unless he opened a major artery, she should be able to heal any incidental injuries. *Good thing he doesn't know that.* It felt like cheating, but her hidden resilience meant she'd finally get to kill him.

Dred smiled. "Call it, Tam."

"Before these witnesses, the terms are set and the battle is joined. Begin!"

She lashed out, but he was faster than he looked. Vost ducked, whirling, and came in with his blades. Dred leapt to avoid the slash at her knees. While that strike might not kill her, it would've crippled her. She snapped her teeth at him as she danced back a few steps to give herself more room to work the chains. His mercs called out encouragement, whereas Tam and Katur were silent. Remembering the friends Vost had killed added to her resolve, and she already had strength and speed from Jael. Dred whipped the chain at his head, but somehow, she missed him again. She cocked her head, puzzled, because with any other man, she would've already knocked him down, at least once. He was quicker than he should have been.

"Should I have told you? I'm augmented," he said, as they circled.

Behind her, Tam drew in a breath, which told Dred that he knew the answer. "What does that mean?"

"Fortified bones, reinforced joints. I've had supplements to my reflexes as well."

"I didn't even know they were doing that."

"They'll do anything for sufficient credits," Tam muttered.

She didn't let the merc disrupt her focus though she gave him credit for trying. "So you'll be a little tougher to kill than anticipated. I'm not afraid of hard work."

"Not according to your dossier. I've been curious, though.

Did they tally up your body count? I've always thought it seemed low."

She slashed a chain toward him, but he was already sliding to the side, and it slammed into the wall behind him in a cascade of sparks. "Sorry, not telling. I have my secrets."

If I can't fight him the normal way, then I need to shift my attack strategy.

"You can trust me."

Dred laughed at that. "The only person on station I trust *less* than you is Mungo."

"That's the one who eats people?"

"Then you understand your place in the hierarchy."

"That's harsh. The crazy one with the bone chair doesn't seem as if she could be relied upon in a crisis."

The conversation made it hard for her to focus on killing, doubtless what he intended. He had been circling, watching her defenses, and soon he'd go on the offense. Since this fight could *not* end in clemency, she had to figure out how to take Vost out.

"He drops his shoulder when he's considering a strike," Tam said softly.

"Unfair," Vost chided.

She smirked. "It's not interference. It's an insight."

"Thanks for the tip." Vost etched a mocking salute at Tam, and then he slashed toward her, each knife slicing the air until she swore it made a sound.

She whipped her chains around as a defensive measure; it would take someone stronger and faster to get inside her defenses when she was braced for a strike. A lesser opponent would already be bleeding from half a dozen cuts. *If I used blades instead of chains, I don't think I could keep him at bay.* She feinted a blow, and he dodged, allowing her to land the true snap at his ankle. He flinched when metal slammed into bone, but he was tough enough to shake off the pain. The strike left her off-balance, and he slashed a cut down her left arm. Hot blood trickled from the wound, slicking the metal length of the chain.

"That looks painful."

She snarled a smile. "How's your leg holding up?"

One of the mercs said softly, "They're pretty evenly matched. Should I shoot her?"

Tam leveled a look on them, and even Dred found his expression chilling. "If you break the terms of the truce before the match is concluded, you will find hell to be a comfort after what I do to you."

"Stand down," Vost said.

An idea struck Dred, and she changed up her tactics. In a move almost too fast to track, she drew the blade from her boot and whipped it at him. Vost spun to the side, but not quite fast enough; it sliced a path down his side as it went by, and his distraction allowed her to land a hit with the chain. She put her full strength behind it, and something in his chest cracked. *Ribs, most likely.*

"Nice," Vost said, spitting blood. "But how many more knives do you have?"

"I guess you'll find out."

But the noises she'd heard a long way off—not a bluff, just enhanced senses—were coming closer. Soon, her people surrounded them, and rifles fixed on the three mercs. The rest of Queensland might not understand, but this was a matter of honor. She'd struck a bargain, so this needed to play out without interference. She glanced around for Jael, but he was focused on her bleeding arm, not listening to her words.

"Stop," she yelled. "Let the fight continue!"

But others were yelling, "Kill the mercs, gut them! Let's finish this!"

Dred tried again. "Queenslanders, this is an official grudge match. Doesn't matter if Calypso's here. The agreement is made, and battle has been joined."

The shouting increased in intensity, drowning her out. Maddened men shoved toward the mercs, screaming bloody murder, and it was a testament to their courage that they didn't cut and run. Instead, they looked to their commander, asking silently, *Stand or fall back?*

A third and final time, Dred tried to leash her people,

but they wouldn't listen. In another second, the walls would be painted in blood, and her word would be dust. She made a split-second decision. Her eyes met Vost's. *Run,* she mouthed.

Unable to believe she was doing this, Dred turned and deliberately blocked the path with her body, so the mercs could escape, the only way to keep her promise.

◄ 40 ►

Last Resort

For the moment, the battle was over.

Bodies lay all around them, more than Jael could remember killing in one go since he became a merc. Instead of feeling exhilarated or even relieved that they'd won, he wondered if there would be anyone left to clean this mess up once the dying stopped. For a few seconds, he imagined maintenance bots like RC-17 banging repeatedly into decaying corpses and eventually scanning them, then cleaning around them.

Can't decide if that's hilarious or grisly.

Jael dragged in a deep breath. It had been a long time since he was simply . . . tired. In a way, it was a welcome shame. His designer body had limits now, boundaries that could be crossed. If pushed hard enough, he imagined he could even collapse from exhaustion.

"What're you smirking at?" Martine asked.

No percentage in telling the truth; it didn't do to show weakness even to your allies. So he shared his thought about the cleaning droids. When he finished, both Martine and Calypso were shaking their heads.

"You are not right," the smaller woman said.

"You must admit, it's quite a picture." Calypso was grinning. Apparently, she had a bit of a taste for the macabre.

"If they succeed in wiping us out," Martine's voice chilled. "Then those assholes can tidy up this mess."

Calypso offered, "The rodents would eat the corpses down to bones by the time the new owners arrive."

"Cheerful notion." Jael shook his head as he cleaned his weapons.

Jael was about to suggest they move on when the bot they'd just been talking about rounded the corner toward them, all lights flashing in a blinding pattern, but it wasn't playing the standard unauthorized personnel warning that Ike had programmed. The thing was beeping in sequence, but the lights and sounds made no sense to Jael. It circled his feet urgently, and he glanced at the two women.

"Any clue what this thing wants?"

She shook her head, kneeling to look at the unit. "No idea. I haven't seen it in days, actually. Not since Ike died."

All the lights on the RC unit turned green at the same time. "Pass phrase recognized, playback authorized."

A chill ran down Jael's spine as Ike's voice came out of the droid. "If you're hearing this, I'm dead. Sorry about that. Wills told me a while back that I didn't have long. In this place, I'm guessing I didn't die of old age. Whatever got me, I hope it was quick."

"I'm sorry," Jael said quietly.

The message continued, oblivious to the living. "You must be wondering what's going on with 17 here. I recorded this and programmed him to locate you and play it if I didn't tune him up on schedule."

"You clever bastard," Calypso said.

"Don't know what's going on, but I have some secret stashes that might be useful. I've been sitting on them, but now that I'm gone, there's no point in hiding them any longer. You know what they say, you can't take it with you. If you follow the RC unit, he'll take you to where I've hidden some goodies. So I guess that's it. Thanks for being good to an old man, and . . . I'll see you around."

"Message complete," the RC unit added. "Play again?"

"Holy shit. This is like finding buried treasure. What do you think it is? Parts? Food? Weapons?" Considering the state Queensland was in, Martine seemed pretty damn excited.

Calypso lifted a palm. "Hold up. I can't believe *I'm* saying this, but we can't tear off and leave Dred to fight these assholes alone. Once the blood dries up, there will be time to see what Ike left us."

Jael said nothing at all. This felt like hope from beyond the grave, a quiet promise that things were never as bad as they seemed.

DRED let *Vost get away.* The thought echoed like thunder in Tam's head. He didn't understand why, but he suspected it had to do with the unfinished grudge match. *This is why we need the formality of the circle.* If the others had come upon the fight within the usual arena, they would've known not to interfere. But regardless of Dred's honor, he needed to know where the mercs were holed up. *I'm not much of a spymaster without proper intel.*

"I'll track them," he said to Dred.

Other Queenslanders got in his way, pushing and shoving, as they tried to chase the mercs. But Tam slid past them. *One of the benefits to being small.* A few aliens moved as if to accompany him, but Katur shouted, "Stay! Follow Keelah's commands. I'll be back soon."

With each passing second, Vost got farther away. "You don't have to—"

"I disagree."

"Find out where he's hiding. This isn't over between us." Dred gave clearance for the mission, then she beckoned the rest of the Queenslanders. "Looks like we won. And you thought it couldn't be done! Shall we take the fight to Mungo?"

Since he and Silence had been mounting mobile strikes on Queensland for days, it was time. *She has this in hand.* Soon, they'd control the whole facility.

Until the next squad arrives.

But impossible things were never achieved by fixating on their insurmountable nature. Tam didn't try to change Katur's mind. He could've explained that this wasn't an assassination; silent executions were best left to Silence and her cadre. No, Tam excelled at gathering information and deciding the best way to make use of it, and he hadn't made up his mind about Vost. Doubtless, Katur felt differently after the massacre in the Warren.

With the other male lending his expertise, he tracked Vost. The walls were dirtier than usual here; they were encrusted with grime after turns of neglect. Tam knew all of the best places to hide on the station. He was an expert at scouting out hidey-holes and secret spots that offered shelter in an emergency. Currently, there were four that even Martine didn't know about.

And Vost found one.

With injuries like Vost had sustained, the merc couldn't go far. He must be in dire straits, especially since he'd harmed enough of Mungo's and Silence's people that they would be hunting him as well. It had to gall the mercenary commander to realize that his life might end in such a way. Men like him expected good and honorable deaths, not to be whittled down by convicts or to starve like rodents in a rotten wall.

"What do you plan to do with our enemy, once we find him?"

But that question would never be answered. Blood burbled from Katur's mouth, and when his body fell, it revealed the Speaker's crouched form. His blade was stained red and his eyes were bright with malice. He wasn't a large man, but he was tall, giving him better reach, though Tam had fought better men and lived. He didn't waste breath with accusations, and he tried to strangle the throb of rage deep inside him. A cool head prevailed in a fight. Yet he was already imagining the conversation with Keelah, a distraction he could ill afford.

"This has been a long time coming," the Speaker said

with icy calm. "I fight for the Handmaiden. *You* spy for your queen." Tam didn't realize he'd reacted until the Speaker went on, "We know that you watch us from the shadows. But it didn't save your friend."

This is where I'm supposed to be baited into a poorly considered lunge.

Instead, he circled, observing the way the Speaker moved. There was a reason why this man had risen through the ranks to speak for Silence instead of dying in her infernal web like the rest of her victims. The Speaker moved with serpentine speed, but his eyes flicked just before he struck. Tam banked everything on his reflexes and spun to the side just as the knife would've skewered him through the heart. The forward momentum pulled the Speaker off-balance, and Tam took full advantage. He came in with a strike from behind, just as the bastard had done to Katur. His blade struck true, a clean kidney shot. The assassin actually looked surprised as he fell, right next to the alien he had murdered.

The Speaker's chest rose and fell for a few seconds. Tam expected a moment of truth or clarity, but instead of smiling as some people did in death, the man's features tightened into pure horror, as if what he glimpsed waiting for him was terrible beyond belief. *If there's any justice, that's true.*

"Mary curse it." Tam clenched a fist, watching as the Speaker died.

The trail to Vost was cold now. And he had to return to carry the grim news.

LOST him.

It was a stroke of luck that the two trackers had been attacked. Without that break, Vost didn't think he would've escaped. His wounds throbbed, making each breath more difficult than the last. Nausea rose in the form of bile, but he held it together until he made it to where he and his two surviving men had been holing up. Vost was also well aware that he wouldn't have made it back without Redmond and Duran supporting him on either side.

"She's tough as hell," Redmond said conversationally.

Duran grunted in acknowledgment. "I didn't expect her to last as long as she did. But I really don't understand why we didn't just kill them all."

"Because we might need them down the line. When our clips run out, things will look a lot worse then. We'll be better off if we can make allies out of the least crazy ones." It went without saying that he couldn't consider teaming up with cannibals or the death-heads. Sometimes the choice came down to the lesser of all evils.

And that's the one they call the Dread Queen.

This was more of a rats' nest than a command post, but the space was too small for the enemy to lay traps. It would also limit the firepower they could bring to bear in here. They had little gear left anyway; the convicts had been stealing and breaking in since their unit arrived on station. That was more initiative than the suit had said they would possess. Vost choked a laugh at the memory of that interview; it seemed so long ago now.

As they settled, Redmond powered up the medibot, one of the few resources that remained to them. The thing went to work on his injuries, but the pain sent a raw shudder through him. He closed his eyes, weary to his soul.

"Well, damn," Duran muttered. "So what's our next move?"

He was lucky they weren't ready to kill him in his sleep. Any two other men in the unit would've refused to follow his lead once the rest of the squad got blown to shit. *Through their own stupidity.*

Reluctantly, Vost admitted, "The situation is this: We've whittled down their numbers, but the loss of the transport hurt us. As of now, we have no chance of completing the original assignment. Which means the rules have to change."

"Level with me. Are we dying in here?"

"Not if we're smart. And careful."

"You've been both so far, but we're still in this fucking mess," Duran muttered.

Vost wished the man didn't have a point, but he'd done

everything he could to succeed in this hellish place. The usual tactics had failed. And it would require all of his ingenuity to get out alive, now that he'd accepted the original mission parameters were impossible, regardless of the payday.

"I'm sorry," he said quietly. "I wish I could report better odds."

Duran shrugged. "Hell, if we'd turned and gone with Casto, we'd be in chunks. At least with you, we're still breathing."

Redmond nodded. "This job rang all my alarm bells, but I took it anyway. I should've known better."

"Me too," Vost admitted.

"Greed got the better of us. Move on." Duran looked like he wanted to pace, but the crazy, silent woman had trained killers crawling all over the station in search of them.

"I have a plan," he told his men. "From what I've seen, the reason these Queenslanders have lasted this long is because their leadership isn't psychotic. And she proved it when she was willing to fight to save two of her own."

"That's true," Redmond said.

"I know what the Conglomerate told us. But the only way we get out of this alive, going forward, is cooperation."

Despite the fact that the Dread Queen had covered their retreat to satisfy the terms of their bargain, his men seemed less than delighted with the plan. *Too fragging bad.*

"So what do you want us to do?" Duran asked.

"I need a few days to heal up. If she takes my proposal badly, I need to be in better shape. Gather some supplies—"

Redmond cut in, "There's a Kitchen-mate in one of the abandoned zones. We could make a run, produce some paste."

It was good idea since paste didn't require preparation or cooking facilities. None of them were thrilled at the prospect of eating it for three days straight, but it would keep them alive. "Get water, too. And be careful. There are still combat zones all over the station. I don't want my claim to fame to be that I got every single one of my men killed."

Redmond laughed wryly. "Trust me, we're not eager for that either."

"Can you give us any intel?" Duran asked.

Vost ran down all of the info he had as to where the pockets of aggression were highest. He concluded, "If you stick to the perimeter, you shouldn't have too much trouble though those silent freaks are stealthy. Keep an eye on your six."

Redmond nodded. "Will do. Let's go, D."

Once the men moved out, Vost peeled the broken armor away from his skin. It had taken every ounce of his self-control not to show how much pain he was in. He hissed in reaction as he studied the lattice of bruises and the slice on his side. The light trousers and shirt he wore beneath had holes revealing the damaged flesh. Even the air hurt. His men didn't know that the acid from the strike had chewed through to his skin or that the wounds were festering.

The medibot beeped in dissatisfaction. "Running low on antibiotics. Less than 10 percent of pain medication remaining."

Vost made a fist, but he didn't slam it into the wall. Every particle of his being objected to their next move, but it was the only play he had left, and he couldn't let anything prevent him from getting out of here alive. Everything hinged on the Dread Queen's response to his proposal, and he hated how powerless that made him feel.

Survive. Whatever it takes. He's waiting.

Unexpected Favors

It had been two days since Dred let the merc commander get away. Things had gotten worse since then, with raids more or less constant from the surviving cannibals while Silence led kamikaze strikes when Queensland could least afford it. The madwoman seemed to think this was her chance to wipe everyone else off the station.

And she's not doing a bad job of it. But she wasn't the primary threat at the moment.

"Is it true eating human flesh drives you mad?" Keelah asked as she slashed a small blade across the enemy's gullet.

Dred killed another before she replied. "Sometimes. But Perdition does that, too."

A normal group of murderers would retreat.

Dred found that thought macabrely amusing as she fought. While Mungo had the numerical advantage, Dred's people were better equipped and trained. But the cannibals were utterly insane, and Mungo was the worst of the lot. It was a miracle his own men hadn't killed and eaten him turns ago. But maybe that was the method to his madness.

"You can't take Queensland," she shouted at the mob.

"You're not even close to our borders, and there are defensive measures."

They can't take your territory, but they can gut you.

It was just bad timing that they'd managed a strike as her squad limped away from a battle with Silence's assassins. There weren't many aliens left though they were fighting valiantly all around her. The last Rodeisian roared in challenge and took out two mongrels in one blow. Dred was close enough to catch the snap of bone.

Mungo's orders came as a snarl. "Cull the Dread Queen. Then kill her."

His cannibals responded at once, surging toward her in a massive wave. There were a lot of men fighting, and now all of them wanted her head on a pike. Keelah and the Rodeisian stepped into their path, then the rest of the Queenslanders followed suit. The sight might've been unlikely, but they were set on defending.

"Go. We'll hold them here."

"I can't," Dred protested.

Keelah snapped, "If you fall, Queensland is lost. It's your will that holds the place together, and my people will have no refuge. This madman is clever enough to know that if he can take your head, he wins. So *go.*"

As Mungo snarled in frustration, Dred sprinted for the hallway. The chains weighed her down, but she didn't let them slow her. At this moment, she felt every sacrifice that had carried her to this point, as if they were etched upon her skin. The battle rang out behind her, and she put distance between herself and Mungo's red tide. Memories haunted her of what she'd seen in Munya: necklaces of teeth and the knives sharpened from human bones, cups carved of the skulls of their victims, red blood drunk down from the grisly goblets while laughter rang out.

Maybe we're wrong to fight. Maybe it'd be best if the Conglomerate ended us.

But she couldn't make that choice. Not now. Not when so many lives had already been dashed on the cliff of impossible hope that some of them would survive. *We have to beat the odds, or it's all been for nothing.* She had faith that the Queensland force could defeat Mungo and his goons now that she wasn't there as a target.

Should make my way back to Queensland. I think it's—

Dred skidded around a corner, her boots loud against the metal flooring. So it wasn't noise that gave the other woman away, but more of a feeling. She whirled low, just in time to avoid the garrote. Silence sprang at her, undeterred by the near miss. Dred read death in the other woman's eyes. She'd known the bill would come due for the way she'd rejected the Handmaiden's offer of alliance.

"Fine, let's have this out now." She lashed the chains before her, keeping the other woman at bay.

Dred scanned Silence from head to toe, checking for poisoned blades or other hidden threats, but the length of wire was the only weapon she spotted. *That doesn't mean she's not dangerous.* She was ready for the fight of her life. The woman hadn't earned the title of Death's Handmaiden by letting her enemies live. Then Silence's gaze flickered over Dred's left shoulder. It was obviously a ploy—and she thought so until the other woman sprang away, putting some distance between them. Her retreating footsteps were eerily quiet.

Fear quickened her heartbeat as Dred turned to greet the new menace. Vost stood with two of his men. All three of them were armed, laser rifles trained on her chest. *Mary curse it.* But there was nothing to do but feign composure. If they wanted her dead, they'd have opened fire when they came upon her and Silence.

"It appears the odds are in your favor." Sounds of combat came from a few corridors away, where her people were fighting Mungo. It was a few paces to the cover of the corner. Chances were good that she'd take at least one hit, but the armor might compensate. But if she retreated the way she'd come, she had no way to be sure how the battle was going. She might end up crushed between Mungo's forces and the mercs from behind.

They like that tactic.

"Appearances can be deceiving, especially here. For all I know, this is a trap, and your men will unload on us in a few seconds or bomb us from above."

"Anything is possible," she said.

It was a bluff, obviously.

"What the hell's going on?" a merc demanded.

Vost held up a hand. "There's a reason you're not in charge, Duran."

It was a handicap not to be able to see their faces when they could read hers, so she tried to maintain a neutral demeanor, hoping they'd assume this was a trap. "Why don't you find out my intentions? Take one step closer. Just one."

"Bullshit," the other merc said. "You're alone. You only have those chains."

Dred smiled. "Bet your life on it? Your transport made a beautiful boom."

"That was clever," Vost said. "Ruined the docking bay, too."

"Why are we talking?" she asked.

I'd give a lot for the rifle I gave to Martine. But even if I were better armed, my chances wouldn't be good against three. I barely made it out of that first fight with Vost.

"I'm taking your measure. And you're taking mine." There was a grudging respect in the merc commander's tone. That surprised her. "But we have unfinished business, don't we? Weapons down, men."

Damn. I'm in no shape for a rematch.

The soldiers lowered their rifles without bitching. She supposed they didn't see her as a serious threat, but snap judgments like that had gotten their unit in serious trouble over and over during this conflict. *Time to gather some information about their intentions.* Dred would be surprised if the grunts knew what their commander was about.

"Did you drive Silence away on purpose?"

He parried with a question. "Did you need saving?"

"Hard to say. I've never fought her. I'm competent, but death is her specialty."

Vost inclined his head, as if she'd said exactly what he

expected. "Yes, I intervened, though not out of altruistic motives."

"Welcome to Perdition."

"Hey," a merc snapped. "We don't belong here. We're not scum like you."

The commander sighed. "Did you even *read* the dossier I put together before we dropped on site?" The two mercs looked at each other, then they both shook their heads. That made their commander ball up a fist. "If you had, maybe we'd have fared better in here."

That sounds like he knows it's over for them. Interesting.

"Why? What did it say?"

She listened as she crept incrementally closer to the wall. From a better position, she could definitely spring to safety before they unloaded on her. Vost was aware of her shift, though the other two weren't. Clear to see why he was leading these men and that they were lucky to be alive. When she spotted Tam behind him, along with a half dozen Queenslanders, she didn't give it away, unlike Silence.

"I ranked the prisoners according to threat level. I went over their criminal jackets and provided a list of those we needed to take out first. What the hell were you *doing* on patrol? The dossier had pictures. Old ones, but—" Vost caught himself. "It's irrelevant now."

"It's so frustrating when a mission goes bad due to personnel issues," she murmured with a half smile.

"I think you'd agree that you owe me—"

Ah. Leverage. She jerked her chin, interrupting whatever offer he had been about to make. Her men surrounded the three mercs, and most of them had rifles. Funny how that worked out when Tam was planning the battles.

"That might be a strong word," she said softly. "You did me a good turn with Silence. It could be argued that I saved your ass during the riot, before, and that we're even now. But I'll go one better, which means you'll owe me. So find a quiet place to hide. If you come hunting my people, it won't end well."

"We both know I don't have the manpower to go on the offensive, and there's nobody here I could recruit."

She nodded at that. "Mungo and his monsters will be dead before the day is out. That only leaves Silence, and her people would die before helping you."

"They'll die anyway," Tam said.

Dred aimed a quiet smile at the spymaster. "One problem at a time."

Vost didn't need to think long. "Very well. We'll talk another time. I'll accept your offer of safe passage and withdraw."

"I hope mercy wasn't a mistake," Tam said, watching the mercs move off.

She shrugged. "Me too. But he could've shot me in the back. The fact that he didn't makes me wonder what he's plotting. And how I figure in."

"Seems like he's trying to build up some goodwill," Tam observed. "The only question is why."

Keelah caught up to them then, along with a few surviving men. Beside Dred, Tam froze, his whole body locked in a posture of regret. *Shit.*

Then to Dred's astonishment, the spymaster dropped to his knees and bowed his head. "I'm so sorry. It was my failure. My life is in your hands."

Before Dred could snap at him for being hasty, Keelah pulled Tam to his feet. "I knew. The bond between life mates is such that I felt him go. Whatever happened, he fought beside you of his own choosing. I hold you blameless."

"I don't." Tam's voice broke. "I wasn't cautious enough or sharp enough. I make mistakes, and people die all around me."

Keelah inclined her head, somber and grave. "That's the nature of this place."

◀ 42 ▶

Death of a Cannibal

There was no time to waste. A few hours ago, they had gotten word of Katur's death, but nobody could spare a moment for a service right now. Too many attackers, not enough defenders, and still more coming in. Dred had put Jael in charge of some Queenslanders, kissed him hard, and gone to fight on the other side of the territory.

Dred could look after herself; she'd managed fine before his arrival. It was hubris to imagine she needed him to protect her. *Especially now. She's as tough as you are.*

That thought filled him with both reassurance and unease. What need would she have for him once the fighting stopped? Like a magician with one poor trick, now that he'd taught it to someone else, the demand for his services was sure to drop. Deeper in the station, he heard sirens blaring. Things had gotten so chaotic that he was no longer sure where the main battle was. The fire-extinguishing system engaged, spraying the corridor with water, though this wasn't where the fires were burning. Men lay lifeless at his feet, but this was a momentary respite. The ones Dred had assigned to him were all dead.

Someone stepped out of the smoke, and he brought up his blades. He dropped them when he recognized Keelah. The female had been grim and uncommunicative since her mate's death. Blood matted her fur, but he didn't think much of it belonged to her. The water dripped through her pelt and came out tinged pink, running off down the faintly sloped metal floor.

"You all right?" he asked.

He told himself Dred was fine. *Don't worry about her.*

She ignored the pleasantries. "Just mopping up. But there's a group ahead that's too big for me to handle on my own."

"Is it what's left of Mungo's mongrels?"

Keelah nodded. "They're quite mad. Even more than they were if you can fathom."

"Pretty hard to believe. I'm with you. How many?"

"About twenty, I think."

"You think the two of us can take them?"

"I've seen you fight. As long as they don't have rifles, we should be fine."

"Now there's a terrifying thought."

"You're not afraid," Keelah said. "For that, you'd have to fear death."

He stared at her, astounded by her perspicacity. "You're wrong, I do fear death."

Her liquid eyes held a weight of unwelcome knowledge. "Just not your own. It's worse when you lose someone you love."

I don't love her. But the words stuck in his throat, and there, they fluttered like the wings of panicked birds. Surely there was another name for the prickly barbs that twined him ever closer to Dred. Yet he couldn't bring himself to speak the repudiation aloud. Keelah turned away, apparently losing interest in the conversation.

"We should go mop up," he finally said.

The mongrels were looting. They had found one of the stashes that had belonged to the Warren and were rooting through the crates like animals. Jael found them disquieting because they had devolved to the point that they mostly communicated in gestures and grunts. He'd heard a few of them form actual words, but most didn't bother. Their time in Perdition had turned them into lower primates.

Jael brought his rifle up and dropped two of them as quick as breathing. That alerted the others, and they spun as a mob, charging with primitive snarls. He shot another one as Keelah readied her weapons. His rifle beeped, indicating an imminent venting of heat, so he hurled it at the charging cannibal. The others bared their yellowed teeth in aggression and surrounded Keelah and him in a slavering pack. This group had sharp, untended nails with blood and filth caked beneath them, so long that they'd started to curve. A glimpse he soon regretted at their bare feet revealed toenails in the same state. And the smell alone was nearly enough to kill him. The plus side of these beasts was that they didn't waste time with threats.

One snapped at him with fetid teeth, while two more lunged. He'd seen how they operated before. Two held the prey while another tore out its throat. But that wasn't happening here today. He avoided the two grabs, then slammed the mongrels together. As one stumbled, Keelah's small blade lashed out and sliced from throat to thigh. Blood gushed from the wound, and the man fell. His comrades kicked his corpse out of the way.

They'd eat you later, mate. But that's not happening, either.

Jael had been afraid Keelah would get in his way, but she proved an able partner, finishing up when he disabled one. Her blade flashed again and again in swift, accurate kills.

Jael lashed out with a kick and followed with a wheeling blow that ended with a broken neck. Another enemy hit the ground. Though his reflexes weren't what they had been, it was child's play to anticipate their strikes. They seemed to be moving in slow motion, and Jael was everywhere. His hands and feet blurred into endless death, and when he finally stopped moving, there was a pile of bodies at his feet.

"You have the battle madness," she said.

"I have *all* the madness. Shall we see if we can find the others?" He considered for a moment, wondering about something belatedly. "Why *were* you on your own?"

"I thought it would be better to die in battle," she said quietly. "I miss Katur."

"I don't think he'd be very pleased if you just gave up."

Her muzzle pulled away from her teeth. "What do you know? Our faith teaches that lovers are reunited in death. He would be happy to see me."

That seemed backward, but Jael had been courting death for a long time, enough to understand where she was coming from. It had taken being sent to a place like Perdition for him to learn how to live. Now he was fighting, not just to find a way out of here, but to do something other than kill people who deserved to be put down. That was a tempting idea, actually, but playing judge, jury, and executioner had gotten Dred sent here in the first place.

To Keelah, he finally said, "Then I hope you find a worthy death if that's what you're seeking. Do you know where the others are?"

She shook her head. "Dred was fighting on her own when I saw her last."

Dammit. Despite himself, he remembered what had happened to Einar. The Dread Queen might have half of his healing ability now, but neither one of them was invincible, and Vost had given them a hard fight; Mungo and Silence hadn't made it any easier. She had to be exhausted since she still possessed a full human's need for sleep.

"Hurry." He tried to pretend he wasn't worried, but from the sharp look the female sent him, she wasn't fooled.

"I hear something . . ." The alien cocked her head.

Jael listened, but he detected nothing besides common station noises. It was unusual to find someone with sharper senses than his own. "What?"

"Combat. It seems there are a few stragglers who don't mean to surrender."

"They're animals," Jael muttered.

"I've heard your people say that about mine, more than once."

"*My* people?" He smiled slightly. "You're mistaken. I have none."

"You're human, aren't you?" She stepped closer, as if he'd piqued her curiosity, and she circled him, whiskers prickling as she investigated by scent.

"Not exactly."

"Interesting. There's another layer."

Do I smell different? Cleaner than Mungo or Silence's lunatics, definitely. In any case, it wasn't the time for explanations. "We should move."

Keelah led the way since he couldn't hear the battle. They ran two hundred meters, then the sounds reached him. Jael closed his eyes, listening for Dred's voice, but he heard nothing that made him think she was nearby. Then a muttered curse rang out. *That's Tam.*

"It's Mungo, with the last of his holdouts," Keelah said, as they closed the distance.

"You know what Mungo smells like?"

She shivered. "I could never forget. His people hunted us for food. With Grigor, it was hate . . . and sport."

Before he could reply, the hallway opened up. This was abandoned territory, claimed by no one, and Mungo's crew had already soiled it. Scraps of flesh, bits of skin, and gnawed bones littered the floor. *I'll be so glad when this asshole dies.* At the moment, however, Mungo had a hand around Tam's throat and was squeezing the life out of him. Four of his men looked on with slavering anticipation. They were so focused on the kill that they didn't spot Jael or Keelah.

"I've had enough of this shit," Jael whispered.

He dropped to one knee, got out his rifle, and shot Mungo in the face. His hands went slack as Tam dove away. The rest charged as Jael fired two more bursts. *One cannibal down.* Keelah killed one with a vicious swipe of her knife, and Tam jabbed his blade into another's back. The last one left alive tried to run, and Tam tackled him. The spymaster wasn't usually much for hand-to-hand combat, but from the bruises and bite marks on him, he wanted the pleasure of this death, so Jael stood back while he worked.

"That was a timely arrival," the smaller man said a few minutes later, wiping his blade. "Thank you."

"Thank Keelah. She heard the fight."

A few seconds later, Dred ran into the room, covered in blood, but from what Jael could tell, she was in one piece. She seemed almost disappointed by the fact that Mungo was already on the ground. "I guess you don't need me after all."

Jael crossed to her and leaned his forehead against hers. "That's a filthy lie, and you know it. Back to Queensland, love?"

Not So Quiet Riot

It should've been easy from there. With the enemy defeated and Vost in hiding, where he'd either starve or be killed by Silence's crew, Dred expected to stride home to a heroine's welcome. After the fight, Keelah had asked for solitude to mourn her fallen mate, leaving the others to return without her. Outside the checkpoint, they met up with Martine, who was bloody but not too badly injured.

"You all right?" Dred asked.

The other woman nodded.

By now, Cook should be preparing a welcome feast. Instead, the chef was up on a table, using up all the words he'd saved over long turns inside.

"The time is now! Join me and be among the lucky five. I'm not dying here." The huge man's eyes focused on her, and he leveled a finger in her direction. "Stand with me and kill the Dread Queen."

Dammit.

She tried to shout, "Vost's men are dead, the transport's blown," but the growing shouts of agreement drowned her out. She cursed the need for secrecy now, the fact that the men wouldn't have understood Tam's decision to sabotage the ship. In trying to prevent a mutiny, she'd ended up causing one. Some things were, apparently, inevitable. The nearby Queenslanders looked at her small group speculatively, violence brewing in their eyes. Then someone threw a knife. It sliced past her ear and embedded itself in the wall behind her. As if that was the spark the kindling needed, the fighting broke out in earnest. It was hard to tell who belonged to what faction unless the men attacked her directly.

"Mary curse it," Tam spat. "Are they truly this stupid?"

"Most are." Jael ducked a punch and threw one of his own.

"We have to rally the defenders," Dred said.

"How?" Martine asked.

"I'll clear a path," Jael said.

True to his word, he hurtled like a madman into the teeming crowd. Now and then, men lashed out at him, but most of them had learned not to mess with him. He didn't carry the title of Dread Queen's champion for nothing. Dred charged after him; the armor she wore would protect her from most attacks, but Queenslanders were dying left and right in the scrum. Blood spattered from a man's mouth, scenting the air with a coppery tang. The noise was overwhelming, snarls and screams overlaying whimpers from dying men, and those who were being trampled underfoot.

"This keeps up, it'll be a handful of us against Vost and the rest of Silence's crew," Tam growled. It was the first time she'd heard such obvious temper in his voice.

"It's not your fault."

Jael pushed through the melee and headed down the hall to her quarters. At first, she wasn't sure why, but then the answer became obvious. While the four of them were armored and had good weapons, they were too few to put down a rebellion without the body count becoming astronomical. Silence would swoop in and mop up. Dred couldn't let that happen; everyone had fought too long and hard for the tale to end that way.

Tam shook his head, not letting himself off with the absolution she offered. "I'm in charge of intelligence. I should've seen the betrayal coming. There were likely signs among the men—"

"Cook was always too quiet for anyone to know what was going on in his head," Martine put in. She sounded breathless from the run, and her blade was slick and red with blood. The drops spattered on the dented floor as the other woman dragged it against the wall to scrape it clean.

"Keep the hall clear if you can," Dred said.

There was no point in assigning blame. It was possible Cook had always been crazy—or at least desperate to escape—he just didn't communicate his feelings. She ran off down the hall, leaving Jael to stand watch with Tam and Martine. She lost precious seconds keying in the security code on her door; she'd taken to locking it while she was out, mostly because she kept spare weapons and ammo in here.

Along with the remote for the Peacemaker.

Without Ike to maintain it, if the thing was damaged in this firefight, Dred wasn't sure if anyone could put it back together again. *But that's a risk I have to take.* There was no other way to shut down the riot fast enough. The Peacemaker delivered shock and awe along with heavy ballistic rounds. When it stomped into a room, men took notice.

Vost's voice came over the loudspeakers, as if he *knew* about the riot. When a drone cam zoomed by, Dred realized he probably did. "My offer's still open. When your numbers dwindle to five, I'll take you with me."

Cheers rang out, then Cook shouted, "See? We made it to the final round. Now it's time for sudden death."

"Lying bastard," Jael bit out.

"Which one?" Tam asked.

Dred understood the question. Did Cook *really* believe the bullshit he was peddling? There was no question that Vost was stirring things up, hoping more convicts would kill each other, so he stood a better chance of getting out of this alive.

Got news for you, asshole. Nobody else has so far.

Jael ignored the spymaster's question. "Look there, he's with Pietro. I knew there was something off about him—"

"Who the hell is that?" Dred demanded.

"One of Grigor's. He's been slipping around, stirring the pot. I had an . . . odd encounter with him, but there was so much other shit happening, I didn't think to mention it."

She bit back the urge to swear. It was certainly understandable that Jael might've had other shit on his mind . . . or maybe he hadn't realized just what Pietro was up to. Either way, they had a hell of a situation to handle. *It only needed this.*

Someone shouted, "They're breaking into the armory."

"I'm on it," Martine said.

The dark-haired woman shouldered her rifle and took off at a dead run, leaving Tam and Jael waiting for orders. She made a snap decision. "Back in the common room. Get me to the throne. I need people to *see* me send in the Peacemaker."

Tam nodded. "Remind them who the queen is."

Theoretically, it shouldn't be too tough, but there were only three of them amid a roiling mass of bodies. Jael shoved toward the large, scrap-metal chair, but men quickly surrounded them, makeshift weapons in hand. Dred thought for a few terrible seconds that she could make them turn away, tear into each other with mindless violence, but—

I can't do that to my own people. If I do, I truly am the monster everyone said I was back on New Terra.

"Defensive posture," she ordered. "Ready weapons, but try not to kill any of our men." She cut a look at Jael. "If you say 'I was born ready,' I'll shoot you."

"We don't have time for sex-pain games right now, love."

Tam made an uncomfortable noise in the back of his throat. "How are we supposed to know which ones are still loyal?"

"They'll be the ones *not* trying to pull our heads off," Jael replied cheerfully.

She drew her laser pistol but before she had to fire it,

loyalists attacked the men facing her and the circle faltered. "Go," one of them yelled. "Get clear!"

It wasn't a question of whether she could win the fight, only that some of these men still believed in her right to lead. That had to be enough. Quickly, Dred scanned the room. They had to fight to the throne without killing or maiming too many loyal Queenslanders. Just as she was trying to figure out how to make that happen, Jael grabbed her gloved hand and towed her toward the throne. The remote felt heavy in her palm; this would probably be a massacre, one that could be laid directly at her door.

What kind of person are you if you can lose track of how many you've killed?

Jael and Tam laid down fire behind them, keeping the men from pushing too close. The warning shots were effective, as most people couldn't absorb a laser blast—one shot, and the target went into shock. It was rare for a victim to die of the burns.

A man lurched into her path, and she tried to move around him, but he lunged at her eyes with a knife. No helmet. Damn. She pistol whipped him in the face, then kicked him back so she could shoot him. She unloaded while taking hits from behind. Jael tried to block for her, but she shouted at him over her shoulder.

"I'm wearing armor, you idiot."

"Ah, your words of love and dulcet tones never fail to enchant me."

Tam's voice was dry. "Should I leave you two alone?"

A hard shove rocked her, and she stumbled forward. "Please don't."

Before her loomed a man with broken yellow teeth and a mad look in his eyes. He looked strong enough to snap her neck, so when Jael called out, "Get down," she dropped without hesitation, giving him a clean shot, and he took the bastard through the head.

Bodies shoved against her, and she tried not to think how many of them were trying to kill her. She just had to press forward until she got to the throne. Someone had started a fire somewhere—that always seemed to happen during a riot, and if the station emergency system didn't kick in soon, they'd all asphyxiate. Her eyes burned from the chemical fumes wafting in lazy spirals, but she couldn't spare the time to dash away the tears. They collected on her chin, dripping down to her armored chest. Four wounds burned in a low, constant throb: shoulder, left arm, thigh, right flank, but she could feel a tickling tingle from where they were starting to heal.

Thanks, Jael. Leg still hurts like a bitch.

She lashed out with a kick to clear the rest of the way— so close now—but her weak leg buckled. She went down hard. Somehow, she held on to the remote, even with three enraged Queenslanders who were ready to rip her apart attacking, so she popped the closest one with her laser pistol. The red power meter on the side said she had fewer than five shots left. As Jael and Tam took aim at the other two, one of them cracked her in the head. The blow made her head wink black spangled with the old gold of ancient stars interspersed with white-hot sparks.

She kept the pistol in her hand, even on the ground. Dred swept with her good leg and knocked one of them down. Prone, the enemy was clumsy, buying her time to shoot. He died writhing like a worm on his back. The other lunged, and she rolled, then crawled toward the scrap-metal throne.

◀ 44 ▶

Garden of Evil

Jael shot the Queenslander chasing Dred.

The common area swarmed with men. At this moment, Jael missed Einar. The big man could clear some space with a few, casual swings. Without him, the battle was tighter and more chaotic. Most of their best fighters had gone down in other sorties, so at least he wasn't squared off against pure talent. These were desperate men with nothing to lose. Or so they thought.

The situation can always get worse.

He flashed to days on Nicu Tertius, thigh deep in mud and walking on the corpses of his comrades as their bodies built a bridge the survivors used to scramble to higher ground. To this day, he couldn't stand in the rain with soft ground under his feet without imagining that the earth was churning with the bones of the dead. With effort, he fixed his vision on the melee all around him. The distraction cost him a slice across his ribs, another invisible scar.

"We can't let them wear us down," Jael said, parrying a lunge and breaking the arm of the man who tried it.

Tam said, "I agree. If our numbers get too low, Silence will kill us all in our sleep."

Fortunately, their side had the better weapons and armor. Dred was wearing one of the suits at the moment; Tam and Martine had the others. Vaulting onto the throne, the Dread Queen brought up her pistol and took aim as a mad-eyed Queenslander charged. The laser blast caught him in the chest, sizzled, and stopped him. His body tripped a couple of his fellows.

"There's only one way to end this quick," he said. "You have to do it."

Nodding, Dred pressed the button on the remote and deployed the Peacemaker. He'd never imagined she'd use it on her own people. Their unit had solid plating and two different heavy weapons, one on each arm: laser gun and Shredder. It limped these days, and the repair work they'd cobbled together after Ike's death left it half-assed effective, but it would be enough to strike fear in the hearts of the traitors.

The mech lumbered in, warning the dissidents in indifferent, electronic tones. "You are guilty of civil disobedience. This scene will be pacified. To avoid bodily harm, desist and vacate the area." It paused a few seconds to let that sink in, then added, "Countdown commencing."

"If you're with us, get clear," Dred shouted. "I don't want any of my people harmed."

Her men stopped fighting at once and ran for the exits in all directions while she jumped down and took shelter behind the shield provided by the scrap-metal throne. Jael ran with her, though he could probably survive the attack. No point in wasting his healing power, though; it made more sense to marshal his strength. When the mech reached zero, it sprayed the room with a relentless ballistic onslaught. The rounds were old-fashioned but effective, especially against unarmored targets.

Dred tapped his shoulder. "Find Martine. Get to the hydroponics garden and don't let anyone inside. You two defend it, I'll hold down the fort here."

They wouldn't last long without the fresh food growing in the garden, so he took off right away, dodging the barrage the Peacemaker unloaded in his direction. By this point, the common room was almost clear apart from one man trying to crawl away in a smear of blood. Bullets sprayed the floor as Jael ran, pinging in sparks off the metal flooring. He dove for the hallway, came up in a roll, and sprang away.

"Martine," he yelled.

"Over here!"

The men who'd fled from the common room had her cornered in a storeroom. *Son of a bitch.* Martine crouched behind stacks of supplies; the fact that she had a laser pistol kept them from rushing. Jael breathed in the lightning cordite zing from her weapon and the char of flesh. *Two bodies on the ground. Eleven left. Here we go, lucky thirteen.*

She shot one in the head at point-blank range. His flesh sizzled and burned, puckering into a black sore in which his mouth was a soft pink hole. The man screamed and clawed at his melting eyes, giving Jael the chance to break his neck. Blood fountained from his nose and hit her faceplate in a messy gush. Martine swiped a gloved hand across her helmet as Jael backed up for a running start and launched himself into the mix.

He swept the legs out from under one and immediately dropped on him, jabbing an elbow into his neck. As the enemy wheezed for breath, Jael rolled forward and snapped his arm. The pain incapacitated him, and Martine finished him with a shot to the chest. He couldn't see her expression, but she gleefully opened fire around him. The men couldn't get past him to touch her, and he let her use his body as a blockade. Jael took out two more in quick succession, leaving the others to scatter. Martine shot another one in the back as he was running away.

"Glad you could join me," she said, hurdling the crates she'd used as cover.

"Dred wants us posted outside the garden."

"Makes sense."

She cocked her head, probably listening to the distant

rat-a-tat-tat of the Peacemaker. It fired intermittently, likely clearing the common room as enemies ventured in to check on its ammo status. Dred didn't need to worry as long as it was functioning properly. With time and laser rifles, the mercs had taken out Mungo's units, but the Queensland rioters weren't so well equipped.

"Let's go," he said.

From the click of her boots, Martine was with him. The fighting had already reached the hallway leading to the garden. There were bodies everywhere, and until they attacked, Jael had no way to be sure which side they were on. Ahead, ten Queenslanders scuffled, slashing at each other with jagged blades.

"Coming through," Martine shouted.

He wouldn't have given warning, but a few of the men—too few—acknowledged her words with a jerk of their chins. "We have to help them."

Seven others whirled to face the woman, who whipped out her laser pistol. "You want some? Come on then, bitches."

She fired two quick shots, dropping opponents on either side of the scrum. From the light on her battery pack, she didn't have too many more shots, but the traitors didn't know that. The men who had been defending took the chance to stab a few more, neat kidney shots that would leave their targets dead in minutes. Now the odds were downright favorable.

Jael launched a kick at the nearest traitor, snapping his knee back, and when the man dropped, he finished with a blow to the temple. He had the strength to fight efficiently, and he used it. That kill flowed right into the next; he broke that asshole's neck cleanly. There was one man left, and one of the defenders cut his throat in a wet slice. His blood jetted onto the wall, slowing as he toppled and died. The wet rasps of breath ceased.

"You came just in time," a man said. "They were on their way to the garden."

"There will be more," Martine predicted.

Jael nodded. "We have orders to hold this ground. Want to help out?"

"Why not? It pisses me off when they fuck with my dinner," a big guy muttered.

"This way, then."

He rounded the corner and came up on a scene that chilled him. Vix and Zediah were defending outside the doors, while the enemy shouted, "Take the garden. If we control the food, we own Queensland."

At this point, Jael had no idea if this was about the merc pardons or if it was a coup within a riot, fueled by silent Lecass supporters. Fifteen more men surrounded them, and while his five could thin them out, it wouldn't be fast enough. Still, he ran toward the mob as Zediah took a blade in the gut, opening him up like a fish. Still, the kid didn't drop; he was defending Vix with a shaky blade. They stabbed him two more times before he went down, then they sliced her from throat to thigh. She felt for Zediah with a blood-smeared hand, and his fingers twined with hers in one last convulsive movement.

In a few more steps, these bastards would have possession of the hydroponics bay. With an enraged snarl, he threw himself at the lot of them. Jael took multiple stabs and slashes, but he ignored the pain as he had learned from a lifetime of doing just that. He didn't a need a weapon to end them. Their bones popped and cracked in the rush of his fury. Separated from him, Martine fired with caution; she didn't know about his regenerative abilities. The other Queenslanders waded in to mop up the ones who were still twitching when he moved on.

Jael was barely breathing hard when the last one fell. His shirt already had so much blood on it that the others couldn't tell how much belonged to him. Martine narrowed her eyes, but the superficial wounds had already closed. The deeper ones would take longer, but none were serious enough to bother him.

She plucked at the rent fabric on his shoulder. "I guess you got lucky, huh?"

He flashed a smile even as his gaze settled on Vix and Zediah, their hands intertwined even in death. "Always do. It's other people that need to watch out around me."

Yep. Lucky as hell. Now he didn't have to worry about what Zediah knew. Or keeping secrets from Dred.

"Is that a threat?" she asked softly.

"No, just a shitty reality."

She nodded. "Poor bastards. If only we'd been a little faster."

While their deaths solved a personal problem for Jael, Zediah and Vix had known the most about running the hydroponics garden. Ike might've known a bit about it, but he was gone, too. That left Jael, who'd spent fewer than ten hours tending the plants before the pair went full psycho on him. *If the garden stops producing, we'll run out of food.* After that, there was only Mungo's solution—cannibalizing the populace either directly or indirectly. But that was a distant concern, not something to worry about while they were still putting out fires and tallying the dead.

"How long are we supposed to hold here?" Martine asked.

"Until Dred or Tam comes to advise us of the all clear."

She nodded. "I wouldn't trust anyone else."

It was hours before the Peacemaker fell permanently silent. During that time, they drove off two more runs at the garden and killed even more rebels. The body count had to be astronomical by this point. Jael piled the enemies away from Vix and Zediah; it was the least he could do, given that he hadn't really tried to save them.

At last, Dred strode down the blood-streaked hall toward them. Her chains were crusted dark brown, her face smudged with soot and weariness. But resolve shone from undimmed eyes. "It's over. You two can stand down."

The RC unit beeped and circled in her wake, and a light went off in Jael's head. *Dammit, I completely forgot.* Belatedly, he told her what they'd learned from Ike's bot. With the constant chaos and attacks coming from all sides, it had been impossible to spare the men to track them down, then

Jael had forgotten about it. The unit was standing by, ready to lead them to his cache the minute things settled down.

On hearing the good news, she actually smiled. It seemed like ages since he'd seen that expression on her face and felt like she wasn't faking the look for the good of the zone.

Martine went off to check on Tam, leaving them alone.

"You all right?" Dred asked, checking him for wounds.

And it broke something in him, that despite the purple shadows beneath her eyes that he knew indicated she wasn't sleeping well, she'd still ask after his mental health. He didn't think she remembered how to do anything except solve other people's problems. The Dread Queen was sucking the life out of her, bit by bit, and it killed him to see it happen.

I have to get her out of here. That can't be another of my quick-patter bullshit promises. This one, I have to keep.

"Yeah. But you're not."

To his surprise, she didn't deny it. In the guttering light from the tetchy fluorescent, her face was pale and soft, faintly shadowed, so that he could only see the glint of her eyes, but not the color. Her hair fell in a dark swath against her cheek, moon and night. The poetry of that contrast compelled him to lift a hand to her cheek.

She leaned infinitesimally into the touch. "You sure about that?"

"I don't think Tam and crew have noticed. But you can't fool me."

"I'm going through the motions," she said at length. "Saying the right words. Making the moves that might keep us alive, but I'm *so* fragging tired."

Her words struck him like a barrage of rifle shots, burning through his emotional shields. Jael felt her exhaustion as if it radiated from his own body. That was how deep she'd burrowed inside him. The emotion resonated, kindling an ache as though she tapped a thousand crystals, all singing the same mournful tune. Distance showed in the slope of her cheek, the delicate shadow of her lashes. Such fine details to notice; he cataloged such minutiae about everyone, every day, and it only mattered when it was Dred.

"It's bullshit how much weight you carry, love." His voice contained more gravel than he'd expected, and he cleared his throat.

She shrugged. "I'll do what I must. And it helps to have you here. I can't talk like this with anyone else."

"I'd want to kill him if you did."

"That's us, ever spinning through a cycle of love and death." Her mordant expression yielded to surprise when Jael kissed her. "What was that for?"

"You'll figure it out. Let's catch up with the others."

◄ 45 ►

Sympathy for the Devil

There are so few of us left.

Eight hours later, Dred glanced around at the smoldering wreckage left over from the riots, char marks on floor and walls. The survivors were piling corpses to be sent down the chute with numb efficiency, supervised by Martine and Calypso, who came out of the last battle with a gash in her side, but she was strong, and it should heal.

Dred and Jael had parted ways to oversee repairs, partly because they needed him elsewhere and partly because she couldn't lean on him too much. The Queenslanders left needed her to be strong. At last count, Mungo's men had been exterminated completely; she had a less-comprehensive idea of how many of Silence's assassins had survived the slaughter. That would probably come back to haunt them, but she lacked the energy to care at the moment.

Jael found her a few minutes later as she went to work with the rest of the cleaning crew. She hadn't slept in days, and she wouldn't until Queensland was back in order. A new set of mercs might arrive anytime, and she knew they didn't have the manpower to repeat this defense of the station. *Next time, they wipe us out.* That awareness rendered the victory bittersweet. He pulled her away from the others and drew her to him. The kindness of the gesture almost brought her to her knees. People didn't console the Dread Queen.

Except him.

"We're doomed," she said softly. "And now we're just marking time."

"This thinned the herd, right enough."

Resting against his chest, she couldn't see his face. "I can't help but wonder what's the point. I can put everything back together, but no more supplies are coming. When the mercs don't return and report the place clear, they'll hire more and send them in."

"Then we need to make sure we're not here when they arrive."

"This again," she said with a growl of impatience. "You know, at this point, I'm ready to call your optimism insanity. Tam blew the transport, remember? To kill a bunch of mercs. And the docking bay is now sealed off from the rest of the station."

"We're actually better off than we were, love."

She frowned at him. "What are you *talking* about? Look at this place."

"It's a wreck, yeah, but the mercs cleared out most of our enemies. Apart from Silence's crew, everything here belongs to us now. It will be easier for us to stockpile resources. The powers that be are sure that they removed *everything* we could use to escape, yeah? But they couldn't have foreseen we'd end up with the run of the place like this."

To Dred, it sounded like clutching at straws. "That's true, but—"

"But nothing. Tam and I will scour all decks from top to bottom. If there's anything we can use to get some of the old machinery spaceworthy, we'll find it."

"You're seriously proposing to build a ship from scrap parts. Before they send a second team."

"Do you have a better idea? I suppose we *could* retire to your quarters and shag until they come for us. I can think of worse ways to go. But personally, I think that'd be a shocking waste of our potential."

Before she could reply, Martine strode up. "The bodies are loaded and ready. Did you want to say a few words? Just so the men feel better about the mass dumping."

Dred wasn't in the mood to be inspiring, but she knew the other woman was right. She told Jael with her eyes that the discussion wasn't over, then moved to the center of the common room and vaulted up on top of the throne Artan had built. Even more than usual, it seemed like a ridiculous affectation, for she was so obviously the empress of nothing.

Just a few tired convicts, beyond any real hope.

"Our people fought bravely," she said. "The outside world wouldn't expect it because they threw us away. They decided we were too broken for fixing, but to me, they were all warriors defending their homes. Going into this fight, I would've said there was no way we could win. The mercs had all of the advantages. But we did what we do best, what we *always* do when the odds are stacked against us. We put our shoulders in and pushed."

"Damn right," someone shouted.

"Who are we?" she asked softly.

"Queensland!"

"What's stopping us?"

"Nothing!"

"I commend these warriors to the next world, where I hope there's plenty of liquor and laughter to keep them out of trouble."

A cheer rose from the assembled men, and she hopped down from the throne to accompany Martine and Jael, who were guiding the hover dolly, groaning beneath the weight of their dead. Cook was on that pile, a man she'd never guessed would turn, but the promise of freedom had been too much for him. She wished she could've explained to him that even if he *had* been among the last five prisoners standing, the mercs didn't intend to honor the deal they'd made. It was a ploy, nothing more, a carrot offered to stupid brutes.

Silently, the three of them unloaded the dead until she

was sweaty, and her back was sore. Queensland had once had a couple of hundred citizens; now they were down to fewer than fifty. The station seemed to echo with silence, each deck deserted, full of traps laid by men who had died before their cunning could be fully realized. That would make exploration tricky, but she had faith in Tam's and Jael's ability to circumvent static defenses. She mustered less confidence in the idea they could cobble together a ship fast enough to escape the next death squad. Even though the mercs had failed in their mission, there were so few prisoners left that it could almost be counted a win.

"That's the last of them," Martine said.

Dred nodded her thanks. "You've earned a break. Get some rest . . . or whatever."

"If I was smart, I'd snatch some bunk time, but who the hell's a genius up in here? I think I'll get drunk instead." Martine flashed a roguish smile, laced with faint menace by the glimpse of her pointed teeth.

"Have at it," Jael said, watching the other woman go. Then he turned to Dred, but whatever he might've said was forestalled by footsteps, *not* coming from the heart of Queensland but from the corridors leading from other areas of the station. Jael stepped in front of Dred, a move she would've protested if she wasn't already watching the corner with chains in her hands. When the merc commander eased into view, helmet off, she pushed out a shocked breath. For once, his men weren't with him.

He left them behind in case things went bad. More proof he was a good commander who cared about those who served under him. And it made him much harder to dismiss.

"Come for a quick death?" Jael asked politely.

Vost shook his head. "I came to make a deal."

Dred laughed. "What could you possibly offer that we'd want, after what you tried to do here?"

"Transport codes."

She froze, exchanging a look with Jael, whose infinitesimal nod seemed to indicate he thought she should hear more. "What're you talking about?"

"The docking bay they use for supplies isn't the only one on this station. You haven't been able to get to any of them because of the blast doors and force fields. But I hacked the mainframe. It's glitched as hell, and it doesn't work all across the station, like it's supposed to, but I checked. I can turn off the automated defenses and unseal the secondary docking area. If we come to an agreement, and you ensure I get there safely, we can leave here together."

"I don't believe you."

"Then look at this." Moving slowly, he produced a drone cam and powered it on.

She peered at the grainy image on the tiny display. Though the footage was shaky, it was clear the little spy bot had penetrated a part of the station no convict had ever reached; the supplies and parts shown in a casual sweep of the docking bay made that obvious. The drone flew all around the room, peering into all corners; and then she saw the faded warning. DOCKING BAY 4: TAKE ALL PRE-CAUTIONS IN OPENING HANGAR DOORS. They still needed a ship, but if Tam and Jael could cobble something together, as he seemed to think, then Vost held their exit pass.

If I believe he can get us in there.

"So your drone slipped in through some tiny air vents," Jael said. "That doesn't prove anything."

Dred considered the odds that Vost had actually hacked the mainframe. If that was possible, Tam would've figured out a way. But she wasn't sure because she recalled that odd Monsanto announcement they'd never heard before.

But she couldn't seem to yield too quickly. "I think you're bluffing. All transport codes were wiped before they sent the first prisoners to Perdition."

"To a cursory inspection, yes. But there are always frag-mented data packets, hidden caches of information, backups hidden on remote servers. They didn't hire the best to scrub the system." Vost met her eyes, his gaze a pale and icy green. "Can you afford to assume that I'm lying? From what I've seen, you can't withstand another assault, and it's not like you can bolster your numbers."